Secret Lives of Men

BJT Ledet

JOZEF SYNDICATE
An imprint of Jozef PA of Louisiana LLC. Louisiana

First published in the United State of America by Jozef Syndicate
Copyright (c) 2022 by Betty B.J.T Ledet and Candace J. Semien

Summary: Follow the second phase of The Christians from the honeymoon of Rev. Donald Grant
and Mary Jean Grant through the scandalous entanglements of Rev. Mical, his deacons, and female
friends--all who set out to destroy Rev. Grant

ISBN 978-1-944955-32-2
Library of Congress Control Number: 2022905368

Visit us online at www.jozefsyndicate.com
Follow BJT Ledet @BettyThomasLedet

This book is dedicated to my family and dear friends
who have been instrumental in encouraging me to complete
this second book of The Christians series.
I also thank my editor who has worked tirelessly
with feedback and many discussions.
Thanks to all of you.
I really love and appreciate you.

Table of Contents

New Love

George told the kissing newlyweds to buckle up as he backed out of the Basin Reception Hall's newly paved parking lot. His brother, the Reverend Donald Grant, and his new sister-in-law, Mary Jean, embraced on the backseat of his deep brown Lincoln Continental. Mary Jean's sister and best friend T.P. sat in the front seat. For a moment, George watched them in the rearview mirror, longing for the innocent love his brother now possessed.

"Hey, you two save all that for your honeymoon. Let me hurry up and get you to the airport!" George said, and everyone laughed.

For the forty-seven-minute ride, George hummed and nodded to the evening music mix by A.B. Welsh on Q106.5 FM. *Man, that A.B is smooth tonight.*

George glanced at T.P.

He smiled when he noticed she too was enjoying the music. By now, she had gotten comfortable and removed her wedding heels. She loosened the two hair clips decorated with lace and fresh-cut baby's breath. Her curls bounced with the car. George admired how feminine and soft she appeared. The scent of her and Mary Jean's perfume filled his nostrils and sealed the moment in his memory. He loved the scent and feeling of new love.

When they arrived at the New Orleans International Airport, George helped Rev. Grant get their luggage out of the trunk. T.P. helped Mary Jean get out of the backseat without tearing her wedding dress. They had struggled for nearly thirty minutes trying to remove the gown's train and reveal the simply laced dress. Damaging it at the airport was not an option.

Once they were situated and the luggage had been checked in, Mary Jean hugged T.P. and promised to call her as soon as they were set up in Paris.

"Girl, you better not call me!" T.P. joked. "Enjoy that man of yours."

The brothers shook hands, and the newlyweds walked into the airport. George held the car door for T.P. and caught the tail of her dress to help her slide onto the seat.

"Thank you, George," she said, catching his eyes and his broad smile. At first, T.P found his stare distasteful and ogling, even though she was accustomed to men leaching over her.

"And, why are you looking at me like that, Mr. George Grant?" She asked.

George smiled.

"You are a very pretty lady." He closed the door before she could respond. T.P watched him walk around the front of the car. His stride was confident, quick, and bold.

When he sat in the car, he slammed the large car door and adjusted the radio. "I would like to get to know you better if that's okay with you." He said as he pulled away from the airport drop-off ramp.

T.P. didn't respond.

They rode in silence through four songs until George asked, "So, Ms. T.P., what do you do for a living?"

"I work out of my house as a beautician, and I'm working longer hours to open my salon soon." Half-heartedly, she hoped that would deter him from asking her for a date.

"Um," George said with a grin glowing across his face. "I find beauticians to be artists. Did you do your hair for the wedding today?"

She touched her curls and said "Yes. I did mine and Mary Jean's."

George watched the road carefully although he wanted to look into her eyes. "It's beautiful," he said.

When T.P. didn't respond, he continued, "You have to have gifted hands to create all the different hairstyles and then customize them to your clientele's faces." This time, he glanced at T.P.

She had never thought of herself as an artist with gifted hands, but the sound of it felt good; so, she decided to use that term when describing herself next time.

Silently, they cruised down I-55, both of them wanting to say more.

"So, Mr. Grant, what is it that you do for a living?" T.P. asked.

"Right now, I'm working in a men's merchandise store. Have you heard of Lloyd's Men's Clothing Warehouse on LaSalle Avenue?"

"Yeah, I have heard of that store. It's extremely popular. What's your position?"

George was not proud of his position and thought that he should be a manager by now, but to expect that as a Black man in Louisiana was a lot to ask. He was lucky that old man Lloyd liked him.

"Right now, I'm the assistant manager of sales."

"How long have you been working there? I heard your words 'right now and that means you are really saying 'for the time being, but I have something else on my mind'."

George thought for a moment and then he could not believe that he had been there so long. "I've been there ten years. I never thought about the time until I just said it to you. I've been thinking about opening my own boys' and men's clothing store. Honestly, it's time for me to find another job because I'm not ever going to be the manager. Right now, Lloyd's son is the manager. You and I both know there is no way they are going to hire a Black man over a white man's son to manage a store whose main clientele is white men. What's worse is that I can't do a darn thing about it," George shook his head and switched lanes to exit towards Basin/Port Hudson.

T.P. knew exactly how he felt. She worked for herself so that she did not have to face the racial discrimination and intimidation that many Black people had to deal with daily, especially since boycotting the buses in Baton Rouge nearly ten years ago. Things were still tense throughout the state. The conversation made the remaining drive to T.P.'s house a quiet one.

When they arrived at her home, George was still quiet. The large car swallowed the parking space in front of her home. Rosemary and lemongrass grew from two shining navy-blue rustic pots which sat on each side of the concrete steps leading to her front door. Night was falling and he didn't want to keep her out longer than needed. He pulled a used envelope from the car's visor and asked T.P. for her phone number. She wrote the seven digits and gave them to him without writing her name.

George got out of the car and opened her door then he followed her up the steps to her door. He quickly surveyed the street and the perimeter of the houses nearby.

T.P. fought the two deadbolts. The door was sturdy but worn. George noticed how easily the door could be kicked in and didn't like the thought of a pretty lady like T.P. having such flimsy protection. He decided to fix the door as soon as she would allow him.

"There!" T.P. said when the lock clicked.

Once the door opened, the house released its natural scent of sweet shampoo and burnt hair.

"It's been nice getting to know a little about you, Pretty Lady, and I will be getting in touch with you soon," George said quickly before she stepped into the house.

T.P. turned and studied his eyes.

"Sleep well. Goodnight," He said and rubbed her shoulder and arm, afraid to attempt to hug or kiss her.

She stepped into the small house, locked the door, and flicked the outdoor lights to let him know that she was safe.

—————————

After giving George her phone number, she expected a call from him the next day; however, he did not call, nor did he call the following day.

By the third day, she stopped anticipating his voice every time the telephone rang. On the following Saturday morning, her phone rang.

"Good morning, T.P.'s House of Beauty," she declared.

"Hi, Pretty Lady," George responded. "I've been thinking about you since we met."

"Yeah, I can tell," T.P. said laughing.

"Well, you know," George chuckled. "I didn't want you to think I was desperate."

T.P. shifted the phone to remove an earring.

"But, on a serious note how are you, Pretty Lady? Were you busy?"

T.P. thought about how thoughtful it was for George to genuinely inquire about how she was doing. He appeared to be a perfect gentleman, but then, of course, he is Rev. Grant's brother and an apple from the same tree.

"To answer your questions, I'm doing well and yes, I am busy. I am in the process of curling a client's hair," T.P. said, trying to sound nonchalant.

"Oh, let me be quick. I called to see if you would be free later tonight. I would like to take you out, that is, if it is okay with you," George said hoping that T.P.'s answer would be yes.

"It depends."

"Depends on what, Pretty Lady?"

From under the hairdryers, Mary Lou and Cassie stopped laughing and talking with each other to hear what T.P. had to say and to try to guess who was on the line. T.P. balanced the phone between her shoulder and ear while she rolled her client's hair with the smoking curling iron. She stared back at the ladies in a way that told them to mind their own business. Then, she answered George. "It depends on where you are taking me."

"We are going to paint the town. You will be pleasantly surprised!" George said as he tried to think of what they would be doing later."I'm going to let you get back to your clients and I'll pick you up at seven."

"Okay," T.P. said.

She turned Mary Lou to the mirror to see the finished style, then motioned for Cassie to take the chair next.

"Bye, Pretty Lady," George said smiling.

"Bye," T.P. said as Mary Lou stood from the chair, admiring the length and bounce of curls.

"Girl, you are something else with those curlers! I wish I could do this to my hair. It's beautiful, T.P!" She gave T.P. two, twenty dollar bills and added a five for two bottles of rose oil. "I can't wait to see this oil in the stores, T.P.!" Mary Lou said as she sashayed towards the door like a new woman. T.P. smiled with pride. This was exactly why she loved the life she had created for herself.

When she finished with her last customer at five-thirty, she decided she would have to leave the shop unclean–something she had never done before--if she wanted to be dressed and ready by seven. She rushed into her bedroom and looked in the closet to find something sexy, but not too revealing.

She selected the pink dress that always brought compliments. She laid it across the bed and grabbed a pair of green heels from the closet floor. She dropped them near the dress and walked to her dresser. Her top drawer squeaked open and she selected a pink, lace bra and panty set along with a pair of hosiery and tossed them on the bed. She decided to take a quick shower.

Within ten minutes, she was back in the bedroom applying a light coat of Fashion Fair foundation to her face. She mixed lotion and lemongrass oil inside her left palm and then rubbed her body making sure she did not miss a spot. She slid on her panties and hosiery, then gently sprayed perfume between her thighs.

The time was 6:45 PM. She had fifteen minutes to be ready. She clipped on her bra and lifted the dress off the bed, raised it over her head, and let it slide down her body. It clung to her curves and fit her perfectly. Feeling sexy, like Mary Lou had been feeling earlier, T.P. smiled and then walked to her dresser.

She unclipped her hair, grabbed a wide-tooth comb, let her hair fall to her shoulders, and ran the comb through it from front to back. She threw her head forward and then back as her hair fell into a full bounce style.

George knocked on the front door.

"This man is right on time," she whispered to her reflection, raising one eyebrow. Walking toward the front of the house, T.P. kicked off her slippers and grabbed her heels off the bed. She slid on the left heel in rhythm with her stride, then the right one. Once on, they lifted her three inches off the floor.

Out of habit, she peeked out the window. This time she lingered to admire the fine man whose head nearly touched the porch's overhead light.

He held a bouquet of sunflowers and daisies. *That's quite a unique bouquet, Mr. Grant.* She smiled at her thoughts then quietly closed the curtain. She opened the door and stepped backward, allowing him entrance to her home which she normally did not do on a first date.

"You look amazing," he said, offering her the bouquet. She smiled knowing they would make a perfect flower bath.

"Thank you," she said. "They are beautiful."

George looked around the small beauty shop as she walked quickly into the kitchen to put the flowers in water.

"You're welcome!" He shouted behind her.

"I'll be right back," she said.

T.P. rushed into the kitchen, grabbed a ceramic vase from the windowsill, filled it with water, and quickly re-arranged the flowers into a wider spread. She would give them more care when she returned. She walked back into the beauty shop and found George standing in the same spot. When he saw her, his body warmed at her beauty. He opened the door for them to leave and followed her out. He closed the door which shook on its hinges. The constant opening and closing by T.P.'s clients had worn the entire frame. T.P opened the door again. When it caught its hinge, she jerked it and slammed it securely. Then she locked the deadbolts. George moaned out his disgust at the shape of the door and became more determined to fix it.

He scanned the street as he followed T.P. down the steps. The porch light sparkled on the blue flower pots sitting against the porch.

It is a perfect night for a date.

The sky was clear.

The moon was full, illuminating the sky.

He was ready for new love.

From the front seat of George's Lincoln, T.P. noticed the stars shining and twinkling off the hood of the car. She could tell that he spent a lot of time detailing the car inside and out. She held her smile when she noticed her reflection on the dashboard. As soon as he started the car, "Reunited" by Peaches and Herb poured from the speakers and filled the car.

George chuckled and said, "I thought this song would fit our first date. What do you think?" He stretched his long arm behind her seat and drove with one hand.

T.P. smiled but didn't quite agree. "I like Peaches and Herb. And, I have that cassette."

"How about jazz? Do you like jazz?" George asked.

T.P. thought about it for a moment, trying to name a jazz artist just in case he asked her which one she liked. Instead of waiting for a response, George continued, "I thought we would have dinner at Fred's." He stopped at the light and looked T.P. in the eyes. "And after that, if you are not too tired, I thought we would go by Club Maxima and catch a live show where I can get a chance to hold you in my arms as we dance."

This man is serious and cocky.

It made her interested in him even more. She could not remember another man who had ever taken her to so many places in one night, and places like Fred's and Club Maxima were high-class. Fred's Fine Dining was one of the most upscale restaurants in north Basin, and Club Maxima was a jazz place where the most popular musicians randomly sat in on other musicians' gigs. With all the work T.P. does, she had never had the chance to enjoy a night out at either place, but she had heard a lot about them.

Fred's Fine Dining

Fred's Fine Dining proved to be a very exquisite restaurant with a variety of ethnic foods. T.P. was surprised to see such a high-scale establishment serving collard greens and spicy fried chicken but under the names Kallad Greens and Deep-Dipped Peanut Chicken.

The round, cherrywood tables were decorated with gold-plated chargers, golden vases holding fresh-cut magnolias, and shiny gold utensils. Posters of the owner and celebrity guests donned the walls. T.P. recognized the pictures of Rev. T.J. Jemison and Gus Young from Baton Rouge but couldn't quite put a name to the women in the other photos. George led them toward the private booths on the left side of the restaurant farthest from the entrance.

T.P. flipped through the menu and quickly decided what she would try, thanks to the photo on the menu. When the waitress walked up with hot buttered rolls and cornbread, George motioned for T.P. to order while he served them each a roll.

"I'll have your strawberry barbecue turkey wings, your Kallard Greens, and a slice of peach-n-apple pie, along with a glass of water."

George smiled at her decisiveness. "I'll have the country-fried, lamb steak and the special Fred's salad. What's in it?"

"It has our homemade dressing, lettuce, tomato, almonds, and apple cubes."

"Sounds good to me," George said. "I'll have that and a slice of chocolate pecan doberge cake."

After the waitress left, they looked around the restaurant.

Both of them watched as their waitress carried meals to the couple one table from them.

"Look at that!" He said.

After the couple said their grace silently, George gave them a moment to taste their first bites. "Excuse me. I hate to bother you but your food looks so good. Can you tell me what it is so the next time I bring my lady back here we can order those dishes?" George asked politely.

"Sure," the older man wiped his mouth with the gold cloth napkin. His hands shook unnaturally.

"For starters, we are having chitterling sausage with apple slaw and cornbread brioche. She's coming back with our oxtail rillettes with foie gras mousse, pickled vedalia onions, muscadine gelee, and truffle toast points."

His wife raised her cocktail and said, "And we have the Green-Eyed Bandit."

"Oh, is that what that's called?"

"Yeah, man, and it's delicious," the older gentleman said.

"Everything at Fred's is delicious," his wife said. T.P. noticed how she gently touched his hand then squeezed it.

"No doubt," George said with a head nod that show appreciation and ended the conversation.

T.P. smiled at the couple and hoped they would be leaving before her food arrived. She took note of how George enjoyed having people's attention and extending any conversation that he can—much differently than she did.

As more customers arrived, the more uncomfortable T.P became. She whispered, "George, Why did you choose this booth?"

George was caught off guard.

"I don't like feeling like I'm being watched, especially when I eat," she tried explaining.

George tried to reassure her. "It's the best seat in the place. I love this booth. I get to see the people as they pass by and they get to see me enjoying an exquisite meal with the prettiest lady in all of Louisiana."

Seeing that his words offered no comfort, he asked if she wanted him to pull the privacy curtain or select a table.

She shooked her head. "No. It's okay." She leaned towards the table and added butter to her roll. Looking into his eyes, she said, "Thank you for asking. I'll be fine." She declined mostly because closing the curtain would appear too intimate for her liking although she wanted the privacy.

George tried switching the conversation to something he knew T.P. would enjoy: history. "Fred's has a strong commitment to our culture. When you taste this meal, you will see how much respect and pride they put into preparing the food. The chef tonight has inventive ways to elevate the flavor without it being too overbearing." George bit into his second roll. T.P. watched–*Damn his teeth are beautiful*–and waited to hear more.

"You'll be able to tell that the food is just a higher class of culinary art, T.P. It represents the soulful recipes that we know and love."

"I like the sound of that, George."

She wondered if Mary Jean and Rev. Grant knew about Fred's or if they knew that this was one of George's hangouts. She watched the way he sat upright in the chair. He was in his element. Solid. Comfortable. Sure.

The waitress walked over with their food and George was relieved at the timing. He didn't know how much longer he could talk to T.P. with the discomfort he saw on her face.

Her body seemed stiffer and he desired to see her softer side. The waitress gently placed T.P.'s meal on the charger and uncovered the plate.

"Wow," T.P. whispered.

She moved her water glass away from the plate. "This is beautiful and it smells divine."

"Wait until you taste it," George said and smiled at the elderly couple as they left.

The old man rested his hand on George's shoulder. "Take it easy, young man."

"Yes, sir," George said proudly.

Throughout the rest of the meal, they ate silently only speaking to share how tasty the food was. T.P. found it to be more modern than necessary for a restaurant in the smallest incorporated city in south Louisiana, but man was it delicious.

They savored their entrees and T.P. resisted the urge to mix her cornbread with the Kallard Greens. She became more comfortable through the quietness of the meal especially when she could not recognize any of the faces in the restaurant.

As they waited for the check, George complimented her looks again. He imagined touching her face and pulling her toward him for a kiss.

"This was so very nice, George."

He paid the check and tipped the waitress before gently moving T.P.'s chair for her to stand and leave.

"Are you ready to enjoy a little jazz, Pretty Lady?"

"That would be great."

For the fifteen-minute drive to Club Maxima, they listened to a series of Rhythm and Blues on the radio. They tried guessing the next song and artist before it aired. T.P. won each time. Listening to music was a standard at the beauty shop. She enjoyed having melodies playing in the background of the beauty shop while she worked. Most times, she was the only one who could hear the music over the continuous chatter and laughter of her female customers. It was a pleasure riding with George and singing new and old songs. So far it was a date unlike anyone either of them had ever experienced, and George was looking for more.

They settled into a booth against the wall to sit as close as they could get to the right stage. George could tell that T.P. was exhausted. Nervous that she was ready to end the date, George quickly walked to the bar and ordered drinks for the two of them. T.P. felt a little put off that he was ordering a drink for her and had not asked her preference. She decided not to say anything considering all that he had done to make the night special.

She glanced around at the people filling the club and the band setting up for the midnight set. She hadn't realized that even though it was late for her, most of the adults in the city were just getting started for the night. She was glad that she still had not bumped into a client, yet.

Pictures of Miles Davis, Louis Armstrong, Billie Holiday, Steve Reid, and Billy Harper decorated Club Maxima's blue walls. There was a section to the right of T.P. with tables and chairs just beyond the dance floor. The seating was placed in a circular design so patrons could equally view the band and dancers while being served. T.P paid more attention to how businesses were designed now that she was seriously looking to design her new beauty shop. She had never seen a place set up like this, but she liked it.

Large, oval, gold chandeliers hung from the ceiling. Each section of the chandelier held ten candlelight bulbs that reflected small kaleidoscopes. She knew the light bouncing off the walls of the chandelier would cause amazing color changes. At the far back of the building, large mirrors hung behind the bar, and she could see George talking to a lady who sat wide-legged on a bar stool. By his body language, T.P. could tell that George knew the thin, light-skinned lady. T.P. initially thought the woman was pale and fragile.

While she and George talked at the bar, he touched her shoulder twice during their brief conversation. T.P. adjusted her body, rocking her hips in the seat to release the tension she suddenly began feeling.

Okay, T.P. girl, you just met the man. Do not start getting jealous now; you don't even know him and you don't know if you even like him.

A barmaid placed a brown bowl of nuts in front of her and quickly walked away once she realized that T.P. was distracted and not ready to order. When George returned to their booth, he placed a small tumbler filled with brown liquor, two ice cubes, a slice of lemon, and a cherry. T.P. took the drink and sipped the thin liquid.

"This is nice. What it is?"

"It's my favorite drink. Whiskey sour. I thought you might like it, so I took the liberty of ordering one for both of us. That was okay with you, right?" He asked raising his glass for a toast.

T.P. clicked her glass against his. She knew she should have responded; however, since she had already had a date like none other, she decided not to say anything at least not at this time.

She sipped the drink again, this time tasting it fully and feeling a slight burn in her throat. She could hear Mary Jean admonishing her: *Since you do not drink hard liquor, Sister, why didn't you tell him that so he could have gotten you a glass of wine?*

She watched the disco ball spinning above the dance floor and sipped her drink. George rocked slowly to the music. When they finished their drink, George took her hand and guided her out of the booth and onto the dance floor where they swayed to the slowest jazz she'd ever heard.

T.P. could smell his cologne and the strength of his embrace was the comfort she desired. He moved his right hand a little lower down her back to her waist area and pulled her closer. Feeling his manhood against her waist, she took her hand and gently pushed his hand back up to the middle of her back as she stepped half a foot away from his waist.

Oh no, my brother. She didn't want to feel him so soon and did not want him to think that tonight would end in bed. *Who does he think he is? I don't care if he is Rev. Grant's brother who, at this moment, he is not behaving like. I'm not going to allow him to disrespect me.*

Her shift reminded George that she is a minister's daughter. George quickly understands and in order to apologize, he adjusted the way he held her. His behavior allowed her to relax more in his arms.

After the dance, they move back to the booth and T.P. watched the strobe lights once more at the ceiling as George ordered another drink for them.

"No. I'll have a glass of Chardonnay or any white wine you have."

T.P. spoke up.

George smiled, knowing she'd pass his first test. From the moment T.P. sipped his whiskey sour, George wondered if she had a mind of her own or if she was going to allow him to run her as so many other women had before her. T.P.'s quick response to the barmaid was another indication to him that she was her own woman. And, he liked it.

As the club filled, guests began to share booths which gave George the perfect reason to move closer to T.P. and wrap his arm around her shoulder even though no one had joined their booth yet. T.P. liked him more than she realized, but to her, he could tone down his assertiveness. This was their first date, and she did not want him behaving or feeling that it was their tenth.

While the band changed sets and the club was relatively quiet, she decided to tell him before he got beside himself.

"George, I have really enjoyed our date up until now." She looked him squarely in his eyes. "I do not like how you pushed yourself on me while we danced. I am not a loose woman." She raised her hand to stop him from interrupting. "I did not like you taking it upon yourself to order a drink for me that only you enjoy. I don't drink hard liquor. I like wine and not a lot of it. So, if you expect a chance at a second date, you're going to need to treat me like the lady I am." T.P. took a sip of her wine.

George was impressed. He always liked women with spunk. It made it so much more interesting to woo them.

"I'm sorry, Pretty Lady. I apologize," he said. "It's just when I held you in my arms, we felt so good and natural. I forgot my manners." T.P. felt he was being genuine.

"I feel like I have known you for a long time, and I'm so comfortable being with you. If I've offended you, we can leave and I can drop you home if you are ready to go."

T.P. looked at her watch and decided it was a good idea to head home now that it was after two am and the date was no longer fun. "Yes," she said. "I'm ready to go home."

George grabbed his glass and gulped the rest of his drink. He slid out of the booth, reached for her hand, and helped her out. It took them five minutes to weave through the early morning crowd. George held her hand tightly until they were outside of the club unbothered. The streetlights on Avenue D were bright and lit the parking lot evenly. They crossed the street quietly and the sounds from the club muffled behind them. Both were in their thoughts about the other.

George listened to her heels tapping the pavement. Her walk was sexy and much more deliberate than that of the women he had been dating. He opened her door and watched her cross her legs after sitting in the car. Her calf muscles flexed, showing off her strength from the hours she stood standing at work. He closed the passenger door and walked around to the driver's side. They rode quietly back to her home.

They were quiet even when they walked to the door of her small row house. After unlocking the door, T.P. turned and looked him in the eyes. "Thank you, George, for a beautiful night. I enjoyed myself, the fresh flowers, the exquisite meal, the jazz, and the wine. It was nice, and I look forward to more time together."

George leaned down and kissed her lightly on the forehead. "So do I."

Before they could say good night, they noticed a sheriff's patrol car driving slowly down the street. George found it odd for patrols to be in this neighborhood so late. He noticed T.P.'s body shift. She seemed to have stepped closer to him.

"What is it?" he whispered.

"Something ain't right about that hick sheriff," she said as a matter of fact. "He and that car stir my spirit like they are full of sin and evil secrets," she said almost forgetting she was talking to George and not one of her female friends.

"You might be right, Pretty Lady. You Christians always know folk's secrets," he said, half-jokingly. She didn't know how to interpret his statement so she didn't respond. It was late and she didn't want to spark a long discussion that could lead to an augment. She watched his eyes watching hers.

She knew he was smarter than he put on. Not only was he especially attentive to his lotioned skin, tailored slacks, crisp-ironed shirts, and shining Stacey Adams, he was attentive to her and the things around her. She liked his attention to style and finesse but it also concerned her although she didn't know why just yet.

The sheriff's car finally reached the end of the street and turned left out of the neighborhood.

"He's made it his business to canvas more frequently," she acknowledged before pushing the door open. "Don't forget to pick up the newlyweds." She reminded him. She reached beyond the door frame to turn on the inside lights.

"No, I don't have to. Mable will get them. Some things were brewing at the church and she said it was important that she talked with them as soon as they returned. Besides, I figured they'd want to continue their love without me as a witness." George smiled and stepped back from the door.

It was time to end the date.

He winked goodbye and walked down the porch steps.

T.P. watched him get into the car and start it before closing and locking her door. George didn't drive off until the porch light flicked and the lights went off in the living room. Both were signs that she was safe. Then, he looked left and right for the canvassing Cracker.

She walked to the back bedroom and removed her heels then slid out of the dress. She smiled and clicked on the radio. It played George Otis Redding and she hummed and danced-walked to the back door. She double-checked the locks and windows then went to start a bath. She enjoyed George's scent mixed with his cologne but she did not want the empty spot in her bed smelling like that sexy chocolate man—not tonight anyway.

Shelia's Recovery

On the day Shelia was found, a caring young white man was searching every nook and cranny of New Orleans for his father. It was the luckiest day of Shelia's life. He found her curled in a fetal position and moaning. Blood covered her face and legs. "I'm going to get you some help,"

Instinctively, he began to look for any identification. He noticed she had a tarnished silver locket in the shape of a heart around her neck.

He tried to open the locket.

"Ma'am, can you hear me?" He gently touched her right shoulder. Her sleeve raised revealing a ridged tattoo of a nine-square grid with numbers in each square and one at the bottom right outside of the grid. He remembered his father bore one on his right ankle. His father had confided in him during the last time he was able to get his father off the streets and into rehab. He'd said addicts would use hot needles to burn the phone number grid somewhere on their bodies. He lifted his pants to show his son the nine-digit phone number. He would be the person to identify his father's body if the call was ever to come.

It was the most morbid thought he'd ever have to bear, and there he was looking down at the grid on Shelia who was nearly lifeless.

His father had explained the grid's number sequence so he could see his phone number in the glyph. Start at the top left. Read right, down, left, down, right, the last number off the grid was the first digit.

The young man tried to remember the numbers in order on Shelia's shoulder. He flipped over the locket. There, he found the same numbers in order but barely legible. He lifted Shelia from the ground and carried her to his car mentally repeating the numbers. Once he got her to lie down on the back seat, he found a piece of paper and pen to write down the phone number. He quickly drove to the emergency room of the New Orleans Charity Hospital. He apologizes repeatedly to Shelia each time the car hit a pothole. But, he was glad to hear that she was still alive,

When they arrived, the emergency room triage nurse questioned if he was family. He said no but he had a number for someone to call.

"Get her family here," the nurse said. "We are rushing her to surgery."

The young man decided to call the number he saw on Shelia's locket. He found a pay phone in the family waiting room and pulled out a quarter before taking a deep breath and dialing the number he had written down.

"Hell....o", Stella said in a sleepy voice.

"Hello, ma'am. I am so sorry to wake you like this. My name is Joey Mixon. I was looking under bridges where drug addicts live trying to find my father who is a drug attic, but instead, I found a young lady off Burbon Street in a New Orleans alley. She had this phone tattooed on her arm and I thought it might be the number of someone who loves her."

Stella couldn't catch her breath to respond.

"Ma'am? Ma'am, are you here?"

He heard her breathing deeply and continued, "She's in bad shape. Somebody beat her in a bad way."

Stella started to cry.

"Ma'am, she's at a great ER. These doctors are the best in the state. You may want to be here when the doctors stabilize her. And once she leaves here, she will need to go into rehab for her drug addiction." Joey said sadly.

"Thank you, son." Stella took a deep breath. "That's my daughter Shelia Woods. She's been out in the streets on that stuff for years, maybe tonight will be her turning point. You were a Godsend for my child. How can I repay you?" Stella asked wiping tears from her eyes.

"No ma'am. You don't owe me anything. I'm just glad I was able to help her because since I have been searching for my dad, I have seen so much misery and bloodshed over drugs. I just pray that I will be able to find him before it's too late."

Stella thought about this nice young man who alone was looking for his father in some of the most dangerous places. "You keep looking Joe and I will keep praying for you to find him. What's your father's name?" She asked knowing she would call every police friend she had in New Orleans to help find Joey's father.

"His name is Dr. Bradford Mixon from Gary, Louisiana," Joey said. He did not bother to correct Stella for the mispronunciation of his name. "I'm going to be here for a while. I can keep checking up on your daughter if that's all right with you," Joey said although he was tired and sleepy. He needed a long hot bath to clean the stench out of his clothing from all the places he had been that night.

"Of course, you can, son after all you saved Shelia's life," Stella said. "Thank you so much and I am on my way there."

Joey waited nearly two hours for Stella's arrival. How she spotted him out of all the family members waiting, he could never know but she would later explain that she recognized the spirit of the man God led to call her.

They hugged their greeting and then sat together. While sipping coffee, Joey told her stories about his father before he became an addict and how he was afraid that his faith was failing."

Stella took his hand and quietly prayed for him and his father.

Dr. Steven Lincoln and three other doctors worked on Shelia for hours. They collected all samples needed for a viable rape kit and removed fragments of glass from her clothing and skin. Without any identification, Dr. Lincoln asked his nurse to closely monitor Shelia until she stabilized and could identify herself and her family. The burns on her hands and body indicated to him that she injected heroin and would need additional support from Social Services, so he had the nurse prepare the papers while he went to the hospital family waiting room to try to find the young man who brought in his new patient.

When he entered the family waiting room, Joey quickly walked over and led him to Stella. He introduced them, hugged Stella good night, and left to rest and gather strength to continue searching for his father.

"Hi, Mrs. Stella Woods." He extended his hand to shake hers.

"Yes, I'm Shelia's mother. How is she doing, Dr. Lincoln?" Stella asked.

"Well, she came through the surgery very well and we've given her much more blood to sustain her loss. She has a black eye that will heal and some hair missing from the top of her head, but that will also grow back. It took quite a bit of time but we were able to gently stitch close the tears to her clitoris and rectum. It was brutal and we notified the authorities who will want to speak to her when she is more alert. She is in a lot of pain and will be with us for a few more days."

Stella cried hard and long. The doctor guided her to the hall to sip from the water fountain. He waited patiently for her to quiet down. "Whenever you are ready, you can go in to see her. I'll have a nurse bring more paperwork to you and answer any questions you may have."

"Thank you, Doctor."

"You are welcome. Good day, Mrs. Woods." He walked down to corridor toward the hospital's chapel.

Stella walked slowly to Room 93 and peeked in. Pain soared through her chest and she closed the door quietly and leaned back against the wall. The day had come for her to take her daughter back and never lose her again.

She lifted her head back to the wall, cried quietly, and began praying with every drop of faith she could muster.

The next morning when Shelia woke up, all she felt was pain throbbing throughout her entire body. She tried to get out of bed because she knew if she could get some heroin, she would feel better. She looked around and realized she was in a hospital, but she couldn't remember why. She tried to throw her legs out of the bed to sit up, but the pain was unbearable, so she started screaming until and nurse arrived.

The nurse gently pushed Shelia back on the bed, "Just lie still darling, you have had a rough night. I am going to give you something in your IV for pain and Dr. Steven Lincoln will be in to speak with you soon." The nurse said as she administered the drug into the IV.

"You are one strong woman," the nurse said, rubbing Shelia's arm. "You hold on to your mother's prayers. She's a mighty good Christian lady and she's prayed some powerful prayers over you right here in this hospital. Now, you listen to her, okay,? And you will be okay." She encouraged Shelia as the medicine took control.

"Mommmmaaa–," Shelia whispered then fell asleep.

Four days later, Shelia was transferred to Brainbayer Addiction Center, a well-known center with a recovery rate of ninety percent. There she underwent treatment for her complicated withdrawal from heroin.

Shelia recalls sweating profusely and her whole body had a new ache that made her cry out in pain.

"We are going to have to strap her down to keep her from hurting herself," one of the rehab nurses said and they buckled both Shelia's arms and legs and then gave her a shot of Valium.

A detoxification program was established specifically for Shelia's addiction to safely remove the drugs from her system. She was supervised day and night and given medication when needed.

Shelia would sweat, become nauseous, vomit, and hallucinate during these episodes she would be given drugs for her pain.

———

"Brainbayer Addiction Center, how may I help you?"

"Good afternoon. My name is Stella Woods. I believe my daughter is a patient at your center and I'm calling to see how she's doing and to pay for her care."

"What is your daughter's name ma'am?"

"Shelia Woods."

The dusty-haired secretary began to search through a file cabinet labeled "Patient Records". Once she found Shelia's file, she pulled the record.

"Hello ma'am, yes she's here and she's in treatment. I don't know much about the patients, but I can give you the cost for our services are five hundred dollars a week and if you are unable to pay this amount, we can have her transferred to the Catholic Sister's Detox Center in Lafayette. They are a charity service. I will ask Dr. Ocean to call you and give you more information."

Stella wondered why when people heard a voice and knew that the speaker was Black, they were so quick to assume that you were unable to pay for what you or your family needed.

"No, young lady, the five hundred dollars will be fine. I will have my bank process a check for one-thousand dollars and you have Dr. Ocean call me as soon as he is available to discuss my daughter's care. I prefer to be first on his list if you can arrange that. Thank you and goodbye." Stella was upset.

By dinnertime, Dr. Ocean called Stella. "Good evening, this is Dr. Ocean am I speaking to Mrs. Stella Woods?"

Stella wiped her hands on her apron before replying, "Yes, this is she."

"Mrs. Woods, we are honored that you have chosen us to care for Shelia. Your daughter has moved past phase one quite quickly. We have been able to remove the drugs from her digestive system so now she will enter rehabilitation. Our next step is to monitor her liver and blood, get her to eat healthy foods, and have her rest better since she has not slept well. Then, we will move into phase two where she will participate in group therapy daily and we will ably work with her individually.

"She's not eating?"

"When they are going through detox sometimes, they can't eat, they don't crave food they crave drugs, so we have to feed them through a needle until they can restore their gut."

"What made my daughter dependent on drugs?"

"Addictive drugs change the way the body functions. The more she used them, the more her body became accustomed to them and soon the body depends on them to function properly. Once she stopped using the drug, she experienced painful symptoms of withdrawal. That's what happened here when we detoxed her. However, if she had not come to us when she did, her heart, brain, and liver would have been damaged—possibly severely damaged. Going through detox she became nauseous, she couldn't sleep. She was in a lot of pain. She had tremors and headaches and she was hallucinating, but she's moved from that stage as I mentioned before."

He paused.

"We monitored her vital signs to assure there was not a medical emergency. She was given benzodiazepines to aid in her withdrawal and I am also going to prescribe valium for her now that the worst part is over and we can start addiction treatment. Are there any other questions, Mrs. Woods?"

"Will she be able to call me soon?" Stella's voice cracked.

"Yes ma'am, but please be patient with this process. We want her to do so well that she does not have to return here again. Do you understand what I mean?"

Stella could tell that the young doctor was hopeful.

"Yes, I do. Thank you for caring for Shelia, Doctor."

"Thank you, ma'am, Good night"

In the next week, Shelia's nurse explained to her the rehabilitation courses. "You'll have life skills training, relapse prevention and education, coping skills education, counseling, and meetings on aftercare and discharge. Then you will be finished and can finally leave and go home."

"Life skills?" Shelia turned her nose up.

"Yes, the life skills training covers a set of psychological and social skills that you will need to adapt in your daily life once you leave here. There are three main areas of life skills: Cognitive skills which allow you to make better decisions; next, there are personal skills that will help you to manage yourself; and finally there are interpersonal skills which allow you to communicate and interact with other people. When developing a healthy routine, you must develop a basic daily routine that will include a sleep schedule, exercise regularly, work and of course your commitment to family and work. You will also learn how to properly interview for a job, and write a resume. You will need a job to help boost your self-esteem and your self-sufficiency, this will give you confidence. In this meeting, you will learn to budget your money, you will also learn to pick a hobby, and your communication skills will be utilized. This is what we will discuss two days a week."

Damn, I'm never going to get out of here! I guess I'll just try to learn as much as I can. This place sure has a lot of free services.

Shelia left the meeting and went into the cafeteria for lunch, she had a sandwich and juice. She wanted coffee but didn't see any. *I guess you are not allowed coffee.*

She had a peaceful rest and then went to her next meeting on relapse prevention with Dr. Lonnie Golden. He was well-built and stood five-foot-six with a graying hairline. He was soft-spoken with a friendly demeanor.

"Good afternoon class. I hope you are all doing well."

Five of the seven students nodded quietly, and to Shelia's surprise, all of them seemed to like him.

"I will be relaying a lot of information and resources to you quickly, so if you need clarity just raise your hand and I'll stop and answer your questions. I will be talking about how to not relapse. You must have a relapse plan to prevent you from going back to your old habits. These plans are documents on paper that can be shared with your individual treatment team and your support group. In your plan, write down the things and people who are triggers for you, everything you crave, coping tools that truly work for you, and support group information."

Shelia raised her hand.

"Yes, Miss Woods, what is your question?"

"How do you stop these cravings? Because I still want the drug."

"Good question. We have different models to help prevent future relapse, they are not perfect, but they help most of our patients. The next thing you will need is educational coping skills along with counseling and finally aftercare and discharge planning. We are here to help you through the entire process, so, please don't get overwhelmed."

Shelia tried her best to relax but couldn't.

As a group, they worked through four scenarios to manage cravings. She appreciated the time Dr. Golden spent guiding each of them through fearful thoughts, triggers, and conflicting behaviors. After closing out the session with applause and meditative breathing. He said, "If there aren't any other questions then you are released for the day and I will see you in two days to go over what we've learned and how you've incorporated it this week."

This isn't bad at all. I hope they keep these meetings as short as they are. I have time to go to the cafeteria and get a salad. I've gained a lot of weight, and I feel heavy, so I'm going to eat light from now on. Shelia walked to the dining hall. Doing so made her miss Stella's call again.

For the next four weeks, Shelia had to take notes, take the test, sit in a circle group, and talk about her problem. The other patients shared theirs without hesitations, but Shelia didn't because she'd convinced herself that her only problem was heroin. Her skin had begun to look healthy, and her hair was growing back. She decided that when she left the center, she would return to her mother, find her daughter, and change her life for the best.

The night of Mary Jean's wedding, Shelia's memories flooded her with so much emotion and gratitude while she stood in Stella's bathroom, taking off the most beautiful dress she's ever worn. Her daughter, Mary Jean, was now married and soon to return from her honeymoon as a whole, Christian woman. The dress would forever be a reminder of how wonderful sobriety and love feel. Shelia whispered a prayer for more. And, she admitted, a part of her believed now that God brought the biggest blessing out of her biggest hurt and deceit. She had her mother's love again and would soon know the love of her daughter, son-in-law, and grandsons. *Ain't God good.*

Returning from the Honeymoon

When Mary Jean walked through the airport's exit and stepped onto the ramp, she knew instantly she was back in South Louisiana. The sun glowed and radiated heat hot enough to fry an egg on the concrete. The wind had hidden and not one breeze blew. She instantly began to sweat. She could feel her deodorant melting under her arms and sticking to her dress.

After living in Louisiana for 30 years, she knew the temperature without a meteorologist's report. *It's 90 degrees and the humidity must be 105.* She chuckled and looked down the breezeway as her new husband pushed their luggage cart toward her. Even though Mary Jean enjoyed her honeymoon, she was elated to be home again despite the blistering heat. She was exhausted from the trip and lovemaking.

Now that she was home and Rev. Grant would soon be back at work, she knew she would be able to get some needed rest at least during the day. She wondered what their nights would be like at home as husband and wife.

Within five minutes of waiting, Mable pulled up to take them home. She hugged Mary Jean, "Look at you, Mrs. Grant, glowing and whatnot!" She complimented Mary Jean and smiled the most genuine smile Mary Jean had ever seen. After Rev. Grant loaded the luggage and gifts into the car, Mable gave him a stack of office files and copies of *The Baton Rouge Newsleader.*

"Rev. Grant, hold on to these tonight and read them after you are well-rested and well-fed. You're going to need a clear mind." She said.

To help the process, she prepared two days of meals for the Grant family and arranged for the Women's Auxiliary to clean the home while the men manicured the yard. It was clear to them that those files should be his sole focus.

"That'll be fine, Mable," he smiled. "I will call you once I sit down to study the files."

"Call me after you study them." She stressed the word 'after'.

Mary Jean looked out the window before the cool air condition and rhythm of the ride made her dose off. Rev. Grant looked back at his wife, smiled, and whispered another prayer for wisdom and protection. He reassured Mable that whatever it was, he would handle it all expeditiously. Then they rode home silently.

The next day when the telephone rang, Mary Jean knew it had to be T.P.

"Hello, T.P.," Mary Jean said, smiling into the phone.

"Hey, Sister! Are you by yourself because I want to hear all the unedited details of your honeymoon!" T.P said quickly.

"Yes, I am," Mary Jean laughed. "Everyone left to grab lunch at Moxy's. She has the last pickings of strawberries from Ponchatoula and made her famous custard and pies. The boys just had to have some and Donald needed more files from the church."

"Ohhkay. And I can't wait for the details, so spill it," T.P said.

"I'm exhausted, T.P! We were constantly on the go every morning until late afternoon. Donald wanted to see everything, and I went along with him, but I was so tired by the time we returned to the Hotel Celine, I took a hot shower and went to sleep. Donald stayed up a lot of nights until later enjoying the view from the balcony and writing sermons."

"Girl, don't tell me the man was in Paris and still thinking about the church. Did he jump your bones while you all were there?" T.P. asked laughing.

"Every night after he came in from writing his sermon, he made love to me and it was simply amazing. I have never experienced anything like it before," Mary Jean said still recalling how she felt.

"Of course, you haven't!" T.P. laughed even harder." You only had one piece of a man in your life before Rev. Grant, but now you have a full-grown man who knows how to please a woman! And, to think, girl, you are going to have that every night now that you are married."

Mary Jean thought about how exhausted she was throughout the whole time and knew she would not be able to handle this type of lovemaking every night. "No, I know I will not want it every night, but I could handle it every other night," Mary Jean said laughing.

T.P. was bending over laughing. Then she thought about Paris, a place she had heard so much about and always wanted to see for herself, so she began questing Mary Jean. "What was it like there? No. first, what did you bring me?"

"I brought you some chocolate and a Louis Vuitton bag. I bought purses for Granny and Shelia. I even bought Mrs. Agnes a little gift," Mary Jean said trying to remember where Rev. Grant put the packages.

T.P. thought about remarking about Mary Jean bringing Mrs. Agnes a gift, but she changed her mind. "I'll be right over to get my gifts," T.P. said. "No, I'm just kidding I will see you tomorrow. Now what was the weather like?"

"It was warm but not as hot like it is here. I guess it's because the air blows over the Atlantic Ocean and into the city. Did you know that the name Paris came from the Celtic Parisii tribe? Most people think the name came from Greek mythology, but it does not. One of the shop-keepers told me this."

"What was your hotel room like and why do they call it the city of lights?"

"We had a one-bedroom with a queen-size bed, a fully equipped kitchen, a fireplace, and a shower bathroom. We also had washer and dryer units in the suite and there was a private balcony where we were able to see the Eiffel Tower while sitting on the balcony."

"One of the maids told me it was called the city of light because Paris was one of the first large European cities to have gas street lighting. Girl, I wish you could have seen the Eiffel Tower. It was magnificent, and Rev. Grant insisted that we attended services in the Notre Dame cathedral."

"Isn't that a Catholic church?"

"Yes, it's a medieval church, and it's the tallest church I've ever seen. They had mass just like other Catholic churches."

"Rev. Grant was fine with that?" T.P. asked as she poured boiling water over loose tea leaves into a bright blue pottery mug.

"You know how Donald feels about other religions. He is comfortable in any religion as long as it's about God."

"Where else did the two of you go?"

"The Aquarium de Paris-Cineaqua had more than five hundred species of fish. They had one nearly transparent fish. They call it the glass catfish. They had a lot of electric eels and electric rays. Did you know that a fish can drown in water if there is not enough oxygen in the water?"

"How is that?" T.P. asked as she sipped her tea.

"They'll suffocate, girl," Mary Jean chuckled. Mary Jean always finds the simplest things so entertaining. T.P. loved how happy Mary Jean sounded. "There's this beautiful museum called the Louvre Museum, which houses the most impressive art statues. We saw the Mona Lisa, the Ship of Fools, the Raft of Medusa, and Saint John the Baptist. Their artwork is exquisite." She said.

"Well, don't tell me any more about the museum because you know I'm not into that kind of art, painting yes, but statutes no," T.P. decided to sit in the living room and continue the conversation, "Now, tell me what you had to eat."

Mary Jean soaked the dishes while talking to T.P. and took a bag of fish out of the freezer to thaw for dinner. "We ate salmon and steak Frites which is steak with a green sauce poured on top and with French fries. I don't remember what that green sauce was, but it tasted good. I do not like tarts, but Donald had a lemon tart. He said that it was sweet and sour and topped with lemon candy. He also liked the roast chicken and fries. You know how much I like tea cakes and they had some called financiers. They were delicious almond cakes. I wish I could order some of them now."

"Wow, girl, they must be good," T.P. said crossing her legs.

"We tried their ice cream and we liked the salted butter caramel and strawberry much better than the ice cream here. The crepes were good also. They were stuffed with meat, cheese, and vegetables and wrapped in brown buckwheat. We also had some American food like hamburgers. They make their candy with almonds and sugar, not pecans. I didn't like that. There was so much more food, but I know you don't want to keep talking about that."

"Yeah, you're right, but how did they treat the Black people? You know these Americans are mad with all the protesting we have going on. How did the French treat you?"

Mary Jean deliberately avoided talking about the racial tension that was seeping across the nation. She was angry and afraid especially with Baton Rouge being so close. She prayed constantly for peace. Instead of answering T.P., she started washing the dishes.

T.P. took notice. "Well, did you two drink any liquor?"

"Yes, we did, we had beer—a lot. The French drink a lot of wine. Everywhere we ate, everyone drank red wine with their food. We mostly drank smokey Charbonnier, and it was okay for me, but Donald liked it more." Mary Jean said. "We even bought a bottle of Rose and took it to our room with us for later in the evening. "

T.P. struggled to imagine Mary Jean drinking any kind of alcohol.

"Before we left, we went to another place with more than three hundred wax figures. They had Michael Jackson, Superman, the Pope, Jimi Hendrix, Madonna, the Queen, and many more. They look so lifelike that a couple of times I thought it was a living person. They said it takes forty-two hours just for the makeup team to complete the reproduction of one celebrity using oil paints." Mary Jean said while turning back on the water.

T.P. heard the noise of the dishes being washed and decided to play with Mary Jean, "Girl, are you taking a bath while we are talking? Don't you know that you can electrocute yourself while talking on the phone with me?" She laughed.

"Now, T.P. you know I'm not taking a bath, I just finished washing dishes and taking some fish out of the freezer for dinner tonight."

"Can I come?"

"Sure! You're always invited here even without an invitation."

"I was just playing, girl. I don't want any fish, but thanks for the invitation. I'll see you tomorrow." T.P. knew she wanted to tell her baby sister about George and their first date, but decided to tell her later. Mary Jean smiled and hung up the phone.

Jealous Deacon Tomas

Deacon James Tomas entered the back door of The Greatness of Christ Baptist Church. The Louisiana heat had scorched the doorknob making him fight to open the door without burning his hands. He nodded hello to Sis. Dorothy Martin before entering Rev. Mical's office. She quietly greeted him with a wave but didn't stop him since the older deacon had been permitted to enter and leave the back office without announcement.

Before Deacon Tomas opened the door completely, he could smell cheap perfume. He stepped into the large office suite and noticed Carla Knotts sitting across from Rev. Mical. Her legs were crossed high and open. Her red polka-dot skirt laid high on her hips revealing her right butt cheek. He never liked this girl and he wondered why Rev. Mical kept her around if not for sex.

"What are you doing here?" Deacon Tomas asked, staring directly at Carla.

"We are minding our business which is what you should be doing, Tomas," Carla said uncrossing her legs and throwing the right leg across the arm of the chair, being sure to flash him a peek of her womanhood.

She knew Deacon Tomas didn't like the fact that if any woman could get the esteemed Rev. James Mical into bed, it would be her.

Deacon Tomas slammed the door and stepped toward the oak desk. He turned to Rev. Mical. "I don't deal with those kind, Mical, and neither should you," he said sternly. *This little slut thinks she's able to change Mical but that will never happen and especially won't happen with her fast ass.*

"No need for the hostility, Deacon Tomas." Rev. Mical gave him a knowing look. "We were just finishing up." He shifted forward in the large-back executive chair, leaned on the desk, and adjusted papers. His voice was professional and direct. "Carla, only you can make this happen. He can only hold out for so long." He gave her a wink.

Carla stood from the chair with her skirt rolled revealing her naked behind.

This gal is mentally ill. I don't know why Mical can't see that!

Deacon Tomas opened the office door, signally for her to leave. When she did, he moved her chair to the window and exchanged it for another. He had a mind to throw hers away seeing that she had just soiled the seat and the arm in his eyes. He curled his nose. For any other man to do so, it would have been an ugly expression, but Deacon Tomas was suave naturally, even his ugliest face was handsome to many—including Rev. Micah, the newest senior pastor at the church.

"Mical, why do you entertain that gal? You know her type. They were all over your former church. Isn't that one of the reasons why you joined this ministry?" He asked rhetorically. "You know she's marked with sin and she has mental problems and demons that torment her just like her mama. You better hope she never turns on you because it would be awfully bad." He chastised.

Rev. Mical straightened the Bible on his desk. He was a neat freak and could not stand anything to be out of place. Sometimes it took him a long time to leave his house because if he saw a picture on the wall that wasn't straight, he would stop, and align it, or if his black Stacy Adams didn't shin smoothly, he'd spend hours rubbing the shoes until they screamed perfection.

"I'm not worried about Clara Knotts talking about me or trying to hurt me. I have her taken care of. She waddles in secrets and scandals. Her mind is on Grant and she will do anything to try to get him in bed. I think that nut is in love with him, poor fool," Rev. Mical boasted. Deacon Tomas had heard enough. He rubbed his hand down the front of his shirt, stood, and headed to the door.

"Well, let's go if we are going to get a good table at Moxy's for lunch," Deacon Tomas said as he held the office door open for Rev. Mical. The older man easily noticed Rev. Mical's erection as he stood stretching his back. He tucked in the back of his shirt and snapped his suspenders behind. *So that's how you respond to sluts.* Deacon Tomas's anger barely allowed him to follow the cocky, forty-five-year-old pastor out of the office, past Dorothy's desk, along the corridor, and out to the back parking lot. They drove separate cars with Rev. Mical leading them down Hwy 90 then onto the two-lane dusty road that led to the front door of Moxy's. The lunch crowd had left and out of the corner of his eye, he saw Rev. Grant loading food into his car with his sons.

Rev. Mical grinned. *Welcome back, Grant. Hope you enjoyed your young wife. You won't have that little family of yours for much longer.* He was so deep in his thoughts he had to slam on the brakes just in time to not hit Mac Brown's clanky pickup. Just a tap against that monstrosity would have totaled Rev. Mical's car. He killed the engine quickly and met Deacon Tomas inside as if they hadn't already seen each other.

Bar-B-Que at Rev. Douglas's House

After enjoying a few special trips out alone with their new stepfather, Lawrence Junior and Robert Michael were excited to meet Aunt T.P.'s family which was now their family—a concept they hadn't fully understood and didn't care to. For them, everything was going wonderfully now that they were all a family. The Grants.

The boys spent very little time asking questions about who everyone was. They accepted calling Rev. Douglas "Papa Douglas" without explanation. They had even adjusted to longer visits with Lawrence now that he was more reliable.

This August Saturday seemed to be perfect for a barbeque gathering. The temperature was seventy-five degrees and the wind blew steadily giving a cooler breeze. The sky held a beautiful overcast and even the trees seemed happy as they swung back and forth in a cool rhythm. The city and nation were quiet even though everyone knew more sit-ins and boycotts were being planned. Even hurricane season took a break this weekend.

For more than a week, Mary Jean tried to get her mom to take the hour's drive to Rev. Douglas' home. The family was hosting a summer feast for Mary Jean to meet the rest of her family. She had convinced herself that Rev. Douglas would publicly apologize to Granny and Shelia for the years of denying Mary Jean as his child and causing Shelia a life of shame and abandonment.

But, Shelia was adamant that she would not be in his presence publically nor alone, despite Granny's pleas to forgive as Christ forgave. "Baby, you've got to try and keep a steady heart before God. It will heal our hearts," Granny pleaded. Shelia was far from Granny in the world of forgiveness but she genuinely wanted Mary Jean to be whole and complete in her relationship with her father and his family. She even encouraged Mary Jean to meet her other siblings, especially now that she had T.P. as a best friend and older sister.

"I don't know how many years I have to live, but I do know that when I'm gone and Shelia is also gone, I want Mary Jean and her boys to have other family members that they can turn to. I will never forget what Rev. Douglas did, but I could not hold on to those bad feelings. It was destroying me and hindering my walk with the Lord. Ain't nothing Christian about unforgiveness and bitterness," Granny said. "I do not have to forget, but I do need to forgive and so do you, Shelia, if you truly want to move on with your life."

"Momma is right that the boys need to know their family, but them Douglases ain't no family of mine." Shelia would tell Mary Jean with finality.

Mary Jean placed water and RC Colas in an ice chest in the trunk just in case they became thirsty. She and T.P. both had on Bermuda shorts, Stella had on a Kente print momo dress, and the boys wore blue shorts with gold short-sleeve T-shirts. Mary Jean drove them to the Douglas's home while Rev. Grant stayed behind to oversee repairs to the church. Part of the roof in one of the classrooms had suddenly caved during the last thunderstorm. The insurance company had denied his request to contract members to repair the damages, instead, the agency sent over a crew from Livingston parish with a sketchy reputation. So, Rev. Grant was determined to oversee them. When it came to the church, Rev. Grant was all hands-on.

After driving an hour, Mary Jean asked, "Which way now, T.P.?"

"Girl, I'm not going to let you miss your turn; for the third time, turn left on Route 53 about two miles ahead," T.P. said still playing and giggling with the boys.

"The scenery is beautiful. I recall all these pretty tall trees. I haven't been back to Tucker, Louisiana, since you were a little girl," Granny said.

I wonder how many of these colonial architectures still exist. They look like they could have been the Big House of some horrid plantation. Mary Jean thought while noticing the outside of each home was white brick and wooden as if someone had just painted them.

Driving up the long driveway to the house, Granny glanced at the house but she was not surprised."Well, this place still looks the same, The only thing that is different is that they added more shrubbery," she said. Memories resurfaced and Granny held in her emotions.

When they parked in front of the house, T.P. jumped out pulling the boys along with her. As soon as she got to the door, Cynthia Douglas greeted them with hugs and T.P. took the boys inside. Cynthia waited for Mary Jean and Stella to walk up the walkway. She noticed Shelia had not come with them. She breathed a sigh of relief. "I'm so happy you all were able to come," she said as she hugged Mary Jean and Stella. Then she stepped back and opened the door wider for their entrance.

Mary Jean looked around, taking in all the beauty. She felt a little down because she saw the large house T.P. was raised in and remembered the small house she was raised in without her parents. She shook the thought out of her head. She was here to start a new life with her father's family, and she refused to allow bad thoughts and the secret lives of men to ruin that.

"Your home is lovely," she said to Cynthia.

"Thank you, sweetheart." Cynthia smiled. "Let me show you the rest of the house. You will probably remember all of this, Sis. Stella, because we haven't changed much since you were last here."

Stella remembered all the times she and her husband had been to this house for various functions. She remembered how close they all were and the love that she and her husband had for this family. The heaviness of grief fell on her.

"This is the living room," Cynthia said as Mary Jean looked around at the massive wood-burning fireplace, two baby blue sofas faced each other and an easy chair faced the fireplace. The chair was floral with a touch of blue. Hanging on the wall behind the fireplace was a large painting of Cynthia and Rev. Douglas. On the mantelpiece, there were family individual portraits. Mary Jean walked up to look at each picture. She recognized a picture that T.P. had taken of her and Granny a few Christmas ago. There was a picture of a lady who looked a lot like T.P. and two gentlemen who appeared to be in their late thirties or early forties.

"Are these your other children?" Mary Jean asked.

"Yes. They are your brothers, Demetric Douglas Junior and James Gordon Douglas. And that is Lillian Cynthia Douglas Matthew. You'll meet them soon. All of them live out of state, but they flew in to meet you," Her excitement made her talk faster than normal.

She led them from the living room through a door and into the white kitchen and sky blue with a white refrigerator, a white huge stove, sky blue cabinets which Mary Jean thought looked strange, a counter in the middle of the floor with bar stools surrounding it. The cushions on the chairs were checkered blue, white, and black. There were no kitchen curtains and Mary Jean did not see any in the living room either.

"Your kitchen is nice. What's that in the middle?" Mary Jean asked.

"A cutting board. Demetric built that a year ago because I hated that I didn't have something handy to cut ingredients or sit my pots on. Other than the wall counters, everything was too clustered, so he built it. Did you know that he's a carpenter by trade? His father taught him everything."

"No, I didn't."

"He went to Tuskegee to learn architecture and changed his major in his third year and decided to switch to Shaw University Divinity School. He still makes pieces for some church members and our home from time to time. If you need something made just let us know, and he can make it. In fact, he can duplicate many pieces that you see in the furniture stores."

"He made our bedroom set," Granny said solemnly.

Mary Jean remembered Granny's bedroom set and it was beautiful, old but beautiful. They walked out of the kitchen into a formal dining room. The room was stunning. The cherry wood table was rectangular and seated ten people. The legs were broad, and the bottom of each leg formed a large clawfoot. The designs cut into each piece of furniture were exquisite. The chairs' seats were brown leather, and the backrests were covered in white leather. It made the cherry wood more distinguished and royal.

Sitting on the table was a fresh flower bouquet. Underneath the table was a large throw rug with the colors, brown, white, and a touch of red. Matching drapes hung from ceiling to floor. They pulled back revealing the backyard. A cherry wood China cabinet was filled with beautiful crystal glasses and gold trim china plates. It and a sideboard spread across one wall. On the adjacent walls hung a large rectangular mirror and a painting of the Last Supper.

"We use this room for Thanksgiving, Christmas, and all other special occasions," she said, slowly moving a bang of bouncing gray curls from over her head. T.P's gifted hands had grown her mom's hair back after depression and bitterness began making it fall out. Now, Cynthia loved her graying crown more than ever. She led them out of the dining area and down a hallway next to the stairs.

"We could go up the back stairs to the upstairs bedroom, but it will be better if we took the front stairs because they are wider," Cynthia remarked.

"I'm going to wait for you all in the living room. I'm feeling a little tired," Stella declared.

"I don't have to see the upstairs, Granny. I can stay here with you," Mary Jean said.

"No, baby, you go see the rest of the house. While you all are gone, I'm going to just sit here and rest my eyes. You know I normally go to bed early so I'm a little tired. While you are gone, I'll get T.P. to get me something to drink so I can take my medication."

"Are you sure, Granny?" Mary Jean asked. Stella nodded, then delicately turned away from them. Stella was not feeling well, but she did not want to ruin Mary Jean's big day.

Even though Rev. Douglas had done her family wrong, what kind of Christian would she be not to be able to forgive him? She had convinced herself that forgiving him did not mean she would forget, and besides, she believed Mary Jean needed to know her family—the good, the bad, and all the secrets.

As they headed towards the stairs, Mary Jean saw Stella take a seat on the sofa and she could tell that her Granny was not feeling well, but she knew there was no way she would be able to drag her away from this event, for her sakes.

The carpet on the stair steps was brown cushioned and soft. When they arrived on the second landing it was carpeted the same as the steps.

"The rooms to the left were the boys' rooms and the ones to the right were for the girls' and ours. So, let's check out the boys' rooms first," Cynthia said.

When they opened the door to the far left, Cynthia stepped inside.

"This is Demetric Junior's room."

Mary Jean was looking for something grander than this, but then she thought maybe Demetric was like T.P.: Plain Jane. The room was mid-size, with a three-piece walnut bedroom set. Behind the headboard were beige drapes and Mary Jean could see that there were windows behind the drapes. She wondered why they covered the window, maybe it was because there was a sliding glass opening leading to the outside balcony. The headboard of the bed was in square sections and inside each section was a padded leather square. The dresser had nine drawers with a square mirror on top. The nightstand was rather larger and had three drawers. On top of the nightstand was a beige octagon lamp. The floor was hardwood and a large beige throw rug covered most of the room.

"Nice room," Mary Jean lied.

They left the room and walked a few feet.

"This is the boys' bathroom that they shared. When Cynthia opened the door, Mary Jean was shocked because there was blue floral wallpaper on the wall.

Who puts floral wallpaper in a bathroom for men? Mary Jean thought.

It was a small bathroom. There was a blue toilet, blue curtains covering one window, a blue vanity top with a sink inside, and a white cabinet underneath. There was a large mirror on the wall and a long rectangular light overhead. The bathtub sat on legs. The towels on the towel rack were blue and white. Mary Jean did not like this room, either.

"The wallpaper is hideous, but the boys picked it out when they were younger, and I didn't have the heart to tell them that it was not for boys. I think they liked it because my mom had similar wallpaper in her bathroom. One day I'll move it, but I don't see the hurry now that everyone has left home and is living on their own," Cynthia said.

Cynthia opened the door next to Demetric's room. She walked inside with Mary Jean on her heels. This room was nice. A four-piece, black walnut bedroom set with a full-size bed, short column footboard bedpost with carvings, and the headboard with two thinner posts was centered by an arch. Directly under the arch was a lattice that stopped short of the bed, and the bottom of the bed was solid wood. There was a dresser with three long drawers in the center and three shorter drawers on each side and in the center was a mirror made of the same material as the headboard of the bed. Beside the bed, there was a nightstand with three drawers and on top of the nightstand was a brown football lamp. Over the bed were two nature paintings. Mary Jean walked up to the bed and looked at the drawings.

"James painted those when he was ten years old. We were so sure he was going to be an artist, but his mind was not totally on art, but we sent him to school for it and even today he's quite a good painter. His apartment is covered in his artwork. I think Demetria has a few of his paintings," Cynthia said.

Mary Jean remembered the artwork in T.P.'s house and wondered where they came from because they did not fit with her décor. Then she saw a doorway next to the bed and when she walked to the door, Cynthia brushed ahead of her and opened the door to another beautiful outdoor balcony.

They exited the room and the next door they walked to was opened by Cynthia and it was the linen closet. It was stacked from the floor almost to the ceiling. With sheets and towel sets. Mary Jean wondered how Cynthia was able to reach the sheets at the top.

"As you can see this is the linen closet. We keep the kids' sets at the top and the things I need middle ways and at the bottom the only time we need to change their sheets is when they come home and then we tell them to make up their beds because we don't put sheets on the bed until someone is going to sleep in the bed," Cynthia said as she moved to the next room and opened the door. Mary Jean knew this had to be Lillian's room because T.P. would never have liked anything so girly.

"This was Lillian's room," Cynthia said.

"Cynthia! Cynthia!" Rev. Douglas yelled from the back of the house.

"Demetric, I'm upstairs showing Mary Jean the house!" Cynthia yelled.

"Well, hurry up! Everyone's hungry and the food is getting cold! It's getting late and the boys are looking for their mother!"

"Okay, Demetric. We'll be down in about five minutes," Cynthia said. "This is Lillian and T.P.'s bathroom," Cynthia said as she opened the door to the room.

The room was dark pink. The toilet was light pink; the sink and the tub were all pink. The tub had floral light pink shower curtains and the window curtains were solid light pink. There were dark and light pink towels on the towel rack. On top of the toilet tank was the prettiest pink floral arrangement. Mary Jean wondered if Cynthia changed the arrangements often, or if it was changed because they were coming. Cynthia closed the door and rushed Mary Jean to the next room.

When the door opened Mary Jean knew instantly that this was T.P.'s room. Everything was off-white.

"This is T.P.'s room," Cynthia said.

"I know," Mary Jean said. "I know she likes white." A full-size bed sat in the center of the room. A canopy connected to the headboard extended over the top quarter of the bed. Mary Jean was shocked to see that there was lace around the edge of the canopy.

"Did T.P. like the lace around the canopy?" Mary Jean asked.

"God no, I glued that on the canopy after T.P. moved. I thought it matched the beds and purchased it when I bought all new bedspread sets and curtains for all the rooms. "

The dresser had two small top drawers two side drawers and three middle drawers with a plan mirror attached. The end table by the bed had a plain white lamp on top and in the far-left corner of the room, there was a dressing table with different types of perfume. When Mary Jean walked over to the table Cynthia felt she needed to explain.

"I bought more perfume to replace the ones that T.P. took, so when she came home, she would always have perfume because I know how much she loves perfumes," Cynthia said.

There was also a door leading to the balcony, just like in the other bedrooms. They rushed out of T.P.'s room and into this room. Mary Jean knew it had to be Cynthia's and Rev. Douglas's bedroom. The first thing Mary Jean saw was this huge, brown cherry, four large, posted bed that looked Egyptian style. Surrounding the bed was a gold rod that would be used for sheers if she ever decided to place them around the bed. There was a large dresser with the same post that the bed had, and an oval mirror attached. There was an end table, but it was not next to the bed it was off to the right side of the room and on top of it was a lamp whose base was an Egyptian goddess. Mary Jean knew that Rev. Douglas had made this even before Cynthia told her. In the far-right corner of the room, there were a palm tree and balcony doors. As Mary Jean walked into the room her feet sank into the beige and brown carpet.

"Let's hurry into the bath so we can get downstairs before Demetric yells at us again," Cynthia said.

Suddenly they heard.

"Cynthia! Cynthia! We are all hungry. How much longer must we wait? The food is getting cold," Rev. Douglas yelled.

"If you want to eat go ahead and start without us!" Cynthia walked onto the balcony and yelled.

"The barbeque is for Mary Jean, her sons, and Sister Stella, so why would we start eating before they got the first plate!" Rev. Douglas yelled even louder.

"We'll be there in a minute, Demetric!" Cynthia yelled and came back inside. "Mary Jean, let's look at this last room quickly, so we can go downstairs before Demetric have a heart attack!"

When Cynthia opened the master bedroom's bathroom door, it was nothing like what she expected. It didn't fit with the room. The walls were covered in green floral paper and the curtains were dark green. The tub sat on silver legs and the outside of it along with the double vanities and toilet was mint green. Leaning against the left wall was a decorative ladder painted dark green and on each step were towels of different sizes. Mary Jean planned to do the same in her master bathroom now that she's seen it.

"Let's rush downstairs," Cynthia said moving down the stairs quicker than when they went up. When they reached the bottom step, Stella came out of the living room and met them. "What time is it?"

"It's about four o'clock," Cynthia said.

Stella shook her head. "I can't believe I slept that long. I was really tired." They walked down the hall towards the backdoor. Mary Jean knew the boys must be having a great time because they had not come looking for her as they normally do when she brings them around unfamiliar people.

Pictures of popular ministers hung on the walls. Granny recognized them all since she spent most of her time watching church services on television or listening to them on WXOK 1550AM. She saw Rev. Gerald Pope of Christian Light Center and Rev. Mason Dupre of Christ First Gospel Baptist Church, but what surprised her the most was the last photo on the wall. She glanced ahead and noticed that Mary Jean had not looked at the portraits and she was now pushing through the back door.

Stella stopped briefly to look closely at the last picture frame. It was a familiar photo of a minister holding the hand of a young boy. Both wore matching black suits with thin black ties. She was certain the boy was

Donald Grant—her new grandson-in-law. *Now, why would this photo hang here?* She wondered. *And how long has it been there?*

Stella held her thoughts to herself and slowly stepped through the backdoor. When she and Mary Jean walked around the corner of the house into the spacious backyard. Thirty or more voices shouted, "Surprise!"

They were shocked because they expected to see family members only. Surely all these people were not Mary Jean's people, Stella thought. Now, she knew why Cynthia was taking so much time with Mary Jean throughout the house tour.

The family prepared a grand celebration. Decorations were everywhere. Lanterns hung from four massive trees. One was wrapped with white lights and the others were wrapped with multicolored lights. Strings of paper ribbons and balloons hung from the corner of the house and any place one of the younger kids could stick them.

Six long tables were covered with a different color table cloth. Each table had a small basket of dinner rolls and two homemade cakes. Freshly-cut bouquets of pink Morning Glories sat as centerpieces. A bricked barbecue pit stood in the far corner of the yard. Mary Jean knew it was another construction project of Rev. Douglas. She looked around the yard trying to spot T.P. and the boys. She'd wondered where they'd run off to.

When she saw all the guests, she knew that T.P. was talking the entire time she was touring the house. Mary Jean smiled, knowing T.P. probably had already introduced her nephews to each and every person there. She also knew that was just what the boys needed to get them comfortable. She finally spotted the boys on a bright red swing set. To Mary Jean's surprise, Lawrence Junior was already swinging with two taller boys, while Robert Michael went spinning down the metal slide with a piece of cake in his hand. She was focused so much on them at that moment that she did not notice the guests walking over to her and Granny.

Stella touched Mary Jean's hand when Gertie Sims and her granddaughter walked up. Although she tried to put on her best Christ-like behavior, Stella's body told her true feelings. Mary Jean noticed Granny's stance stiffening and her body shifting when certain people came to greet them. She knew her grandmother had some endearing conflict with the smiling guests. All of which probably stemmed from the years of Stella being a faithful member of Rev. Douglas's church.

Lillian could see that her new sister Mary Jean was uncomfortable with all the people trying to shake her hand, so she came over to get her.

"Sorry, ladies. Let us all eat first and then you all can socialize," she said.

"Thanks," Mary Jean said as Lillian led them toward the serving tables.

"I felt overwhelmed," she whispered to Granny.

"Umm-humm," Stella moaned.

"Since Daddy has already blessed the meal, let's eat everyone!" Demetric Douglas Junior yelled over the sound system. This was the first time Mary Jean had seen a son who looked so strikingly identical to his father. If not for their age difference, the two men could have been twins.

He handed the microphone to one of three women who stood on a makeshift stage no more than a foot off the ground. They rose their mics and began bellowing the new hit, "Oh Happy Day" by Edwin Hawkins Singers. The two speakers carried their voices and the music across the yard. Everyone knew then that the celebration had officially begun.

Kids ran to the food table and the servers placed hot dogs or hamburgers with potato chips on their plates and then gave them a cherry soda. Adults danced in line waiting to get their food. Mary Jean and Stella were first to get a plate of barbecue ribs, potato salad, and baked beans. With their free hands, they picked up bottles of Coca-Cola then headed to the center table which had been set up for them and the immediate family.

Lillian, T.P., Demetric, James, and their parents soon joined Stella and Mary Jean at the family table. The boys sat nearby with Lil' James and Lilly Dee, their new cousins. Everyone's plates overflowed with hamburgers, chicken, ribs, rice dressing, and sweet peas.

For a moment the music overpowered most of the conversations but T.P. shouted and formally introduced her siblings to Mary Jean. When she got to James, Rev. Douglas walked up and interrupted.

"How's the food, Mary Jean?" He asked. He kneeled between her and Granny, pulling their attention.

"It's…it's delicious..umm, Rev. Douglas," She quickly took another bite of the tender ribs. She was unsure of how she would address him. So far, saying "Rev. Douglas" was all she could muster.

He watched her hesitancy and whispered, "Please, can you call me dad instead of Rev. Douglas?"

Mary Jean wiped the barbecue sauce from her cheek, "Okay, I'll try." She tried to whisper also. "It's just that all of this is so new to me and I forget, but I will try."

He nodded his appreciation, "And you, Sis. Stella, how is everything?"

"The food is good, Demetric, but you are going to have to go awfully slow with Mary Jean. She has just gotten to meet all of you. She's comfortable with T.P. because they have known each other for a long time and I'm sure she'll be the same way with the rest of you as soon as she gets to know you." Mary Jean liked seeing the feisty side of Stella.

Rev. Douglas could tell Stella was still very protective of Mary Jean and he couldn't blame her only now he needed her to allow him to love his daughter properly. It wasn't enough that he had secretively sent Stella money for Mary Jean. The first time Stella received the bulky envelope of cash, she attempted to return it and he pleaded to the point of tears for her to keep it and never utter a word to anyone. She promised and watching him at the barbecue was the first time in a long time that she'd remembered doing so.

Rev. Douglas touched their shoulders and returned to his seat next to Cynthia.

"Are they okay?" She asked.

"Yes. Yes. I think everything will be all right."

The conversation at the table was light and quiet as everyone ate their food and enjoyed watching couples dance and laugh. Once they finished their meals, Cynthia cut the cakes and gave everyone a slice. Stella declined hers and offered it to James instead. He enjoyed having a double portion. Cynthia gave the grandkids vanilla ice cream with their slices.

Mary Jean got up from the table and went to get another drink. As she walked past a table of elderly women, one lady wearing a wide-brim, straw hat stopped her. "You turned out to be a very good-looking, fine young lady considering where you came from," she said condescendingly.

"Yeah," another lady remarked. "None of us thought that you would turn out to be much considering who your mother is by the way where is your mother? Why didn't she come?"

"Girl, you know that little fast ass wasn't going to come here to her bell maw's house," They laughed.

Mary Jean did not know how to answer them without insulting them, but she decided she needed to tell both of them something.

"Aren't you two Christian ladies from Rev. Douglas's–I mean my daddy's–church?" Mary Jean asked.

"Of course, we are! Why else would we have come here?" The straw hat lady said.

"That figures because you couldn't be part of the Douglas family behaving like that. So, first ladies, let me tell you that my mother is doing well and what happened here years ago happened to her and not with her. She was a young impressionable girl and was taken advantage of, but my mother has moved past that and I know now why she chose not to come because she knew there would be some unchristian folks like you! And as far as me, I'm fine also and I am at my father's house and you too are just at your minister's house, so who belongs here more? You two or me?" Mary Jean asked.

By this time, her voice carried across the yard. She hadn't realized how loudly her voice had gotten. Stella put both hands on the table to lift herself, but before she could Rev. Douglas had b-lined around the table and put his hand on her shoulder. He took the microphone from a young musician and stepped on the stage.

"Mary Jean, please come up here and stand with me. Come here, boys," Rev. Douglas said and motioned for them all.

"Thank you, everyone, as the evening comes to a close, I pray that each and every one of you enjoyed the evening. Now, let me let you know why you were invited. For those of you who know, but chose not to accept, allow me to introduce my daughter, Mary Jean Grant, who I love and the rest of my family loves, also. I would like everyone in my family who loves Mary Jean and my grandsons, Lawrence and Robert, to please come and stand next to me."

Demetric Junior led the way, Lillian and Cynthia followed holding hands, and James walked to the stage last. Each one of them hugged Mary Jean and each of the boys.

"After all these years, there are some of you from the church who still blame this innocent child and her innocent mother for the sins I committed. My wife forgave me," He stopped and put his arm around Cynthia and she nodded. "And God has forgiven me. Now, I publicly beg Mary Jean and her mother in her absence to forgive me. I love you with all my heart and hope to share the rest of my days as a good father to you." He took Mary Jean's hand and kissed it. She held back her tears and nodded.

"I also would like to apologize to Sister Stella for ruining her and her husband's lives and I'm certain that my actions brought incurable stress on his health and for that, I can never forgive myself. Sister Stella, you and Brother Rob were two of my best members and I have not had anyone of your spirit in my presence since we parted. Please accept my soul's apology and please come up here and stand with our family," Rev. Grant said.

He was the only one Robert Woods would allow to call him "Bro. Rob". Hearing Rev. Douglas saying his name, warmed her body. She still missed him decades later. Tears filled her eyes. She knew there had been enough hard feelings on both sides of the family, and it was time for everyone to heal. She rose from her seat, walked to where the family stood, and put her arms around Demetric Junior.

Rev. Douglas looked out at the members he knew were still tongue-wagging about his indiscretions and he needed to address them.

"There are some of you still here who are members of the church and continue to talk about and against me and my family; yet, when you see me you are quick to shake my hand and tell me you are praying for me. Well, after tonight if you are unable to keep my transgressions out of your mouth, do not pray for me, but pray for yourselves. And if you are unable to stop this evil chatter, then please find another church to attend. I have heard every word you have had to say and so have my wife and my kids, so if you are unable to find something constructive to talk about, then please, please, leave the church and you may now leave my yard. For you, this party is over, oh and thank you for coming," Rev. Douglas said.

When the two ladies, who had talked to Mary Jean, passed Rev. Douglas and the family they murmured.

"Well, I never!" Straw hat lady said.

"I've been thrown out of classier joints than this!"The other remarked.

"No problems ladies, just exit my yard."

The family started laughing. Then other guests laughed until everyone was laughing and cheering. After a few rounds of charades and karaoke with the remaining guests, Mary Jean could tell Stella and the boys were exhausted.

She walked over the Cynthia and told her it was time for them to head back home. "May I use your telephone?"

"We're family, of course, you can use the phone. There's one right in the hallway through the backdoor," Cynthia said.

Mary Jean went into the house and called Rev. Grant.

"Hello," he answered quickly.

"Hi, Honey. We are getting ready to leave the barbecue and I just wanted you to know so you can be looking out for us. I think I'm going to get Granny to spend the night with us unless she doesn't have her medicine, and in that case, would you take her home for me?"

"Of course, darling, you know I will. When I finished up at the church, I started to come out there, but then I changed my mind. I thought you and Granny needed this time for closure and forgiveness."

"You were right," she admitted.

"Well, tell me more when you get home, okay?"

"Gladly," she smiled. She loved having him to come home to.

"Take your time. Drive carefully and I'll see you soon. Love you."

"Love you, too." She hung up the phone gently.

When Mary Jean went back outside, the boys were laying their heads on Stella. Lawrence Junior rested his head in her lap, and Robert Michael's head rested on her shoulder.

Mary Jean was surprised when Demetric Junior and James walked up and began to walk the boys to her car and buckle them. T.P. took Granny by the hand. They joked privately and hugged before Granny got into the front seat. Mary Jean was so proud of T.P. She had been low-key all night. Mary Jean prayed that this barbecue was also closure for T.P.'s anger.

T.P. squeezed into the backseat again and they waved goodbye. Only she and Mary Jean stayed awake for the drive but they stayed quiet.

With T.P. in the car, Mary Jean decided to drop Granny off then T.P. before getting the boys home. She'd rather have the extra time with Rev. Grant than send him out again.

Gail Calls Mrs. Agnes

"Gott-dang-git!" Gail snatched off her straw hat and scratched her scalp aggressively. She wasn't completely in the house before she was reaching for the telephone. She snatched the receiver from the wall and punched the numbers.

Mrs. Agnes wondered who could be calling her house this late on a Saturday evening. Everyone knew she went to bed early so that she could get up Sunday before Sunday School. "Hell....o," She said groggily.

"Agnes, this is Gail, wake up! I have something to tell you," She practically shouted.

"Gail who?"

"Woman, wake up! It's me, Gail! TweetyBoy's sister from Rev. Douglas church."

Mrs. Agnes moaned and turned on her bedpost lamp."What is it, Chile, don't you know what time it is?"

"Yeah. Yeah. But listen, Agnes. I went to that barbecue over at the Douglas mansion tonight! Chile! His brand new daughter was there!" She smacked her lips and Mrs. Agnes cringed. How many times had she told Gail Holmes that that lip-smacking was unChristian and just plain ole unwomanly? "Chile, his new daughter was your Mary Jean Grant!

That girl you are always telling me about! Why you never told us? We know you of all people knew that was really his daughter all along."

Mrs. Agnes sat up in the bed, "What! What did you say?"

"Remember the girl you told me about and you showed me her picture, you said her name was Mary Jean. Well, she came to the special barbecue at the Mansion tonight." She stressed *the Mansion* knowing the thought of the beautiful home would get under Mrs. Agnes' skin.

She cleared her throat, "So, what, Gail? Her husband is a minister, and she was probably there with him."

"No, Agnes! You don't understand, she's Rev. Douglas's daughter. Daugh-terrr. Do you hear me? His daughter," Gail said practically screaming.

"That girl's not his daughter! You so nosy you got it mixed up!"

"Okay. Let's see." Gail put her hand on her hip to mock Mrs. Agnes. "Is her grandmother named Stella Woods?"

"Yeah, her grandmother is Stella."

"Well, me and Alma recognized Stella at the barbecue and we knew that girl with her was her daughter's daughter because she has her momma's figure and Rev. Douglas' eyes. It was clear as day who she was. Stella's little trashy daughter—I can't even remember her name—tore our church up with her little fast behind. She was having an affair with Rev. Douglas inside the church and everyone knew it but his wife! Can you believe that? I remember it like it happened yesterday. We lost a lot of members because of that. So, when Alma and I figured out who the granddaughter was, we asked her where her momma was." Gail took a deep breath and waited for Mrs. Agnes to respond. "Do you know she got indignant and insulted us right in front of everyone!"

Mrs. Agnes was shocked but knew only half the story could be true. In all the years she'd known Mary Jean, she rarely got indignant and Lord knows Mrs. Agnes has pushed every possible button Mary Jean could possess.

"Agnes! That gal told us that her mom was young and impressionable and that Rev. Douglas took advantage of her. Point blank. Right there in front of all those people!"

Mrs. Agnes was speechless.

Gail continued, "Well, why didn't she say 'no'? That's what I wanted to say but Alma jumped in. Anyway, she said her mom chose not to come because she knew there would be unchristian people like us who only came to see how she looked now. She even had the nerve to say that she was at her Daddy's house and that we were just at our pastor's house, so I guess she meant that she had more right there than us!" Gail said making herself more upset.

Mrs. Agnes laughed. "Well, Gail, if that is her daddy, then she was right about that!" She laughed again. "I kind of recall something about her and T.P. being sisters but I thought they meant sisters in friendship or sisters in Christ. I did not know they meant biological sisters." She paused and visualized the two women together. "Well, I be darned! Those girls do look alike now that I think about it!"

She shifted in her bed. "What else happened, Gail?"

"That girl was talking so loud everyone heard her. I believe the little musician even stopped playing his song because she was so loud. Then, Rev. Douglas heard her, so he called her and the rest of his family to come to stand by him," Gail smacked her lips again and Mrs. Agnes rolled her eyes and released a loud huff into the phone.

"Girl, Agnes, he told all of us from the church off!"

Mrs. Agnes laughed.

Gail's anger wouldn't let her respond and Mrs. Agnes kept laughing.

"You mean he told you and Alma off," she said struggling to talk, laugh, and breathe.

"Rev. Douglas introduced her as his daughter who he and his family love!" Gail shouted, then calmed herself.

For a moment, they held the phone while Mrs. Agnes composed herself.

"I felt sorry for his wife. I know Sister Cynthia just went along with him to keep peace in the family even after all this time. More than forty years for sure. But, I know she didn't like that and in front of her children." Gail said.

"What else did he say, Gail? You and Alma are just alike. You have to add all your opinions and theatrics to the story before you can finish telling it. What else happened?" Mrs. Agnes was reluctantly fully awake.

"He said he invited us to let us know that he loves his daughter and his grandsons. Then, his entire family all got up and went and stood with him and hiiiissss daughter. Even the children that moved out of state. They came hugging and smiling like all is well at the Little House on the Prairie. Rev. Douglas said he had committed a sin and he apologized to her, her momma who wasn't even there, and her grandmother for hurting them all. Now, I wonder what he had in that cup because he did not sound like himself."

She paused and Mrs. Agnes stayed quiet.

"Then, he said those of us from his church who still felt the need to talk about his daughter and his family should find another church to attend immediately!"

Mrs. Agnes gasped.

"Exactly! He said he has heard all the gossip so if we didn't like what he was saying or the decisions of his family, then find another church! So, Alma and a few others of us got up to leave and as we were leaving his family and everyone else were laughing at us."

"No, Gail!"

"I ain't lying, Agnes. Before you put this on me. I am telling you the whole truth! And I'm not going back to that church! He didn't have to talk to us like that!"

They both took a deep breath.

"Gail, I'm sorry, but he was right. If you felt the need to talk about the girl and her momma, you should not have done it to her face. What did you think was going to happen?"

"But, Agnes! Her momma sinned inside the church! A man is going to be a man and a woman has to keep him in his place." Gail said.

"Look. Thanks for the information. I know someone who will be happy to know this but it's time for my beauty rest, Dear. Thank you and goodnight." Mrs. Agnes quickly hung up the phone.

That darn Agnes hung up in my face! That's the last time I tell her any-thing. Gail slammed the phone on its receiver then closed off her living room for the night.

Lallia's Desires

T.P. was glad so many women from the church stayed to help clean up after the barbecue. It gave her just enough time to get home and unwind before meeting George for drinks. She wasn't sure where the time with him would lead but since the shop was already closed for the day, she decided to enjoy the company of a confident, Ralph-Lauren-Champs-smelling man.

Once she arrived at Club Maxima, George greeted her with a simple hug and motioned for her to sit in the same booth they'd selected two weeks ago. T.P. noticed how the women and a few men watched them move through the crowded space. A jazz quartet played a fast song that neither of them knew. George seemed to move uncomfortably in the small booth and T.P. watched his eyes survey the club more times than she thought necessary.

"Let me get us a drink, Pretty Lady. That's what we came here for, right?" He feigned a smile.

"Sure. That's one of the reasons," T.P. said.

"Yeah," he tapped the table. "I'll be right back. Do you want a glass of white wine or a little more whiskey sour?" He smiled.

"I'll have my wine, please sir." She said returning his flirt.

As he walked away, she took note of the distance to the bar, the ladies' restroom, and the exit. She scanned the room then turned her attention to the band. She was glad that she had an opportunity to shower and spritz her hair otherwise she would've smelled sweet like her brother's honey barbecue sauce and sweetly like her two nephews who obviously didn't have enough friends their age.

Next, the band played the sultry Aaron Neville and "Tell It Like It Is." T.P. was entranced, rocking and humming the new hit song. She only knew a few random words but that didn't stop her and the other women from singing the chorus.

The band had set the perfect mood for the night ahead.

T.P. swayed and hummed as the band extended the four-minute song to six minutes.

While George waited for the drinks, Lallia Walker swooned behind him, rubbing her body on his back and pulling his arm. George quickly jerked his arm from her grip. The force against her long nails tore along the inset of his sleeve. He was furious. She rubbed his arm sliding her finger into the hole she'd made.

"Hey, George, whheeere yoooou been, babeee?" She said pulling on him, stepping closer, and gyrating her hips. He caught her shoulder quickly and resisted the urge to shake her. He remembered where he was and who was watching and decided it would be better to whisper in her ear. "Look, Lallia, it has been over for us for a while now get over it and if you ever put your hands on me again, I will forget where we are, and you will be sorry. Do I make myself clear?" George looked at her sternly.

Her eyes widened, and she stumbled backward. She was high, again.

Seeing that, George turned toward the booths along the wall. He could not see T.P. or the booth beyond the dim lights and thick smoke surrounding the bar. He shifted to the left then right but did not see her. He'd hoped she'd gone into the ladies' room and hadn't seen any of Lallia's touching.

He turned to the bar and shouted, "Joe! Where's my Chardonnay and whiskey?"

From the other end of the bar, the short man nodded. He was dressed in tailored slacks, a white shirt with thin red stripes, black suspenders, and a red and black bowtie. His Stacey Adams were black, shining, and clean. For a quick moment, George admired how good he'd made Lil Joe look wearing a combination of rejected orders from the shop. *Man, I made that brother look sharp!*

George turned his back to the bar and looked for T.P. to return to the table. Once the drinks were placed on the bar, he paid for them and then headed back to the table. The band started playing their third set and George rocked and walked to the beat. He looked forward to dancing with T.P. in his arms. He weaved through the crowd careful to not spill the drinks even while sipping his own. When he returned to the empty booth, he put the drinks down and looked over his shoulder to see where T.P. went.

He searched the dance floor, then looked towards the ladies' room. He positioned himself in the booth to be able to see her when she returned. After five minutes and no sign of T.P., he sipped more of his drink. He wiped his lips to hide his frustration as Lallia stumbled toward his table. *I hope I don't have to knock this girl on her behind to get rid of her.* He gave her a harsh look and she kept walking toward him.

"Y....ou don wan..tt mmmeee, but sheeee donttt wantt you, eeeether!" she said pointing her finger in his face. Her fake nail dangled from her finger. Tearing his shirt also snapped her manicure, too. She stumbled from him laughing. George sat back and then it dawned on him what Lallia meant: T.P. had left.

Playing it cool, George drank his whiskey and gave T.P.'s drink as a tip to one of Club Maxima's barmaids. He wondered what he would have to say and do to get T.P. to go out with him again. He knew he had better think of something quickly.

He stepped out onto the parking lot and sure enough T.P.'s car was gone from the space she'd secured earlier. He walked to his car contemplating what he would say to her as soon as he got home to call.

T.P let the phone ring seven times before walking out of the bedroom. Before she made it to the kitchen, the phone rang again. She refused to answer. He called two more times back-to-back then decided to wait ten minutes. On his fifth call, her line was busy and stayed that way until the next morning.

George was furious. He could not believe T.P. had left the club without saying a word and wouldn't take his calls for days. No woman had ever handled him that way. He was a lady's man, a charmer, a casanova. Because of her stubbornness, he took it as a welcome challenge to pursue her more. He had to see her again. He also knew he had to straighten Lallia out. This relationship that she continued in her mind had to end even though it was his habit to keep her hanging on between relationships because he secretly needed a woman who was willing to do anything and everything for him. But right now, though, she was standing in his way of moving forward with a very good woman.

Thinking about how hard he was going to have to work to win T.P. over, George snatched his phone from the receiver and punched in Lallia's number. She answered on the first ring.

"Hello," Lallia said anxiously.

"We need to talk," he said.

She was happy to hear George's voice. "Sure, George, I'll be here waiting for you," She said, softening her voice. "When will you be here?"

George started to put it off for a couple of days, but what good would that do. "I'll be there in the next hour."

Lallia smiled although George hung up without a goodbye. She rushed to the bathroom to get ready. She needed to take a shower, perfume and oil her body, and put on makeup just the way George liked it. He always told her how Ebony's Fashion Fair made her look so soft and feminine. And it should have because she paid top dollar to cover her skin that was becoming more dehydrated because of her drug use.

George arrived a half-hour later than he said he would. She was a little upset but nonetheless very happy to see him. "Hey, baby!" She said.

She opened the door in a black negligee, smelling sweet.

George brushed past her and went straight into the living room and sat on the sofa. Lallia closed the door and rushed over to the sofa. She attempted to sit on his lap before he maneuvered her body onto the sofa next to him.

"Lallia, what the hell were you thinking at Club Maxima?" He questioned her.

She hated him looking angrily into her eyes.

Oh shit, I was hoping he had gotten over that. "I'm sorry, baby, I was just a little tipsy," She said trying to laugh it off. "I never would have torn your shirt if I hadn't been intoxicated."

"A month ago, we talked and we decided that we would go our own separate ways. Do you remember that?"

"George, you were just here a week ago. Do you remember that?" She snapped back. She hated when he talked to her like she had bad understanding. "So what do you mean by, 'going our own way, George? Which way is that this week?"

"I'm serious, woman. I ain't got time for all this with you. You need to get yourself together," he was incredulous. She looked at him, knowing exactly what he meant.

"George, you said you would help me, and—"

"No, Lallia." He interrupted her and ignored the tears forming in her eyes. "It's over. Do you hear me!"

"George," she smacked her lips, then crossed her leg over his. She leaned towards him enough for her negligee to expose more of her breast. "You don't mean that. You will be right back here next week and want to roll our bodies all over this house, so I'll just wait until you are truly not ready, and I'll believe you then."

He looked down at her naked thigh and pushed it off of his.

"Umph," she grunted. "I know what it is. It's that little beautician you were with at the bar. You want to try her out for a while and then you'll be running back to me! You always do." She was arrogant.

He stood up and walked towards the door. "Don't call me and if you see me in the street, pretend you don't know me. Okay?" He opened the door to leave.

"Sure, baby! Suit yourself! She shouted as he slammed the door and walked out of her life.

Past Comes Back to Haunt

Getting clean proved to be the easiest part of her addiction; however, staying clean, resisting temptation, and missing old enemies were the worst parts. After having completed the addiction program and leaving the Come Dirty Leave Clean Center in Alexandria, Shelia felt like a new woman. Her body felt lighter, and her head was clearer. The thoughts of where to find the next hit and the money to purchase the heroin were no longer in the frontal lobe of her mind, but she still thought about them.

Thanks to the Center, she was able to properly explain her decision to not attend "D.D's barbecue". No matter how or who he was with others, he was still just "D.D." to her. And so far, having him in Mary Jean's life has not tormented her too much.

When she walked into her mom's house, she was certain that her past was farther behind her and that a new life was just beginning. The first few weeks there were difficult for Shelia. There were times when she wanted to leave the house and go get back with her old enemies. The taste of heroin stayed in her mouth, but as the days passed, the taste became fainter. She bought a pack of cigarettes hoping that would help the urges pass and even shift her taste.

"Shelia put that cigarette out," her mom would demand. "You know I can't stand smoke and besides it's bad for your lungs, too!"

"Okay, Momma you're right, but I still have these urges. I thought smoking these cigarettes could help." She explained. "Im just trying to hold it together, Momma."

"Baby," Stella said patiently. "You need to pray and ask God to remove any temptation out of your life and He will, that is if you are serious." She shifted in the recliner so she could see Shelia's reaction.

Shelia put out the cigarette. She hesitated twice but finally threw the pack in the kitchen's trash can.

For a little more than a month, everything went well until Shelia and Stella went to Schwegmann's Grocery in Gentilly just outside of New Orleans. As they got out of the car and headed toward the store's entrance, a pair of hands suddenly covered Shelia's eyes and Stella continued walking.

Shelia quickly removed the hand and swung around to face whoever had grabbed her. Immediately, her body shook with fear and took away her natural reaction to yell. Stella turned to notice Shelia was not walking with her. She began walking back towards Shelia.

She was fear-ridden. Looking into her eyes with a sly grin on his face was Monster Hopkins.

"Well, hi there, Redbone," he said jerking her head backward by her hair and pulling her body close to his.

"Young man, take your hands off my daughter!" Stella threatened.

Still holding Shelia's head back, he looked at Stella and tried to see where the old lady had come from so quickly, then he jerked her head harder.

"I certainly will as soon as your daughter pays me for her last little package. Baby girl took the goods from me and promised to pay me back by turning tricks for a week," He said laughing. Stella was shocked to hear what her daughter had to do to get high and she was pissed that this monster of a man had no respect for his elders.

White shoppers passed by them while going in and out of the supermarket. They stared at the commotion but dared not to help.

"How much does she owe you?" Stella asked unafraid.

"Old lady, you don't have the money she owes me, so I'd advise you to stay out of this and her to get down to the business of paying me back starting right now," Monster said showing his yellow teeth. "She'll just come with me until she pays off her little debt."

Stella took a hard step toward Monster. "Shelia's not going anywhere with you!" Her words were laced with anger. "Now I will ask you again, young man, how much money does she owe you?" Stella said loudly, which pissed Monster off.

He turned Shelia's head a loose and faced Stella, "She owes me three thousand dollars, old lady, now what are you going to do?" He asked so sure that this inflated amount would shut Stella up.

"I will give you your money, but if you ever approach my daughter again and try to bring her back into your lifestyle I can promise you that you will be truly sorry," Stella said pushing Shelia towards her car.

"Where do you think you're going!"

"To the bank! You can follow me or you can stand here looking ignorant. It's up to you." She pushed Shelia again, "Get in the car!"

Shelia obeyed.

Once the car began moving, Shelia began to cry. " Mama he has a gun."

"I know that, child. So do I. But we are going over to this bank and getting him out of your life forever."

"Momma, even if you give him the money he's still going to be coming after me. I'm sooooo sorry for bringing this to you!"

"Shelia, you are my daughter and I love you more than life itself. There is nothing that I won't do for you and don't worry after I give him this money and he signs off that the debt is paid, he won't be coming back of that I am certain," Stella said smiling slyly.

Stella knew a few powerful people in the city that could make him disappear if he double-crossed her. And she was prepared to do whatever she had to do for her family. *That lil boy is judging me by my cover but what he doesn't know is I am not Shelia, I am Mrs. Stella Will Tear*

Your Ass Up If You Harm My Baby. She thought to herself. She looked in her rearview mirror to ensure that Monster was still following them.

When they arrived at the Gentilly Bank and Trust, Stella parked in the parking lot and he pulled alongside her car, she then beckoned him to follow her into the bank. He stood outside the door and refused to walk in. A young man leaving the bank opened the door for the two of them. Stella walked to the counter and asked the teller to go get Mr. Peter Henderson.

"Tell him Mrs. Stella Woods is here to see him."

He held the door for Monster who chose to stay outside.

He was uncomfortable and needed to stay in control. He thought the inside looked like a ritzy hotel but he would never put his money in a bank that would always question how he got his money. He was close enough to see Stella's every move. Shelia watched from the car.

"Why, hello, Mrs. Woods," Mr. Henderson said as he approached Stella and shook her hand. "What can I do for you today?"

Monster read the name tag on Mr. Henderson's suit coat and he was surprised that she had gotten the bank president to come out and wait on her. He was impressed and decided to step into the lobby and stand next to Stella.

Maybe this old bitty might prove to be useful to him after all she was willing to cough up three grand for Redbone perhaps she had more to pass out.

"And your guest?" Mr. Henderson asked.

"He's no guest of mine. My daughter owes him some money and I'm here with him to settle her debt and I would like for you to assure that this is done in a legal manner," Shelia said rolling her eyes at Monster.

Mr. Henderson knew Stella for a long time and he also knew about Shelia and where she had been and that she was at home now trying to get her life back together. So this character standing beside Stella had to be one of the shady pimps or drug dealers from Shelia's past who was getting money to punish and probably rob Stella. *Over my dead body,* Mr. Henderson vowed to himself.

"Shall we go over to this desk and take care of this transaction?" Mr. Henderson asked as he turned and led the way to a desk in the back of the bank with a typewriter.

Stella and Monster took a seat in front of the desk and Mr. Henderson sat in front of the typewriter and begin setup to print.

"Now how much money are we needing today?" Mr. Henderson asked.

Stella looked Monster sternly in his eyes and back at Mr. Henderson, "Three thousand dollars."

"In small bills," Monster said. He heard that when banks gave you money in large denominations, they marked the bills, so he wanted his money clean. The thought of this made him want to burst out laughing.

"I see, and what is your name, young man?" He asked.

"She told you. It's Monster!" He said as he leaned back in the chair.

"Well, Monster, what is the name on your birth certificate?" Mr. Henderson asked looking at Monster like he was a pile of dung.

Monster wasn't sure if he should give his real name so he called his bluff. "Nah, all you need to know is Monster. She's handling this. I'm just the pickup man."

He felt smart.

"Can you proceed, Mr. Henderson? Shelia's out in the car and I probably should get her on home safely."

"Sure, let me have Wayne check on her while I retrieve your funds." He stood and walked to the young teller. Mr. Henderson went behind the counter and Wayne walked quickly out of the bank to Stella's car.

Mr. Henderson returned with a sheet of paper from the printer along with a stack of money.

"Mr. Monster, this paper states that three thousand dollars is all the funds Shelia Woods owes you and once you receive this money then Shelia Wood's bill with you will be clean and you and your associates will no longer contact her. Is this your agreement?"

"Sure, once I get this money I'm finished doing business with Shelia," He said. *This dude is a banker, not judge nor jury he can't make me agree to nothing. Like hell I'm done with Shelia. That's prime redbone meat at least for another six years!*

Monster, Stella, and Mr. Henderson signed the paper, and Mr. Henderson counted out the cash, laying each bill neatly on the desk for Monster to pick up.

Monster grabbed the money and shoved it into his pockets and then Stella picked up her copy of the papers and shooked hands with Mr. Henderson and followed Monster outside the bank. Once outside Monster was smiling from ear to ear so Stella startled him when she touched him on the shoulder.

"I hope you meant what you said back in the bank and that this is all you want from my daughter. I'm a Christian woman, but I also know how to deal with the devil, so go in peace, Robert Wilbert Hopkins. I never want to see you alive again," She said and walked back to her car where Shelia and Wayne were waiting.

The ladies agreed to return to the supermarket to purchase enough groceries that would allow them to stay put for at least a month. They wanted to be sure Monster would not find them out again. That night while Shelia cooked dinner, Stella made calls privately in her room. She had two very close friends who lived in New Orleans and hated drug dealers and abusers. She explained what happened and gave them Monster's alias and birth name. They assured Stella that she had nothing to worry about. Not only would she get her money back soon, she would also be able to sleep soundly every night knowing Monster would be taken care of.

"Mrs. Stella, if you have any other problems stemming from Shelia's past, call us before you pay or shoot another soul," they joked.

"That was a long time ago," she quipped.

Mrs. Agnes Confronts Rev. Grant

For nearly two months Rev. Grant had been inundated with paperwork. He was sorting through details with the church's accountant after having another three-hour phone call from the Internal Revenue Service. Anonymous calls were being made to the New Orleans offices demanding an audit and accusing Rev. Grant of fraud and theft. He was standing by the window, mentally surveying everyone who knew to try to determine who had it out for him and his ministry and also had the time available to make repeated calls. He watched the children throw balls to each other and heard the girls counting off their rope jumping. He crossed his arms and mindlessly fingered the buttons on the inside of his suspenders. He looked at the pleats in his pants. He remembered how beautiful Mary Jean looked while ironing them. The thought of his loving wife soothed the rage boiling in him.

Who's behind this? His mind scanned the faces of his church, his neighborhood, the city.

Just then, Mrs. Agnes walked through his office door already talking, "You know, Rev. Grant. This church could use more scripture," she walked quickly to the only chair without a stack of files and binders. She was waving a lace fan to cool off from the hot walk from her car. She pulled her chair closer to his desk. "This place is not like any church I've ever seen," she said sarcastically before noticing him staring out the window.

"That's because it is not like the churches you've been to. Well, not in the sense of what you and a lot of others are accustomed to. You see here we work to help the inner and outer man. We are more concerned with helping people to live in this world, here and now." Rev. Grant said as he stared at Mrs. Agnes. He knew she had heard him say all of this before and not just from the pulpit.

"But you are not saving souls! And that is your job from God to do."

Rev. Grant turned around and walked to his desk, then sat facing her. She stared straight into his eyes. "When God called you, I know He told you to take care of His sheep. You were called, weren't you?" Mrs. Agnes asked smartly.

"No. Mrs. Agnes. I never said that God called me. No, He did not. I chose to be a representative for Him, and how I represent Him is how I live my life and how much I care for His people. And by caring for His people, I mean how I can help them in the here and now." Rev. Grant said. *Now, why in the world are you even here, Agnes, and where is Mable when I need her?!* Rev. Grant was getting agitated. He only had a few minutes to continue this conversation and knew it would take much longer than that to get Mrs. Agnes to understand the purpose of this church—of God's church. She had been a member for two years, and she seemed to spend every moment trying to transform T.E.A.M. and Rev. Grant into The Greatness of Christ Baptist Church which she had discretely left to chastise more than forty others.

"I'd like to continue this conversation with you Mrs. Agnes, but I have a two o'clock appointment. If you don't mind on your way out, check with Mable and make an appointment. We can continue this conversation at a later date," Rev. Grant said as he walked to the door and opened it for her.

Surprised by his sharp tone, Mrs. Agnes scrambled to get her huge purse off the arm of the chair and stumbled out of the chair, nearly tearing her hosiery. "I can't believe you are putting me out of your office when I came in here to give you some much-needed advice!"

Rev. Grant knew Mrs. Agnes was an old horse and it was not going to be easy to teach her anything new, but that was the job he had volunteered for when he decided to become a pastor. He needed to talk with someone who could calm him down, so, as Mrs. Agnes stumbled out of the door, he walked over to his desk, picked up the phone, and dialed his home number.

Mrs. Agnes Calls Mary Jean

Storming through the front door of her home, Mrs. Agnes wasted no time getting to the kitchen phone. She snatched the handle from the wall so hard that her purse swung and hit her side.

"What did you forget this time?" Mary Jean laughed, expecting to hear her husband's voice again.

"Hello, Mary Jean. This is Mrs. Agnes. How are you?" Mrs. Agnes's anger seeped through her teeth.

"Oh hi, Mrs. Agnes, I'm fine. I thought you were someone else." Mary Jean said thinking back to her twenty-minute conversation with Rev. Grant. He seemed bothered by something but wouldn't say it. She would have driven to see him if she weren't preparing for the upcoming fellowship. She cleaned her hands with a wet towel that hung from her apron and glanced over at the table. She counted the chicken quarters she had cleaned and estimate how many more to clean before Mother Jones came by to pick them up. Lord, what did I get myself into with this woman? Mary Jean shook her head and returned her attention to the phone call.

"Now, Mary Jean you know I never say anything about anyone that I can't say to their face, or in your case, their family's face. So, I'm going to just be direct and tell you what I feel about your husband." Mrs. Agnes said irately.

I really don't have time for this! Mary Jean thought. *I have too much to do to just sit here and listen to Mrs. Agnes complain.*

"Mrs. Agnes, can we talk about this later? I'm in the middle of cleaning chicken for the social tomorrow. I can call you later tonight if that's okay." Mary Jean said.

"No! We need to talk now!" Mrs. Agnes demanded. "And anyway I don't see any reason to be having a social at the church. Christians should not be having events like we are of the world! That's the problem with the church now! You all spend too much time socializing and holding those people's hands. Stand up and be Christians!" She yelled, slamming her purse down. It crashed and half its contents spilled on the floor. "You need to be more like the other churches and spend more time in the Word of God and then maybe those heathens could stand on their own feet!" Mrs. Agnes said still fuming.

Mary Jean was silent. She knew it was best to allow Mrs. Agnes to blow her top than to try to talk sensibly to her. Instead, she stretched the phone's cord as far as she could to return to cleaning and cutting the chicken.

"But, that's not why I called! I just want to tell you that your high and mighty husband put me out of his church today and I don't feel that he had a right to do so. All I was doing was trying to tell him he needed to preach more of the Word and spend less time being a social worker for all those people in the church. Your church only spends twenty to thirty minutes on the Word on Sundays and the rest of the time is spent on social affairs. That needs to stop!"

Mary Jean cleared her throat and gave herself time to think before she said something that she would regret later. "I'm sorry Mrs. Agnes that you feel that way. I'm certain that Rev. Grant didn't mean to say or do anything that would hurt your feelings nor insult you. It's just not a part of his nature. Maybe, he was just tired." Mary Jean said moving toward the kitchen, table hoping to soon hang up the phone.

"Well, he could have fooled me. I'm a member and he treated me like an outsider. Maybe some of your former trash is rubbing off on him," Mrs. Agnes snapped. "I saw Lawrence passing by the church when I was leaving. I know you remember how that fool used to act and look, well he looks like his old self and is probably pulling your husband down in that pit of hell that he lives in, causing him to act the same fool as that boy." Mrs. Agnes said smiling to herself. She could tell from the quietness on the other end of the phone that she had told Mary Jean something that Rev. Grant hadn't told her and she was happy to be the one who brought her the news. I wonder what she thinks of her precious husband now. "You didn't know that did you?" Mrs. Agnes asked.

"No. Mrs. Agnes, I don't keep up with Lawrence's whereabouts whether it's near the church or in the church. And Rev. Grant doesn't discuss his meetings with me and I prefer it that way. If there was something that I need to know, I am more than confident that my husband will tell me himself, Besides I'm sure that Rev. Grant can handle anything that Lawrence or you send his way." Mary Jean said. Now she was agitated and tired of standing with the telephone hooked on her shoulder.

"You need to talk to your husband and tell him that he needs to take into consideration ALL his members and what they think and feel. The church is not his! It's OURS, so you better get him straight and let him know that I'm not a member who will tolerate his foolishness. Do you hear me, Mary Jean! Just like I came there I can leave there and take away all the members who joined because of me!" Mrs. Agnes shouted, hoping her threat would upset Mary Jean even more.

Of all the things going on in the world right now with these boycotts and protests, she's bothering my husband about this? Really, Woman!

Mary Jean breathed deeply and said, "Mrs. Agnes, first, the church is God's church, and second, Rev. Grant and I work very hard to help the members of the church. However, both of us know that we will not be able to please everyone. We are aware that many of the people are not there with good intentions, but with the intention to destroy the good that Rev. Grant has built. You see, whenever you are doing well, there will always be someone in the midst trying to destroy it. I'm sorry to hear that you are so upset and that you are contemplating leaving the church and taking the members who joined because of you. Nevertheless, if they joined because of you, then let me suggest that you do just that. You and them. All of you should go wherever you will be happy." Mary Jean said and threw the knife on the table.

"No need to get a hair up your rump, Mary Jean," Mrs. Agnes said defensively. "I'm just saying that I contribute to that church and I'm a member, so your husband needs to keep that in mind. I do have a lot of pull in this town, and I can always kick up enough smoke for you and your precious husband to know that there is a fire somewhere. Do I make myself clear?" Mrs. Agnes said thinking,

"Thank you, Mrs. Agnes, for that bit of information. If you would like to discuss this further please feel free to call the church and make an appointment and speak to him." Mary Jean said.

Mary Jean hung up the phone.

No, she didn't! Mrs. Agnes thought. "That little hussy hung the phone up in my face!"

Mary Jean chuckled. She was glad the conversation was over and pretty proud of herself for standing up, again, to the church trouble rouser.

By the way Mrs. Agnes reacted, Mary Jean knew she was preparing to stir up as much commotion as she could but little did she know Mary Jean would protect her family by whatever means she needed to. That was one thing she could agree with that Malcolm X had boasted. Even though he was a member of the Nation of Islam and not a professing Christian, Mary Jean agreed with his pronouncement: By Any Means Necessary.

And I mean that, Mrs. Agnes. Mary Jean continued chopping the leg quarters. This time with an extra snap to her wrist.

Mrs. Agnes Calls Sister Joyce Smith

"Well, I be damn!" Mrs. Agnes was surprised. Never did she think that Mary Jean would ever do such a mean thing and especially not to her. After all, she was the one who was instrumental in Mary Jean being where she is today, if it had not been for her, she'd still be next door, scuffling. Mrs. Agnes picked up the phone and dialed Sister's Smith number. "Hello. Joyce?"

"Oh, Hi Agnes," Joyce said, thinking, *I really don't have a lot of time to talk to Agnes today.* "How are you doing today?"

"I guess I'll do for an old lady, who was just insulted and hung up on by our pastor's wife."

"What? Sister Grant hung up on you?" Sister Joyce laughed.

"Who else Joyce? I swear sometimes I wonder if your elevator goes all the way up to the top. Of course, it was Mary Jean's fool. She's his wife, isn't she?" Mrs. Agnes said becoming more agitated. "I called that fool to tell her I had spoken to her husband and she got mad and hung up in my face."

"I find that hard to believe, Agnes! Mary Jean is a fine young lady! What did you do to get her to that point?" Joyce asked, even though she knew that this would upset Mrs. Agnes even more.

"Look! She told me not to call her house anymore and hung the phone up in my face. Can you believe that?"

Joyce snickered under her breath, because she did believe it, and it was something she had always wanted to do—even today. "Agnes, these youngsters are not like us, but she's the pastor's wife and she should be an example to all the other young ladies in the church and that isn't no way to treat the members of your husband's church. After all, they are the ones who keep food on your table," Joyce said annoyed more at Mrs. Agnes than at Mary Jean.

"I had planned to help her with the food for the Senior Citizen Dinner next month, but I refuse to help someone who insults me!" Mrs. Agnes said in a huff. "You know what I'm going to do? I'm going to tell everyone I know in that church about her little behind!"

Sister Joyce did not say anything. *Is there no length that Agnes won't go to trying to destroy someone's character?*

"Did I tell you that she once lived on the same block as me?"

"Yes, Agnes, I knew that. Remember I know Stella, her grandmother," Sister Joyce said, knowing that Mrs. Agnes was going to continue telling her anyway.

"Right before she met and married Rev. Grant. I remember when she did not have a pot to piss in, or a window to throw it out of. All she had was a whoring man and two little bastards. Did I tell you that she and that half-sister of hers—who she didn't know was her sister at the time—saw me in the street where I fell and those two were peeping out of their windows and neither one of them came to help me up off the ground!"

"NO! Get out of here, Agnes! She did that?" Joyce said although her thoughts were louder: *I would've left your butt on the ground, too.*

"Now, there you go again, Joyce, who are we talking about?" Mrs. Agnes said. *It's so hard talking to this woman! She has such a bad understanding.*

"Sister Grant?" Sis. Joyce said.

"Bingo, Joyce. You got it! Finally! She thinks because she is the pastor's wife now, that this makes her special, but you and I know better. Right?"

"Not me, Agnes. I don't know the lady personally." Sis. Joyce said. "But I have a dinner cooking, so I have to go. I will call you tomorrow. Okay?"

"Okay. Don't call me during my stories." Mrs. Agnes said.

After Mrs. Agnes hung up the phone Sis. Joyce thought more about their conversation. She knew that if Mary Jean Grant hung the phone up in Agnes's face, then Agnes deserved it. Everything she had heard about Sis, Grant was good and only Agnes had something negative to say. Sis. Joyce felt it was time that she let her friends know it was time to really watch Agnes or stay away from her.

Mary Jean and T.P.

After putting dinner in the oven to cook and sending the boys pulling their red wagon down the street to Mother Jones with the last crates of raw chicken, cut sharply, and seasoned to perfection, Mary Jean took a hot shower then plopped down on the bed. The thirty minutes of quiet would be more than a treat, but she had to be careful not to fall asleep. To her surprise, Mrs. Agnes had gotten under her skin this time. She took five deep breaths, then called T.P.

"Hello."

"Hey, Sis. I just had to call you about Mrs. Agnes. Do you have time to talk now?"

"Sure, my last customer just left and I'm about to eat my dinner so we can talk awhile. What did old Sister-I'm-So-Righteous Agnes do this time?"

Mary Jean shifted to her side, still lying across the bed which was un-usual for her to do now that she was married. "You do know that she has been complaining–almost berating to–Donald about things that she is unhappy about. She has had two unannounced meetings with him and in both, she tried to tell him her thoughts about what was wrong with the church and some of the members. So, she decided to call me after storming into his office, and I was not in the best mood. After complaining to me, she then told me that she brought a lot of members to the church and she and they could leave just like they came."

"No, Girl! You are kidding!" T.P. laughed but wasn't surprised, "I always told you that Mrs. Agnes is a demon. You never believed me." She stuffed her mustard greens into a corner cut of cornbread and slurped it down like she had since she was a child. Smacking her lips in pleasure, she continued, "I found Mrs. Agnes out a loooong time ago." T.P held the "o" long like it was part of a song.

"I don't know if I told you this, but Mrs. Agnes's husband was bedridden before he passed, and his brother came and stayed awhile to help take care of him. Well, Sister Agnes took the liberty of having Ole Brother-in-Law for her husband." T.P. said, stuffing a fork full of greens and seasoning into her mouth. Absolutely no one in the state of Louisiana cooked nor ate mustard greens like T.P. She swore her people didn't eat slop meat and oil but used herbs instead to enjoy their own crops.

"Stop it T.P.! Just, st….op it!" Mary Jean said and held in her laughter.

"No. I am not kidding. She did. She started having a relationship with her brother-in-law," T.P. said.

"How do you know that, T.P.?" Mary Jean asked.

"Girl, they don't call me 'Times Picayune' for nothing," T.P. boasted, then laughed. "I saw it for myself!" Mary Jean laughed. Her sister had gotten her to feel better just like the best friend she was. T.P. continued, "I remember because it was the fourth of July and my parents held a barbecue in the park. They had so much food left that they gave me some to bring home. I thought about giving some to clients but I didn't want the hassle, so I remember Mrs. Agnes and her husband and decided to give enough for a few days so it wouldn't go bad. When I got over there with all that food, I rang her doorbell and waited, but no one came to the door. I knew someone was there because her car was still in the garage and she'd said the hospital told her someone always had to be there with her husband. I went to the side by her kitchen window and tapped on it and there was no answer there, too. I was tired of carrying the food so I went on to the backyard, thinking that perhaps she was back in there and had not heard the bell. Well, when I got to the back door, I could hear giggling and murmured voices. I knocked on the back screen door, and after I didn't get an answer, I peeked through the screen. Guess what I saw." T.P. said.

"I have no idea, but I know you going to tell me." Mary Jean said.

"Sister Agnes and her brother-in-law were entering the kitchen. His arms were wrapped around hers. She was adjusting that famous wig she still wears when she does not have time to go to the hairdresser. They were so engrossed in each other, it was like I was invisible. He started opening her dress and feeling her breast and then guess what else he did?"

"Stop! Stop it T.P. spare me the details. I can guess the rest. Why didn't you tell me about this before now?" Mary Jean asked.

"I haven't told you the half about Sister Agnes! There's a lot more I could tell you but I am a lady and a Christian," T.P laughed mocking Mrs. Agnes who made certain to remind people of her self-professed status with The Lord. T.P. wiped her mouth and put her fork in the empty ceramic bowl. "I didn't tell you before because you always thought that Mrs. Agnes was a saint. You found out quick enough that she wasn't what you believed her to be, and you haven't finished learning yet. I'll tell you more when you are ready to hear it." T.P. said. "By now you should see that that old woman's not a person who you can trust. I bet you she's doing a whole lot more than we can imagine with her evil ways. What's sad is that she claims she is the ultimate Christian. Psht!"

"Oh, I thought about that T.P., but what more can she be doing and who with?" Mary Jeans asked.

"Who else but that old flaming Casanova whose church she used to attend. I know that they have been close from the day he walked into that church, claiming his wife had passed. I'm surprised Mrs. Agnes didn't try hooking you up with him. She's tried with so many other people on both sides of the pendulum." T.P. said in a manner that made Mrs. Jean question T.P.

"What do you mean by pendulum?"

"You know. He swings both ways," T.P. said matter-of-factly.

"T.P. girl you are so crazy. You are never going to change." Mary Jean said and laughed, also.

"Sure won't," T.P. said. "I still haven't gotten my little Paris gift from you. Mind if I swing by tonight on my way to Baton Rouge?"

"Sure, T.P. But promise me that you will be careful. It's 1967 and these people are cutting up," Mary Jean pleaded.

"I promise, Sis. You just have my goodies ready." T.P joked and hung up the phone just as Carla walked in for a quick curl set.

T.P. and Carla Visit Mary Jean

When Mary Jean opened the door, she was surprised to see T.P. walking toward the house with a client. She was an attractive woman in her late forties who walked with an extra bounce to flap her fresh curls. Night would fall soon and Rev. Grant would be home for dinner. Mary Jean made a quick note of T.P.'s guest's outfit, then hug T.P. as she entered through the front door.

"Hi Sis, this is Carla. Carla this is my sister, Mary Jean. Oooh, what's smelling so good?," T.P. brushed past Mary Jean and headed straight toward the kitchen. *It's just like T.P. to leave her friend who I don't know and run to my kitchen looking for something to eat*, Mary Jean thought.

"Come in," Mary Jean said to Carla, "and excuse my sister's manners." She led Carla into the living room and extended her hand for her to take a seat.

"That's okay." Carla said as she took a seat on the sofa, "Your home is lovely."

"Can I get you something to drink? I have RC, water, and juice."

"I'll take an RC Cola," Carla said. As Mary Jean walked into the kitchen, Carla looked around the living room at the art and artifacts that presented The Grant's cultural taste. She was impressed. These pieces are authentic, she thought. Carla knew art well because she had been in some expensive homes when the wives were away. Their husbands always enjoyed teaching her about their art while bragging about their expensive taste. She knew one of the pieces was Jacob Lawrence's "The Library" and the masks were from Ghana. She stared at them, trying to recall the village and artist when Mary Jean returned with a glass of ice and an RC Cola.

"You have some lovely pieces of art, and these artifacts are from Ghana, aren't they? I cannot recall the artist's name," Carla said as articulate and posed as possible.

"Well, I won't be able to help you with that. My husband is the art lover in the house. He purchases them from a friend in Detroit. I don't know anything about the artists. Please make yourself comfortable while I drag my big sister out of my pots," Mary Jean joked and left to get T.P. Mary Jean didn't feel up to entertaining any guest, especially one she didn't know. And from the attire Carla wore, Mary Jean could tell that Miss Carla was not in the mood for her female attention. Mary Jean entered the kitchen and laid the gift on the kitchen table. T.P. was sitting at the kitchenette table nibbling on a cold, roast beef sandwich.

Mary Jean opened the refrigerator and took out another RC Cola, opened the cabinet drawer, and found the bottle opener. She popped off the top, then walked over to sit the drink beside T.P.

"T.P., I took your friend a drink but I have a lot to do tonight, so I don't have time to entertain and socialize," Mary Jean said watching T.P. take the last bite of her sandwich, then she grabbed her gift and sat it next to her.

"No, that's okay, Mary Jean. I don't want you entertaining us. I only came for my gifts," T.P. said and walked out of the kitchen into the living room. "I'll be ready in about fifteen minutes, so by the time you finish your drink, we can leave. Okay?" T.P. asked and quickly returned to the kitchen as if Carla's "okay" didn't mean anything.

As soon as T.P. left the room, Carla heard the front door open and smiled, recognizing the most stunning man she had seen in a long time. Welcome home, Rev. Donald Grant. From where she sat, she could see him but he couldn't see her until he fully entered the room. Carla thought to herself that this was the kind of man she had dreamed of all her life and here he was walking right into her grasp.

Rev. Grant entered the room. Not expecting company, he quickly began untying his tie and loosening his shirt collar. He had seen T.P.'s car in the driveway but expected her to be alone or with George. He never looked up while walking into the living room, until he heard Carla clear her throat.

"Hi I'm Carla," Carla said anxiously as her hands began to tingle—a reflex that happens whenever she was instantly attracted to a man.

"Hello," he said, noticing how she turned her body towards him. "I'm Rev. Grant."

Damn. That voice. She smiled, already enjoying his presence. "It's nice to meet you. Where is everyone?" He asked as he picked up the mail on the coffee table that separated the two of them.

"They've just gone into the kitchen for a moment," she answered quickly and shifted her drink on the table. She wanted to feel the heat of his hands. "T.P. never mentioned that she had a minister in her family," she said and crossed her legs, knowing that from the angle where he stood, he would see her skirt lift to reveal her shapely thighs. And he did.

"Well, T.P doesn't see that as being very important. I'm brother-in-law to her; more than I am a minister," Rev. Grant said trying his best not to be curt. He was tired and always preferred not to do a lot of talking when he came home in the evening. He was usually exhausted from talking all day long and the only people he wanted to talk to were his wife and sons. If they had made plans for company, he would have returned home earlier, so that he had ample time to rest before entertaining.

Carla was intent on having Rev. Grant's attention as long as she could. She uncrossed her legs and slowly opened them to reveal farther up her inner thighs. Bare of panties, she'd hoped he had caught of glimpse of what she had to offer him. Anger shot through Rev. Grant's temples. Who sent her here? He stared down at her. Carla watched his eyes but couldn't read his thoughts. If she could have, she would quickly excuse herself and never return. But, she was ready for the challenge she saw on his face.

Rev. Grant held his reaction. Instead, he yanked the tie from his neck. He did not want this unrighteous Jezebel in his home, exposing herself to him, cunning and crafty. Just then, Mary Jean entered the room. With a quick gesture, Carla closed her legs, pulled down her skirt, and reached for the remaining cola on the table.

"Oh, hey baby. I didn't hear you pull up," Mary Jean said and kissed Rev. Grant. She instantly recognized the look on his face, then looked at Carla who was still sitting and innocently sipping the last drops of RC. Rev. Grant walked out of the room without responding. Mary Jean thought something had happened at the church that upset him and she was embarrassed that he left the room in a manner that would make their guest feel unwelcomed. She knew they would discuss it later.

Rev. Grant walked into the kitchen.

"T.P.," said Rev. Grant, before gently hugging his sister-in-law. "Do you know who you just brought into our home?" he asked sternly.

"Well, hello to you, too Rev. And that's, Carla, she's a client and we are on our way to Baton Rouge," T.P. said quickly. She noticed his tie had been removed and he seemed disheveled.

"I would appreciate it if you would get her out of our home and never bring her back," Rev. Grant said looking T.P. in the eye.

T.P. had never seen him upset nor unwelcoming of anyone even on his worse days. And here lately it seems he has been having more bad days than good. T.P. remembered Mary Jean telling her about the stringent reports he was filing with an accountant all the way up in Shreveport. Then she remembered how Carla had sashayed around in her too-tight, too-short skirt as they prepared to stop to see Mary Jean.

Hell! She looked towards the kitchen door and tried to whisper. "Did Carla say something to you?" She placed her bottle in a plastic crate on the floor, next to an empty trash can.

"T.P., you should be very careful of the people you associate with—especially those with demonic spirits. They have other agendas when they start a relationship with you and sometimes you won't know what their agenda is, nor do you know who they are." To calm himself, he ran cold water over his hands. "Be very careful with this new friend of yours and never, ever bring her back into this house."

He looked back at T.P. who was closer to the door.

"Now, go get my wife out of that demon's face." He said, "She is not welcome here. Ever!" Rev. Grant said.

Although she could challenge her brother-in-law with Biblical scripture, Quaran, and MAAT principles to show how ungodly he was behaving, T.P. gave a second thought and didn't question him. Instead, she would easily get Carla to tell her everything after they left.

When T.P. entered the living room, she stumped up to Mary Jean who had taken a seat on the couch across from Carla. She rubbed her back for her to stand up. She gave Mary Jean a quick hug, and whispered "I'm sorry" so softly Mary Jean didn't recognize that was said until later that night. Carla promised Mary Jean that she would be coming to their church on Sunday and what a nice husband she had. The sound of her commitment pricked a nerve within T.P. making her angry.

"Carla, let's go!" T.P. said, storming past the other women. Mary Jean walked Carla towards the door, sensing that something strange was happening. She could not wait to talk to Rev. Grant. As soon as they drove off, Mary Jean walked through the kitchen and peeked out of the window to see the boys practicing their baseball stance. She smiled as Robert Micheal took full form and swung at an imaginary ball. Then, she walked into the den where Rev. Grant was now resting in his recliner until dinner. Miles Davis' trumpet swooned softly from the turntable. At that moment the telephone rang and Mary Jean walked over and picked up the receiver.

"Hello," She said.

There was a long pause on the phone and just as Mary Jean was about to hang up Lawrence spoke. "Mary Jean when can I come and get my sons or when can I come and see them?" He asked.

"Lawrence, I have told you time and time again that you will not be able to take the boys out until you get therapy, but if you are interested in seeing them you can come here, just let us know in advance."

The idea that he had to come to another man's home to see his sons made Lawrence even angrier. "No thanks," he said and slammed the phone down.

Rev. Grant had heard the conversation and knew that Lawrence was being his disrespectful addicted self and he decided not to ask Mary Jean because he knew what had transpired.

Mary Jean didn't attempt to tell Rev. Grant what Lawrence had said because she was more interested in knowing what had made him so angry before the call.

"Honey, Can you tell me what just transpired?" Mary Jean asked. Normally she wouldn't bother him when she saw his eyes closed. She knew how important it was for him to unwind through meditation before settling down as a family. But, she instinctively felt this just could not wait.

Rev. Grant described in detail what Carla had done including being disrespectful. Mary Jean could not believe her ears. She just didn't think anyone could be that brazing to come into her home and try to entice her husband as Carla had. Didn't she know who he was? Mary Jean questioned. She wanted to react immediately until she heard the boys laughing just beyond the window. She would later go into her prayer corner and write before confronting T.P. and Miss Carla.

Carla Tries to Convince T.P.

As soon as T.P. started the car, she pulled out of the driveway abruptly. "What are you doing, T.P.! Slow down!" Carla yelled.

"No, Carla! What are you doing?" T.P turned away from the road to look Carla in the eyes. "What did you do back there in my sister's home?"

Carla told T.P. that she found Rev. Grant to be stunning for an older man, and she boldly told him so. She chuckled and clicked her teeth. "He responded right back, telling me how beautiful of a woman I am." She turned her back toward the window and adjusted the cloth under her. Louisiana was hot and car seat heat was like none other. She was not about to burn her thighs in T.P's car.

"Girl, it was all done in very good taste," she tried convincing T.P. "We were not flirting. It's simply two harmless adults finding one another very attractive." She humpfed. "Until his wife entered the room. Then, he suddenly left the room." She smacked her lips again, "that's all there was."

T.P. knew Carla's type. She'd dealt with them all her life: seductresses in and out of her father's den. She sped through Backtown, behind the Piggly Wiggly warehouse, over the railroad tracks with such fierceness

Carla bounced but didn't say a word. When she got to Carla's street. She stopped in the middle of the street.

"Get out," T.P. commanded.

"This is the middle of the street!"

"Get –"

"T.P! I didn't do anything! No more than what I've done with George and that's just being friendly. You, know I'm a really friendly person and I admit I do flirt sometimes, but it's all done innocently, besides I would never do anything in your sister's house. I am not stupid. What kind of person do you think I am?" Carla said, talking faster.

"You really don't want me to answer that, Carla."

"What did he tell you, T.P.?" Carla asked getting more nervous. She had never seen this side of T.P. and didn't want to cross her by any means. She pushed the door opened, grabbed her towel, and exited the car. She slammed the car door. Walking down Kerr Street, Carla cursed T.P, Rev. Grant, and Rev. Mical. She wanted nothing more than to cause the fall of these men—especially those who thought they could just use her for their whims.

That bit… thinks they are all better than me.

Getting Members to Leave T.E.A.M

"That Negro thinks that his large membership makes him indestructible, but he has another thought coming when old hag Agnes and I finish with him, he'll be lucky if he has any members," Rev. Mical boasted.

"By now, the IRS should be ready to audit that fool's books. T.E.A.M will be the first church that they audit in the entire United States, but it won't be the last. When this works out as I plan, I can use it to move a lot of these other fools out of my way. Fraud. Tax evasion. Take your pick, Rev. Grant." He chuckled and rubbed his chin. It was time for a shave but he enjoyed the extra stubble of new growth. Then, he allowed himself to sink into his thoughts while he waited for Mrs. Agnes to join him.

I am so glad Agnes told me that he is investing the church's money in the stock market and earning great interest. I cannot believe that nigger is gambling with the church's money, and those fools are allowing him to do it. There is just no end to what people will not do when it comes to money. I know you are not allowed, to invest money, gain a profit, and still be listed as a non-profit. Before he knows what's happening to him, he will be locked up, paying huge taxes, and once he does that, he'll have to ask his members for more money and since most of them are not used to paying, I know they are going to leave that church. Rev. Mical was so proud of his little scheme. He lit a cigar, placed it in his mouth, and then blew smoke rings into the air. He knew it was not good to smoke in the church but the windows were opened and besides this was his church.

When Mrs. Agnes greeted Rev. Mical, he was proud to see she was fired up. He needed her mad and vengeful. From the way she swung that old handbag she carried, he could tell something was stewing inside of her. There was a deep hatred in her eyes that he was happy to see. The eyes always tell the story; after all, they are windows of the soul. He laughed to himself.

Although she would pride herself on being a proper lady, today she failed to greet him before pulling out a Polaroid picture of Rev. Grant and his new family and demanding, "I want you to have this printed in your church's bulletin."

Rev. Mical examined the picture but kept his thoughts to himself.

"At the bottom of the picture, print the names of the boys. I wrote it on the back. Have their names, Rev. Grant, and Mary Jean—that's his new wife." She looked at him, hoping to read his stoic reaction. She waited for a response. When he offered none, she continued, "When people see the names of the boys, they would know that the proud Reverend has married a younger woman with two bastards, not one, but two!" Rev. Mical knew gossip would start as soon as his members saw the pictures. As Jackie Gleason used to say, 'H......ow sweet it is.' He thought. He truly appreciated that Mrs. Agnes can go spiraling on her own.

————

After arriving home, she dropped her purse by the door, picked up the phone, and called Sister Smith.

"Hello!" She nearly screamed into the phone.

"Oh, Hi, Sister Agnes. How are you?"

"I'm better now that I have taken care of Mary Jean and that old spiteful Rev. Grant," she said as she sat on her French provincial sofa.

"What are you talking about, Agnes?" asked Sister Smith. Lord, what has this demon been up to now?

"I can't say just now, but you'll hear about it soon enough. I'm just call-ing to tell you that you need to change your membership, back to The Greatness of Christ Baptist Church, because things are going to get hot at T.E.AM. And the two of us will need to stay clear of it all. Move your membership as soon as you can! I am leaving in a few weeks! "Mrs. Agnes said proudly. She nodded her head as if Sister Smith could see her. Then, she removed her heels, bent over, and rubbed her toes.

"Look, Agnes, you just remember that when you dig ditches, dig them deep, so you can be comfortable in them right along with the other people you threw in," she snapped.

"Oh. I'm not worried in the least bit. Those two won't know what hit them when we finish with them." Mrs. Agnes said as she smiled to her-self.

Sister Smith had heard the "we" and intuitively knew that Mrs. Agnes and Rev. Mical were in cahoots and she would need to do something quickly before Mrs. Agnes blew down all the Holy walls of Jericho.

Mrs. Agnes's laughter broke Sis. Smith's thoughts.

"Agnes, you know why I left The Greatness of Christ Baptist Church in the first place. That man has too many secrets and we only knew of the one for sure. He was out there bleeding all of us members dry. Using our money–God's money–for himself and his cronies. Have you forgot-ten that, Agnes?" She asked and waited for a response. Mrs. Agnes rolled her eyes and smacked her lips. "When your husband was sick, the great Rev. James Mical came to see him only one time and gave him an envelope with three dollars in it. Do you remember that, Agnes? Your husband had been a member of that church for twenty-five years and was a head deacon, and that's all he did for your husband!" Sister Smith said, disgusted that Mrs. Agnes had conveniently forgotten that.

"What's that got to do with the cost of tea in China, Joyce?" Mrs. Agnes asked. You can't ever keep to the subject. Here you're bringing up something that happened years ago. "Look, Joyce, you take things too personally! My husband and I did not need any money from Rev. Mical nor the church. We have never needed anything from anybody. My husband worked up until he retired, and we saved our money. Rev.

Mical knew that we did not need his money, and it was more than three dollars. Everybody isn't destitute like you, Joyce!" Mrs. Agnes said, irritated that she had even called her.

But Sister Smith was not going to let it go this time. She decided, since Mrs. Agnes brought up the subject, she was going to let her have it about her precious Rev. Mical. "Agnes, do you recall the day I left? Remember the straw that broke the camel's back? No? Well, let me tell you. Remember, when we were witnessing on Cherry Drive in the projects we met the lady with the kids who did not have any furniture. She asked if we could help her and her family to get some mattresses because they were sleeping on the floor. Not beds, Agnes, but mattresses. I told her we would. Then I went and told Rev. Mical that she would be coming by the church, to talk to him and that I had told her that we would buy her some mattresses for the family. Well, you know what Rev. Mical did? Not a damn thing!" Sister Smith waited. Mrs. Agnes remained quiet, allowing a fly on her dress to occupy her attention.

"When I saw her a few months later, she told me that she had spoken to Rev. Mical and that he had promised to buy the mattresses but that he never did. Well, the next day I went to see Rev. Mical and I asked him what happened. Do you know what that man told me? He said that we could not be helping junkies. If we bought her the mattresses, she would just sell them for heroin or have tricks on them! I could not believe him. What about her kids? We would be buying the mattresses for her kids, not so much for her, and even if she did sell them, we would have done the right thing, as Christians. As true witnesses of Christ. He didn't care at all. I left the church that day." Sister Smith said.

"Well, why didn't YOU buy her the mattresses if you felt so strongly about it?" Mrs. Agnes asked.

"We did, Agnes! My son and I not only purchased her the mattresses, but we also bought bunk beds and I know you don't remember her, but she is now clean, and she and her kids are members of the church." Sister Smith said.

"Who's church is she a member of?"

"T.E.A.M of course!"

"How were you able to pay for beds for that junkie's family when every time I talk to you, you are complaining about your bills?"

"Agnes, we didn't buy new furniture, but we did get a deal from a white lady who lives in the suburbs, who was selling her kids' furniture. We got a complete set of bunk beds and an extra bedroom set, all for fifty dollars. When I told this lady who I was buying the furniture for, she gladly threw in the sheets and spreads and curtains for nothing, she also gave me a lot of toys for the kids." Sister Smith said.

"Used furniture. Black folks are always so quick to accept hand-me-downs from white folks. They're always right there to lap up any and every crumb that falls from white folk's tables." Mrs. Agnes said. She and her husband never had used items in their house, she would not allow it. She had to wear the hand-me-down rags from the white families that her mother worked for when she was young and she swore that when she became an adult, she would never wear anything that was used by someone else.

Sister Smith knew it was useless to try to talk to Mrs. Agnes. It would always be her way or the highway. She heard her front door open and knew it was her son. This was the distraction she needed to end this conversation. "Agnes, my son just came in the door, let me get back with you later."

"All right, girl, call me later. Bye," Mrs. Agnes said and hung up the phone.

When he walked into the house, James could see his mother's anger. "What's the matter, Momma?"

"Son, I just got off the phone with Sister Agnes, need I say more?"

"Mama, you know that old lady is evil. I don't know why you continue to talk to her. Every time you talk to her your blood pressure elevates. You need to cut her loose. Some people are just evil to the core, and they are never going to change."

Sister Smith nodded her head and tried to explain to him how Mrs. Agnes seemed to be trying to destroy Rev. Grant, his family, and the church at any cost. He encouraged her to tell her friends and decide the best way to confront Mrs. Agnes and protect Rev. Grant. After he left, Sister Smith called each member of the Quilting Club. She told them about her conversation with Mrs. Agnes. They decided that they would talk to Rev. Grant that evening after their meeting and let him know what was being plotted against him and his family.

Problems Between Lawrence and Donna

Mary Jean noticed that the boys did not seem like themselves, after returning home from their weekly weekend visits with their dad and stepmother. Usually, they were full of talk about all the fun they had over the weekend. But this time each boy went directly to their room and did not say a word.

Mary Jean knew her boys and she intuitively knew that something had gone wrong at Lawrence's house. She decided to wait and see if they would confide in her about it. An hour later, Lawrence Junior came into the kitchen.

"Momma." He said standing at the door. He waited for her to turn to face him.

"Hey. I'm warming up some pie. Want to have some with me?" she smiled. His eyes were hard and focused.

"No ma'am," he shook his head. At nine years old, he stood to her shoulder.

"Me and Robert Michael ain't going back over there anymore!" He declared.

"And why do you think you aren't going back?" She asked.

"We're just tired of going over there all the time!" He said. She knew that wasn't true because the boys were spending less time with Lawrence now that they were in school.

"Lawrence, I thought that you boys enjoyed your weekends with your dad and Miss. Donna." She said while sitting the hot pie on a cooling board. Didn't you both tell me that when you are there you go to the movies, frost top, skating and the park," Mary Jean asked

"Well, yes! We did!" Lawrence Junior looked confused. "But we just do not want to go back for a while, if that's okay with you, Momma." He opened the icebox and got a bottle filled with water.

"Well, you need to tell me why you don't want to go, so when your father calls to let me know what time he will be picking you all up, I can tell him why you won't be going." Mary Jean said as she sat at the table. He sat down and looked at the bottle, but didn't look up. She turned his face towards her and looked him in the eyes.

"Lawrence Junior, we don't keep secrets in this house. We share our truth. Don't we?" she asked.

He nodded and she moved her hand.

She cut a piece of the pie and offered it to him. He loves pie but declined, again.

"So, what's the problem with going to your father's house? Why don't you all want to go?"

"Dad and Miss Donna had a bad fight!" he blurted.

"What! What kind of fight do you mean?" Mary Jean asked although she had a strong notion of how the fight went.

"Dad left early Saturday morning and told us he would come back to get all of us for the movies later that day. We waited a long time then Miss. Donna called a cab, and she took us. We still aren't riding the bus since people were boycotting all that time. So when we got back home, daddy still wasn't there. I could see that Ms. Donna was mad about it. She was slamming the dishes and cabinets, but she let us play outside into the night. We went to bed real late, too, cuz we were waiting for him! Right before I fell asleep, I heard doors slamming and daddy yelling. The yelling kept getting louder and louder then something was hitting the wall!"

He looked at Mary Jean. She stared at him, waiting to hear more.

"I'm listening, baby. Keep talking," She reassured him.

"Momma, we heard Miss. Donna scream!" He raised his voice. "Momma! She was screaming! I jumped out of bed and ran to the living room door. Robert Michael was with me too. We peeked in and Miss. Donna was on the floor! Daddy was punching her in the head and mouth!" Lawrence Junior demonstrated, swinging his arms wide and plummeting against the leg of the table.

"Momma, Daddy looked like he was drunk!" He started to get frantic.

"Okay, baby. Okay," Mary Jean moved closer to him but he didn't want her to hug him. "She was bloody, Momma. He's a monster! I wanted to call you, but the phone was in the room with them. When daddy looked up and saw us, he screamed for us to go back to bed before he kicked our A-S-S! He cursed us, Momma!" Lawrence Junior said. He lifted a bottle of milk to his mouth and tried to drink some. He was mad and afraid. His hand trembled and he put the bottle down before drinking.

She put her arm around his shoulder and held him. She took a deep breath and told him to breathe. Together, they took three long, deep breaths. Upset was not the word for what Mary Jean was feeling. She was livid. She instantly recalled all the horrible things that Lawrence had done in the past, and she knew she would not deal with this lightly. She told Lawrence Junior that he and his brothers did not have to go back to their father's house and that she was sorry that they had to witness such violence. She held back her anger and explained what his dad did to Miss. Donna was wrong and that no matter what a woman does to a man, it does not give him the right to put his hands on her except in love. She told him to always remember that, and he nodded.

"You were very brave and smart to tell me," she said. "I want you to enjoy this pie and your milk, okay?"

He nodded as his anger subsided. He loved his mother and how she made him feel stronger.

Mary Jean left him alone and went to check on Robert Michael. He sat on the windowsill, throwing and catching a baseball in an old, worn catcher's mitt he found at Stella's house a year ago.

"Hey, Jackie Robinson, you busy?" She said with a big smile.

He turned and smiled. He adored baseball and Jackie Robinson was quickly becoming an idol.

She didn't want to upset him but she needed to hear what he'd seen at Lawrence's house. Robert Michael had already disconnected his emotions from it. He recalled the situation the same way Lawrence Junior had but with less emotion. Now that he was back home, his mind and heart were on baseball.

Leaving his room, Mary Jean knew this was something she needed to deal with immediately. She picked up the phone and dialed Lawrence and Donna's number.

"Hell…. o." Donna said, in a painfully sad voice.

"Hi Donna, this is Mary Jean. Is Lawrence there?" Mary Jean asked as her foot patted the floor, trying to keep herself calm.

"No." Donna said. As she started sobbing, "I'm sorry, Mary Jean, he isn't. He is in jail. I am so sorry that the boys had to witness all of this mess. I know that's something kids really should never have to see."

"You don't owe me an apology, Donna. It is not you that I am upset with. But, my sons will not be coming over anymore until Lawrence gets some type of therapy. Please believe me I know it's not you. I know that you are good to my boys, and I am incredibly grateful and so are they. They really love you, but I will not have them around such violence. It's not safe there and he can call me when he gets out of jail if he needs to!" Mary Jean said while screwing off the cap on the Tylenol bottle and popping two tablets into her mouth to ease the pressure that was building up inside of her head.

"I don't know how long Lawrence will be in jail, but unless he gets out in the next hour, I won't see him. My people are on their way for me and my things. But I will leave the telephone connected. I'm leaving Lawrence and if he knows what's best for him, he'll stay away from me! I just cannot take any more of this foolishness! He beat me bad, Mary

Jean, real bad." Donna said looking at all the packed boxes in the middle of the floor. She raised her pain-stricken body off the sofa and eased to the window to see if her parents had arrived.

"I'm so sorry, Donna! Would you like to talk with Donald about all of this? Maybe, he could talk to Lawrence and you and help," Mary Jean said, knowing good and well, that this was not going to solve Lawrence's problem.

"No. But, thanks for the offer, Mary Jean. Let him talk to the boys. I really don't know how much they saw or what they heard. I'm to the point now where I just don't want to be married to Lawrence." She sobbed. Her body hurt as much as her heart was broken. "He needs help and, you, Rev. Grant, nor I, will be able to give him the help he needs. It's something he will have to do for himself. I am moving back home, and I plan to file for divorce as soon as next week. I thank God that I don't have any kids for that fool! Oh! I'm sorry, Mary Jean, I didn't mean that the way it sounded." Donna said, instantly feeling like she'd insulted Mary Jean.

"That's okay, Donna. I understand. I wish you well. Keep in touch with us. I know that the boys will want to hear from you, and if there is anything that Donald or I can do for you, be sure to let us know. Okay? " Mary Jean said, sincerely.

"I will. Bye." Donna hung up the phone.

"Bye," Mary Jean said. She hung up the phone and looked around her bedroom, thankful for the love she now shares with Rev. Grant. She whispered a prayer for Donna, for her family who had a reputation for being vigilantes, and for Lawrence. She thought about calling Rev. Grant but instead decided to get her journal and sit in her prayer closet. For some reason, she felt a burden to pray for George, Donald, and their sister, Sarah, who was now living in Ghana with her husband Pete and their sons.

Carla Confronts Rev. Mical

Carla made a B-line straight to Rev. Mical's church. It was time to get smarter or be done with these schemes. It was a waste of energy and gave her no satisfaction, financially, or sexually. Right now, she was losing valuable time. She sped past Sheriff Golepsky who had conveniently parked his patrol car at the vacant Willie's Car Wash. *Ugh, he's a creep. Who let him be a police officer?* She let up on the gas knowing if she hit her brakes he would come behind her. His harassment was so unattractive. She would complain about him to her cousins in New Orleans. "If he wants to be with Black women, he needs to get himself together. Can't nobody work with his potbelly," she would say.

She looked in her rearview mirror and was relieved when she saw that he had not moved. She picked up speed, knowing she needed to get to Rev. Mical before the rumor mill began making calls.

Carla strutted past Sis. Dorothy's desk without stopping to ask her if Rev. Mical was in or busy.

Sis. Dorothy looked up to stop her but decided to not waste her breath. *There goes that demon ready to meet with the devil.* She continued typing, then nosily yanked a page off the typewriter.

Carla opened the door and walked in on Rev. Mical who was ending a conference call. He slammed the phone down.

"Did you stop at my secretary's desk to see if I was free?" He growled.

"No, I didn't! I didn't feel I had to!" Carla said.

Rev. Mical shook his head and then looked Carla straight in the eyes. His lips were pinched. "Don't you ever bring your ass into my office without checking with my secretary first!" He stood and walked around the desk.

"What the hell you mean? I am doing a favor for you and you getting ugly. No, sir, you better correct yourself!" Carla said, keeping herself from shouting. "You asked me to try to subdue Rev. Grant and then to try to find out any incriminating information on him, so don't be yelling and cursing me like you don't know better!" Carla said stepping closer to Rev. Mical. "I'm not afraid of punks." She declared.

"Wench, you have always wanted that man! Everyone can look at you and knows that the only reason you decided to try to seduce him and spy on him is for me. When in reality, what you're doing is for you too, so don't walk into my office and pretend that you are doing me such a fa- vor. The favor is all yours!"

They were face-to-face. Both attempt to show strength over the other. Rev. Mical stepped away first and returned to his desk chair. "Now that we have cleared this up, what did you find out or should I ask what did you do?"

Carla sat in the chair and thought about if she should tell Rev. Mical that she failed, but then he had been failing all the time trying to trap Rev. Grant, so he could not be angry at her.

"Well, I made friends with T.P. Rev. Grant's wife's sister. And, I just wait- ed for her to bring me with her over to his house," she smacked her lips with confidence. "I must say, I was incredibly surprised to see that the place was not elaborate as I thought it would be. I bet your house looks better than his! Anyway, finally T.P. invited me to stop by her sister's house with her and as fate would have it, Rev. Grant came home. He's so handsome, Lord! I sat down in front of him and gave him a peek at MY glory. He instantly got angry and made T.P. leave, dragging me along. I know T.P. has all the details now because she stopped talking to me, and that little mouse of a wife of his has probably heard, too. Can you imag- ine an older man like him with a young wife like her?"

"Yeah, Carla. I can imagine it and that's why your job should have been so much easier. A woman with your experience should have been able to handle that situation better. First of all, it was dumb of you to even try to entice that man inside his own home. That was a crazy move! No man in his right mind is going to accept a sexual invitation inside his home and with other people nearby. Go to the man's damn office when there will be only you and him and no one else will see or know what is being said or done! Are you sure you are capable of handling this because if you are not, I can get someone else to do it!"

"Noooo. I got this. I've never been turned down by a man before because my stuff is magic!" Carla crossed her legs again.

"Well, you can add him as the first one because your ass got turned down by him. Now, I have something else to do so call me when you have some good news and proof, other than that do not come back to my office and waste my time.

Stella's Warnings

Shuffling through boxes of yarn, perfectly cut squares of fabrics, and spools of ribbon, Janie Jones fought through her arthritic pain to find perfect matches for the blue and gold quilt pattern she had imagined. She had arrived at the Blount Road Nursing Home early enough to start a pot of tea and organize the room for the dozen quilters who would gather soon. Out of convenience, Stella had insisted that they meet at the home for the two eldest members to join. Most times they were brought in by a cute orderly who Janie would affectionately call her missing son. He would smile at the old ladies and each time Janie would smile back and tell him, "I am so proud of you, son. Somebody done raised you right."

If the other women heard her, they would laugh, but on this day, no one had arrived on time. After Janie prepared a pitcher of hot tea and a pot of coffee, Stella walked in, carrying a heavy, red quilter's bag full of more fabric. A few years younger than Stella, Janie helped her walk to the table and sit in a brown overstuffed chair. Stella unpacked her bag while Janie poured their tea into matching mugs.

"Stella, I'm so glad you made it. I've been meaning to call you," She placed the mug on the table in front of Stella, then a mason jar of Betty's Beehive Honey. "How's your granddaughter and Rev. Grant doing?" she asked as they waited for the other members to show up.

"They're doing amazing, Janie. I am so happy for my baby. That man of God truly loves her," Stella said taking a sip of her tea. She started quilting. "I'll tell them that you asked about them."

"Yes, please tell them," Janie said and looked towards the door to see if anyone was entering. She sipped her tea and awkwardly looked up. "Stella, I need you to tell your granddaughter and Rev. Grant to be very careful because the buzzards are swarming waiting for them to fall," she said. Stella knew the rumor mill of Baine, Louisiana, would soon come out of their slumber, just like they had when Mary Jean was born.

"What buzzards, Janie? Who are you talking about?" Stella stopped quilting and looked directly at her.

"Agnes and Rev. Mical, of course. One of my dear friends attends Rev. Mical's church and she told me that he, Mrs. Agnes, and some young lady name Carla are all trying to destroy Rev. Grant and the church. She said that he keeps sending the girl to seduce Rev. Grant. They are even trying to mess with Rev. Grant's money." Janie said.

"Who is that close to Rev. Mical to know that much of his business that she would be able to tell your friend?" Stella asked.

"It was Rev. Mical's secretary, but you have to swear to not tell Mary Jean or Rev. Grant that that's where the information came from because the girl could lose her job, and I don't want to be a part of that, "Janie said.

"What's this seductress' name again?" Stella asked.

"Carla, her name is Carla. My friend said that Rev. Mical is livid that his members are leaving the church and going over to TEAM, so he's been conniving with Mrs. Agnes from the first day she joined Rev. Grant's church. He has her over there so she can snoop and find out information. Hell, based on what his secretary said, Agnes has been successful in gathering something that could possibly bring down Rev. Grant, his family, and the church. So, you tell Mary Jean and Rev. Grant to watch their backs because Rev. Mical, Mrs. Agnes, and that gal Carla are all after him!" Janie's voice rose, "And you know what! I never did like Agnes! She always thought she was so much better than all of us on the block just because she had a nicer house. Everyone knows her poor husband worked his hands to the bones to support her high lifestyle and he left her well off when he passed, but she is a snake," Janie said as she took a sip of her tea.

Stella shook her head and raised her hands, "Lord, the devil never stops," she proclaimed. "Thank you, Janie, for this information, but let's not talk about it anymore. Here comes Manuella and Gretchen." Janie turned around and looked out the large window towards the parking lot. She waved both hands as if they could not see her sitting at the only table in the large room.

For three hours, the elder ladies of The Bains Women's Quilting Club stitched seven quilts to fit twin beds. They were just short of their goal but would soon have enough quilts for the youth to travel to the Second District Missionary Baptist Convention in Baltimore this Christmas. While they work, the women talked about their grandchildren, laughed at each other's antics, and hummed as The Mighty Clouds of Joy sang in the background. It was just the amount of activity Stella needed and the only movement her body could take.

As soon as Stella walked into her front door, she dropped her bag heavily, walked to the living room sofa, and sat down. She took the telephone receiver and struck each number to dial Mary Jean's number. The phone rang about six times and she was about to hang up when Lawrence Junior answered.

"Hello." He said.

"Hi, Baby! How are you and your brother?" Granny asked.

"Oh hi, Granny. We are fine. How are you?" He asked, then yelled into the phone, "Momma!"

Stella quickly removed the receiver from her ear.

"Granny's on the phone!" He yelled, then quietly returned, "She's coming, Granny."

"Hello," Mary Jean said. "Hang up the phone, son."

He placed the phone on the hook.

"Hey, Granny. The boys and I were just planning to come over and bring your groceries," she said, smiling at the thought of seeing Stella soon.

"Look, baby, Granny don't have a long time to talk because I just got home, but I had to call you because one of my quilting members just told me that Mrs. Agnes and Rev. Mical are trying to destroy TEAM Church and your marriage with some little wench named Marla or Carla. She was sent to your house to seduce your husband, so I'm telling you that you and Donald and T.P. all have to keep your eyes open. The devil is working to destroy you," Stella said as she pulled the lever on her recliner to lean backward and elevate her legs. The pain from sitting and walking all day was beginning to take a toll.

"Lord, Granny. I've been praying about this every since that woman came over. Thank you, Granny. You've answered my prayer. I'll tell Donald tonight. We know all about Mrs. Agnes and Rev. Mical, but I'm so glad that you called to validate it for us. We will be extra careful. And, that woman who came by here with T.P was named Carla. T.P. is aware of her and so are we, but I have a feeling she isn't finished." Mary Jean stopped and thought about the last time she'd seen Carla.

Stella adjusted her weight in the chair, but the pain in her legs wouldn't let up.

"Now how are you doing, Granny?" Mary Jean asked.

"Baby, I'm just tired, so I'm going to sit here for a while and watch T.V. Then I'm going to get up and go get me some of that apple pie from you and the boys. We can talk more when you come by, okay, baby?

"Yes ma'am. That would be great, Granny. We will see you later," Mary Jean said and Stella hung up the phone.

Mary Jean Confronts T.P.

When the phone rang T.P. was not up for any long conversation but decided to answer it anyway.

"Hello."

"Hey, Sis."

"Oh, hey, how are you?" T.P. perked up. She always enjoyed talking to Mary Jean.

"I'm not going to keep you long, T.P." Mary Jean took a seat at the kitchen table before continuing to talk. "Donald just told me about that disrespectful lady that you brought to our home. He said she was brazening enough to open her legs so that he could see under her clothing. Now that is just nasty and to do such a thing to a minister is such a disgrace. Where did you meet her?" Mary Jean asked.

"What did he say she did?" T.P. asked.

"He said she sat on the sofa, leaned to the right, and crossed her legs in a manner that show far up her thigh. He was so upset. I've never seen Donald get that angry. Then he said she uncrossed her legs and opened them up wide as if what she had just done wasn't bad enough, and he could almost see her womanhood. He said she can never cross the seal of our door again because it was disrespectful to him and to me," Mary Jean said.

T.P. felt so bad. The first time she ever brought someone to her sister's house it turned out to be someone evil and nasty. "I'm sorry Sis I thought she was a better person than that, but that just goes to show you, you never really know people. She's one of my clients, but not anymore. I have never made friends with any of my clients until her and it makes me question my judgment because I thought she was so nice. If I hadn't I would never have brought her to your home. Please tell Rev. Grant how sorry I am and that I was fooled," T.P. said genuinely sorry.

"I believe you and I'll explain to Donald on your behalf, but please do not bring any more women to this house," She said laughing.

T.P. laughed too and was happy that Mary Jean understood and was willing to speak to Rev. Grant on her behalf.

"Well, that's all I had to discuss with you, and you know what I have to go do now," Mary Jean uttered.

"Cook, of course, that's all you do is cook, so what's on the menu for tonight?" T.P. asked.

"Red beans, rice, fried chicken, and a salad. Would you like to come over for dinner?" Mary Jean asked.

"No. Not tonight I'm dog tired and I need to do something with my own hair. I'm so busy taking care of other people's hair that I forget about mine, so tonight's the night that I will pamper myself."

"Speaking of hair, when are you going to come over and do my hair? It's been three weeks," Mary Jean asked.

"I'll come by on Wednesday night, that's my slow night. Okay?" T.P. asked.

"Okay, I'll see you then," Mary Jean said and hung up the phone.

Stella Slows Down

Mary Jean, Lawrence Junior, and Robert Michael ran into Stella's house, laughing, each carrying a canvas bag of produce. Stella was sitting in her favorite recliner, anticipating their arrival. She still loved the noise they made throughout the otherwise empty home. Mary Jean looked at her granny and saw the same thing she saw at the Douglas barbecue. Her granny had aged a lot. She looked tired and her breathing was labored even in her sleep. After they each kissed Stella, Mary Jean motioned to the boys to be quiet. She walked toward the back of the house to find a blanket for Stella to rest more comfortably. Once in the bedroom, she noticed dirty sheets and paper napkins around the room, empty coffee mugs, and an overflowing trashcan. Granny must've been too tired to clean this up. I'll have to get back here more often. Mary Jean took the blanket to Stella, covered her from the neck down, and kissed her forehead as she slept. She went back to clean the bedroom and bathroom before joining the boys.

They took their bags into the kitchen and searched for any sweets Stella may have baked. They found an apple pie cooling on the counter. Lawrence Junior cut two generous slices for them. Robert Michael found a small bottle of milk in the icebox where he had arranged the produce and groceries from his bag. He sat at the table across from his brother.

Although they were twins, Lawrence Junior was much taller and sat poised, while Robert Micheal hunched over and devoured the pie.

"You think Granny's okay?" He asked between bites.

"I don't know," Lawrence Junior answered flatly.

"I hope she is. I want her to come to the science fair and watch me beat all the fourth graders!" Robert Michael boasted.

"She'll be there," Lawrence Junior said.

After they'd eaten their second helping, Stella woke up. She was weak but forced herself to walk into the kitchen.

"Well, look at my handsome young men!" She said. Robert Michael jumped up and ran over to her. He hugged her tightly, then she kissed Lawrence Junior who quickly gave her his seat. "Want some pie, Granny?" he asked.

"No baby, you two enjoy it and save some for your grandma Shelia. She was the one who cut up all those apples for me. Save her a big piece now, okay?" Stella said. She loved seeing her great-grandsons. They were always so happy and courteous. Mary Jean was raising them right, and her grandfather would be so proud. Stella reminisced.

Mary Jean walked into the kitchen. "Oh, Granny, how are you feeling? Did that nap help any?"

"Yes, baby, I am well," Stella said. "Did you see what I put on my dresser mirror, Mary Jean?" Stella asked proudly. She had been keeping up with the commentaries Mary Jean had been writing in the *Baton Rouge Newsleader* and had taped two clippings as high as she could reach. She planned to cover the wall with them until she purchased the perfect picture frames. She was so proud of Mary Jean.

"Granny's so happy to see you all. How are you doing in school?" She asked.

"I made all As on my report card, Granny," Lawrence Junior belted.

"I made one B and all the rest of my grades were As, "Robert Michael said.

"Okay, That's enough boys." Mary Jean said. She could see that Stella was weak.

"Don't stop them, Mary Jean. I love having them tell me about their grades and how happy it makes them. Never stop them from being proud of their accomplishments. They are smart just like you were at that age. Do you know I never had to help your momma with her homework?" Stella told the boys. "Your momma was always able to do her work on her own without my help—not that I could have helped her anyway—and she made all As and was always on the honor roll? I said God knew I could not help her, so He gave her the brains to help herself and me."

Stella turned towards Mary Jean, who stood behind Robert Michael as he finished eating the pie. "You would read my mail for me and write out my bills. Baby, you have always been such a blessing in my life, and I have always loved you for it."

"I know, Granny, you look a little tired," Mary Jean said.

"Okay, you are right. I do feel a little tired tonight. Would you go in my bedroom and bring me that jewelry box on top of my dresser and the Bible on my nightstand?" Stella asked.

"Sure, Granny. Boys finish eating your pie; I'll be right back."

"Lawrence Junior, look in that drawer by the sink and get a pencil and a piece of paper and then I want you to add something for me. Okay?"

"Okay, Granny," Lawrence Junior said as he pushed back his chair and walked over to the cabinet got the paper and pencil then returned to the table.

"Now for every A that you had on your report card I want you to add each A by 100 and give your brother half of the paper so he can do the same," Stella said as Mary Jean entered the room with the jewelry box and the Bible and placed them in front of Stella.

Stella reached into the box and took out her wedding ring and a pair of diamond earrings that her husband had bought her before he died. He had saved for a long time to purchase them. She took them out of the box and looked at them for the last time and then she took Mary Jean's hand and opened it.

"These are for you and don't tell me that you don't want them because I want you to have them," Stella said feeling a heaviness in her chest.

"But, Granny, Grandpa gave these to you why would you want to give them away and why won't you give them to, mama? Are you okay?" Mary Jean asked concerned.

"Lawrence's what's your total?" She asked.

"It's 500, Granny," Lawrence Junior said.

"And Robert Michael, what is your total?" Stella asked looking inside her Bible.

"It's 400," Robert said.

"Come here," Stella said as she took money out of the Bible.

"Hold your hand out Robert and when you go home put this in your bank, Okay." As she counted four one-hundred-dollar bills into Robert's hand.

Mary Jean wondered why Granny had given her the jewelry and was now giving the boys so much money and it made her feel like she was not telling her something.

"Lawrence Junior, you do the same thing, now hold out your hand out," Stella said as she placed five one-hundred-dollar bills in his hand. Lawrence Junior had a big smile on his face.

"Now if you all don't mind, I need to go lie down, Mary Jean," Stella said as she stood up, but had to sit back down because she felt dizzy. Everyone ran to steady her.

Just then the front door opened, and Shelia walked in calling for the boys.

"We're in the kitchen!" Lawrence Junior yelled.

"Momma, come help me get Granny to her bed!" Mary Jean yelled which caused Shelia to rush into the kitchen.

"What's wrong?" Shelia asked.

"I don't know. She was getting up and then she fell back into the chair. Help me get her to her room and let's call Dr. Bloomberg to come to see her. What time is it?" Mary Jean asked as they both lifted Stella off the chair and slowly began to walk Stella to her room.

Once they had Stella in her room, they changed her into a clean gown. Shelia gave her a cool wash towel for her face and neck. With a shaky hand, Stella folded back the bedspread then sat on the bed as the younger woman lifted her legs one at a time onto the bed. Mary Jean went into the kitchen, came back, and placed Granny's jewelry box and Bible on her dresser, while Shelia called Baines's only Negro doctor.

"What did Dr. Bloomberg say? Is he going to be able to come tonight?" Mary Jean asked.

"Yes, he'll be here soon, but if you need to get home, I can call you later and let you know what he says."

"No. We'll wait." Mary Jean considered telephoning Rev. Grant but decided to wait.

"Are you and the boys hungry? There are some leftovers from yesterday that we can warm while we wait for the doctor."

"What do you have?" Mary Jean asked.

"There's some smothered steak with mashed potatoes and broccoli and a green salad. I'll warm the food," Sheila said, "Go check on momma and see if can eat anything."

When she walked into the room, Stella was rubbing camphor oil on her arm and chest. Mary Jean knew the strong scent meant Stella was in some sort of pain.

"Oh baby, I hope I didn't scare you," Stella said. "I'm fine I just have a little gas pain in my chest, but I'm going to be fine." She repositioned herself on a mound of pillows.

Mary Jean knew that Stella was not telling her the truth and she would get Dr. Bloomberg to tell them exactly what was happening once he arrived and checked her out.

"Granny, do you feel up to eating something? Momma's warming leftovers for the boys." She said.

Stella shook her head, "No. No."

Dr. Bloomberg arrived while the boys ate. Shelia opened the door before he was able to step onto the porch and knock on the door. For a man who has seen the worst conditions, he always looked great. He greeted Shelia by nodding his head twice. He spoke slowly.

"What is the problem with Mrs. Stella? Is her heart still giving her problems? I told her a year ago that she needed a pacemaker but she told me she didn't want anything inside her body that God didn't put there," He said as he followed Shelia through the house.

Mary Jean was surprised to hear Stella was having heart problems for a year and hadn't mentioned it. She was more dismayed that she hadn't noticed. Shelia knew her mother was developing heart problems but Stella had reassured her that her only instructions from the doctor were to increase her blood pressure medicines, change her diet and keep taking her diabetes medication on time and she would be fine. As she walked down the hall towards Stella's bedroom, Shelia was having her doubts.

"How long have you known this?" Mary Jean whispered to Shelia once they entered the room.

"She told me something different," Shelia said as the doctor used his stethoscope to listen to Stella's heart from her back and chest. He began asking her questions about her vision and balance, to which she whispered her answers and avoided eye contact.

"I'm going to increase your heart medication and you get this filled as soon as possible. I'm going to give her a shot that will help her for tonight but she will need to start taking this medication immediately three times a day and she can't skip a dose. She also needs to rest more from now on. Do I make myself clear?" He said glancing first at Stella and then at Shelia.

"Okay, Doctor! Okay!" Stella said, patting her lap.

"Stubborn as a mule, is what she is. I told her what she needed to do but she wouldn't listen," he said as he walked out of the room with Shelia and Mary Jean on his heels.

"How long has Granny had heart problems and how bad is it?" Mary Jean asked quickly.

"A little longer than a year that I know about, but she probably had it long before that."

"This pacemaker you spoke of, can Granny get it now and what is it?"

"It's a small battery-operated device that can tell when the heart is not beating regularly and it will send a signal to the heart to beat at its correct pace," He said. "It's too late now to get it. Mrs. Stella is too weak and she would not be able to make it through the operation. Right now, I suggest you two see that she is comfortable, follow the diet that I gave her for her diabetes, and see to it that she takes the medicine I just prescribed." He shook Lawrence Junior's hand as he stepped off of the porch, leaving Mary Jean and Shelia in shock.

The Day After Stella Gets Sick

Shelia slept the night between the middle bedroom and Stella's room. She checked on her mother nearly every thirty minutes. She prayed for God to keep her sober through the mounting stress of seeing her mother aging and becoming ill. She couldn't wait until after breakfast to call Mary Jean. When her phone rang, Mary Jean knew that she had to take this call, because the only people who called her this early were her family and close friends, so she grabbed the phone off the dresser.

"Hello." Mary Jean said as she sat on the bed.

"Hey, Sugar. How are my favorite people in the world?" It didn't matter how Shelia felt, she greeted Mary Jean the same way every time she called.

"We're doing good, Mama. How are you? How did you and Granny sleep last night?" Mary Jean asked nervously.

"She slept like a baby. Much better than me," she said.

"Aaw, Mama. I'm so sorry," Mary Jean said and began planning how she could sit with Stella for a few hours before the boys and Rev. Grant returned home.

"Mary Jean?"

"Yes, Mama. I'm here. I was just thinking. What did you say?" she asked.

"With momma having this heart condition and everything. I'm thinking about quitting my job. I need to be closer here and driving back and forth to clean those dorms at LSU puts me outta pocket."

Shelia took a deep breath.

For a moment, they didn't speak. Both, thinking about the challenge of caring for Stella who has always been the strongest person they knew.

"Maybe I can go to those adult education classes over at the Betty Thomas Tutoring Center and study for my high school certification." She said. She smiled knowing how proud Stella would be to hear her talking about school again.

"That's a great idea, Mama! I remember when we talked about it a year ago, you thought that you were losing your memory and that you wouldn't be able to keep up. Now would be a perfect time." Mary Jean proclaimed.

"Yeah. I agree," she said, feeling a little lighter. "I need to be able to work smarter and not harder. It sure is getting really hard standing on my feet all day and it's far too much racism that I have to endure on that job." Shelia said.

"I don't think having an education is going to stop you from having to have to deal with racism. Educated people are racist also, but they are good at hiding it. Those labor jobs usually hire people who have little education at all and who have no qualms about speaking exactly how they feel. Remember I was cleaning hotels for years. I hate seeing you go back and forth with that job. Has something else been happening there?" Mary Jean asked. She didn't want to overhear any more secrets, so she asked directly.

"I don't want to bother you with my problems, baby, we have enough to deal with than to have to listen to me complain," Shelia said as she let out a loud sigh. "We gotta get momma to do everything the doctor said and that won't be easy!"

"You are right about that, Mama." Mary Jean said, then waited for Shelia to continue. "Mama, I have time to listen and it would be no bother if you would tell me what's happening on that campus. If anything, I'll be worried wondering what is happening to you if you don't tell me."

Shelia thought about it. She listened to hear if Stella had begun moving around. After she didn't hear a sound, she relaxed and sat on the high stool in the kitchen. "Well, I got my evaluation last week from Mr. Cool—you know that's what I call my boss—he had the gall to tell me that I'm not working up to standards. I could not believe my ears! I'm always early for work and I open up the laundry mat by myself each morning. Even though that crazy white bigoted woman from Livingston is supposed to be there helping me. I stand on my feet all day, and most days I'm only able to get a fifteen-minute break, just long enough to grab a piece of fruit or a sandwich and eat, before it's time to clear out all waste bins. There are only three of us working, and most of the time it's just me. Lucy—her real name is Mita—but Lucy is my name for her because she is so loose. She takes off on Mondays and Thursdays and hangs over at the truck stop on Highway fourteen."

"Well, to make a long story short, in the middle of giving me a piss poor evaluation, he had the nerve to tell me something about 'you people.' When he said that, I told him about his people. I told him that his people had stolen most of everything that they have and that they were all crooks, they were brought here from England because the Queen was tired of the law-abiding people having to take care of these criminals, so she sent them here to this country."

"What?" Mary Jean interrupted, laughing. "You told him that!"

"Yeah, and I was just getting warmed up. I told him that when they got here and Indians tried to live with them, all they did was destroyed the Indians, by any means necessary, sneaking around at night and killing them, placing smallpox in their blankets, killing the buffalo, and selling their land." She smacked her lips and continued, "and that wasn't enough for them, so they moved them to reservations where they had more control of the Indians and they just kept on destroying. Making those people walk halfway across the United States and most of them dying along the way. Those were some cruel people," Shelia said.

"I don't believe you, Mama! You told him all that?" Mary Jean said laughing and picturing her mom standing with her hands on her hip as she always did when she was upset.

"Then, I told him that since his people were so lazy, they had to come to Africa and steal my people, who were warriors, agriculturalists, kings, and queens. They put my people in chains and dragged them back here to force them to build America. Then, I told him if it wasn't for racist hiring practices, he wouldn't be one of the campus managers. He'd be working in my place!" Shelia said feeling tightness across her forehead.

"What! He didn't fire you?" Mary Jean asked laughing. She was surprised that Shelia stood up for herself and was more surprised that her mother knew so much about American history.

"No, he didn't fire me! That fool knows better than to fire me! Who is going to do all the work around there? He needs me and he knows it and so do I, but I do not need him at all!" She said. "All he did was turn red in the face and walked out of the door. I haven't seen him all week! And that fool, Lucy, was quiet for the rest of the day. I think she thought that if I talked to him that way, I probably would have done worst to her and she was right I was waiting for her to just say one word!"

Mary Jean laughed more. "Mom, I'm proud of you. You told him right! I know it is not easy working for people who do not respect you as a person. But, if you decide to go back to school, Donald and I will help you with whatever you need. Just let us know. Okay?" Mary Jean said proudly.

"That's okay honey. I think I can make it. I have been saving as much of my check as possible ever since I started working and I know Mama has been putting money into a savings account for me. I'm good and I'm blessed to have a mother who loved me even when I didn't love her, you, or myself. Tomorrow I'm going on Fisher Street to that center and register for the adult education program, and whenever they tell me I can start, I am going to quit that job and be here for my mama." Shelia said as she heard Stella coughing. "Momma's up. I'll call you back, honey."

"Okay, Mama. I'll make some dinner for you and bring it later."

"Okay. I will see you then. Bye, baby"

"Bye, Mama." Mary Jean said. She thought about how their relation-ship had grown and was grateful for the love growing in her chest.

-129-

Lawrence Calls Mary Jean

One month after being jailed for assault and battery, Lawrence finally resurfaced, looking for his sons and any semblance of a normal life. He'd lost his job while in jail and Donna had taken everything out of their bank accounts. When he returned home, only a phone, two pillows, and bedsheets had been left on the living room floor.

He called Mary Jean's home again. This time, he was ready to go to the house if no one answered. The phone rang twice before Mary Jean yelled, "Boys! Will you get that, please?"

"Okay!" Lawrence Junior ran into the den and picked up the phone.

She waited for him to yell out as he normally did but he didn't. She placed the breakfast dishes in the sink and wiped her hands on her apron before taking it off. She thought maybe it was one of his little friends from school, so she started taking meat out of the freezer to thaw for dinner. Then, suddenly she had a feeling that something was wrong and walked into the den. She could tell by the look on Lawrence Junior's face that he did not like what he was hearing on the other end of the phone.

"Who's that, Lawrence Junior?"

"It's Dad!" He tried to whisper.

Mary Jean knew Lawrence was scolding Lawrence Junior. "Give me the phone!" She took it from him but before speaking, she calmed herself. "You and your brother go ahead and leave before you miss the bus, and Honey don't worry about whatever your dad said, I'll handle this. You just have a nice day in school, you hear me?" She kissed him and caught Robert Michael's arm before he passed, then hugged and kissed him. "I'll see you later."

She watched them walk out the door. From the window, she could see them standing at the corner stop. She put the phone to her ear and heard Lawrence shouting.

"How dare you call our home and scold our child!" Mary Jean yelled so loudly that Rev. Grant heard her from the hallway. He quickly entered the living room in alarm.

Lawrence lowered his voice. "Look, Mary Jean, I was just telling the boy that what goes on in my house should have stayed in my house. I called Donna's parents' house and told her off and she told me that she didn't tell you. He told you! All I was doing was trying to teach the boy something about minding his business." Lawrence's speech was slurred.

"Well, let me tell you what you taught him thus far, Lawrence! You taught him that men take care of problems by abusing alcohol and beating women! You taught him that men are violent and not dependable! You taught him that his father can find fault in him but cannot see his own faults. That's what you have taught him!" Mary Jean yelled. "And furthermore, how I handle anything that upsets him is his and my business. Not yours!"

"Look, Woman! I did not call for all this bullshit. I called to ask why the boys haven't been coming on weekends like they used to."

"You're lying, Lawrence, this happened over a month ago and you haven't called, nor came by not one weekend to pick them up because you knew they wouldn't be coming to visit you anymore, but now you call our house after you thought we had cooled off, trying to see what we thought. Well, here is what we know. Do you really think that I am going to let the boys come back to stay with you? You sound like you are on something right now and I will not have our sons exposed to your ungodly craziness. I really thought that you had changed after your near-death experience, but I guess it will take more than that to get you to do the right thing. But I tell you what until you are stable in mind and heart, the boys will not be coming by you. Do I make myself clear?" Now, if you really want to see them, then you can come by here and see them. You will never be alone with them." She shifted her weight from one foot to the other.

"Oh, so now you are a Holy Saint, calling me ungodly? You cannot stop me from seeing my sons, Woman! I will take you to court. I know my rights!"

"Your rights? What rights are you talking about, Lawrence? You have not given me one dime for these boys in years. Are you really ready to take me to court? But, if that is how you feel you just do that, Lawrence, and be sure that you have all of the money you owe them, birthday gifts, Christmas gifts, time that you were not there for them, everything that's due to them!" Mary Jean knew it was time to end the conversation.

"Screw you, Mary Jean!"

"You did that before, Lawrence, but you'll never do it again in this life. Grow up!"

Lawrence slammed the phone down on the hanger, practically breaking the hook. Mary Jean knew what she had just told Lawrence would keep him away from them for a while.

George Tries Again

George was reluctant to call T.P.'s number after having called the last three nights and she hasn't answered. But, he decided to call her anyway because she intrigued him, and he felt sharp with her. Come on, Woman, answer the phone.

On the second ring, she answered, "Hello."

"Hello, Pretty Lady." He paused to see if she would respond. "Please don't hang up. I've been trying to explain the other night." George said waiting to hear if T.P. would slam down the phone. She didn't respond. She wanted to hear the excuse he had for interacting with the intoxicated lady at the bar.

"You still there?" He asked.

"I'm listening," T.P. said as nonchalantly as she could.

"I apologize for the antics. I once dated Lallia and I thought we had both moved on with our lives, but apparently, she has not. We talked months ago and decided that it would be best if we ended our relationship since it wasn't working for either of us. She agreed, so I was as surprised as you were when she decided to rub up on me," George said.

This man thinks I don't know a lie when I hear it. T.P. took a seat at her small kitchen table, stretching the phone cord from the wall. "So, you are telling me that Ms. Lallia agreed to end your relationship, but suddenly that night she became intoxicated when she saw you with me. Then, she decided to let everyone in the bar know how she felt about you? Is that what you want me to believe?"

George thought for a moment."Well, yes, that's the truth. I was as surprised as you were!"

"Who said I was surprised?" She asked smugly. "You see, George, I'm very seldom surprised by people because I start the relationship off by giving you zero, so you have to build it up and earn my trust. A lot of people are the opposite of that, they give a person one hundred to start with and every time they do something that they don't like they lose a percentage. But, I start you with zero and at the rate you are going, it will take quite a long time before you reach one hundred percent with me, so no, I'm not surprised."

George had never had any woman talk to him with such assuredness in herself and he wanted to get to know this woman better.

"So, may I have a redo?"

"I think you need to end your last relationship, before trying to start one with me. I do not have time for games, George. I've been down that road before and, now, in my life, I am looking for someone who is looking for a solid, transparent relationship with one woman. And I, honestly, don't see that as the case with you. You're not ready to be a one-woman-man, nor do you want to be totally open and real with a woman. Your swagger doesn't allow it, yet."

She stopped for effect, knowing he had never heard a woman talk like she was talking even though they would both be turning forty soon. "George, I'm sure there are a lot of women who are interested in you, and many of them have been quite easy for you, but I'm not one of them. So please, lose my number," T.P. said.

She waited, then hung up the phone.

George was taken aback. This woman had hung up in his face. He knew he had to find a way to get to know this woman.

———

When the telephone rang, Mary Jean prayed it was not Mrs. Agnes with more of her conniving. She had less than two hours to get to the grocery store and back before the boys returned from school.

She snatched the phone from the receiver. "Hello," she said.

"Hey, Sister-in-Law," George said feigning cheer.

"Oh, Hi, George. Donald is not home," Mary Jean said quickly. "Would you like me to ask him to call you back or you can try calling him at the church," Mary Jean hurried.

"No. I'm not calling to talk to him. I called to ask you to do me a favor," George said running it through his head as to how to ask Mary Jean such a question and if she would be willing to help him.

"So, what can I do for you, George?"

"I'm sure T.P. has probably told you about our last date and how it ended," George paused waiting to see if Mary Jean would admit to knowing about it, but she was quiet.

"Well, a young lady that I used to date made a scene at the lounge where T.P. and I were on a date. T.P. got angry and left."

"OH?" Mary Jean said, sure that George was still trying to see if T.P. had told her.

"So, now T.P. won't talk to me anymore and I really would love to make it up to her. I really would love to take her out again, and I would like for you to put a good word in for me." George held his breath.

"George, I don't really know you well enough to speak about your character. Besides, based on what you have just told me, you have messed that up yourself and I do not want to get involved in T.P.'s and your business," Mary Jean said whole heartily.

"Come on, Sis, all I want you to do is to tell her to give me another chance," George asked.

"I don't have a reason to do that, George. I don't know enough about you and your relationship with women to give T.P. any advice. So you will have to get creative and redeem yourself if you think you're worthy of my sister's attention." She grinned at her own wit. "I am sorry, but I must go now. Would you like for me to tell Donald that you called?" Mary Jean asked.

"Only if you can get him to speak to T.P. for me," George said laughing, but Mary Jean did not laugh.

"Bye, George." Mary Jean said, thinking *what nerve this man has to call me to put in a word for him. Hump, for all I know, he's a smooth womanizer, and he's not ready for T.P.*

"Okay. Bye, Sis-in-law."

The Seductress Returns

There were four cars parked at the back entrance of T.E.A.M. It was 11 a.m. and Carla knew the men gathered on Tuesday morning to cash out Sunday's collection and validate Monday's bank deposits. She also knew that if Rev. Grant was the pastor everyone claimed he was, then he would soon be alone to prepare for Tuesday night Bible study. She was right. Slowly, the deacons began exiting the church and leaving.

Carla sat in her car which she parked on the side of Broucher Avenue near the bus stop. She stayed there until she saw Rev. Grant get in his car and leave. Since he was empty-handed, she knew he must have been heading out for lunch and would soon return. Impatiently, she watched the door and parking lot, waiting for the owner of the final car to leave. Within moments, Mable exited the building carrying her purse and a workbag. She fought with her car door, then sat with the engine running while she adjusted her makeup and sprayed on perfume. Carla knew that meant Mable was off for the day and was probably heading to see the new history professor at Southern University over in Baton Rouge. Carla slowly pulled closer to the church, opened her car door, exited as if she had official business there, and headed towards the door.

"I hope no one else is in there," she said to herself. She dropped her keys in her purse, rubbed her hands down the front of her dress, and carefully stepped over rocks in her new yellow heels.

When she reached the back door, she found it locked. She placed her purse on the ground and shifted her body to the left to block anyone's view as she attempted to pick the lock.

Carla smiled slyly. She'd picked many doors in her life and this little cheap lock would not be hard. She took out a metal pick and a small hook worked them into the lock and turned them until she heard a click. She opened the door, walked in, and closed it softly behind her.

She had to move fast. She rushed to Rev. Grant's office, picked his door lock, opened it, gently closed it, and swung around toward his desk. The scent of his cologne lingered and she immediately became aroused. *My, My, Rev. Grant. You shol' smell good.* She rushed over to his desk, took off her peach, lace panties, and tried to open the top drawer but it was locked. She looked around the desk for another hiding place. Then, she folded the panties as if they were a man's handkerchief and placed it in the Bible. She returned it to the corner of the pastor's desk. She shifted the notepad and desk phone to make the space appear less neat, then she laughed to herself. I bet when he opens this Bible to give someone a scripture they will both be surprised! I wish I could be here to see how he explains this!

She could not wait that long, so she decided to sit in the waiting area until Rev. Grant returned then she would see how much of a man he was. She closed his office door, locked it again, and sat in the waiting area, flipping through magazines and church bulletins that were on the table. When she was just about to leave, she heard someone unlocking the side door nearest the waiting room. At first, she thought Mable had returned. When Rev. Grant walked into the waiting room, he immediately saw Carla sitting provocatively on the sofa and knew he was going to have a problem with this demon again.

"What can I do for you?" He asked sternly looking back at her as he unlocked the door to his office. His mind quickly noted that she had to have entered on her own which could explain how letters and files connected to the church finances conveniently are moved around in the offices.

"I need to talk to you–privately–for a few minutes, Rev. Grant," Carla said crossing her legs in a manner that revealed her upper thigh. She attempted to sound innocent.

"What is your name?" Rev. Grant asked. He crossed his arms and leaned on the secretary's desk as far away from Carla as he could stand.

"Carla. My name is Carla."

"Well, Miss Carla. I know who you are and I know what you do."

She tried her best not to grin, instead, she lifted her eyebrow and put her hand on her purse although she was not ready to leave.

"I know that you are working with Rev. Mical, and he has hired you in an attempt to manipulate me and destroy this church, but it's not going to work. And you can go back and tell him that I said that." Rev. Grant eyeballed her and waited for a response.

"Hired? I would not take a dime from Rev. Mical to get next to you. I want you on my own and I always have. Now, you are right he does want to destroy your church, but I want you, it has nothing to do with the church." She stood up and bent down for her purse, allowing her dress to reveal the cheek of her behind.

At 35, Carla had the body of an athlete. No man could completely ignore her body, and neither could Rev. Grant. Even he had to admit that this fast little demon was fine, but unlike many of the men who'd succumb to Carla, he knew secrets and temptation came before a brutal fall.

"Miss Carla, let me show you out," Rev. Grant turned back and walked to the door. "You will leave this church and never come back!" Rev. Grant said.

Just then, Mable and Bro. Michael, the church's security guard, walked up to the door.

"Damn!" Bro. Michael said as he looked at Carla's raised skirt. He quickly apologized. "Sorry, Rev.," he said. "Ma'am, what are you doing here?"

"Ooh no! Go on in your office, Rev. Grant. I got this little hussy!"

"Who the hell you are calling a hussy, you old, bitch?" Carla asked stepping towards the door.

"I'm talking to your fast little a...s....s., now come on and get out of this church. Brother Michael, get her out of here!"

Carla swung her hands. "Put your hands on me and see don't I sue you, this church, and Rev. Grant! But not you, bitch! I see you don't have shit!" She stumped past them and out the door swinging her hips in exaggeration, knowing that Bro. Michael would be watching.

Mable and Bro. Michael walked right behind her.

Watching her coke-bottle frame sway, Bro. Michael became more aroused. He could tell that she was bare-assed, and he liked knowing that. As he walked behind her, he thought, *These pastors have all the luck!* She needs to go ahead and offer me some. I'd take so much she wouldn't have any left for any other man. Hell, I like secrets, too."

Before she left the foyer, she raised her dress, stuck out her hip, and patted her bare behind. "Y'all can go to hell," she said to Bro. Michael and Mable. Then she stormed out of the church, slamming the door as she left. This shit isn't worth all of this. I'm finished trying to get this old fool. There are too many other men who want this, so I don't have any more time to spend on this caper."

As Carla drove off the church ground, she thought about her panties folded in Rev. Grant's Bible. She started laughing and couldn't stop.

When Rev. Grant walked into his office, he sat at his desk and he could not believe that Rev. Mical was still trying to tear down the church. He could hear Mable ranting about Carla's behavior to Bro. Michael. Rev. Grant took a deep breath and made himself think about Mary Jean. He pulled on his senses to see her face and eyes, then her hair and neck. He took deep breaths and concentrated on her presence in his heart. He focused until he could hear her voice and feel her hug. Sitting at his desk, he slowly opened his eyes, feeling as if he had regained control of himself and his day. Now, he could begin studying again.

He reached for his Bible and quickly noticed it was flipped over and turned backward. He frowned at the thought of someone moving it. When he picked up the Bible, he opened to the section that gapped open. Right in the middle of Job, Carla's panties flapped open. He almost dropped the Bible.

He swirled the chair around to reach into the desk drawer for a paper bag. He had kept it from his lunch a few days ago. Then, he used an ink pen to pull the panties from the Bible. He threw them and the Bible into the bag.

He pulled his attaché case from under the desk, opened the top latch, and put the bag into it. He would soon take it out and throw the bag in the dumpster when he left. He knew he'd have to tell Mary Jean as soon as he walked into the house otherwise she'd hear it from one of the security guard's female friends. In fact, he knew Bro. Michael's favorite friend, Georgia Stanton, had already begun talking to other members of the church. It took her no time to gossip. He had no time for Mary Jean to think he was keeping secrets or trying to hide any of what is happening.

Deacon Tomas's Wife Meets Rev. Mical

When Deacon Tomas walked into the house, he could feel an awkward chill in the air. Maria didn't come to greet him as she normally did, and the kids were nowhere in sight.

"Honey! Honey!" He called, knowing deep inside that something was wrong beyond his inner turmoil. He had tried to keep his feelings for Rev. Mical in check, but with each passing day, it was getting harder and harder for him to continue lying. Making love to Maria was becoming a dreadful duty.

"We're in the dining room, Fernando."

We? He walked slowly to the dining room dreading which lie she would ask him to explain.

"Why are you sitting in here?" He pushed the dining room door open. To his surprise, Rev. Mical sat at the table holding a mug of coffee. Deacon Tomas scanned the room and searched his wife's eyes for answers as his mind swirled. *What is he doing here? I didn't see his car. Why would he come to my house and sit with my wife and hide his car where I cannot see it? What has he said?*

Deacon Tomas walked over to his wife and gave her a quick kiss.

"What do we owe this pleasure of your company, Rev. Mical?" He looked at Rev. Mical who slyly sipped from the mug. He shifted under Deacon Tomas's glare and faced Maria.

"Tomas, I was told that there's some ridiculous lie circulating about my love life. Not only am I offended but I feel the need to make certain the leaders of my congregation and their spouses know better. I came to talk personally to Maria and let her know that this is not the first time members have made up some fabrication. Truth is, they never see me with a female and they never will. The reason I do not bring my lady to the church is because they will fill her head up with gossip like they are trying to do now. My lady is a member of Rev. J. L. Lee's church in Alexandria. We see each other out of town, but I plan to propose to her at the end of this year and if I decide to stay here then and only then will I bring her to the church." His tone was fearless and steady.

Damn. Mical can lie. Tomas looked at his wife.

"What's her name?" Maria wasn't convinced.

"I can't tell you that because you might just let it slip," Rev. Mical teased, then said, "But after our engagement, I will bring her by so that you and Deacon Tomas can meet her."

"Okay. It just makes me so darn mad every time they tell me that foolishness. They even tried to bring my James into relations with you. I try to tell them that you are simply good friends and that's. all, but they said I needed to open my eyes," Maria looked at her husband then at Rev. Mical and shook her head.

"Let me ask you something, Sis. Maria, who told you these lies?"

"I'm sorry, Rev. Mical, I can't tell you that because you might let it slip." She smiled, showing a pair of beautiful dimples. He could see how Deacon Tomas had fallen for her.

He smiled back. "I understand, Sis. Maria." Checking the time, he said, "Deacon Tomas, would you see me to the door and I'll let Sis. Maria get your family dinner together." He pushed his chair from the table and stood. He touched Maria on the shoulder and headed toward the door. Deacon Tomas walked quickly behind him.

"Man, what the hell! Why did you come to my house and tell my wife all those lies?" They stood just beyond the doorway.

"You should be glad," Rev. Mical turned and faced him. His eyes shot over Deacon Tomas's shoulder to see if Maria had followed them out. He checked the windows to see if she or one of their children was looking out. "I knew your ass wouldn't be able to convince her, but she believed me, so keep your cool! And, oh, I do expect an amazing birthday gift as a result of this, Tomas."

He looked his young lover up and down, licked his lips, turned, and headed out of the yard.

Deacon Tomas watched Rev. Mical pick up his pace, turn the corner, and cross the street into the parking lot of The Newsleader, Bordelon's Pharmacy, and Lloyd's Unique Men's Clothing Store. He's doing everything he can to tear down that man. How could I ever love someone like that? Deacon Tomas rubbed his beard and returned to the house, hoping to have a quiet sexless evening.

Quilting Club Tells Rev. Grant About The Plot

"Rev. Grant we need to meet with you," Mother Mavis led five women into Rev. Grant's office. He'd begun spending more long days in the office tending to calls from accountants, investigators, and the Department of the Interior. He'd begun to wonder how much longer would he have to defend his accounting before his accusers would be revealed. He was so wrapped in his thoughts, he had not noticed the women entering his office. When the door closed, he looked up and saw Mother Mavis towering over his desk with a group of women behind her. He could only brace for what was running through their minds.

"We think you would be interested in knowing what we've been told." Mother Mavis's voice was firm. The other ladies shook their heads in agreement. Sis. Joyce stood the farthest way, holding the doorknob.

"Ladies, please have a seat, and let's talk."

Chairs were situated throughout the office and each deaconess sat where they could. Mother Mavis and Sis. Willow sat directly in front of Rev. Grant's desk.

"So, ladies, what's going on besides the beautiful quilts that you all are making? Oh, let me tell you again how much my wife Mary Jean and I love the beautiful one you all made for us. We keep it at the foot of our bed."

"That's good to know, Rev. Grant." Sis. Willow was nervous.

Never one to sugarcoat her opinions, Mother Marvis was quick to say, "We came to tell you Rev. Mical and Mrs. Agnes are plotting to get you arrested on federal charges to get your members to leave T.E.A.M and move to his Greatness of Christ Baptist Church."

For a moment, Rev. Grant was quiet. "How did you find out about this?"

"Dorothy. She's Rev. Mical's secretary, and she overheard him talking on the phone to the IRS about you using church money to invest in the stock market, and she told my daughter who told me, but I'm not the only member who has heard this. Sis. Willow said she heard it, too. Didn't you, Sister?"

Sis. Willow turned so that she was facing Rev. Grant and looked him in the eyes. "I sure did. I heard it from one of Agnes's so-called friends, who said Agnes told her that our church was doing some unhanded illegal stuff and that she was going to get to the bottom of it!"

"Well, ladies have anyone else heard any damaging gossip?"

"Pastor, we all have heard some gossip at some point or another," Mother Mavis said.

"Well, ladies, you do know that it is legal for me to invest in the stock market. There are no laws that prevent our ministry from investing. You've seen the work that we do as a result of those investments. We are the only Black church in south Louisiana helping our people the way that we do. Our destitute members, our senior members, and our homeless friends do not have to worry about giving the church anything and we can help them more." For once, Rev. Grant was boastful. "Jealousy comes before the fall, ladies. Haven't you heard that before?"

"Yes, Pastor, we know all that," Sis. Willow shook her head and waved her hand toward him.

"Pastor, we just wanted you to know about those evil people who are trying to destroy you and this church, but we won't have it! Will we, sisters?" Mother Mavis looked at the other quilting club members who all shook their heads. Two of them mumbled, "Um-hum" in unison, and another said, "Yes, Lord."

Rev. Grant was honored by their seriousness. He knew very well the result of crossing one of these fire-brimstone praying women. "I appreciate you ladies caring so much for me and this ministry as you do. Coming in to tell me about this was the best thing you all could do. I assure you I am handling this problem, so you can go back to your quilting knowing that it will be taken care of, and don't you all worry one little bit, okay?" He looked into each of their eyes.

They had just confirmed for him why he had received letters and calls from the federal government for the last six months. Although he wasn't convinced that Mrs. Agnes was capable of participating in a scheme that destructive, Mary Jean was certain Mrs. Agnes was part of this plot. Both agreed that Rev. Mical was capable of any evil and spiteful scheme.

Mary Jean reminded Rev. Grant how she'd had to hang up the phone on Mrs. Agnes the day after he escorted her from his office. They agreed that that gave her added to continue joining forces with Rev. Mical.

Before he could hang up the phone, Mother Margaret stormed into the office and slammed Rev. Mical's Greatness of Christ Baptist church bulletin on the desk. She had circled pictures of Rev. Grant and his family. With her arms crossed she held in her anger and tightened her lips closed. She wouldn't allow herself to say a word, knowing she would say something ungodly and full of hate. She refused to disrespect God's House behind Rev. Mical and Church Folk mess. When Rev. Grant lifted the two-page church newsletter to read the caption, Mother Margaret turned and stumped out through the door and back down the hall. Rev. Grant looked at the picture intensely, laid the bulletin face down on his desk, leaned back in his chair, and closed his eyes.

He prayed and asked God to settle his anger and give him clear guidance. He knew the entire city would judge his reaction and he had to maintain what he knew was the countenance of Christ. After sitting quietly and breathing deeply, Rev. Grant felt reassured, knowing that the church's accounting was in order and that every cent that the Church made on the stock exchange was accounted for in two different systems. For a moment, he was concerned about the fairly large savings the church had amassed and he wondered what the government would do about it, although he was prepared to pay additional taxes if needed. He repeated to himself what he had told the board: God had seen fit to allow every investment to grow; not once had the church lost money on the stock market. It seemed that each time he felt led to sell their stock and re-invest it, it was always in the nick of time and the stock grew. So, he was sure that God was in on this plan and if He did not like the plan, He still took care of the planner. The money funded all the needed programs, school, and church activities.

The character assault against his family that Rev. Mical saw appropriate to publish in his bulletin had crossed the line. But, he was convicted to not make a big issue of it. Doing so would make it more important than it was. People knew him and his family, and he believed the community would not be quick to believe the trash that Mrs. Agnes and Rev. Mical were cooking up.

Nonetheless, it greatly disturbed Rev. Grant that some of his brothers and sisters got so much joy out of destroying each other. If they would take this energy and place it into something constructive, like helping each other, they would all be better for it.

Rev. Grant Confronts Rev. Mical

Because of the rumors, Rev. Grant decided it was time for him to speak man-to-man with Rev. Mical. When he arrived at Rev. Mical's church his secretary was so busy she didn't see him enter the office. When she looked up, she was stunned to see him standing there, which told him that she knew who he was.

"Good afternoon, Miss."

To his surprise, she rushed out of her seat, walked over, and shook his hand. "I'm Sis. Dorothy. Dorothy Martin. I assume you are here to see Rev. Mical. Please have a seat and I'll let him know you are here." She walked to the Pastor's study and gently knocked on the door before opening it.

"What is it now, Dorothy?"

She smiled knowing that he would be upset when she told him who was here to see him. "Rev. Grant is here to see you."

Rev. Grant could tell by the way Sis. Dorothy was standing in the doorway that Rev. Mical was trying to signal for her to get rid of him, so he walked to the door and looked over her shoulder. He could see Rev. Mical shaking his finger at her as he entered the office.

Rev. Mical quickly hung up the telephone and stood. "Well! Well! What do I owe this honor to?" He approached Rev. Grant with his hand extended. Reluctantly, Rev. Grant shook his hand and then walked to the chair in front of Rev. Mical's desk. Rev. Mical followed and walked around his desk to his lush chair.

For a few moments, both Reverends sat staring locked-eyed at each other.

"Rev. Mical rumors are spreading around God's church from your congregants to mine and everyone in between." He didn't blink. "As I understand it you have consistently telephoned the Internal Revenue Service in an attempt to criminalize me and the leaders of T.E.A.M." The top of his head itched as it did every time he became angry. He refused to scratch it in Rev. Mical's presence. "I've come to find out if this is true and to set the records straight once and for all."

"What are you trying to insinuate, Grant?" He leaned back in his chair. " I find it insulting that you would come over to MY church and accuse me of such an ungodly thing! "Why would you believe such asinine lies, Man of God?" He was sarcastic and belittling.

"Why would I waste my time calling the IRS? How would I know anything about the finances of your church? " He wiped the sweat off his brow.

Rev. Grant started to feel his blood pressure rising. He knew Rev. Mical was behind everything, including Carla's seductions.

"Your partners in crime, Mrs. Agnes, and Carla, for starters." His words seeped with the same sarcasm. "I have known that you and she were plotting to destroy T.E.A.M., but you can rest assured that destruction will not happen. Every aspect of our Christian ministry is done above reproach and well within the law for God's church."

He leaned towards Rev. Mical. "Did you hear me, Mical? It's not my church. It's God's church. I'm sure your contact at the IRS has told you—just like they told us a decade ago—that no law prevents a church from investing in the stock market. Maybe, this information can help you a little and you can invest and grow as we already are.

"What makes you think that Agnes and I are in cahoots? After all, she is your member now along with the others."

"I never asked your members to come to TEAM. They chose where they wanted to serve the Lord. Don't blame us."

Through the walls, Sis. Dorothy could hear their arguing. Every time Rev. Grant told Rev. Mical something she punched her fist forward wishing he would punch Rev. Mical in the mouth.

"It's good riddance to any of the members you think may have left here. I'm sure they were all the troublemakers, so have at them, they are going to lie on you just like I'm certain they have lied on me. You'll see and you'll wish they would come back here." Rev. Mical smiled.

"Rev. Mical, Mrs. Agnes has never been a member of God's church. Just because she joined and put her name on the church's roll and pays tithes does not mean that she is a Christian and that goes for you, too!" Rev. Grant scratched his head.

Rev. Mical jumped up, causing the chair to bounce against the wall. He made so much noise that Dorothy thought they had begun to fight. He walked towards the door, opened it, and waved his hand in a gesture for Rev. Grant to leave.

"Oh, I will leave, Rev. Mical, but you nor Mrs. Agnes nor Carla will be successful in destroying TEAM because it is God's church, not MY church, unlike YOUR church," Rev. Grant exited.

When he passed Sis. Dorothy's desk, he nodded and noticed the smile on her face. She was happy to hear someone speak to Rev. Mical in the same way he daily spoke to her.

When Rev. Grant got in his car he sat there for a while and prayed. *God, I know that the devil is always in the midst of chaos and disdain. Rev. Mical is one of his workmen who is trying to tear Your church down, but I ask you to remove the chains that bind him and allow him to return to be a worker in Your midst as the truth of T.E.A.M is revealed.*

He started the car and drove off the church's parking lot.

Third Time's a Charm

Two weeks had passed since George tried to get T.P.'s attention even though every day he picked up the phone to call her. Once while hemming Judge Lyles's slacks, he accidentally called her T.P.'s name. Luckily, the old white lady was more concerned about the safety of her 1967 Mercedes Benz being parked in this neighborhood than anything he may have said. Once he finished the pants and boxed them for Brenda to give to the judge, George went into the back of the shop and dialed T.P.'s number. It rang four times before he realized it was Monday and T.P. ran errands on her off day. He had to figure out how to make her interested in him again. He decided then that he would keep calling her until she gave him another chance.

On Wednesday, he waited until 2 p.m. to call T.P again. He knew she would be working and she would not disrespect him in front of clients if she didn't want to talk with him. On the first ring, a young woman with a raspy voice answered.

"Hello, T.P.'s House of Beauty," she said.

"T.P. please," George said pretty certain that the woman answering wasn't T.P.

"Hold on a minute," she said. George was nervous and being nervous made him insecure and he hated feeling insecure. He could not believe that he felt this way. He had never had a woman to make him feel the way he was feeling for T.P. *Dang George, Get it together.* He cleared his throat.

After a few minutes, T.P. answered, "Hello."

"Hi there, Pretty Lady, how are you?" He asked.

"I'm fine. How are you?" T.P. asked as she sat back in her chair and started rolling Macy's hair.

"It's good to hear your voice. I have not heard from you. I was really hoping that you would give me a call," George said.

"Sorry to have disappointed you, but I meant what I told you the last time." She tried to sound indifferent but stern. "I see you decided to make the call instead." T.P. knew he would call again, but she was a little surprised that he had taken so long.

"I know you are busy working, but I was hoping that you would allow me to take you to dinner tonight—no strings attached," George said crossing his fingers.

"You had strings attached before?" T.P. asked. She moved the phone under her left ear so she could part the front sections of Macy's hair. She also noticed Carla's cousin Cheryl watching her every word.

"No. No. I didn't mean for it to sound like that. What I meant was that I would love to see you again and we can go anywhere that you would like, how about that?" George asked sounding worst by the minute.

She decided to go out with him.

Normally his ego validated his every move. But, when it came to T.P., he couldn't assume anything.

"So, will you go out with me again tonight?" He asked.

"What time?" T.P. asked surprising him again.

"How uhh about eight?" He asked.

"Okay. Where did you have in mind?" T.P. asked.

"Have you been to Old Joe's Seafood Restaurant?" George asked.

"Yeah. That's where the N- double A -C-P meets on Thursdays. That's fine, I'll meet you there." T.P. said. Her body felt lighter, warmer. She had to be careful or it would choose him before her mind did.

"Oh. Okay." George said although he wanted to pick her up. but still glad that she had decided to see him even though it wasn't on his terms.

"Okay, see you there," He said hoping that she was not setting him up to be stood up.

T.P. hung up the phone and focused on getting the next three heads done in time to shower, dress, and get to dinner on time.

Macy tried to hold in her opinion, but she had to say something.

"Girrrrrl, you were hard on that man. I'm unaware of who he is, but I'll bet my check that he messed up and now he's trying to get back in your good graces. Now, you're giving him a hard time!"

"Mind your business, Miss Macy! Besides, you don't have a check, you are still living with your momma," T.P. said and everyone in the shop laughed except Macy.

T.P. finished her last customer five minutes to eight. She knew when she told George that she would meet him at eight that it would be nearly impossible.

Although she had every intention of making dinner, she just couldn't make it. Let's see how he handles this. She thought about the last conversations and time spent with him—from the first car ride through the last call.

She quickly swept the shop, unplugged every cord, and wiped down every chair and counter. She even cleaned the dryer heads, shampoo bowl, and telephone. She double-checked the door, making sure it was locked before heading to the back of the house.

She walked into her bedroom and picked up the phone from her nightstand and extended the cord as far into the bathroom as it could go. She placed it on the toilet seat next to the tub, then she turned the crystal knob to fill the large tub with hot water. She dropped cubes of salt into the bath, then searched the cabinets for the Avon bubble bath her sister brought from Chicago. As the scent filled the bathroom, she undressed, throwing her royal blue smock in the basket with all her blue beauty shop towels. She tossed her underwear in another hamper.

Then, she eased into the bubbles and water. Steam rose. T.P. was so tired and soon she fell asleep until the sound of the phone awoke her.

"Hello," She said.

"If you didn't want to meet me, all you had to say was, 'no,' T.P.," George said.

"I apologize, George," she said. Sleep had taken her voice. She cleared her throat and sat up in the tub. She couldn't remember if she'd bathed before falling asleep so she quickly lathered soap in a lukewarm towel with her left hand and held the receiver in her right hand. "My last client left close to eight and I didn't have your telephone number." George could hear her moving in the water and his imagination pulled him into the bathroom with her. "So, I wasn't able to call and let you know that I wouldn't be able to make it, but I'll make it up to you soon," She said as she stood up and stepped out of the tub on the mat.

Hearing T.P apologize and saying the word "soon" gave George a little hope.

"So, Pretty Lady, when do you plan to make it up to me?" George asked full of ego.

"I said soon."

"Soon can mean tonight, tomorrow, next week, next month. So when?" George said beginning to think that T.P. thought this was a game.

"Okay. How about Monday night? Once you finish suiting up your last customer, we can go out. My treat." T.P. said, drying her body and carefully oiling her legs and feet with a camphor-coconut-oil blend she had crafted to soothe herself after standing for long hours in the beauty shop.

"Why do we have to wait for Monday night, why not Saturday or even Sunday?" George asked.

This is why I can't let myself go with this guy. He knows I work in my shop and he should know that Saturdays are my busiest day, but he is all about himself, and on Sundays, I'm in church and I rest. I pushed myself tired on a Saturday night to go out with him before and he messed that up, so I'll only go out with him on my terms. She chuckled. "Hold on," she said and placed the handle of the phone down. She slid on her gown and brushed her teeth. The bath had worked its magic. Her body was less tense. Skin soft. She was ready to get in bed and dream.

"I'm going to ask you one more time, George," she said "Would you like to go out Monday night, my treat?" T.P. asked knowing he would say yes.

"Okay, if that's all I can get for now, I'll accept it," He said and began thinking about how he could make the day special since he had several days to plan.

"Call me Monday, and I'll let you know where we are going to meet," T.P. said.

George's heart sank again. Here she goes with that meet again. I'm a man who picks up my woman. He thought, resisting the urge to say it.

"Okay."

"Okay. Good night, George, and I apologize again for tonight."

"Good night, Pretty Lady."

T.P. hung up the phone. She took the phone back into her room. Before falling asleep she read passages from the Quran. By the fourth page, she had fallen asleep.

Beauty Shop Gossip Brings A Little Truth

T.P.'s House of Beauty always smelled like a mixture of burning hair, lavender, mint, and soap. Every woman was given an orange smock to cover their clothing. For a while now, T.P. debated having them embroidered with the beauty shop's name but paused knowing she may change the name once she finally moves into a larger place. Now that she has been in business for more than twelve years, it was time for her to expand. She had her eyes on new equipment, a display case to sell products from Bonner Brother's shows, and she wanted to bring on three more stylists from Nature's Crown Institute before they were lulled into New Orleans. Every time she was overbooked, she'd long for an extra set of gifted hands.

In the middle of curling Sharon Dupre's hair, Marylee, and Maggie started their usual gossiping. Each one sitting under a hairdryer and talking loudly to the other.

"Girl, that man or should I say 'that lady' thinks he—she—is fooling all the members of the church, but I can tell you for sure that he's not fooling me, nor any of the ladies that I know. Christian women are smarter than the Great Reverend thinks!" Marylee smacked her lips in over-exaggeration. "Have you ever seen how he walks?"

Maggie laughed. "Yes. I've seen him strutting around town and he even preached for Rev. Smith's anniversary. We all laughed because we knew that Rev. Smith would never ever never have chosen Rev. Mical to preach had he known who that man truly was. Now, don't get me wrong. I'm not one of those Christians who think that people who are gay are evil. I feel like that's God's judgment and I just stay in my lane."

"Yeah, you're right about that! I won't judge nobody about who they're sleeping with."

Did she just say she won't judge people? What a hypocrite! All they do is talk about other people's business. T.P. held her thoughts.

"But I thought for sure he was dating Lydia. I used to see them together at different social events but suddenly that stopped after a few months." Marylee surveyed the beauty shop to make sure the other women were listening even though they pretended otherwise.

"Girlllllll, Lydia told me that that man never wanted to have sex but one way and that was oral! She said she began to think he was just using her as a show to make people think that he truly liked women, but she never saw or felt him on a hard."

Both women tried to muffle their laughs until Sharon Dupre laughed loudly. She was taking in every drop of gossip, readying her mind to re-write and retell what the women shared about Rev. Mical.

Marylee moved from under the dryer and tried to whisper to Maggie but the sound of the hairdryers made her talk even louder. "I heard he was married before and that he has a daughter, but that his ex-wife doesn't let him see his daughter."

"How do you know that's true?"

"One of his deacons is married to my husband's sister! She said Rev. Mical went through a bitter divorce and child custody battle, and if that wasn't enough, the church he was pastoring asked him to leave. That's when he came here."

"I don't like him," Sharon Dupre interrupted, as T.P. curled her hair. "He's a snake and the reason I say that is because Cherie–y'all know Cherie, Rev. Lewis's sister–said he made a play for her when he first got in town, but her brother who is the pastor of that church Rev. Mical came from. Ya'll know the name. Anyway, her brother had already heard about Rev. Mical even before he arrived, and schooled her."

"I bet he don't even try to see his daughter!" Maggie shouted.

"You're probably right," Marylee said. Sharon Dupre stood up from the chair and turned to the mirror behind T.P. She played with her curls a second, then pulled out a check to pay T.P. "Sharon Dupre is pleased!" She gloated, and the ladies chuckled that a grown woman would still refer to herself in the third person.

T.P. beckoned for Maggie to get into the styling chair. Marylee turned off her dryer, stood up, and wrapped her hair with a long silk scarf. She was careful to hide the soft black rollers behind the scarf. She'd planned to wear her rollers two days until Sunday morning services. Marylee had a confidential arrangement with T.P. for partial payment for her wash and set, so before she left, she would sweep the beauty shop, put away all trash, and wipe down all surfaces. As a dishwasher at the Baton Rouge Country Club, she was able to thoroughly clean the beauty shop in twenty minutes when it took T.P. nearly forty-five minutes.

It didn't take long for T.P. to feather out Maggie's curls and spray-holding sheen throughout. Once Maggie finished checking her hair, she added a layer of Fashion Fair foundation and lip gloss before paying T.P. and leaving. Soon T.P. had completed all the ladies' hair.

T.P. took off her smock and admired how clean Marylee had left the beauty shop and how much time her cleaning saved T.P. So, she decided to drive over to see Mary Jean.

"Hi, Aunt T.P." Robert Michael smiled, looking like a younger image of his father. "Mom's in the kitchen so I came to answer the door." He hugged her.

"That's nice of you. You're so thoughtful." T.P. entered the house and walked into the kitchen.

"Hey!"

"Hey, sis. You're just in time for dinner."

"Girl, you are always cooking." T.P. walked over and hugged Mary Jean. "It's very seldom I come here, and you are not in the kitchen. All your family does is eat." T.P. sat at the counter. "I came over to tell you who my customers were talking about today. Guess who."

"I don't have to guess 'cause you are going to tell me." Mary Jean dished Salisbury steaks into a serving platter, then picked up a large bowl and started scooping mashed potatoes.

"Since you are so smart maybe I shouldn't tell you anything."

They laughed.

"Girl, they were talking about Rev. Mical. Did you know that he was married before and has a daughter that he's not allowed to see?"

"No T.P. I didn't know that, and you don't either because it could be a lie." Mary Jean sat a bowl of lima beans on a carrying tray along with the other food.

"Well, they also said he was asked to leave his last church and that's when he came here.

"I will tell Rev. Grant about this later tonight, but I won't allow it to interrupt our dinner this is our family time, so don't you say a word. Now, go get the boys to wash up while I get Donald. Then, we can all have a nice dinner."

Monday Night With George

Monday night seemed to come quickly. All day while running errands and cleaning her home, T.P. contemplated canceling the date. She just did not feel up to seeing George, but she had given her word and she did like him a little. On Sunday, she'd confirmed the date and told him to meet her at Krystal Burgers on Lexington Street at 7 p.m. It was outside of the city, heading towards Kenner. She felt it would be better for them to put some distance between him and another one of his female acquaintances. If something like what happened with drunk Lallia happened again, T.P. could promise things would not turn out nicely.

She pulled into the parking lot at 6:55 p.m., checked her makeup in the mirror, and touched up her lip gloss. She recited beauty affirmations in her mind while looking in the mirror. She loved that her skin still required very little enhancement and that her lips were naturally tinted.

When she stepped out of the car, she noticed George standing outside the door of his car waiting for her. He walked towards her. She was wearing a pair of denim jeans with a tan tank top showing off her small waist. She wore a thin necklace with a charm of a symbol he had never seen. Her hair was pulled back into a bun revealing her beautiful, smooth face with soft pink, juicy-looking lips. The gladiator sandals she wore matched her outfit perfectly. She looked so gorgeous to him. He stared in amazement at her beauty and when they met, he gave her a friendly hug although he wanted more.

"Hi, Pretty Lady."

"Hi, Mr. Grant. How are you?" T.P. asked as he took her hand and headed towards the door. He wondered why she picked such a cheap place for them to eat, maybe because she had offered to pay. Could it be that she was one of those tight women?

They walked inside and T.P. slid into the booth and placed her purse by the window forcing him to sit across from her.

"So, how have you been? How are things in the shop?"

"I've been good and I'm still fighting the stupid door to the shop. Every time I think about asking my dad to fix it I am in the middle of something and I forget." T.P. answered. Then, she decided that she would let him do most of the talking. Besides, men loved to talk about themselves. "How have you been, George?"

"Wait, let me go order our food first." He said forgetting for a moment that this is what got him in trouble before.

"No. I'm going to look at this menu and then I'll order for me, but you can go order what you want now if you would like to do that," T.P. took the menu and began to peruse it. She did not have to look up at George to know that he was not going to leave the table and that he would also look at the menu.

After a few moments, T.P. laid the menu on the table and pointed to number five which was the hamburger platter. George said he would have the double beef burger platter and then he went to the counter and ordered their food.

When he slid back into the booth, he was full of talk. "I've had a semi-good week."

"Why was it only semi-good?"

"I finally got a raise, but I don't think that's enough. I want a position to go with it. I think Mr. Gonzalez recognizes that I am not happy with the job and he knows that I secure a huge volume of sales. His lazy son just sits back while I bust my behind making most all of the sales and doing all the measurements when he's supposed to be helping me."

T.P. looked away and saw the cook waving at them to get their food. "Our food is ready."

George got up, walked over to the counter, picked up the brown tray holding their platters, and returned with a smile. T.P. was beautiful and he couldn't wait to tell her. The booth was uncomfortable for his long frame but he didn't complain. He adjusted the table to be more comfortable sliding back into the booth.

"Well, you did get a raise on this semi-good week. I'm sure you are learning about the business so that you can one day open your own clothier. Our brothers sure do need their own men's store. Soon you will be calling on some of those same clients, and they will visit your establishment." She placed their plates on the table and moved the tray to the other side.

"You'll enjoy working for yourself, George, because you are never making any money until you work for yourself. All the other times, you are making money for someone else."

George thought about that for a moment. He liked that T.P. was full of genuine wisdom. It was one of her sexiest traits. He caught her hand while she blessed their food.

"You're right, Pretty Lady." He stuffed four French fries into his mouth. "I think I'll look into that. How did you start your shop?"

T.P. bit into her burger and carefully ate it before replying.

"I wrote it down first as I do with most things that I'm interested in. I wrote down what I would need. I made some calls to find out the cost for the equipment and all supplies that I needed, then I made my own business cards and started giving them out."

"You gave out business cards before you opened your business?"

"Why yes. I set it into motion to hold myself accountable because now I had to open the business. Not only did I expect it, so did others." She sipped her RC Cola and waited for his reaction.

"Wow! "George said. "I don't know if I could do that. What if you failed?"

"I didn't fail because failure never crossed my mind or lips. I had people who were depending on me and besides, I knew I could do it,"

This is one smart chick. George had been so engrossed in T.P., he had forgotten about his food. He sat across from her, staring almost in a trance. He finally took a bite of his burger. Then looked back at T.P. This woman intrigued him. He was on a date in a burger joint, of all places, and falling hard for a woman who walked out on the first date and stood him up on the second. It was something about her that made him want to be better. When she looked up from her food and noticed him watching her, she smiled and her face lit up.

"I'm going to look into that and write down what I know. I already know the suppliers we order from. I know how to create stellar suits, tailor and alter them, or even reconstruct slacks from torn fabrics. I know the price and suppliers' costs for suits and materials. Hell, everybody knows I can dress a brother to the nines and make him look like a whole 'nother man so much that his momma won't recognize him! I can match style to his physique and that brother will leave with swagger like Sam Cooke!" He was almost shouting.

T.P. chuckled, "Well, now there you go, Brother. You have a gift, so go use it." She said behind a broad smile. He knew at that moment that he had to have this woman—she was the one he had been searching for all his adult life. He knew it was not going to be easy and karma was always around the corner. He had caused women hurt and pain in the past and he knew there would inevitably be some type of payback, but he did not care. If T.P. was going to hurt him, he was ready to risk it.

T.P. checked her watch. She was enjoying his company, but at 9:45 pm, she was ready to head home and prepare for a busy and profitable week in her beauty shop. George did not want their time to end, but he could tell by the way she looked at her watch that she was going to be leaving.

"Sorry. I must go now. I have an early client tomorrow morning and some other business to take care of," She slid out of the booth, walked to the counter, and paid the check. George left a tip between their empty plates, then they walked outside. He walked her to her car and opened the door. He kissed her on the forehead.

"Thank you, Pretty Lady, I enjoyed our short time together."

"I did too, George." She got into her car and he closed the door. He stood there until she drove off. It was still early for him, but he knew it was time for him to start doing things differently if he wanted to be with T.P. Doing things differently started tonight with him deciding to go home instead of to Club Maxima as he always did. He knew the type of trouble he would most likely get into all night and he would rather think about T.P. and the possibility of owning his own business.

Lawrence Asks to See His Sons

Every time Lawrence called Mary Jean, he was drunk so she refused to let him see his sons. She had determined in her heart that she would protect Lawrence Junior and Robert Michael at all costs, so she did not budge. He had called her so much that now he was at the point of begging to just take the boys to a movie. His frustration was beginning to get the best of him. He decided it was time for a man-to-man conversation with Rev. Grant. Lawrence expected him to be willing to change Mary Jean's mind and create a routine to see the twins.

When the day of his appointment arrived, Lawrence pressed a new pair of dark brown slacks and a matching collared shirt. He had convinced a new lady friend of his to let him borrow her car while she was at work. He claimed it was important for him to pick her up and get her home safely since reports were growing about women going missing. Once he saw that his new girlfriend was fearful, Lawrence knew he could control where she went and how freely he could move in her new car.

"Hi, I'm Lawrence Roberson Sr. I have a meeting with Rev. Grant for one thirty." He looked at his watch but did not acknowledge that he was late.

"I'll let him know that you are here." Mable walked to the door, knocked, then opened it. She stayed in the office less than a few seconds and returned. "He'll see you now, go right in."

When Lawrence entered the room, Rev. Grant was watering a large plant. Instinctively, Lawrence frowned at the pastor doing what he believed was a woman's job.

"Good afternoon," Lawrence spoke.

"You're forty-five minutes late. We had a 1 p.m. appointment." Rev. Grant turned towards Lawrence and pointed to the chair for him to sit. To Rev. Grant, Lawrence had shown that he was irresponsible once again.

"There was a lot of traffic coming out of New Orleans." Lawrence lied.

Rev. Grant walked to his desk. "So, what can I do for you, Lawrence?"

Lawrence cleared his throat and pulled his chair closer to Rev. Grant's desk as if he thought someone could hear them. "I know that you are aware that Mary Jean won't let me see my sons." He held on to the word 'my' for emphasis. "They should not have seen what happened with Donna, but that has nothing to do with how I treat them." He tried to read Rev. Grant's expression but he had none. "I came here to ask you to instruct your wife to let me see my boys." He leaned back in the chair.

"First, Mr. Roberson, I don't instruct my wife to do anything. She is a grown woman and she's capable of making sound decisions. I agreed with her to not let our sons come back to visit with you until you get some help." Rev. Grant paused, making sure Lawrence heard him refer to the boys as his own. "Did you just hear what you said to me? You show no remorse for what you did to your wife and in front of our sons. What do you really believe I can tell Mary Jean that will make her change her mind? If you can come up with something that I am certain will change her mind then I will tell it to her. And! Without your lies, Lawrence." Rev. Grant knew there was nothing that Lawrence could think of that would accomplish what he wanted.

Lawrence thought about it for a few minutes and decided it was best for him to just leave. As he rose from the chair Rev. Grant made an offer, although he knew it would never happen.

"If you agree to see a therapist—for the sake of our sons—I will pay the fees and you can pay me back as soon as you are on your feet. Then, you and Mary Jean can schedule a routine for the boys to visit you indefinitely."

Lawrence left, angry that he would not see his boys again.

Stalking Donna

Lawrence was angry and desperate. Not only had Donna left him with nothing, he no longer had his boys, and his new girl was as much of a drunk as he was. When she wasn't at work, they were fighting, smoking weed, and drinking daily. He didn't know why she drank so much and he didn't care. He blamed Donna for his excessive habit.

"That bitch thinks she can just leave me and live her life normally while mine is hell? Well, that's not going to happen!" Lawrence yelled as he sat alone in the car. He'd parked outside of the hospital where Donna began working.

She should be coming! Where the hell is she? I know she isn't working overtime. His rage had him to the point of nearly screaming. It was five-thirty and he resisted the urge to honk the horn until it got someone's attention.

When the hospital doors opened, out stepped Donna with Dr. Frederick Mortez.

"You're off this weekend, Donna?" Dr. Mortez asked.

"Yes. Finally, I have a weekend off. I am going to enjoy it resting because I have worked overtime all this week." She smiled at the older doctor as she searched her purse for her keys. Lawrence looked on and his anger boiled.

"I wish I could say that. My in-laws are coming into town this weekend and I am going to have to slave over the barbecue grill so that I can save my wife from having to cook so much. I hope you enjoy your rest," He touched her shoulder and walked away.

"You too, Doc, try to enjoy yourself. It's better than being here the entire weekend." She walked towards her car and began looking over her shoulder, feeling like someone was watching her. Fear began to creep up and she quickly got into her car and locked the doors. She took deep breaths as she started the engine.

I knew it! She's been seeing that guy that's why she left me, but she won't enjoy her new life with him if I have to live a life in pain. Lawrence followed Donna out of the parking lot. *I bet she'd going to meet him somewhere.*

He kept a distance but followed her for more than fifteen minutes. Donna pulled up to her parent's home and parked in the driveway. Lawrence quickly parked, jumped out of his car, and ran towards her just as she was reaching across the seat for her purse. When she turned to open the door, she was looking at his angry face.

"So, that's why you left me!" He snatched the door open and pulled her from the car. "You left me for a doctor, Donna!" He grabbed her around her neck and pushed her against the car. "He will never have you!"

Donna fought to pull his fingers from around her throat. Lawrence squeezed harder. His eyes had more fury than she'd ever seen in a human. She bore her weight down into her hips and legs as her brothers taught her to prevent an attacker from lifting her from the ground. Lawrence had underestimated her strength. She kicked the car door and kneed Lawrence as close to his groin as she could but she was losing consciousness. Then, Duke jumped the back fence and ran to attack. His bark was loud and fierce. Lawrence let her go, ran to his car, and jumped on top of the hood until he noticed Duke pacing around Donna. Lawrence got into the car and yelled over Duke's constant barking, "It's not over, bitch! If you think you are going to have a life with that doctor, you got another thought coming because if I am not happy, you won't be either!" He sped away.

Duke nudged and tugged on Donna who turned and lifted herself from the ground. Her mother came running.

"Donna! Donna! What happened, baby?" Her hands and apron were covered in flour and yeast. "I heard Duke barking!" She held Donna up and helped her walk into the house. After catching her breath and holding a cool towel to her neck, Donna rubbed Duke's head, "I'm so glad you came when you did, Duke." Her mom returned with Donna's purse on her shoulder and her hands full of all the articles that had dropped out, then she walked Donna and Duke into the house.

Tears formed in Donna's eyes, "Momma, that fool probably would have choked me to death!"

"Is this the first time he had followed you?" Her mom sat on the couch beside her.

"No, I've been seeing him off and on following me, but I didn't see him today because when I left the hospital, I was talking to Dr. Mortez. That took my mind off of looking for him." She thought back to when she was walking through the parking lot. " I did have a feeling that someone was looking at me, but I didn't think it was him because normally he parks in front of the hospital so I can see him, but not today. I did not see him until he pulled me from the car! Mom, that fool is crazy, do you know that he was choking me with one hand and holding me against the car with his other hand and all I could do was bend my leg back and hit the car. I guess that's what Duke heard," Donna rubbed her throat. Tears fell onto her lap. "He thinks that I'm seeing Dr. Mortez. He is married and loves his wife and family." She cried, "Even though it's been six months, I'm not seeing anyone because I might get another one like him."

Donna's mom gave her the cold towel again, "Put this towel back on your throat to help minimize the swelling."

For a moment, she watched her daughter cry. Duke laid his head in Donna's lap and waited quietly. "Your brother will be here soon and I don't want him to know nothing of this, okay? You know these men of ours are protectors, and he especially will do something crazy! You saw how he reacts every time he hears about those girls going missing."

Donna nodded her head. She wanted to be protected. She wanted to be loved.

"First thing Monday morning, you go down to the courthouse and put him under a peace bond. And from now on when you get off from work, your daddy or me, and Duke will be outside to walk with you to your car, okay?" She felt sorry for her daughter even though she'd told Donna not to marry that boy. She knew Lawrence had too many problems for Donna to handle, especially after Gertrude's husband pulverized him with a bat. "If it ain't kill him, it shol' knock sense outa his head," she would try to convince Donna. She stopped talking against him only to honor their relationship since he had vowed before God to care for Donna.

Still, her heart broke knowing how hard it must be on her only daughter to always have to look over her shoulder. "Okay, baby, I've got to finish these dumplings. You go upstairs and lie down, but keep this towel on your neck. I'll call you when dinner is ready."

Once Donna walked into the bedroom, she leaned against the door and prayed. She wanted it to be a genuine Christian prayer of forgiveness and repentance like the ones she'd been praying for six months, instead–behind her tears and shaking hands–she prayed for immediate death to fall on Lawrence Roberson Sr.

T.P. and George Become More Serious

It had been three months since their first successful date, and T.P. and George were enjoying each other's company more and more. George planned dinner an hour away in Lindon, Louisiana at an upscale Japanese restaurant owned by one of his clients. They would head to the concert and he would surprise her with front-row seats at the hottest concert of the year. All T.P. knew was the concert would be amazing and George didn't like Gospel music. "Whatever he has planned would be thoughtful and romantic," T.P. told her mother.

They arrived at the restaurant and were ushered straight to their reserved table. The restaurant was dark and intimate with candles, chopsticks, and two small bowls on the table. After they were seated, they looked over the menu quietly. "This place is owned by one of our clients. Tonight, they host new customers in order to branch out and grow," he explained. Apparently, they were part of the early crowd because the restaurant was empty.

T.P. looked around the small restaurant and then returned to reading the menu. George noticed her reaction as she scanned the menu. T.P. waited for George to offer guidance, but George had learned better and he decided to allow her to order her food. When the waiter arrived, T.P. asked for the ingredients of the three entrees she found most appetizing.

"What's in the crab and avocado salad?"

"It consists of crab meat, cubed avocado, mayo, sesame seeds, and lemon juice." He was polite although George's smile showed that he was laughing inside.

"Good. I'll have that." T.P. closed the menu and handed it to the waiter confidently.

"Are you sure?" George knew the waiter had not told T.P. all the ingredients. He left out the chili sauce and caviar. He knew T.P. would probably not want the caviar if she knew but she would probably enjoy them if she didn't know. So, he decided to wait and see.

The waiter took her menu and asked George if he would be having the same. George shook his head and ordered a sashimi salad made of mixed greens and thinly cut raw salmon. Then, he added sake as his drink.

"What is sake?" T.P. asked.

"It's a rice wine and very tasty. I think you would like it." It's not served in wine glasses like we are accustomed to but in a sakazuki which is a ceramic cup." George nodded for the waiter to bring two. He was careful to be considerate of ordering for her he wanted the night to be perfect and end with the two of them making love. After the waiter left, T.P. smiled and shifted in the chair. He loved how graceful she always was.

"So, how was your day, Pretty Lady?" George asked.

T.P. thought for a moment and decided not to tell him that she had to stop a fight in her shop between a wife and the outside woman, who just happened to meet up at her shop. Instead, she opted to omit it. "I had a good day, lots of clients, and lots of interesting conversation."

"Everybody knows that in beauty shops all the women do is talk about what their men are doing wrong. I just hope you haven't said anything bad about me."

"That's not true!" She held in her laughter. "We don't talk a lot about men, and we definitely don't talk politics and religion."

The waiter returned with their salads and drinks. T.P. nodded her head to George and reached for his hands. He quickly blessed the food. T.P. considered using the chopsticks but decided it was best if she used the silverware that was wrapped in a bright red cloth napkin. She looked at the salad and wondered what were the black balls sprinkled on top. She decided to taste it first. It was okay, but she didn't like the salty taste of the balls. She scooped a few with her fork. "What's this?"

George smiled. "It's caviar." He continued eating hoping she would not question him more. "Taste your sake." He motioned toward the cup.

"Is this raw caviar?"

"Yes." He refused to look up from his salad.

"What's that pink meat on your salad?"

"It's raw salmon." He showed her the meat then ate it with exaggerated chewing.

T.P. scraped as much of the caviar as she could off her salad. She ate as much as she could then tasted the wine. It was stronger than she expected so she decided to drink it slowly.

Soon the waiter returned for their entrée orders. T.P. was careful in her ordering this time. She ordered Chicken Teriyaki, which was a grilled chicken breast topped with teriyaki sauce. It came with clear soup and grilled vegetables.

George ordered Shrimp Teriyaki which was grilled fresh shrimp and scallions on a skewer served with teriyaki sauce, clear soup, and grilled vegetables.

T.P. was pleased with her entrée. "Sorry, George, I was so into the food that I forgot to ask you about your day at work."

"I always have a good day at my job because I go in with a frame of mind that no matter what happened, I'm not going to let people destroy my day." He looked into her eyes. "Besides, most of the time, I'm thinking about you. I know I'm going to talk to or see my Pretty Lady, so that makes my day beautiful."

T.P. ate the sweet chicken and smiled. "It's very nice to know that you think about me at work."

"Pretty Lady, I'm always thinking of ways to make you happy. That is why I really want you to consider attending the Bonner Brother's Hair Show. It will blow your mind." He pulled out an advertisement for the national show. "I'll get you there safely and you won't have to spend a dime. Look, it's the perfect environment for creative stylists and businesswomen like you."

T.P. held the advertisement and read it front and back. He was right. It's the place she should be but she would have to consider if she wanted to travel with him. "I've heard a lot about this show. Rumor is that Russell Chew in Lake Charles is planning an amazing showcase."

George nodded and waited to see if she would agree. When she didn't, they ate quietly until he announced, "We have thirty minutes to finish our meal and get out of here if we want to be on time for the concert."

T.P. could see his excitement. "Who is the artist?"

"It's a surprise. You will see when we get there," He said as he beckoned for the waiter, so he could pay for dinner.

When the waiter arrived, he placed the bill on the table.

T.P. heard him mumble sternly, "Cash only."

Yeah, they are clients but not friends. We will pay your cash, sir.

George. When he returned George gave him a tip and then they left the restaurant for the concert.

While in the car T.P. tried to guess who the artist would be at the concert.

"Is it Shirley Caesar?"

"I'm not saying." George noticed how soft her exposed thigh looked.

"I know who it is!" T.P pulled her dress to her knees and adjusted in the seat. She enjoyed how he couldn't resist looking at her but she wanted to control what he saw and when. "It's Staple Singers!" She laughed at her excitement.

"I'm still not saying, so you may as well stop guessing. Sit back, relax, and wait to see."

Her smile was warm and more gentle than he'd seen from her before.

After a few minutes, she broke the silence. "Donald seems like he was probably a preacher even when he was a kid."

"Yeah, he was the good boy in the family. He was the one who made my mom and dad proud, and yes, he did start preaching at an early age.

Every time the church door opened, he was in the church with my parent," George swayed around a truck that suddenly began slowing down.

"Sounds like my parents and my older sister," T.P. said solemnly. Her voice cracked, attempting to hold in an unexpected pain in her throat. She coughed, hoping he hadn't noticed her weakness. "Were you in the church every time the door opened?"

"Nah. Too much was happening to me then."

T.P. wasn't sure but it looked like tears were building in the corner of George's eye.

Otis Redding stepped onto the stage singing T.P.'s favorite song. He swooned. "I've been loving you too long to stop now." He sounded even better in person and she had a perfect view since George purchased two middle seats on the fourth row.

George was a little uncomfortable because the velvet seats were too close to each other and the lady sitting in front of his seat kept jumping up and plopping down in her seat and each time she did this, the seat hit his knees. If he had been by himself he would have left, but he could see that T.P. was happy and that's all that mattered.

George nudged her. "You really like this song, you seem to know every word by heart." He was happy to see that T.P. was having a good time.

"Yeah, I know a few songs off his album, I play WMRB radio station in the shop and they play his songs a lot. The audio and acoustics are great here. This is my first time here," T.P. said as she swayed to the music.

Otis Redding looked a little thinner than the pictures she had previously seen of him, but he still sounds the same. A handsome, deep baritone sexy voice. Then she hears, "I'm the man on the scene. I can give you what you want. But you gotta come home with me," T.P. stood up singing to this tune, and George smiled he was certain this was the right choice he made, and he planned to surprise T.P. with many more concert dates.

As George looked around the auditorium he checked out the exits—a habit he had learned a long time ago. When something went left, he wanted to make sure he knew where his escapes were. Just then the band went into intermission.

"What would you like from the concession stand?" He asked lovely.

T.P. thought for a moment and then replied, "Popcorn, a lemonade without ice, and a Mr. Goodbar." They walked down the aisle to the outer area.

"I'll be back," T.P. said.

"Where are you going?" He asked, but T.P. just kept walking. She hated it when she knew that he thought she should explain that she was going to the lady's room, which she was not going to do, if she said she would be right back then that should have been sufficient for him.

As she walked away George was so engrossed in her body. The dress clung to her hips and buttocks and that small waist. The heels she was wearing made her shapely legs look toned and sexy. He imagined throwing them over his shoulders. He did not know that the line had moved up until a lady nudged him on the shoulder. Even then, he kept looking to see T.P.'s sassy walk again where she slung her hips from side to side. He bet she was not even aware that she walked that way, and he was not going to tell her because she might stop doing something he loved about her.

When she returned from the restroom he was waiting with the snacks and he stood aside and allowed her to lead them back to their seats.

He did not remember much about the second set because by this time T.P. was out of her seat like her sister in front of her and they were swaying to the music. Her hips and behind were so tempting that he almost touched them twice but thought better of it.

The concert ended and it took them thirty minutes to get out of the parking lot, but he had the tape and when he pressed play, T.P. was happy again. On the way home, she sang the songs and he smiled

knowing that he would be privileged to another date after this successful one.

"I hope you enjoyed yourself."

"You know I did and thank you." T.P. opened the door and kissed him gently on the lips before walking into the house.

Rev. Mical Visits George Work

After a long evening with T.P., enjoying dinner and George Otis Redding, George finally felt he was in a good place. He believed he now had a chance to experience love just the way he needed. When he walked into work, he was nearly floating. He checked the client log and notice three new customers had scheduled appointments. An asterisk was next to the name of one customer indicating the customer was given a gift to shop at the store. George made a point to remember names so he could welcome the patron formally. He somehow knew the name with the asterisk –Rev. James Mical–but didn't recall the face.

When Rev. Mical walked to the door. He noticed the smooth, gold etching on the door that read Lloyd's Unique Men Clothing Store Where Every Man is Unique. He smiled to himself. *Ain't that the truth. Every man is unique and full of secrets.* He pulled open the door. Let's see what this can do for me. The store smelled like a mixture of fabric, black coffee, and men's cologne. The scent was arousing.

"Welcome to Lloyd's," Rev. Mical looked around. "George will be with you shortly," Brenda greeted him from the opposite side of the counter. He nodded and walked over to the closest rack of suits. Rev. Mical had never purchased a suit from this establishment and was surprised that the quality matches the high cost. He was equally impressed that Deacon Tomas had arranged for him to purchase any two suits in the store.

At first, he felt the suits had no better quality than Bonner Brothers or Sears Roebuck but Deacon Tomas made a show of giving him a memorable gift: two custom suits tailored by the city's best men's store. And, Rev. Mical proudly decided to accept it along with Tomas's incredible bedroom performance.

He walked around the small store while George measured the hem for Mr. Banks. Once he finished, George walked over to Rev. Mical with his hand extended to shake. He looked at George and liked the way he walked and the span of his shoulders.

"Good evening, what can I help you with?" When their palms touched, George felt a shock through his hand. It must be from this carpet. George started to apologize but decided not to when Rev. Mical seemed to not notice.

"You could help me with a lot." Rev. Mical's voice was deeper than usual, "but right now I'd like to see your Brooks Brothers navy blue suits." He looked under-eyed at George. It was a look George had seen a lot as a child and didn't like it then nor now.

Rev. Mical's behavior took George back to a place he'd long ago fought to forget. So, he quickly refocused and extended his hand toward the far left wall where the suits hung. Rev. Mical sassed in front of him and headed to the display of suits. Once he'd shown an interest in a few selections, George removed one of the double-breasted suits, then, hung it on the display pole for Rev. Mical's approval.

Rev. Mical looked at the charcoal three-piece, blue-gray Herringbone-Flannel suit.

"I don't like this one at all, what else do you have?"

"Well, I would recommend this particular four-button suit because it's a versatile wardrobe staple. Which is perfect for a man who has multiple commitments and appointments." George opened the vest to show Rev. Mical the exquisite fabric used for the lining. "What makes it a good addition to your wardrobe is this blended charcoal that can be worn with black and brown leather shoes and belts. With your skin complexion, it won't wash you out."

This boy knows about suits. I like him. Rev. Mical nodded and touched the suit's sleeve.

"The shoulder is soft, slim cut and the side has a vented jacket with flap pockets. Even though the lapel is slim, it's still conservative which will work well with most neckties." George said looking for a reaction in Rev. Mical's eyes, but the reaction he saw was not the one he was looking for, so he focused on presenting the suit as he had practiced. "These trousers are flat-front and will give you a clean look especially since they are non-cuffed."

Rev. Mical took off his jacket and handed it to George then took the jacket off the hanger and slipped it on. He was surprised that the jacket almost fit him. The sleeves were a little long, but the slim-cut jacket fit nicely over his shoulders. It buttoned perfectly catching around his waist.

George folded each sleeve. "The suit can be altered to your specific size."

"How long will that take? I'd like to wear it in two weeks."

"I can check our log and get an idea of when it would be completed based on the amount of altering we would need to do."

"Okay, you go do that and I'm going to try on these pants. Where is your dressing room?"

George pointed toward the back of the store. As Rev. Mical headed in that direction, George walked to the sewing room to check Brenda's alteration schedule. When he walked into the small room, Brenda could tell he was not pleased with this customer.

"Brenda, can you have a suit ready within two weeks?"

"Depends on what all needs to be done." If he didn't want the client, she definitely didn't.

George was trying so hard to not become unhinged that he had forgotten to collect measurements before they could estimate how long it would take.

"Damn." He took a deep breath. "I forgot. I do know that the sleeves are two inches too long. I will go check the pants. I hope they fit," he mumbled and grabbed the measuring tape from his work table.

Another customer had entered the store while Rev. Mical changed into the new slacks. He stood in front of the three wall-high mirrors. George greeted the new customer and offered him a seat. He said he would return soon, hoping this would be the case.

"These pants are too small!" Rev. Mical hadn't allowed George to walk up before complaining. "How can that be? The jacket almost fit perfectly and the pants are too small."

"We don't sell our suits as separates. There's a six-inch difference between the jacket and the size of the pants. We call this the drop. We can accommodate your size, just let me measure your waist and lengths." George's tone soothed Rev. Mical's frustration. He stepped onto the tailor's stage, and George stretched the measuring tape, then placed his arms around Rev. Mical's waist. As George's right hand reached behind Rev. Mical, he rubbed the back of George's hand and glided his fingers up his forearm.

George's body became ridged as memories suddenly flashed around him. Rev. Mical felt George's tension and eased his hand back in place and waited while George measured the inseam and, then, down the outer side of each leg. Instinctively, he clenched his thighs as he watched George kneeling to measure the hem.

When George stood, the disgust in his eyes frightened Rev. Mical. For the second time, he decided to behave, knowing George could easily send him out of this place on a stretcher.

George wrote down the measurements and told Rev. Mical to leave the suit inside the dressing room. "Then, you can check out at the front with Brenda to have it ready in two weeks." He walked away; never looking back nor thanking Rev. Mical for his business. He completely abandoned all customer service etiquette to hold his mounting anger.

Brenda stood at the checkout desk watching the men's interaction. When Rev. Mical walked up, she took the gift certificate that was signed by M. Tomas, wrote down Rev. Mical's contact information, and carefully signed the receipt with the pickup day and time. She handed it to Rev. Mical. He folded the receipt and placed it in his wallet. Then, he asked her to let the owner know how pleased he was to be helped by "such a very astute tailor." She smiled and thought What the hell? She made a mental note to tell George exactly what the debonair pastor with the generous gift giver had said of him. When Rev. Mical left the building, she watched George storm into the back office with his jacket and keys in hand.

"Joel. I'm going home."

Joel laid across an old beat-up brown sofa. He looked up at George, then took a long drag of his cigarette.

"Not unless you're sick." He blew out a long stream of smoke, "And you don't look sick to me." Joel knew his dad would never let him fire George especially since he was the best employee and top salesman they ever had. George turned and walked out. He took broad steps towards Brenda on his way out of the store.

"Here are hissssss measurements." He hissed.

"Are you, all right, George?"

"I will be." He walked out the front door.

Never had she seen George leave work early even when he was sick with pneumonia he still stayed at work until his doctor told him he had to be on bed rest for a week. She knew something about Rev. Mical had triggered him.

Lord, help that man. Demons are all around.

She looked for a bottle of Pastor Pate's Holy Water and sprayed it on his chair. That man got some secrets, God. He needs your help. She shook her head. George took deep breaths before starting the engine. He needed a drink.

George is Triggered

On the way home, flashbacks haunted George. The memories were relentless and vivid. He could smell the stinky liquor of his uncle's breath kissing his neck as he violated him. The pain was still imprinted in him. His behind hurt in the seat and the hurt enraged him.

He started to go to Tabby's Night Club, but his anger drove him to the convenience store where he bought three bottles of Old Grand Dad and two, one-liter bottles of Coke. He would rather go home and drink to help him forget those terrible years.

When he arrived home with his bottle, he walked into the kitchen and retrieved a tall drinking glass from the cabinet. He quickly grabbed two ice cubes from the freezer, dropped them into the glass, then opened the bottle and filled the glass half full before adding an ounce of cola. He stirred the liquid with his finger and headed to his bedroom where he took a large drink and then sat the glass on the end table by the bed.

The liquor burned his chest as it traveled downward, so he took another drink and kicked his shoes off, and headed to the bathroom to take a long bath and he brought his glass with him.

By the time the tub was half-filled with warm water his glass was half empty and he was feeling good, there were no more flashbacks and for that he was thankful. He slid into the tub and took the last swallow of the liquid which was still burning his chest, but he felt relaxed and warm in the water. He soaped his body and then leaned back against the tub and closed his eyes.

"Georgie, you are so cute. All of the little girls must fight over you at school." Uncle Matt said as he pulled George's pants down and jerked his body closer to his. Then he bent George over and began violating him painfully and moaning and still talking as he did it.

He licked his neck fondling his private with his left hand as his right hand held his body tightly to him.

"Don't ever forget, your father is myyyy brother and they will never believe anything you say and if they do, before I go to jail I'll kill the whole family. Do you hear me, boy!" He said moaning louder.

"You are so tender, Shhhh," He said as George began to cry, "Ouch," a little loud," And you are mine, and don't you ever forget that. Awwww, Oh yeah," He said and then he pushed George away from him and told him to go clean up and do his homework before everyone came home.

George, suddenly felt water in his face and he jumped and woke up to the discovery that he had slid down in the tub and could have drowned, so he decided it was time for him to get out because the water suddenly felt cold as he tried to lift his body out of the tub it felt extremely heavy and each time he tried to rise he'd slip back into the tub splattering water all over the floor.

He had to get out of the tub, so he wrapped his toes around the chain and pulled letting the water out of the tub. Once the tub emptied, he found it easier to lift himself. He stepped out of the tub onto the wet rug which slipped under the pressure of his body causing him to fall hard on the floor.

The pain was severe so he laid there for a while, holding his breath until it subsided. Then, he stood unsteadily, grabbed the towel off the rack, wrapped it around his waist, and limped into his bedroom before collapsing across the bed.

He reached the end table and grabbed the Old Grand bottle and gulped down a few swallows, sit the bottle back on the table and turned over in the bed, and fell asleep.

The dream was so real and the pain was back. He felt his throat being stretched and a feeling of wanting to gag, but being struck on the top of his head.

"You better hold it boy, in fact, you better not bite me or I'm going to knock your head off. That's right, keep it up, you are doing good. The more I show you the better you get," George recalled.

Suddenly, George heard, "Bang!" and watched Uncle Matt's body hit the floor. When he looked up he saw his dad grab his hand and pull him off his knees. The old preacher took the tail of his shirt and wiped the tears from George's eyes and wrapped his arm around him.

"Do not rinse out your mouth and this wasn't your fault. Do not be afraid. I am going to take care of this. I'll be right back," he said then left the room.

George laid on the bed looking at the ceiling when he heard the door open and in walked Donald who stretched out on the bed beside him. He didn't say a word, but George knew that his older brother knew what happened and he also knew that he was angry.

Soon he found himself explaining to the police all the times that Uncle Matt had violated him. Listening to the details of his pain, George's mom cried. His dad was furious and cursed which was something he had never heard him do. Donald cried and scratched his head in anger.

George later found out his uncle had confessed and was going to jail.

When George woke up he had a hangover, but since it was Saturday and a day the business was the busiest he had to go to work, so he got up, drank some tomato juice, took two aspirins, and then left for work.

When George got to work, he felt awful. He made a pot of coffee and had drunk most of it by the time Brenda arrived. He didn't have to worry about Joel because he never came to work until around ten or eleven most mornings.

When Brenda walked into the store, she smelled the liquor scent from George. She had never smelled liquor on George before and she knew that something had happened the day before that had upset him.

"Good morning, George, did you have a good time last night because it's bouncing all over the store," she said.

At first, George didn't understand what she meant, but as soon as his brain caught up he knew he had to do something to get that scent off him.

"No, Mrs. Brenda, I had a terrible night. Do you have anything that will help me?" He asked.

"Yeah, I have something in the back that might help you a little bit, spray it on your clothes and maybe people will think it's a bad cologne and not a bad hangover," She said laughing.

Most times George laughed with her, but not this time. When she got to her workspace she reached into the bottom drawer and reached George a small bottle of English Leather. George poured some into his hands and then rubbed his hands over his clothing.

"You'll need this too," She said reaching him some lavender mints.

George opened two and threw them into his mouth and placed the others in his pocket.

"I'll buy you some more of these, Mrs. Brenda." He said as he heard the bell ring in the front, indicating that someone had entered the shop.

"No need to do that George," She said as George headed to the front of the shop to wait on his first customer of the day.

The day went slowly and George was anxious to get home and pour out the liquor. He felt so bad he didn't want another drink, but deep down inside he knew that would not be the case because the dreams had come back again with a vengeance to disturb his life.

Stella Dies

Shelia called Rev. Grant first. He was at the church meeting with the accountant and signing the fourth letter to the Internal Revenue Service. It was another stressful day for him and Shelia could hear it in his tone. She kept the call brief and then, she called her daughter Mary Jean. With the calmest voice she could muster, Shelia told them "something" was wrong at the house and they needed to come over quickly. She deliberately didn't tell them that she'd found Stella unresponsive. She didn't want them driving with this burden on their minds or sorrow in their hearts.

Rev. Grant arrived before Mary Jean and when he saw Stella, he knew her spirit had left this world and was now a part of the world that God has established for Believers. He placed his hand on her head and said a prayer, then thanked her for the love she had shown him. "Rest, Mother, your work is well done."

As he talked, Shelia groaned and moaned, tucked in the corner of the sofa.

Just as Rev. Grant finished praying, Mary Jean rushed into the house. She stopped on a dime when she saw Rev. Grant's face and sank to the floor. She knew the worse had happened: her sweet grandmother was gone. Shelia was still sitting on the sofa and talking out loud, with her head hung low and tears streaming down her face.

"Oh My God! Oh No! Not Granny!" Mary Jean sobbed into Rev. Grant's chest. "Why? Why my Granny?"

He stroked her back. For the first time in his life, he had no words which had always flowed so easily when he was speaking to a grieving member. But, Stella was his granny, too.

He held Mary Jean until she quieted. "Where are the boys?"

"They are with T.P." Mary Jean rested in his chest.

He looked over her shoulder and out the open window hoping the coroner would arrive soon.

"Mama was sitting in her favorite chair- in front of the television as she did most days," Shelia rocked and talked facing Stella's body. "When I arrived home and entered the room, I could see her eyes glued to the screen and knew that it would be useless to talk to her while she watched General Hospital; I figured she would say something as soon as a commercial came on." Shelia's legs shook and tears streamed down her face.

"So, I went into my room, changed my clothes, washed up for dinner, then came back in here. When I came in, I saw a commercial on so I asked, 'What do you want for dinner, momma?' She didn't answer but I didn't even realize it until I had walked all the way to the kitchen table. So, I looked back and saw that her eyes were fixated on the screen and that she was in the same position that she was when I first walked through the door. I knew right then that my mama was gone! I couldn't do anything for a minute. I just looked at her. Then, I walked over to her chair and kneeled and place my head on her lap and...Oh, God, how I wished at that moment that I could be a little girl again and my momma would pick up her hand and rub my head and tell me that everything would be okay, but she never moved! She just sat there with this peaceful look and a smile on her face. I don't know how long I stayed there before I remembered to call you two."

Rev. Grant knew that Shelia felt that she needed to explain what had happened. He also knew that her talking was more for her benefit than theirs. When the coroner arrived, Mary Jean and Shelia tried to stop the attendants from moving the body. They knew she was dead but the finality was too great. Gently, he had to pry Mary Jean's hands loose from Stella's while Hercules Millican and his youngest son had to carry Shelia back to the sofa.

It took the men forty-five minutes to remove the corpse and lock it down in the hearse. When the doors closed, Mary Jean stared quietly at the door and Shelia rocked and cried and mumbled to herself. After nearly an hour of Mary Jean staring and Shelia rocking, Rev. Grant decided to call Dr. Bloomberg to come over and examine the women.

Dr. Bloomberg arrived about thirty minutes later and determined that the women were in shock but they were otherwise okay. Their pupils were normal, heartbeats steady, and blood pressure near normal. He gave Rev. Grant a sedative for Shelia and Mary Jean to take half an hour or so before bedtime. He promised to call in a prescription for more if Rev. Grant felt the women needed it.

He extended his condolences again and suggested that Rev. Grant discussed Stella's passing with the boys only after Mary Jean had come to herself. Rev. Grant agreed. He called T.P. and told her that Stella had passed and that he would be coming to pick up the boys soon. He did not think that Shelia should be at the house alone, so he told her to get a few outfits so she could be with them for a few days. She resisted, but eventually gave in when she saw that Rev. Grant and Mary Jean would not be leaving unless she left, too.

When they arrived home, Rev. Grant guided Mary Jean to their bedroom and Shelia stopped at the porch and stared at the sky. He let her stay outside while he got Mary Jean undressed and in bed. He gave her a cup of tea and the sedative from Dr. Bloomberg. He knew she was in no shape to explain to the boys that their beloved great-grandmother had passed. After hearing Shelia close the front door, he walked down the hall and knocked on the guest bedroom door. Shelia mumbled that she was okay.

"I have some tea to help you sleep if you are ready for it." His voice was gentle.

Shelia knew he was referring to the sedative and she had already decided to stay away from any drugs or alcohol, especially now. "No." She sat on the bed and had not moved to open it.

"Okay." He placed his hand on the door and whispered a prayer of comfort. "I'm going to pick up the boys from T.P. and we'll get Mary Jean's car later."

"Can you call Mason for me?" He could barely hear her request. "Yes. I will call Mason."

He walked into the living room and quickly called the school, knowing Mason had probably left for the day. Luckily he was able to catch the night janitor who agreed to call Mason at home with the news.

Rev. Grant opened the front door, turned on the porch light, and locked the house behind him. His mind raced through the names and faces of people he would have to begin calling about Stella Woods' death. He let the car engine roar and took a few deep breaths before pulling out of the yard.

When Rev. Grant arrived, he quickly noticed how drained the boys looked. T.P. explained that she had broken the news to them and that they had taken it extremely hard. She felt that it would be better if she did it; because she knew that if they broke down in front of their mother, it would make it even harder on her. Rev. Grant felt that it was his and Mary Jean's responsibility to tell the boys but he admittedly was grateful that T.P. had handled it and fed them their favorite pizza. He was exhausted and now, he could get them straight to bed.

For several miles, the three of them rode quietly. Robert Michael held the box of leftover pizza. Other than tapping the box with his index finger, he sat motionlessly. Lawrence Junior stared out the passenger's window. Rev. Grant was sure his son was still crying. Father, guide me.

"Why do people have to die?" Lawrence Junior hit the door.

Rev. Grant thought for a moment and tried to craft the best words to explain it to children—his boys. "When we get older, our bodies are not as healthy as it was when we were young. We get different aches, pains, and diseases. These diseases cause problems with different organs in our body and even though we take medicine to help us with the problems, it does not always help and that is what happened with Granny. Her body just couldn't take anymore so she went to sleep with God." Rev. Grant said looking in the rearview mirror to see if their faces reflected their understanding.

"Your mom and Grandmother Shelia are at the house and both of them are very sad and we guys will have to try to help those ladies keep it together if we can, you understand?"

Both boys nodded, but Rev. Grant knew that they did not fully understand.

When Rev. Grant went into the bedroom, Mary Jean was spread across the bed she had cried so much until she was just staring at the ceiling. He knew he had to let her know that Stella was better off where she was than being here, so he picked her up in his arms and held her like she was a baby. He looked into her eyes and began to speak.

"Remember this, Darling, The bible says, 'for whether we live, we live unto the Lord and whether we die, we die unto the Lord: whether we live therefore, or die we are the Lord's, so Stella is in the best of hands," He said holding her tighter.

"I feel your pain. I too loved Stella. She was a wonderful, caring human being. She is no longer with us in the flesh, but she is with us inside of you and your mother. She is at rest now, and she knows nothing. It is like a deep sleep and believe me, Sweetheart, one day you will see her again and it will be a day of jubilation for you, your mother, the boys, me, and all of her other family and friends."

He sounded like he was convincing himself more than comforting her. She wrapped her arms around him although she was weak with sorrow.

"You know Granny was godly, and she will be missed, but you must hold on to the memories of her. We must hold on. The memories will help us get through this time of grief. It is not going to be easy, but as time passes, so will the deep-rooted feeling of doom. You will know that she is in a better place; she has no pain, no worries, and no cares, for she awaits the awakening that God will one day raise her and everyone like her from the grave."

He allowed his tears to fall while Mary Jean began to doze off.

"Our world changed as soon as Granny closed her eyes. She has been such an intricate part of our lives. She made up a large piece of our world. We are going to miss her for a long, long time most likely as long as we live, but we must live in the knowledge that she is with us, just not in the flesh. There are going to be times when you will think of her and have an overwhelming feeling inside and outside of you, but you know that her soul will live forever in God's presence."

He held in a cry that sat deep in his throat. "She is in God's love."

Mary Jean quietly nodded and fell asleep. Rev. Grant held her until he was certain she was asleep, then he laid her gently on her pillow and covered her with the bedspread. He turned off the overhead light and walked to the boys' room. He tucked Robert Michael under the covers and moved his baseball mitt to the dresser. Lawrence Junior was sound asleep. He turned off their light and checked to see if any lights were on down the hall as he walked to the kitchen.

He was tired, but he knew he needed to start working on Stella's arrangements. He took out a tablet from the telephone stand and began making notes of what he would say if he decided to speak. He compiled a list of the people he would need to call to be on the program and those who would need to hear directly from him. For two hours, he sat at the table writing before he returned to the bedroom. He laid on top of the bed, placed his hand on his wife's back, and prayed until he fell asleep.

The next day, Rev. Grant and Mable worked on the funeral program with minimal input from Mary Jean and Shelia. They called everyone they thought would not mind being on the program and received a definite yes that they would be there and happy to speak. So many people in and around Blaine and throughout south Louisiana thought highly of Sis. Stella Woods. He even telephoned Rev. Douglas and asked him to eulogize Granny for the family. Soon, the program was completed and he read over the final copy. He asked Mable to add three scriptures to the program: *I am the resurrection and the life. He who believes in ME, though he may die, he shall live. John 11:25; We were therefore buried with him through baptism into death in order that, just as Christ was raised from the dead through the glory of the Father, we too may live a new life.* Roman 6:4; and Nehemiah 8:10, *Do not grieve, for the joy of the Lord is your strength.*

Rev. Grant was proud of the work they had done on the program and went home to share it with his grieving family.

Stella's Homegoing

On the day of Stella Woods's homegoing celebration, it was cold and gloomy. The clouds were dark and still as if waiting to fill more before bursting open into rain. The trees on the street looked strange to Mary Jean as did the houses. Everything was familiar but unfamiliar. She had cried so much that she was certain that she had no more tears within her to shed. She had tried to hide most of her grief for the sake of the boys because they each had taken Granny's death hard and she knew if they saw her breaking down it would make them cry even more. Granny was her mother and her grandmother. The grief felt particularly unfair and she quietly struggled to accept God's will in this death. She tried comforting herself with the thought that Granny was no longer in pain, but she had been hiding her illness so well that Mary Jean wasn't convinced that Granny was suffering on earth other than being tired all of the time. Every time she thought like that, she would reprimand herself, *That's not Christian, Mary Jean, cut it out.* Then, she'd cry and wrap her arms around herself in the way she knew Stella would if she were still alive.

When the family arrived at T.E.A.M. they saw cars lining the aisle of the parking lot. Mary Jean's dad Rev. Douglas was waiting by the front door to greet them. He embraced Mary Jean and whispered in her ear,

"God loves you and so do we. You will never get over this loss; however, you will learn to accept it and we will all be here to help you." Then, he shook Rev. Grant's hand and walked into the church to think through the eulogy.

As soon as Marry Jean arrived T.P. rushed over to her, grabbed her around the neck, and started sobbing, Robert Michael and Lawrence Junior started crying quietly. The services had to be delayed for twenty minutes while the funeral director and ushers consoled the family.

When the family finally returned to the vestibule, Lawrence was sitting on one of the pews. He walked over and reached his hand out for Lawrence Junior who hesitated but still took his father's hand then hugged him. Robert Michael moved from the deacons and embraced his father and brother. Mary Jean looked back as the three of them stood in the family procession to enter the sanctuary. Rev. Grant shook Lawrence's hand and put his hand on Lawrence Junior's shoulder. "Do not leave out of this church." He looked sternly at his son then at Lawrence before returning to Mary Jean's side. He braced his arm under hers to hold her up for this was the most difficult walk of her life.

As Mary Jean sat on the front pew, she opened and looked at the program through tears and read:

Prayer

Brother Joshua Melon

After a moment of soft music from the old organ, Brother Melon walked to the podium and bent the microphone to speak. "Heavenly Father, we come to you today in this hour of bereavement over the loss of our dear Sister Stella Jean Larson Woods. We ask that you place your loving arms around this family and—-"

Mary Jean's mind went blank until mid-way through the choir singing "Amazing Grace." Her tears began to flow again and her body shook. She could feel Rev. Grant's arms around her, but they felt limp.

Mary Jean listened to all the kind words and loving memories being shared. She was comforted to know how many people loved Stella. Some of the things that were shared, Mary Jean knew nothing about. These people had long memories of all the work Granny had done for different churches and the city. It gave her a warm feeling to know that there would be many others who would also long for her grandmother.

Then she heard a familiar voice. "The Life of Sister Stella Jean Larson Woods" and when Mary Jean looked up, she saw her friend Lucille who looked as sad as she did. Lucille cleared her throat and read from the program: "Sister Stella Jean Larson Woods was born on July 3rd, 1896, in Natchez, Mississippi to the parents of the late John Henry Larson and Martha May Jones. She was married to Robert Michael Eugene Woods, and from this union, one daughter was born Shelia Mary Woods. Sister Woods was baptized at the age of twelve at Mount Calvary Baptist Church by the late Rev. Jimmy Joseph. She leaves to cherish her memories: her daughter, Shelia Woods, her granddaughter Mary Jean Woods Grant, Rev. Donald Grant; two great-grandsons, Lawrence and Robert Michael Woods."

Lucille's voice trailed. Mary Jean did not hear anything except her mom sobbing. Her body felt cold. She began to tremble and Rev. Grant removed his suit jacket and wrapped it around her shoulders.

"Sister Woods lived a life of giving and serving Jesus Christ and others. She was a member of the Quilting Club, the Bereavement Ministry, the Sunday School Ministry, the Pastor and First Lady's Ministry, the Women's Auxiliary, and the Youth Ministry."

When Mary Jean looked up, she saw Lucille's eyes were red with tears. She had just made it through reading the obituary before bawling. Lucille had always been very fond of Mary Jean's grandmother. She knew that this loss was devastating to her friend. As hard as she tried, she was unable to stop the tears from flowing and had to be ushered off the podium.

Sis. Susan Illes stood in the middle of the choir and sang in the strongest alto voice. "Soon I will be done with the troubles of this world" and the entire church went into a frenzy, sobs could be heard outside the front door.

Stepping to the pulpit microphone, Rev. Douglas wiped his eyes and adjusted the microphone. He opened his Bible and softly cleared his throat. Sis. Illes quietly ended the song and then sat with the choir.

"I have known Sister Stella Woods for over fifty years." He wiped his forehead and took a deep breath. "She has always been a child of God and was always working for the Lord, helping in any capacity that was requested of her. I recall when her husband passed, she came to me and I thought I was going to have to console her, but it ended with her consoling me. What she told me was that she and Robert had had thirty happy years together and that the memories were as fresh in her mind as yesterday. I recall her exact words. She said, 'Reverend Douglas, I hope when I die, I go as peaceful as Johnny did. I don't want to ever be a burden on my kid or have to suffer as a lot of people do.' Well, I say today that Sis. Stella's wish came to pass and she went to sleep watching 'Guiding Light' and woke up with the Lord."

The congregation chuckled. Even Shelia had to smile. Stella made certain to watch her soap operas every time they came on whether it was a replay or not.

"Church, what Sister Stella Woods has done we will all have to do one day, so I say to you all gathered here in this church this morning that you need to get your life in order. Tomorrow is not promised to any of us!" He raised his voice then went silent. He looked down at the gray casket covered in white flowers.

"God almighty." He shook his head. "To the Woods family, I say, There is no sorry that God cannot heal and weep not for Sister Woods because she has crossed over and I'm sure that she is happy."

For the first time, Mary Jean looked at her dad and saw him as the preacher he was and not as the man holding the secret sin of impregnating her mother. She looked at Shelia and followed her eyes. She stared at the flowers in front of her and never looked at her daughter's father. Shelia had rehearsed and feared the day that she would have to see Demetric Douglas, the man, in the pulpit again. Yet, here she was and she was barely holding herself together. Somehow, Mary Jean understood. She looked at the pew behind them and Mason nodded twice. He would be right there when they needed him.

"Church members and visitors, our text for this morning comes from Ecclesiastes verses one and two. Verse one says: 'Where a man has lived to earn a good reputation the day of his or her death can be a time of honor'. In verse two, Solomon argues that mourning and adversity are more beneficial than the pursuit of pleasure because they bring a measure of wisdom in contrast to the surface happiness that foolishness produces. It also brings a person face to face with the reality of his temporal life."

"Therefore, it is important that your name is one that when spoken, family, friends, church members, associates, and co-workers all remember you in a meaningful loving manner. Today, we remember the name Stella Woods and the honor it carries."

He wiped his forehead again and looked at Shelia. Her eyes stayed fixed on the flowers, but the sound of his voice pulled more tears than she wanted to shed. Rev. Douglas focused back on the eulogy.

"The Scripture states that the day of death is better than the day of birth because after birth you will encounter many trials and tribulations, but the day of death means that you are now finished with the pain and heartaches. You are now ready to go to our Father who has prepared a place for us. So, weep not for Sister Woods because she is in the arms of our Master and she is no longer suffering in any manner."

The elderly women shouted, "Amen," "Yes, Lord," and "Thank ya" from every corner of the building. Their shout startled Lawrence Junior who turned around to see who had called out.

"Death is the destiny of every man and every woman!" He raised his voice and the organist began to strum keys. "We will all die one day and how we live our lives will determine our faith in what God has in store for us. And, it is truly something amazing! There will be no more sorrow!"

The organist jammed the keys four times and Rev. Douglas shouted, "No more pain! No more pain! No more pain! No more pain!"

Then the fingers banged five times on the keys and slid back.

"We will live forever and without any diseases, won't that be glorious, my brothers and sisters? We are going to be happy forever. Everyone in this place should take this to heart and if you have not gotten your life in order then let me suggest today that you do that because Sister Woods, got her life together years and years ago and now she is going where we all want to go one day to be with God!"

As the family followed the casket out of the church, Rev. Grant reached his hand out to the boys and they both moved from Lawrence and took Rev. Grant's hand.

This man has taken my sons. Lawrence watched them get into the family car. As it followed behind the hearse, Lawrence watched and his anger grew. He walked to his car, lit a joint, and drove off.

Community Responds to Granny's Death

Walking through the gravel and rocky paths of Mt. Olive Cemetery to get to the burial site was tedious. The memory of it would linger within the boys and Mary Jean. The family sat beside Stella's casket for the final time. After Rev. Douglas ended the final reading and prayer, Mary Jean and Shelia were exhausted.

Back in the family car, they sat quietly as Rev. Grant shook the hands of ministers and deacons who had traveled from Mississippi and were heading back before nightfall. Lawrence Junior stood by his side with his hands in his pants pocket. As they walked back to the car, Rev. Grant explained that they could return anytime the boys wanted to feel close to Granny.

Rev. Grant told the driver to take them to the King's Children Banquet Hall on 80th Street for the repast. Mary Jean was surprised to hear that they were not going to T.E.A.M so Rev. Grant explained.

"Apparently your mother," he nodded towards Shelia, "and your grandmother had helped Mr. James Moses and the Freemasons purchase the land and build the hall years after Mr. Woods had passed. So, Mr. Moses, had all the food and preparations moved over to the building to accommodate the crowd of people that he believes will show up out of respect for Granny." He lifted Mary Jean's hand from her lap and kissed it.

"Did you know that Mary Jean?" Shelia was surprised.

"I sure didn't, but after everything that was said today I am really not surprised." Mary Jean looked at Robert Micheal, then Lawrence Junior. "Granny was truly an amazing woman."

When they arrived at the banquet hall, they were exhausted but honored to see nearly a hundred cars wrapped around the building and down the street in both directions. When they walked past the office and bathroom, they entered a room that was full of people waiting to comfort them. Every table in the room had food on it.

"That's a lot of food!" The boys exclaimed in unison.

"Yeah, I think they prepared too much."

Rev. Grant winked at her.

Then they walked into the large ballroom and saw that it was almost full of people.

"Who's all these people?" Shelia tried to whisper. "They were not at the cemetery and I didn't see them in the church."

"You know any of these people, honey," Rev. Grant asked just before Mrs. Gertrude Garrett led them to the front table. She gave Mary Jean an orange patch quilt, then returned with one twice the size and full of colorful patchwork for Shelia.

Shelia looked at Rev. Grant as if to ask what was going on. She gestured at the mic stand and podium. "Are you planning to speak, Donald?"

"No. Not to my knowledge unless they have me on a planned program," He said as Rev. Douglas and his family slid into the chairs next to them.

"What's the microphone for?" He asked Rev. Douglas.

"Demetria, what's the microphone for?" He asked T.P. She looked around the room. Every chair was occupied and people were standing around the wall. "Look," She shifted her eyes towards the crowd.

"Mary Jean, who are all of these people?" Shelia was surprised. "I recognize some of them from the church and T.E.A.M but there are people in here that I don't know." Shelia's heart smiled when she saw Mason sitting two tables away from her. A woman who could've easily been his twin sat next to him.

Mr. Moses walked up to the podium using a hand-carved walking stick and began to speak. "I know the family is wondering why we have a microphone at the repast, so let me tell you. Stella has helped so many people in this community and they did not know if you all knew, but I knew that you did not! So, I called them and asked them to tell you what an amazing mother, grandmother, great-grandmother, mother-in-law, church member, and friend she was. I'll start with me."

He cleared his throat then took a piece of paper out of his pocket and began to talk more.

"In 1956, I wanted to buy this land and build this edifice that you are now sitting in. I wanted a home for our Mason brothers and Eastern Star sisters. I had saved up what I thought was enough money for the down payment, but I found that I was two thousand dollars short. Stella had been preparing dinner for me and my boys after my wife Eunice had passed," he held back tears.

"I would buy all these ingredients and she would prepare enough food to last me and these greedy boys for the week and for holidays she had all of us over for dinner, and she would not take a dime from me. But, back to the purchase of this hall. I went over to Stella's house that Friday and she asked me how it felt to be the owner of my own business. I then told her that I was two thousand dollars short and that they had raised the price when they saw how bad I wanted the place, and my color didn't help either. They were not ready to cooperate with any Negroes in 1956," Mr. Moses said.

The crowd murmured in agreement. Mary Jean vaguely remembered Granny cooking for the Moses boys. He chuckled and continued, "When Stella heard what I said she told me to wait a minute and she came back and gave me an envelope and said you can give me this back to me one hundred dollars a month. When I looked in the envelope there was money, and I knew it was the two thousand dollars I needed. The rest is for you to use to clean or buy what you need for the place. I was so happy, and I was struck that Stella trusted me enough to loan me that kind of money without any written form of security, but that was Stella, trusting and loving. I'm going to miss her because she was a great lady."

Everyone clapped.

"Okay. Mr. Colbert Mickens the third, you're next." Mr. Moses handed the microphone to a neat-looking young man.

"I know Mrs. Woods because when I was homeless she fed me every Tuesday and Thursday. When she knew she wasn't going to be home at lunchtime, she brought me my lunch on her way out. There were days that I would have starved if she had not fed me and last month, she asked Mr. Moses if he would take over for her. She told me to go see him and he has been feeding me ever since. She even had him hire me to keep the property looking nice and cut the grass. In the winter when it was cold, she would bring me one of her special blankets and Mr. Moses let me sleep in the hall. I am doing better now because of Mrs. Woods. I know I do not look like it today, but soon I will have enough money to get a place. She helped me even though my own people wouldn't help me. I do not know if there is a heaven, but I do know if there is one then Mrs. Woods is there. God bless you. You all had an angel in your midst." The tall, thin 25-year-old held back tears.

Shelia felt like she should have known some of this, but Stella was good at keeping her and others business to herself.

Mr. Colbert looked at the paper and said, "Deloris Myers will speak now." George rolled Miss. Myers in her wheelchair to the podium and he gave her the microphone.

"Hello everyone and to the family, I say I am so sorry about Mrs. Stella's passing. I knew something was wrong when she did not call or show up two weeks ago. You see, Mrs. Stella came and helped my grandmother take care of me on Monday and Friday mornings. That must've been days after she took care of Mr. Colbert. She knew my grandmother was sick, so she would come and help me twice a week. She would help us with our hygiene. She would cook a few meals to help my grandmother out because my mother is dead and the only person I have is my grandmother. My mema and Mrs. Stella went to the same church. I miss the long talks we would have when Mema would doze off. But what I really want you to know is what she did two months ago! We didn't even know it until after it was done. Somehow, Mrs. Stella got the state to send a home care nurse to help me with my baths and granny with the housework. She also got the deacons to fix the ramp going up to the front porch so it would be easier for me to roll the wheelchair outside. Then, she got a lady–Mrs. Manuella–to come to cook for us for pennies on the dollar. I see Mrs. Manuella back there! Hey, Mrs. Manuella! Thank you for taking care of us. Wave, Mrs. Manuella, so everyone can see you!"

The guests looked around and saw a short, elderly white woman waving proudly. They applauded her.

"So, I say to all her family, thank you for all the thanks I didn't get to say to Mrs. Stella. She will truly be missed for her kind heart and good works." Miss Myers blew kisses to each family member and George rolled her back through the crowd. T.P. felt a sense of pride while watching George so gently handle Miss. Myers. She hadn't expected him to show up to the services since he had started having difficulty sleeping. His stride was still strong and deliberate, but his eyes were worn. *I could use a hug myself, too, George.* T.P. decided to pass by his house on her way home to check on him.

Two servers began to serve food at each table using gold-painted serving carts. Fried chicken, French fries, lettuce and tomato salad, and cake were on the top shelf of the cart. On the middle shelf were plates of sliced roast beef, potato salad, peas, rolls, and cake. The third level of the cart held plates of sliced ham, baked macaroni, string beans, garlic bread, and cake.

The program continued with six other people speaking about the goodness of Stella Woods in their lives. Everyone ate silently as music played.

"The food is delicious, and I think we need to thank these people who spoke so nicely about Granny," Mary Jean said to Shelia.

"You speak baby. You and Donald represent this family well. I can't say anything." Shelia shook her head.

Mary Jean asked Rev. Grant if he wanted to speak.

"No, I feel this is a time that you or your mom need to address these good people. It will be heartfelt coming from either one of you.

Mary Jean knew that he was right, and she stood up, walked to the podium, and picked up the microphone. "Ladies and Gentlemen, on behalf of me and my family we would like to thank you from the bottom of our hearts. The words that have been spoken today will remain with us for a lifetime and more so because we did not know any of the good deeds that Granny was doing and being the kind and giving person that she was, she never mentioned a word to any of us. Of course, sometimes we were unable to reach her, but when we questioned her, she let us know that she was an old woman who was grown and did not answer to anyone about her whereabouts. I say again, thank you, thank you, and if you ever need help please feel free to come to TEAM Church and we will do our best to help you. For those of you who do not know about our church and do not have the address, we are in the telephone directory and, we are going to ask Mr. Moses to give anyone who asks our church phone number and address. We are going to also ask him to place the address on his sign in front of the hall. We pray that all of you will have love, peace, and prosperity. Thank you," Mary Jean said. She returned to her seat and began eating.

Mr. Moses took the microphone and announced, "As you are leaving each person can pick up plates of food for your family because we have a lot left." Then, he walked over to Shelia and said, "We have boxes of food for this table for each of you. You will not have to cook for a long time."

Cynthia and Rev. Douglas, along with T.P., were surprised that Mary Jean was able to make the speech and they were all proud of her.

After people had eaten, they passed by the front table and each one said, "I'm sorry for your loss; I'm praying for your family; Please know that I loved her; We are going to come to your church; and many other nice and kind sentiments. Most of the families who walked to the table gave envelopes of money and cards to Mary Jean and Shelia. Even, Lawrence Junior's classmates came to the table with cards and hugs.

Robert Michael's baseball coach had members of the team walked over and hugged or patted him on the back before they left the repast.

Rev. Douglas and his family left along with the crowd after hugging and kissing Mary Jean and the boys, then shaking Rev. Grant's hand and getting their boxes of food. Shelia had intentionally walked away with the little league team to avoid contact with the Douglas family. She still wasn't quite ready to be friendly with them.

It was almost 8:30 pm. The life of Stella Woods had been celebrated the entire day. Everyone had left the banquet hall and the family was tired. Two servers loaded Rev. Grant's and Shelia's cars with boxes of food and a cooler of canned drinks.

"Thank you, Mr. Moses. We appreciate your kindness," Shelia said.

"You are welcome. I loved Stella and I am still in shock. It seems like she put so much in place just in time for us all to care better for each other." Mr. Moses put his hand on her shoulder. "You let me know if you or your momma needs anything. I'll be checking on you every month, you hear?"

Rev. Grant attempted to give Mr. Moses a hundred dollars to pay Mr. Colbert and a friend to clean the hall. "No, Rev. No, no. I wouldn't have you paying for my dear sister's services and Stella and these girls of hers are family." Rev. Grant put his money away. They shook hands.

"Be blessed, Brother."

Just as they walked to the car, a detective from the New Orleans Police Department walked over to them.

"Ms. Shelia Woods?" He tilted his hat at Rev. Grant and shook his hand.

"Yes, officer. May I help you?"

"I'm so sorry for your loss, Ma'am but I am happy to have found you again."

Shelia took Mary Jean's hand."What do you mean, again?"

He didn't believe it was appropriate to discuss those details after burying her mother, instead, he handed her an envelope. "Your Grandmother made this happen for both of us."

She looked inside the envelope and quickly closed it. The shock on her face scared Mary Jean. She took it from Shelia, opened it to her surprise, and asked, "What's all this, officer–" she read his badge. "Officer J. Mixon."

"Stella was robbed of this years ago but before she passed, her testimony in court helped us put away, umm, a very bad man." He squinted his grey eyes in a manner to trigger Shelia's memory. For a moment everyone was silent.

He tilted his hat and walked away.

"Wait," Shelia said.

He took another step then turned around.

"I don't understand. What? What am I supposed to do with this?"

His eyes searched her face. "Monster is dead." He said flatly and walked off.

Mary Jean put her arm around her mother's shoulder. She had no idea who Monster was but she could see her mother was relieved at his death.

Mrs. Agnes Offers Late Condolences

For weeks after Stella's death, Mary Jean forwarded all the calls from her home phone to the church for Mable to handle. She wanted time to rest and Granny's popularity kept the phone ringing with people grieving and offering condolences. Most of the time Mary Jean did not feel well. After realizing she couldn't write or pray her sorrows away, she asked Dr. Bloomberg to help. He gladly prescribed valium although it hadn't helped her much just yet. She felt bad about adding more work on Mable, but there was nothing else she could do at this time. Even taking care of the twins had become physically tiring Once they were out of the house and on their way to school, Mary Jean went back to bed.

When the telephone rang, she was surprised that she'd forgotten to forward the line. Reluctantly, she reached over and picked up the receiver. "Hello," Her voice was faint.

"Is that the way for a Pastor's wife to answer the phone?"

Mary Jean rolled her eyes but did not respond. *I'm really not in the mood for you today, woman. Jesus, help me.*

"Mary Jean, Mary Jean. Are you there?"

"Yeah, Mrs. Agnes, I'm here." She scooted back into the bed. *Lord, she always calls at the worst times.*

"Sister Smith told me that your grandmother, Mrs. Stella, passed. I am sorry to know that. You have my sympathy. I would have come to her funeral if you would have called me."

"Granny's death was in the newspaper and the church's bulletin. Did you stop reading the obituary every day?"

"Well! I do not read it every day. I read the paper three days a week and on Sundays."

"The obituary was for seven days, so which days did you miss?"

"Oh, I don't know. I just know that I didn't know and if I had I would have attended the funeral, but Joyce let me know all about it."

"Well, I'm happy you had someone to get you caught up, now you can feel like you were sitting right there in person." Mary Jean knew Mrs. Agnes was lying but decided to just let the old biddy get caught up in her web of lies.

"Joyce told me you let Sister Susan Illes sing a solo. I fell out laughing when I heard that because everyone knows that woman does not know how to sit down once you let her start! How long did she hold up your program? Joyce said she checked her watch before and after and that Sister Illes sung the same song for five minutes and she would not have sat down then but everyone who knew her knew they had to fall out to get her to stop. You know she has to have some bragging rights..." Her words trailed into laughter.

"I don't recall that part, Mrs. Agnes." Mary Jean interrupted

"That's right you were overcome with grief. You also had Brother Mc-Nasty do the acknowledgments," Mrs. Agnes snickered.

"Who is Brother McNasty, Mrs. Agnes?"

"He's the one who is always looking at the young girls in the church. I've seen him myself lusting after some of our youngsters—even the boys." She felt good knowing something that Mary Jean didn't know and she wondered what the other church members thought when he walked up to the podium.

"Well, if you saw Brother McN...alty" Mary Jean held the "alty" sound to correct Mrs. Agnes's pronunciation "doing something inappropriate, Mrs. Agnes you should have brought it to Rev. Grant's attention because no one else has expressed this to either one of us," Mary Jean said and yawned.

"Your husband knows everything so I figured he knew that too, so why should a little old lady like me go and tell your husband something that I'm sure he should have known?"

Mary Jean didn't have the strength to reply.

"How is your mother doing now that she has to live alone?"

"She's fine."

"Well, how're the boys and your husband?"

"We are ALL doing fine, Mrs. Agnes."

"I don't know about all of you because I heard that you are not doing well and that you are experiencing some type of emotional breakdown."

"Well, Mrs. Agnes, we all experience grief differently. I'm sure you remember the death of your husband and how you responded. Thank God I don't result to drinking and I am feeling much better. You can tell your friend that for me."

"I'll do just that, and—"

"Goodbye, Mrs. Agnes. Take care of yourself, okay? Mary Jean slammed the phone down. She had had it with Mrs. Agnes. She quickly dialed star-67 and forwarded the calls to Mable. Four minutes later, she'd fallen asleep.

Mason's Family Visits Shelia

It had been two weeks since the family buried Stella, and Shelia's grief had intensified. Mason couldn't find the right words nor do the right things to get her to snap out of it. Thankfully, the Adult Education Program had ended and it would be another month before her final night classes began. He worried over her and stayed as close to her as she would allow so that she would not disappear from him as she had before. She would walk the house, aimlessly cleaning. She cleaned the walls, the floors, windowsills, tops of closets, and behind all the beds. She only stopped the day when Mason said, "Baby, you can't clean your grief away. You need family around you and friends to love on you a little." Then, she finally agreed to meet his family, but she wouldn't venture out. They would have to come to her, and he didn't mind those arrangements.

When the day arrived, Shelia did not know what to expect from Mason's people. "Tell me what they are like, Mason. You know I don't have any siblings or true friends, so this is all new."

"Honey, it'll be okay." He gave her a sly grin, "Just don't you wear your feelings on your sleeve. My people are some fun-loving people, and they don't have any muzzles on their mouths or masks across their faces. Do not let what they do upset you. And, remember we can fix everything the next day. Okay?" She thought about what he said and wondered how bad they could be and what would they have to fix the next day. Mason hugged her from behind while she washed the dishes. His body and arms swallowed her medium frame in a way no other man had. He was a big teddy bear, and she felt safe in his arms.

"What time are they coming?"

He kissed her neck. "Well."

Before he could answer, a horn blew repeatedly. It did not sound like a normal car horn. Then, someone rang the outside doorbell six times quickly. All the commotion made her feel like someone was hurt and they ran to the door.

When Mason opened the door, Shelia was right on his heels. Outside was a yellow school bus with animals painted on it. The harder Shelia looked at the bus the more she realized that she did not know the names of half of the animals. The ones she recognized were cows, hogs, raccoons, squirrels, and rabbits, but the other venisons she didn't recognize. She knew Mason came from a family of butchers but this market bus was a bit over the top for her. When Shelia looked up, she saw a group of people climbing off the bus and coming towards her. The leader of the group was a large man who stepped sideways off the bus. His grin was wide and his teeth looked like someone had painted white gloss across them. His handmade overalls were two large sizes perfectly stuck together. Right behind him walked a young child who looked like his twin. Smile, size, color, and clothing matched.

"Hey, Bro! Ya'll come on in!" Mason waved his arm. Shelia stood behind him in the doorway. She was shocked. Who the hell are all these people?!

"Hey man! How you doing? I brought the gang, and we brought the food. You don't have to do anything." The two burly men shook hands and hugged. "Oh! This must be your sweetness?" Before Shelia could respond he'd stepped around Mason and wrapped his arms around her waist so tight, she instantly felt the need to go urinate.

"Yeah, Bony, this is MY Shelia," Mason said as everyone else stood in line to hug her and Mason.

"Bony?" *This man is not bony!*

Then a woman only slightly smaller than Bony stepped onto the porch, picked Mason up, and kissed him three times on his right cheek. "Hey there, little brother! I have missed you," She swirled Mason around. "You look good! This lady has been taking good care of you," She grabbed Shelia and lifted her off the floor into a big hug. The floorboard creaked and adjusted under all the new weight. Mason led them into the house while Shelia adjusted her shirt, feeling flustered.

As the rest of the family entered the house, Shelia was hugged, twirled, twisted, pushed back, eyed, hand kissed, and picked up off the floor. They offered their condolences. The oldest sister gave Shelia a large, potted ivory plant with a card dangling from the inner stick. A total of fifteen people—young and old—all large-bodied entered the house. They all had the same wide grin as Mason. After they scattered to the kitchen, den, and dining room, some went out to the backyard to begin setting up the table to prepare the food they brought with them.

"You okay, honey?" Mason asked as he saw that Shelia's eyes seemed larger and she seemed edgy.

"I… I'mmmmm, okay. I am just a little surprised. Are all these people your sisters and brother? I know you said you came from a big family, but is this just the sisters and brothers?" She asked.

"Yeah, honey they are all my sisters and brothers. Some of them are twins and triplets. In fact, I am a twin. Mason is my brother."

"Which one was he?" Shelia asked.

"He's the one who you said looks just like me. Before I could tell you that he is my twin, Bird came in and distracted me.

"I remember he was the one who didn't hug me he just shook my hand, which I found odd because everyone before him had bear-hugged me almost to death."

As they entered the kitchen Shelia was shocked. An animal with its neck cut off was being skinned on top of her kitchen table. Its blood had saturated the pile of newspaper under it. Instantly her stomach turned, and she felt her breakfast moving upward as she ran to the bathroom and threw up, then looked out of the window and heard blues being played loudly in her backyard.

"Birda, could you have skinned that rabbit outside? Shelia is not used to seeing animals slaughtered and now she's sick," He said as he headed toward the bathroom.

After Shelia vomited, she looked out her bathroom window and saw a folding table being used to hold the carcass of what looked like a deer, and one of Mason's brothers was moving the coals around on the grill, she assumed he was about to grill and barbecue it. Something she knew she would never want to eat.

Mason knocked on the door, "Are you okay, honey?" He asked.

"Yes, I'm fine. I'll be out in a minute. Go back and talk with your family, I'll be there in a minute," Shelia said.

Shelia opened the door when she was sure that Mason had left. She went into the bedroom where she had a phone next to her bed and dialed Mary Jean's number.

"Hello," Mary Jean said.

"Baby, can you come over here now!" Shelia whispered into the phone all the while looking at the door. She hoped that Mason did not come in and see her on the phone.

Mary Jean could tell by the tone of her mom's voice that something was amiss.

"What's wrong mom?" She asked.

"Baby, my house is full of people, big people. You know I do not have anything against large people, but these people are big and big-boned people and tall, they remind me of Bigfoot. They are in my kitchen killing animals on my kitchen table and they are in my backyard with an animal on a folding table that looks like a deer and two grills are smoking, so I guess it's safe to assume they are going to barbecue the deer. Baby, my stomach is weak, and I do not know if I'm going to be able to put up with this all day. Just seeing the animal on my table made my stomach turn and I threw up my breakfast. Can you come over here?" Shelia asked.

Mary Jean had never heard her mother sound so desperate, but what she had just said sounded like she was having a hard time.

"What people mom? Mary Jean asked laughing inside because she knew her mom did not like being around strangers.

"It's Mason's family they came to try to meet me and try to lift my spirit but it's having the opposite effect. Baby, my nerves are on the edge. Please try to come!"

Suddenly Mary Jean heard through the phone, "Sister-in-Law! Where are you? We need you in the kitchen!"

"Oh Lord baby, tell me that you are coming," Shelia whispered and then answered the person.

"I'll be right there!" She yelled.

"Rev. Grant is on his way home and if he doesn't need to go right back to the church, I'll leave the boys with him, and then I'll come over for a little while," Mary Jean said.

"Thanks, baby, "Shelia said, and as she hung up she heard a loud sound as she walked toward the kitchen Mason met her halfway and hugged her then whispered in her ear, "Don't worry honey I'll fix every-thing tomorrow."

As Shelia walked towards the kitchen she could not imagine what could have been broken because she didn't have an overcrowded kitchen, but when she walked into the kitchen her right foot slipped and she tried to hold onto Mason but her weight was too much for him so he started slipping and they both hit the floor at the same time sliding and slipping in animal blood and- on top of that- they slid into Birda who had fallen first and wasn't able to get up by herself.

Shelia grabbed onto one of the kitchen table chairs and began to pull herself off the floor and as she did, she saw two other large creatures on top of her table with blood running off the sides of the table. Once again, the smell of blood made her start gagging, and as she made her first step after having pulled herself upright to try to make it to the bath-room, her foot slipped, and she landed back on the floor.

"Come on, baby, crawl to the edge of the kitchen in the hallway. I've placed a quilt there, so you won't slip anymore," Mason said reaching his hand out to Shelia. "Bert, as soon as I get Shelia out, I will help pull you to the edge, and then I will mop up the blood."

Mason helped Shelia walk quickly across the bloody quilt. She noticed her brand-new pantsuit was ruined by bloodstains.

"Help me to the bathroom," she ordered Mason.

When they reached the bathroom, Shelia walked in first, reached back and jerked Mason inside, and then slammed the door.

"Ma.....son I love you. I really do, but your family is too much for me. There's blood all over my kitchen and what the hell are they cooking? Now I am going to take a bath, change clothes and then I'm going back to my kitchen which had better be clean of blood and your sister had better be off my floor!" She said stepping out of her pants and showing the body that Mason loved looking at, but he knew he had better get everything cleaned up if he wanted to hold that body again; so he walked out the door and closed it behind him.

When Shelia looked out of the bathroom window, she saw one of Mason's brothers brushing barbecue sauce on the deer or whatever animal he had in her backyard. She then turned the water off and stepped into the tub, sat down, and decided to soak there for a while. Taking a bath gave her the time she needed to think of what she needed to say to George's family when she went back into the kitchen and outside in the backyard.

Mason went back into the kitchen and took the quilt and began moving it over the floor toward Bert who was now sitting up against the back door and Bony was trying to push the door open.

"Bony stop pushing this damn door in my back! I am on the floor and I can't get up. You and Boxer go around to the front door, so Mason can let you in and the two of you can help get me off this floor," Bert said out of breath.

"All right, sis. Come on Boxer, Sister and Mason need our help!"

Mason headed to the front door and found most of his family in the living room watching the game. *Oh, Lord, they have moved into this room and they are drinking and I know what's going to happen once they get drunk, but if we can get that food ready before they drink too much then everything might work out just fine.* He thought.

————————-

When Mason opened the door, Mary Jean stood with his brothers.

"Who are you, little sugar?" Boxer asked looking Mary Jean up and down.

"Boxer, watch your manners this is Mary Jean, Shelia's daughter. She's a pastor's wife, so behave!" Mason said as he ushered Mary Jean inside.

"Shelia's in the tub but go on back there because she needs you right now." He said.

Bony, Boxer, and Mason went into the kitchen where they used the quilt to mop up most of the blood. When they got the blood cleaned as much as they could, they went for Bert.

"Put your arms under her left armpit, Bony. Now, Boxer you put your arms under her right armpit, and I'll get behind her and push up on her. I am going to count to three and then you two lift up and I will push. Ready. One, two, three!" Mason said.

Boxer and Bony pulled up and Mason shoved, and they got Bert half-way up off the floor before she slid back down pulling them down with her.

"Damn, Bert! You feel like you weigh a ton! Can't you do something to help us?" Boxer asked agitated that he was straining.

"I smell my meat burning, so go get Maddy, Monny, and Jay to help. I got to check on my meat that's on the grill." Bony said.

Mary Jean found the bathroom door open so she knew Shelia was in the bedroom. She knocked on the bedroom door.

"Who is it?" Shelia asked.

"It's me, Momma." Mary Jean said.

"Hold on a second," Shelia said as she pulled a pair of jeans up her hips, tucked her blouse inside, walked bare feet to the door, and un-locked it. She pulled Mary Jean inside then closed and locked the door behind them.

Shelia burst into tears and Mary Jean hugged her and then moved them to the bed where they both sit down, and Mary Jean ran over to the dresser and grabbed a box of Kleenex tissue.

Shelia whipped her eyes and then told Mary Jean the entire story from the beginning to the end.

"Let's go see what they are doing in the kitchen. I told Mason to be sure to clean up the floor in the kitchen and pick up his sister, "Shelia said as they entered the doorway of the kitchen where Birda and Maddy were sitting and talking.

"Hi, ladies this is my daughter Mary Jean. Please introduce yourselves because I do not recall everyone's name yet," Shelia said as she looked down and toward the corner of the room. She saw one of Stella's hand-made quilts covered in blood. Angry tears welled in her eyes, but she held them back.

"Hi, Mary Jean, I'm Bertha but everyone in the family calls me Birda."

"Hi, Birda. It's great meeting you," Mary Jean said shaking her hand which was unbelievably soft. Birda was a pretty woman, with long silky hair that hung to her shoulders. Her skin was olive, and her face was clear with long eyelashes and light brown eyes. Her features were more Caribbean than Black American. She was big bonded and stood five feet nine inches tall.

"Hi, Mary Jean, I'm Madison everyone in the family calls me Maddy. It's nice to meet you," She said as she extended her hand to Mary Jean. Madison looked more like Mason. She stood five feet six inches tall and was slightly smaller than Birda.

She had a cream complexion and she, too, had a beautiful face with a head full of hair that was pulled back into a ponytail that hung to the middle of her back. These people must have some Indian in them, Mary Jean thought.

"Nice to meet you, too," Mary Jean said.

Shelia looked in the sink and she did not see any animals the sink was clean and so was the floor, so she was happy about that, but she wondered where the others were.

"Where is everyone else?" She asked.

Birda spoke up, "Some of them went to visit our cousins in town and some are watching the game in the living room and Boxer is finishing up the barbecue, so we can eat. I brought the potato salad and Maddy brought the baked beans and, by the way, we did fix up some chicken and ribs because we were not sure if you like wild meat."

"Thank God!" Shelia said before she could stop herself and everyone looked at each other and laughed.

They all turned and looked, as the kitchen door opened from the back yard and Boxer walked in with two pans stacked on top of each other. He sat the first pan on the table, and it contained some kind of meat that Shelia and Mary Jean had never seen before, then he put down another pan and there were ribs and chicken and it all looked delicious.

"Let me get the potato salad and beans Maddy said because she knew that Birda's hips were hurting her from her fall on the floor. She took the huge container of salad out of the refrigerator and turned off the oven and then took out two even large containers of baked beans.

"What is the name of the meat that you just put in your mouth?" Shelia asked trying to change the subject.

"Oh, this here is rabbit and Boxer has deer and coon with the sweet potatoes on the other tray. You should try it because it's unbelievably delicious," Birda said.

"No thanks. I prefer the ribs and chicken," Shelia said as she reached and took a chicken wing and placed it on her plate alongside a cut of ribs, potato salad, and a spoonful of baked beans.

"Well, how about you, young lady, will you try some of the game meat?" Maddy asked Mary Jean.

"No, ma'am. I will have one piece of chicken because I'm going to have to go home and eat dinner with my family. I just stopped by to meet Mason's family." Mary Jean was anxious to leave now that she knew her mom was okay.

"You don't have to say, ma'am to me baby I'm not that old I just look old from hard work and a hard life," Maddy said.

Soon the rest of the family who was watching the game came into the kitchen and began reaching over Mary Jean and Shelia's heads to get some food and when their arms went forward so did the scent of perspiration without deodorant. She and Mary Jean both looked at each other as Mason spoke up.

"Man, show some manners! Stop reaching over the ladies for the food ask them to pass you the pan and then get your food! Damn, man! Mama didn't raise us like this." He said as he pulled up a chair next to Shelia. He knew that she was upset, and he was sorry that she had to meet his family like this because they really are nice people once you get to know them and because there were so many of us, we ate off the land. So, my family grew up on wild meat and fresh vegetables that we grew on the farm."

"We were trying to get Shelia to try some rabbit," Birda said. "That will never happen," Mason muttered and they all laughed

"I'm sorry, Birda, go on with the discussion. I'll just sit here and eat."

Mary Jean stood up.

"It's been a pleasure meeting all of you and I look forward to seeing you again soon, but I have to go get dinner ready for my family," After she said this she turned, and Shelia and Mason walked her to the door.

"Thanks for coming, Mary Jean," Mason said as Shelia hugged Mary Jean and told her they would talk later. They both watched until Mary Jean drove off in her car.

The phone rang and Mason rushed to answer it. After a few okays, yeahs, and yeses, he hung up the phone and then announced.

"Bubba, Little man, Shandy, and JoJo will be back in an hour and Bubba wants everyone to be ready because he has to go to work tomorrow so he's going to hit the road as soon he gets here, and he said to fix some plates for everybody and they can eat on the bus."

Thank God. Shelia thought. As she rushed to the kitchen to help pack up all the food, except the ribs and chicken which was quite delicious.

"Do you have any to-go plates, sister-in-law?" Birda asked.

Shelia thought for a minute and remembered that she had leftovers from her mom's repast.

"Yeah, let me get them for you." She walked to the hall closet, pulled out the entire box of paper plates, and dragged it back to the kitchen where Maddy and Birda began dishing food onto them.

"Please, leave me and Mason a plate of ribs and chicken, baked beans, and, of course, some of that amazing potato salad," Shelia said knowing that Birda and Maddy would be happy to know that she liked their cooking.

"I left your salad and beans in the refrigerator," Maddy said as she helped Birda up out of the chair. Her hip was still aching even after Mason had given her a pain pill.

As Shelia walked them to the front of the house and into the living room, she hugged each one of Mason's family members.

"Thank you all for coming and I'm certain that I will see you all soon." She decided if she and Mason married, she would not have a large wedding and would be willing to have a reception in Mason's hometown of Greensburg. That way everyone would be satisfied.

Once the guests left, Mason wanted to talk, but Shelia did not.

"Honey I'm sorry about my family. They mean well," He said as he turned off the lights in the living room.

"Mason, I don't want to talk about this now. I have a terrible headache and I am going to bed. Would you please put the quilt that my momma made for me by hand in a plastic bag and put it out with the trash and then put the food up that your sister left for us in the kitchen? We'll talk tomorrow about all of this," Shelia said. She was shaking with grief and anger but managed to slowly walk to the bedroom.

Bronner Brothers Hair Show

George had finally convinced T.P. to attend the Bronner Brothers Hair Show. She had been contemplating it for years but with his encouragement and excitement, she was ready to walk through the large arena of Black stylists and models showing off amazing techniques. She packed modestly but to strut in the presence of beauticians required the best dress, heels, flowing curls, and impeccable blends of Fashion Fair makeup every time she steps into the building. Thanks to a life under the glaring criticism of church folk, T.P. knew she was ready for the challenge. She also packed up styling tools and Dudley products just in case she gets a chance to touch up a set for another cosmetologist.

The hair show was a quick ride to New Orleans but George had decided to handle hotel arrangements so they would not have to drive back and forth to attend. Since she would cover the expense of entering the show, T.P. accepted his offer. "Consider it an even exchange," George said once he realized her hesitancy.

"Look, baby, don't worry about us having a place to stay. We can live with one of my friends in New Orleans, they will be glad to have us. We go way back, and I can't wait to see them," George said grinning from ear to ear. For days leading up to the trip, T.P. couldn't shake her reluctance. Her thoughts went from wondering who George's friends were to wondering where she would lay her head and if he thought she would share a bed with him while with his "friends". The more she thought of it, the more she had to remind herself of how incredible it would be to be in the mix of the nation's most talented Black stylists. Her excitement rose each time.

Nonetheless, she was dumbfounded when George pulled up in front of a small shotgun house, blew the horn, then got out of the car. He walked to the trunk shaking his keys with what T.P. assumed was nervous excitement. She watched him through the car mirrors. When he closed the trunk and began walking to the house, she watched his every step. Since he didn't gesture for her to walk with him or stay in the car, she chose to stay. I know this is not the friend's house where he wants me to stay.

The front screen door creaked open, and a man ran down the steps and hugged George. He yelled, "It's good to see you, man! Everybody's been missing you! Where have you been?"

"I've been working, man, and dating that Pretty Lady you see in the car," George pointed to T.P and looked right into her eyes.

The man looked at George and laughed. "Yeah, right, Man. Come on in! Joan still here. And she's still waiting to see you."

George looked back at the car, wondering if T.P. could hear them.

"No. Man, that's my lady in the car. We are in town because she is a beautician and there's a hair show at the Regency Auditorium and she invited me to attend it with her. That's why I called you to see what you could do for me." George said a little lower in tone.

"How long have you been date......ing her? A minute or two?" The thin man laughed.

"It's been a while and she's my only lady. I plan to marry her soon," George said quietly.

"Man, I can't believe that!" Snake waved his hand and turned George towards the house. He took two steps before George followed.

"You can't believe what, man?"

They walked to the door of the house.

"First, that you are only dating just one woman! You're the biggest whore mongrel in the world, who always said no bitch was good enough for him to commit to and you'd never put a ring on a woman's finger. I guess there is one bitch, right?"

George chuckled. "She's different and it's time for me to tear up my players' card."

"You, being a player? That's going to be the least of her worries, man."

He looked back at the car and finally acknowledged T.P. with a wave. "Step inside. Man, I didn't clean this place. I thought you were kidding when you called and said that you and your lady were coming by. I even told Joan to get herself together." Snake laughed so loud George wanted to tell him to be quiet. "But, I was dead wrong. Wait until the guys hear about you and your one woman. I can't wait to tell them."

George followed him into the room. Joan stood in the kitchen beside the refrigerator, just enough to be invisible. The sound of George's voice warmed the center of her chest but she could see the woman sitting in his car: slim, glowing skin, loose curls that hung just to her shoulders, simple gold studs, and delicate pink lip gloss. Joan knew George's type and that doll waiting for him was out of his league. Still, she stood hidden to wait for him or Snake to call for her.

"Man, if your lady is okay living in a house that's a little dirty and with a few visitors throughout the night, then ya'll are welcome here. I can get Joan to change them sheets. It's not the Starlight Motel but it should suit you two lovers just fine. When folks leave, I'll go on and check on my mom so ya'll have ya'll space and whatnot."

"How much is it going to cost?"

"That depends on you," Joan walked in and handed George and Snake a whiskey cup of bourbon and hyssop. "How you plan on paying?" She licked her lips and took a sip.

"Because it's you, I'll only charge you twenty dollars a day. You two are staying for the weekend, right?" Snake sipped the bourbon. His face relaxed as the burn and flavor flowed.

"Yeah. Twenty. Twenty is good." Without thinking, George chugged down the bourbon.

"Good, Joan will clean the place up for us. I'll get the guys to meet tonight for a round of bones. We can all catch up where we left off two years ago." George gave Joan his cup and walked out of the house to get T.P. He pretended not to notice how Joan's breasts and hips curved under the green dress.

_____

George returned to the car, excited that his plans were coming together. He sat in the driver's seat and reached over T.P's lap to open the glove compartment. He pulled out his wallet and slammed the latch closed.

"Okay, Pretty Lady. We're all set."

All set? This man must think I'm crazy. There is no way in hell I am going to live in this dump for a second. I will catch Greyhound back home first.

He rummaged through receipts and business cards to find the money. "I ran short of money, and I didn't want you to have to come out of your pocket for the hotel, so I called my friend Snake. I mean, Winfred, over there." He pointed at the house. T.P. could smell the hyssop. "I knew Winfred had this house and would rent it to us for little or nothing."

He pulled out the twenty and folded the wallet closed. Then, finally, made eye contact with T.P,

"George, I am not ever walking up those steps to that dump. I'm appalled that you would bring me to such a place knowing how important this weekend is. I know you can do better than this." She wanted to go on about what she deserved and that he could've been more thoughtful about their first weekend together. But, her concern was more on how quickly she could get away from this house and George.

"Keep your money, George, and let's go." Although she was furious, her tone was leveled and calculated.

"Okay. Baby, just let me go tell Winfred that we are leaving, and we will not be using his place after all." He took her hand and kissed it. "I'll be right back."

He checked the gas level to make sure he could leave the air conditioner running since the August air was hot and humid. He opened the car door and quickly headed to the house. He ran up the three steps, walked into the house as if he was at home, and closed the door behind him.

T.P. glanced at her watch it was a quarter to noon.

The house was filled with cigarette and cigar smoke. Liquor bottles were piled on the table. Winfred's girlfriend, Missy, entered through the back door carrying a case of Budweiser and two boxes of fried chicken. Her shorts were too short for a fifty-year-old grandmother who was thirty pounds overweight. But, in New Orleans, men like Winfred "Snake" Wilson III loved their women big-boned and full of liquor. She nodded at George on her way to the kitchen.

"Nah, Nah, girl. Bring all that here," Snake shouted. Missy quickly turned around. George wasn't sure if he was asking for the chicken or her. She sat the boxes on the coffee table, knocking over two pints of Crown Royal. He pulled her onto his lap and gave her a joint. The scent went through George's throat. Joan watched him sit on the wooden end chair. Winfred reached him a freshly rolled blunt. George accepted it a took a deep drag and before he knew it, he felt glued to the chair. "Where's your lady at, man?" Snake tried to look at George but Missy turned his face back to her and blew smoke into his face before kissing him. George took another drag.

Gently, Joan shook ashes off a bag of cookies and offered it to George. Then, she placed another glass of bourbon on the table for him. He didn't feel the smile grow on his face but it was all Joan needed to see for her to stay around a little longer and endure Missy and Snake kissing and rubbing.

Time did not matter.

T.P. looked at her watch and thirty minutes had passed. Although she thought it was uncouth, she pressed the horn and kept pressing it until George ran out of the house. He missed a step and fell hard on the makeshift cement walkway. Winfred ran out of the house and T.P. got out of the car and ran toward them. He grabbed George, clumsily lifting him from the ground. He tried to walk back up the steps.

"No! Put him in the car." T.P. was stern. "We are going back home."

"What! Can't you see that he's hurt? Bloods all on his face and shirt."

"I said to put him in the car." T.P. walked to the car, popped the trunk, and took a towel from the bag she'd packed. Winfred was too drunk and high to hold George up. He struggled to help George to the car. T.P. wrapped the towel around her hand. She wiped blood from the cut over George's eyes, then pressed the towel against the cut on his lip until the blood stopped. Missy and Joan stood watching from the doorway. Missy smoked and Joan leaned on the door frame and ate a drumstick.

"Damn, woman!" Winfred grabbed George under the arm and tried to balance both of their weight. George moaned but didn't try to walk on his own. Winfred dragged George to the car and yanked the passenger's door open. He dropped George onto the backseat careful not to let his head hit the car or the floor. He pushed the front seat back and slammed the door. T.P. pulled off barely allowing him to step out of her way. She was livid but determined that she was not about to allow his trifling behavior to cost her the opportunity to stand in a Bronner Brothers booth.

George's body carried the odor of the weed house. How dare you, George Grant. She could not believe that this would be the memory of their first weekend together: him leaving her in the car to get loaded with the city's top dealer and trying to get her to stay in the rat's den because he didn't have enough money. Not on my watch, son. I'll be damned if I do.

Her foot was heavier and heavier on the gas. She needed to gas up and get to a payphone quickly.

Nine miles up Interstate 10, she came to a beat-up Esso substation. With George asleep on the backseat, she pumped three dollars worth of gas into the tank and walked over to the payphone.

"Donald, this is T.P." Her voice was hot and angry. The noise from the busy highway made her shout.

"Hey, Sis. What's wrong?"

"Can you meet me at my house in about an hour? I need you to get your brother home so I can get back to the hair show."

If he responded, she could not tell because three eighteen-wheelers whirled into the station. Then the phone went dead. Not wanting to waste time nor another dime, she returned to the car and trusted that Rev. Grant had heard her clearly. Rev. Grant knew that they had left that morning for a hair show. Sadly, he wasn't surprised that there was some issue with George less than three hours before their leaving. He knew his brother and he knew sooner or later he would probably mess things up with T.P.

"I'll be there." He heard the dial tone.

He waited forty minutes then told Mable that he would be back shortly. He walked out of the church with no explanation. So much had happened over the last three years between the IRS constantly probing the church's files, members coming and going with good and bad intentions, and even Mary Jean not yet conceiving a child, Mable knew Rev. Grant was carrying more burdens on him than he would ever share with her.

When he arrived at T.P.'s house, she was just pulling up. After she parked, he walked over to the car and opened the driver's door. George was still sprawled on the backseat. Rev. Grant could see a gash over his left eye and his lip was busted and swollen. The blood-stained towel fell under his chin.

T.P. took her luggage out of the trunk of George's car and threw it on the passenger's side of hers. Moving quickly, she gave Rev. Grant the keys to George's car and detailed everything that happened in New Orleans. She suggested that he take George home and get him settled in bed because she had no time to heal another human. She was on her way back to Bonner Brothers.

"I'm sorry T.P. I know how much you were looking forward to the weekend. I'll handle everything here." He wasn't sure if he should hug his sister-in-law or just let her get back on the road. "Take this for gas and food." He pulled a few bills from his shirt pocket. At first, she resisted, then agreed when he reminded her that he is still family.

"Let us know when you arrive and where you will stay, okay?"

T.P. hadn't figured it all out. Now that George had failed to get the room, her only chance of somewhere to sleep was to call her cousin Stephanie who worked at Community Book Center and danced in Congo Square. She started her car and waited for the air conditioner to purr before backing up.

After moving his car off the lawn, Rev. Grant got into George's car and drove off. He decided to take George to his home and have Mary Jean check his head. George moaned and released the wrenched smell of marijuana, bourbon, and chicken grease.

Another Mugging

On most Tuesday nights Mrs. Agnes is in the front and center of T.E.A.M's fellowship hall, waiting on Deacon Miller to open Bible study with prayer. She's never late and always wore a hat, heels, and what she called a widow's scarf. Even though she wasn't sick, it was harder for her to drag herself out of her favorite recliner and head out. Fall had begun and the night seemed to creep up on her. Now, she was thirty minutes late and didn't want Deacon Miller or the other members to think she was too sick to make it.

She plopped her feet into her black pumps and headed to her purse which hung at the front door. Usually, she would leave out the side door and enter the carport near the driver's side but tonight it was easier to just leave out the front.

She clicked on the porch light before stepping out of the house. Straightening her skirt, she looked down the street hoping to see Billy Greenup in his yard. She looked around again, then, turned and locked the door. These are the most boring neighbors, my God. Where is everyone?

She rubbed her scarf and realized that she had not pinned on her mother's rhinestone brooch. To Mrs. Agnes, the brooch symbolized legacy and wealth. Neither of which she could rightfully claim. In a haste, she placed her keys and purse on the trunk of her Cadillac. She dug through the purse, unzipping three compartments with no luck. She shook the purse.

"Got-dog-it!" She slammed the purse down. Then, a hard object jammed into her back.

"Give me your purse!" The voice was deep and muffled.

"What?" Mrs. Agnes turned to face the assailant who anticipated her movement and quickly grabbed her neck and showed her his gun.

"You he…ard what I said bit…..ch!" His voice was shaky but his hand was steady. He pushed Mrs. Agnes by the neck and reached for the open purse. There was no way, Mrs. Agnes would ever let "one of these gangster fools" take her money. She fought back and a scuffle pursued. He hit her in the head with his fist holding the gun and she swung, trying to gouge his eyes. Then she heard a loud explosion before landing on the driveway.

Her new neighbor Sandra heard the sound of gunshots and ran out of her home to investigate. She ran down her steps and saw the silhouette of a man standing with the sun setting behind him. He stood at the edge of Mrs. Agnes's carport with her purse and a gun in his hand. He ran when he saw Sandra. She ran towards the house and found Mrs. Agnes lying on the ground on the driver's side of her car. Blood poured from a cut on her head and her body was shaking. Billy Greenup heard the shot and ran across the yard as quickly as he could.

"I called the cops. Is she okay?" He asked.

"No. She's shaking. Stay here." Sandra ran back to her house, rushed into the living room, and grabbed the quilt from the couch. Her daughter heard her running and ran into the room where her mother told her,

"Mrs. Agnes been hurt!" She ran back out and the teenager followed.

They covered Mrs. Agnes gently with the quilt. Billy Greenup knelled as close to her as he could, somehow cramming his lean body between the car and wall. "Hold on, Agnes. Sandra's here and some help is coming."

Mrs. Agnes didn't respond. Sandra, her daughter, and Billy Greenup watched the street, praying quietly.

Deputy Jones arrived just before the ambulance. He patiently listened as Sandra described the attacker to the best of her ability. Night had fallen and she became more fearful. She watched the paramedics lift Mrs. Agnes on the gurney and into the back of the van.

"Will she be okay, Mr. Greenup?" The teenager asked.

"I don't know, but it don't look good." He said

"Ain't that the truth." Sandra took her daughter's arm and walked back home. She thought about who she should call about the mugging. All she knew was that Mrs. Agnes was a widower with no other family in Basin. She knew that Mrs. Agnes was on her way to Bible study because she was always asking her to visit and Sandra declined every time. The only time Mrs. Agnes was gung-ho to talk to her or offer her anything was when she was trying to recruit her to church. That is what Sandra hated most about what she called "TCF" – Those Christian Folk. They were only nice when it had something to do with the church, but for the most part, they treated everyone like they didn't exist. She would tell her daughter, "TCFs only saw value in you when they thought they could get you to go to church, so they could earn another jewel on their crown and get a little praise from their fellow members for bringing in a lost soul!"

She huffed at the thought of having to call TCF and tell them that Mrs. Agnes had been hurt. She searched the desk to find one of the church bulletins that Mrs. Agnes kept giving her. Once she found it hanging out of the trash can, she dialed the church's number not fully expecting anyone to answer.

"Hello TEAM Church. How may I help you?"

"Good evening. My name is Sandra Brown. I live next door to a lady by the name of Mrs. Agnes. I do not know her last name, but I do know that she attends your church."

"I'm sorry, what is your name, again?"

"Sandra Brown, but the lady I am calling you about is Mrs. Agnes."

"Thank you, Ms. Brown. I believe I know whom you are speaking of."

"Well, She was just robbed and shot in her carport. I didn't know of any family members to call so I decided to call your church just in case you know her family and can make them aware that she has been taken to Charity Hospital in New Orleans."

"Oh, my Lord! Father! You said Mrs. Agnes, right?"

"Yes ma'am"

"Okay, dear. Thank you so much for calling. Bless your heart, dear. I will let Pastor know of this most awful tragedy right this instant. Thank you for calling us. "

Mother Margaret Holloway ran to the door of the fellowship hall, startling the members who were midway through the night's lesson.

"Excuse me, Deacon. Sis. Grant, excuse me, I must speak with you, please." She waved her arm a bit to hurry Mary Jean who quickly got up. Shelia grabbed their purses and Bibles and followed with the boys trailing behind. One of them knocked over a chair but kept walking, eager to hear the news.

Standing in the hallway just beyond the members' hearing, Mother Holloway told Mary Jean about the call. "Go on to the hospital. We'll head on to your house and I'll tell Donald," Shelia said, knowing they needed to be at the hospital for their members.

As Mary Jean drove towards the hospital, she prayed. "You know, God, Mrs. Agnes is a hard person to care for, but I'm sure you know that, Lord. But, Father, she doesn't deserve to be shot or killed. Lord I'm asking you to save Mrs. Agnes. Give her a chance to have a change of heart and to become the Christian you have called her to be if this is Thy will. Thank you, Lord."

Mary Jean felt an eerie sense of fear when she stepped through the doors of the hospital. She was overwhelmed with memories of staying by Lawrence's bedside while he fought to live. She saw his bandages and bruises as clearly as if they were right at that moment. Instantly, tears welled. She quickly wiped her eyes and asked the receptionist for information on Mrs. Agnes. After waiting for an hour, Mary Jean was told Mrs. Agnes was still in the operating room and someone would come out with an update as soon as possible.

Rev. Grant had his hands full trying to manage George's erratic behavior. He wasn't sure if the bump on his brother's head was causing more damage than they knew or if he had relapsed into alcoholism. He was glad he was able to monitor George but the timing couldn't have been any worse. When Shelia and the boys pulled up, Rev. Grant knew more trouble had arrived. Shelia explained everything and Rev. Grant told her George was in the guest room finally asleep. She said she would stay in the boys' room and answer any questions they may have. He hugged her and headed to the hospital.

He was nervous and heavy-hearted. He drove quickly, swerving lanes and flashing lights at vehicles moving too slow. He thought about returning to the hospital where Rona and Ronald died in the car wreck. He pleaded with God for strength and healing. Even though she has done so many things to try to destroy me, my ministry, and my family, Lord, please without death and give her a chance to change. He prayed, then walked straightway to Mary Jean in the hospital's waiting room.

It was six hours before the operation was complete. The doctor told Mary Jean and Rev. Grant that Mrs. Agnes was in critical condition and there was a possibility that she would not fully recover from the head trauma. Rev. Grant wrapped his arms around Mary Jean as she cried. "Let's try to have some faith, Baby. Let's try." He consoled her and whispered another prayer.

Mary Jean and Rev. Grant were able to go to see Mrs. Agnes at five the next morning, both of them were terribly exhausted from trying to get comfortable in the hard seats inside the waiting room. The nurse in ICU told them that Mrs. Agnes was still in critical condition; however, the worst was over and if she stayed stable for the next four or five hours, the doctor thought she just might make it. She told them that there was nothing else they could do for her, so they might as well go home and come back later in the evening. She then gave them the number to the ICU nurses' station so they could call to check on her condition. Rev. Grant and Mary Jean were too tired not to take this offer.

Investigation into Mrs. Agnes Mugging

Sheriff Roger Golespy walked into the station just as Deputy Jones was unhandcuffing Oscar Smith. He'd been detained for committing an assault with a firearm.

"As soon as you finish there, come see me in my office." He told Jones.

"Sure, chief," he answered as he placed Oscar in the jail cell before pulling out the station charge book then he began the write up the charges. He placed a call, then walked into Golespy's office.

"Was that Maude Smith's son Oscar?"

"Yeah, that was him. I know Maude works for your family, so I called her."

"My wife would be upset if I didn't call her and tell her about Maude's son.

"So what crime did he commit?"

"Aggravated assault with a firearm."

"What happened this time?"

Deputy Jones crossed his legs and relayed the story told to him. "Old man Peanut said that Oscar and Louis Gross were gambling in the alley on Elm Street, and Louis won all of Oscar's money. Oscar wanted to borrow a few dollars, so he could try to win some of his money back—now we both know only someone high on drugs would think that! When Louis told him 'no.' Old man Peanut said Oscar pulled out his gun and hit Louis across the side of his head. Then, he shot him in the shoulder. Louis Gross is over at Charity Hospital and I brought Oscar here to book and charge him."

Sherrif Golespy didn't respond, instead, he looked at his watch and calculated the amount of time it would take for him to end this conversation, pack up, and make it to Plank Road to arrest another streetworker.

"It seems like every since he became our informant, he thinks that gives him the freedom to run ramped." He pulled his chair closer to the sheriff's desk.

"You know I'm getting sick of that nigger's shit!" He was so agitated the vein above his left eye pulsed. Deputy Jones could see the blue-green street trailing toward his skull.

"I'll talk with him tomorrow morning before anyone else comes in and let him know that the information he gives us is not enough to keep his Black ass out of jail all the time." With a flat hand, he hit the desk and shouted, "One day, he's going to piss me off and I'm going to let his ass rot in jail and no judge in the state will be able to get him out!"

He leaned back in his chair, lit a cigar, and blew smoke toward the ceiling. Deputy Jones didn't like the smell of smoke and he didn't like Sheriff Golespy, but he knew his assignment in Basin, Louisiana was far greater than a cockeyed, narcissist like Roderick Golespy. Sometimes he would feign a laugh when the sheriff talked about Black people. As quiet as it was kept, Deputy Jones was an Opelousas-born, Creole man who had been passing for white ever since the death of his parents. It gave him pleasure just knowing the sheriff would die during his dinner invitations if he knew he was Black. He sat at the desk intentionally listening for cues.

"Listen, Jones. I called you in here to join me on the Agnes Rosenthal case. I've known Agnes for years and I knew her husband before he passed. He was a good man, so I think I had better lead this case. I'll check the crime scene and question people who know her. She's not able to talk right now since she's recovering from that long-ass surgery.

But, I'm going to question the lady who lives next door and a few of them church friends of hers. Get your pad and be ready in twenty minutes. Let me call Jane before Maude comes storming in here behind that boy!"

"Sure. I'll be outside in twenty." Deputy Jones walked out of the office and the desk phone rang.

"Basin Police Station Sheriff Golespy speaking."

"Sheriff this is Maude Smith. Where's my boy?"

"Maude. I'm on a case. Call back later."

"No, sir, Mr. Roderick. Just tell me what he's charged with so I can come to bail him out," Maude Smith was furious.

"We got him on double assault and assault with a firearm. He hit the guy with the gun and then shot him. You might wanna sit tight. Your boy is going to be with me for a while."

"Oh my, God. Is he hurt?" She wailed.

"Nah, he's laid up in cell block five. Judge Clark will see him in the morning. You know the routine, Maude. So settle yourself down and call tomorrow for the bond."

"Okay, Mr. Roderick."

"It's Sheriff Golespy, Maude, not Mr. Roderick."

"Good. Day. Mr. Roderick." She hung up the phone.

"That's where that boy gets his ways. Both of them are stubborn mules." The sheriff said.

Sheriff Golespy grabbed his car keys and walked out into the booking room. His feet shuffled across the wooden floor and the rubber bottom shoes squeaked under his massive weight.

Deputy Albert Williamson ignored the sheriff's presence.

"Williamson!" He barked.

"I'm taking Jones out for the Rosenthal case. Grab lunch for those boys before they start banging bars and fighting. I ain't call no meds behind them savages this week. Get 'em feed before all of that, hear me?" He didn't wait for a response and Williamson didn't acknowledge his demand. The sheriff quickly walked out of the police station's front door and met Deputy Jones.

Their first stop was Mrs. Agnes's next-door neighbor.

Deputy Jones knocked on the door and briefed the sheriff. "This is the residence of Sandra Brown. She's lived here for some years. Her daughter and husband live with her but he has been away on military duty since they arrived in Basin."

"Was she friends with Agnes?" Sheriff Golespy asked just as the door opened. Her beauty struck him. He had expected Sandra to be overweight and miserable. Her hair was pulled from her face, tucked under a light blue headscarf that rested on her left shoulder. She wore an apron that had globs of flour speckled across the front. To him, she smelled like butter and salt.

"Good morning, ma'am. I'm Sheriff Golespy and this here is Deputy Jones." He extended his hand.

"I know who you are. What can I do for you?" She asked without touching his hand. *I don't like Crackers.* She looked at the deputy, then over his shoulder to the squad car.

Sheriff Golespy took the liberty to move on to the first step. The way she looked at his feet showed him that he was not welcomed any farther.

"We're here to question you about the mugging of your neighbor Mrs. Agnes Rosenthal."

"I told that other deputy—Mr. Williamson—everything I know, so what new questions do you have for me?" She stepped out of the threshold, closed the door behind her, and thereby closing any chance for the men to enter her home.

"It's here," Deputy Jones said. He thumbed through a folder then reached a page to the sheriff. Sheriff Golespy skimmed it before speaking.

"So you heard a shot and then you ran outside to see where it was coming from, is that correct, Miss. Brown?" He asked looking undereye at her.

"It's Mrs!"

"Is that correct, ma'am?"

"I don't remember my exact words but I did hear a shot that sounded so close to my door, so I went to see if someone was shooting outside my door." She said

"That was very brave of you, Mrs. Brown. You are a very brave woman to go outside and look and not call the police first."

She didn't like his sarcasm."Do you see where I live?" Sandra waved her hand back and forth. "You cannot live in this city, in Louisiana, in America, if you are afraid. This is not like the world you live in, Sheriff. It's a good thing that I'm not a person who frightens easily because if I did Mrs. Agnes would still be lying on the ground and dead. So what else can I help you boys with? I'm cooking dumplings and I need to stir my pot."

"One more question, when you went outside did you see anyone running from the scene of the crime?"

"No. I did not see anyone except Mrs. Agnes on the ground. When Mr. Greenup ran from across the street, I ran back here and got a quilt from my couch to put over her. She was shaking like a leaf. My daughter called the police and it took way too long for any of you all to come to help us. After it was all over, I came in and call her church."

"Why did you call her church?" The sheriff asked.

"I'm going to answer this question and then I'm going inside," she said. She wanted to point her finger for emphasis but decided to show more respect although it had not been earned. "Mrs. Agnes usually goes to church on Tuesday nights, so, I knew she was on her way to church and I figured that someone in that big congregation must care about her and would want to know why she hadn't showed up. So, gentlemen, that's why I called her church and that's all I can tell you. Good evening." She turned around, quickly opening her front door and leaving the sheriff and deputy standing on the steps.

"That's a smart ass there. I bet her old man has to whip her ass a lot to keep her in line." Sheriff Golespy said. Deputy Jones knew better than to respond.

"Let's knock on a few more of these houses. See if anyone was looking outside and may have seen what happened. You knock on the doors to the right and I'll go left. Only about five houses would have had a clear view. Then we'll cross the street," The sheriff ordered.

Deputy Jones knew they were wasting time. No one in this neighborhood was going to talk to them and he was certain they wouldn't talk to the Sheriff. They found him intolerable and knew he would lock up their children for the smallest discretions then make them pay a hefty bail or other outrageous fines.

Deputy Jones knocked on the doors of four homes with no answer. At the fifth house, an elderly man opened the door.

"Good morning, sir. I'm Deputy Marcus Jones and I'm investigating the mugging of your neighbor, Agnes Rosenthal. I was wondering if you saw anything or heard anything that could help us find the mugger."

"Yeah. I heard that Agnes had almost been killed and her purse stolen. I was sorry to hear that. This used to be a nice neighborhood until those youngsters started using those drugs that done completely messed up their brains. There's one boy that's always walking up and down these streets and he doesn't live in this neighborhood. Now let me see, what's his name?" He thought for a moment and Deputy Jones looked over his shoulder and scanned the contents of the small brick home. "Hold on a minute. Sadie! Sadie!" He turned and called out to his wife.

"What you want, Norman?" The lady shouted.

"What's the boy's name that I told you I see on our street all the time and he doesn't live around here?"

"I think that's Sister Louise Horne's grandson. I believe they call him Pretty Boy. You know him. That's supposed to be Golespy's son," She said as she walked into the room. She noticed Deputy Jones standing at the door and realized she may have spoken too soon.

Deputy Jones smiled. He could do a lot with that little bit of information. The sheriff was always putting down Blacks but not so much that he didn't mind sleeping and having a child with one.

"So tell me, sir, where can I find this Pretty Boy?" He asked.

"We don't know where he lives, but we think he might live with his grandmother who tried to raise him. That boy got so much hate in him!" Norman shook his head.

"You would too, Baby. If you knew your daddy won't acknowledge you and he has money but you're living in a swallow." Sadie stepped into the door with her husband. She was nearly half his height and weight. Their arms moved similarly when they talked and mid-sentence she caught his hand. "His grandmother lives on Oak Lane. It's an ugly brown house you can't miss it."

"Thank you, Mister and Mrs…"

"I'm Norman Wallace and this is my wife Sadie Wallace." He hugged his wife.

"Well, thank you, Mr. and Mrs. Wallace. Do you mind if I come back and talk to you again if I need to?"

"No problem, young Brother. We'll be glad to help because it could have been one of us."

Deputy Jones walked from their house writing the new information into his pad. He omitted the part about the wondering boy being the sheriff's son, but he couldn't wait to see the expression on Golespy's face when he told him that the possible mugger was named "Pretty Boy." Deputy Jones also made a mental note that the old man had deliberately called him "young brother". He made it across the street just as the sheriff returned from the last house where he questioned an elderly lady.

"So what did you find out?" The deputy asked quickly.

"That was Janie Mae Brewer. She said she sometimes sees a strange young man walking the street at night, but she has cataracts and can't make him out good. Ole bitty wasn't much help." He checked his pocket for a pen and scribbled her name and comments in his pad after noticing Deputy Jones had taken notes while he talked. "What you got? I saw you talking to the couple at the grey stone house."

Deputy Jones opened the patrol car door and got inside. The sheriff scanned the houses down the block and looked back at Mrs. Brown's home. He sat in the driver's seat and caught himself wondering how long her husband would be deployed. Deputy Jones interrupted his thoughts. "Let's go, sir. I am starving!"

Sheriff Golespy jerked on the keys and started the ignition, then sped away.

When they pulled into Jimmy Joe's Diner, the parking lot was packed as it normally is. The place wasn't much to look at, something Jimmy could have made more appealing on the outside if he would invest in a few gallons of paint, but he was too busy making money inside to worry about how the outside looked. The diner was a house built in the early 1800s where his family lived for generations starting as freed Black men who worked nearby sugar cane fields. For as long as residents could remember, Jimmy's family operated some kind of business there. For the last two decades, it was a popular diner by day and juke joint by night that paid for the needs of his ten children. When his wife, Mel, passed, he and his Freemason Brothers added two rooms to the back of the house for the kids. As they grew up, they moved away for a better life. All except for Joe, the youngest, who picked up where his dad left off. He made the entire house into a diner with help from Black Aunt May, the family cook who still works in the restaurant serving up spectacular mouth-watering meals.

Deputy Jones notice the restaurant had white paint that had turned brown over the years from dust, hurricanes, and various other elements. He liked the rectangular shape of the house and the newer windows that paneled from corner to corner on the east side.

He and Sheriff Golespy took their seats at the counter. Looking around the crowded diner, Deputy Jones scanned each table for familiar faces. He recognized Mable and Professor Toldson who both seemed enamored with each other. He smiled at them and at any other diner who made eye contact.

"Damn, we're not going to be able to talk at this counter." The sheriff complained, but Deputy Jones was especially glad that the Joint was busy. He didn't want to talk to the sheriff nor hear him rattling on about random complaints.

"Looks like that couple is finishing up. We can move to their spot." Deputy Jones nodded towards Mable's table. Johnnie Lou slapped a menu on the counter between the two men.

"What will it be, gentlemen?" Her smile was broad and toothless.

"My usual, Johnnie Lou," The sheriff said.

"What about you, deputy?" She sucked her gums and winked.

"I'll have my usual also, Johnnie Lou."

"Hey, Black! Fire up two medium-rare burgers, one dressed fully without tomatoes, side of onion rings and the other mustard, tomatoes, pickles only with fries!" She shouted. As she walked away, she collected empty glasses and plates. She scooped vanilla ice cream into a frozen glass and whisked ice milk and cinnamon into a creamy float. She walked back to the officers.

"Here you go, gents." She said as she slapped two napkins on the counter and placed the floats on them.

"These are the best floats in town." The sheriff boasted.

"They are the only floats in town." Deputy Jones laughed and chugged down half of the float.

"Look. I'm going to have to go over to Maude Smith's house and let her know that we can't keep letting Oscar's ass get off. People are beginning to talk." The sheriff's eyes shifted quickly toward the door which hit a cow's bell every time it opened.

Johnnie Lou placed their meals in front of them. "Can I get you two handsome gents anything else?" She asked.

"No, we're good." They both said in unison.

Sheriff Golespy bit sloppily into his burger while Deputy Jones whispered a prayer of thanks.

Each time the men tried to talk, the crowd got louder and louder. They ate quickly and quietly. Always gruff, the Sheriff peeled seven dollars from his wallet and paid for lunch. Deputy Jones added a tip for Johnnie Lou on the counter. Outside, Deputy Jones noticed Rev. Mical pulling onto the far side of the parking lot where grass led out to the woods. He saw two college students wearing baseball caps in the car. Rev. Mical quickly turned his head pretending to adjust his parking. As usual, the sheriff was the unspoken designated driver. "Let's head over to Agnes' pastor's house." Deputy Jones considered asking why they wouldn't just go to the church which was nearby but he stayed silent to see what was the sheriff's thought process.

As they rode toward the Grant residence, the sheriff questioned Deputy Jones about the couple he talked with down the street from the crime scene. He likes to use the phrase "crime scene" even if a kid stole a piece of gum. That was another flaw Deputy Jones found in the sheriff. He took out his notes although he knew every word in it. The gesture was something the sheriff demanded. He argued constantly that no one can remember everything that a person tells them unless they write it down.

Deputy Jones looked down at the pad. "The neighbor was Norman Wallace. He called over his wife Sadie. They both know Mrs. Agnes as a neighbor and they had heard about the mugging although they did not see anything that night. Norman said there's a guy who frequents the neighborhood. Looks to be in his early twenties. Slim. Matted and curly dusty brown hair. He doesn't live in their neighborhood, but tends to walk the blocks a few times a week."

"Is that right? Did they know his name?" The sheriff asked.

The Deputy looked up from his notes and into the sheriff's face before answering.

"People call him Pretty Boy." Deputy Jones said slowly. Sheriff Golespy's eyebrow lifted and his bottom lip tightened.

"The Wallaces said this Pretty Boy is the grandson of Louise Horne who lives on Oak Lane."

He watched the sheriff shift his body. His fingers clenched the steering wheel. "Shit! Shit!"

"What? Who is he?" The deputy asked.

"Shit! I know Louise Horne, and that damn boy has been nothing but trouble for her since the day he was born. His mammy's an alcoholic and that old lady has tried all she knows how to raise that little nigger but his ass stays in trouble! He better not be mugging people now." The sheriff drove up to the Grant residence.

"I wonder why he's roaming the neighborhood all of a sudden. Most times when young men stay in trouble it's because something is going on in their lives that they cannot control," Deputy Jones said.

"Be a detective, Jones, not a damn shrink!" The sheriff pushed his car door open. He practically stumped with each step up the driveway to the front door.

When the doorbell rang Mary Jean wondered who could be dropping by unannounced, especially at a time when she was alone. She hoped it wasn't one of these new encyclopedia or life insurance salesmen roaming door to door. She closed the notebook she was writing in, then turned down the fire on the stove. The smell of kidney beans, herbs, and pork filled the house and seeped out the door.

She pulled back the curtain covering the small window near the top of the door.

"Yes. May I help you." She shouted.

"It's Sheriff Roderick Golespy and Deputy Marcus Jones. We would like to speak with you about the mugging of a Mrs. Agnes Rosenthal?"

"Wait right there." Mary Jean said. She went to the telephone and called the Sheriff's Department.

"Hi. This is Mrs. Mary Jean Grant and I have two gentlemen at my door who say they are a Sheriff Golespy and a Mr. Jones. Do you have anyone by those names working at your office?"

Deputy Williamson chuckled before answering, "Yes, Madam. Sheriff Golespy and Deputy Jones both work here. Is there a problem?"

"No, that will be all. Have a nice day and thanks for the information," Mary Jean said before thanking him for answering her call. She knew about the sheriff's reputation but had never seen the Sheriff face to face.

Golespy looked at Deputy Jones. "Where the hell is she? You think she forgot we're out here?" He pressed the doorbell again. She slowly walked to the front door, hoping the two officers had left. She needed to take care of other things and they had already cut in on some of her time.

"No, she didn't forget." Deputy Jones scanned the porch. "She's checking out our credentials. She's a well-known minister's wife and I'm sure she won't just invite people into her house that she doesn't know. Just be cool. She'll be back." Deputy Jones said just as the door opened and Mary Jean ushered them inside.

"Have a seat," Mary Jean waved toward the sofa, Then she sat in a chair across from them. "There's not much that I can tell you because I wasn't there when it happened. I was called at the church and told about what had transpired," Mary Jean said as she sat back in the chair. She knew all of this was just a front and that there was not going to be much done about it because law enforcement in this town was strictly for the white. They usually just put on a good show for Blacks, but that's all it was just a show.

"We would appreciate it if you would tell us what you know. Are you related to Mrs. Rosenthal?"

"No, I'm not related to her. I use to live near her and we do talk occasionally because she is a member of TEAM Church."

"You mean that she is a member of you and your husband's church?"

"The church is not ours. It's God's church, not my husband's, and not my church. We are the instruments that manage it and take care of the people in God's name, but we do not own the church it is an entity of its own."

Gotdamn, I hate talking to damn uppity, religious asses. They always have a sermon or break out moaning and singing. Don't they know everybody ain't Christians?

He took a deep breath. "So would you say that Mrs. Rosenthal is a friend of you and your spouse?"

"No, she's a member of the church," Mary Jean said pointedly.

'So, on the night that she was robbed and mugged do you know where she was going? He asked.

"I'm not certain, but maybe she was on her way to the church. She didn't usually miss any of our services."

"Do you know if she has anyone that she may owe money to?"

Mary Jean frowned and looked at Deputy Jones she could tell by the look on his face that he didn't like this line of questioning. He had seen him question Black people many times in the same manner.

"If that's all I'd like to get on with my day," Mary Jean said as she rose and began walking toward the door. with the two of them on her heel.

When they got in the car and the Sheriff drove off, he seemed deep in thought.

"I'm going to drop you off at the precinct and then I'm going to make a run. You see if Oscar has sobered up any so we can get his ass off our docket and out of our way."

They were quiet for the rest of the drive.

Investigation Continues

When Deputy Jones walked into the station, Oscar had sobered up and was raising hell in his cell. Ranting and cursing, Oscar demanded to be released as he normally did. He reminded Deputy Jones of his young nephew's best friends.

"Quiet down!" He yelled. "You know the procedures since you spend a great deal of your time here." He walked to the cell and looked Oscar squarely in the face—a move none of the white officers would dare do. "You also know that what you did to that Gross boy was no misdemeanor. You tried to kill him. So sit on down and make yourself comfortable. You are going to have to enjoy my company for a while even after you see the judge." Deputy Jones had a demeanor that Oscar had never seen from a white man. Even though the deputy reminded him of the pastor with the young wife and twins, Oscar couldn't quite place where Jones was from or who his family was.

One thing for sure, he wasn't going to allow a new deputy to test him. "Yeah, sure, says who? You? We will see about that! You just wait until my mom gets here and Golespy! I'll be out of here in a matter of hours!" Oscar shuttered. He kicked the cell bars, "This place is a pig's sty!"

"It's funny, how you always checking in. I thought you loved the place because we see you at least once a week."

"N.......ow, N........ow......., that's a lie. I only come here about once a month." Oscar said right before vomiting across the cell floor.

"Hey, Williams! Bring our special guest the mop and bucket. Looks like he's got some cleaning to do."

He grabbed a roll of tissue from the storage cabinet and threw it into the cell. "Clean it up because I'll be damned if any of us are going to do it." Deputy Williamson wheeled the mop buck and mop over to the cell. PineSol and water splashed as he pushed the bucket over the threshold and into the cell.

Deputy Williamson laughed.

"Excuse me!" The precinct door slammed. "Where is Mr. Roderick?" Maude Smith's voice was raspy and too deep for a woman with such a small frame. "I came to get Oscar." She reached inside her purse for money to pay the bond.

"I heard about that ole bitty Agnes Rosenthal getting mugged and ya'll better not try and put that on my boy. He ain't that kinda child."

"Mrs. Smith, Sheriff Golespy is out and I don't expect him back until later tonight," Deputy Williamson answered. "And even if he came back now, Oscar wouldn't be released to you. This time, your son has committed a felony and he's not a child. He will have to see Judge Clark tomorrow morning. Bail will be set then."

Deputy Williamson walked Maude between the metal desks and chairs toward the door. "We'll call and let you know how much it will cost and when you can pick him up. Your son's in a lot of trouble now." He knew there would be no bond for attempted murder but he would let Sheriff Golespy tell her.

"Okay, I'll come back tomorrow. Oscar, baby, momma will be back tomorrow to get you, okay?" She turned and waved to him as if he were being dropped off at first grade.

Oscar grumbled. He'd vomited again while cleaning the floor. Now he sat woozy on the bed with a pounding headache.

Deputy Jones pulled back the metal chair leaning against his desk. It released a horrible scratch across the concrete floor causing Oscar to squeal. "Come on, man!"

He ignored Oscar's plea, then dragged his chair under the desk and began typing the day's reports. He added extra punch against the typewriter's keys just to hear Oscar moan.

Meanwhile, Sheriff Golespy drove to Oak Lane to see Louise Horne. Over the last twenty years, she has kept the house immaculate in contrast to the blight neighboring her. Flowers grew on each side of the walkway and bushes were trimmed perfectly by her gardener's hand. The beige and brown paint was still fresh in the hot air. It was not colors he would have chosen for the small rental house, but he had to admit Louise Horne made everything look good. If only she could fix that gal of hers and this boy. He opened the gate which screeched in need of oil, and he made a mental note to tell her to have her grandson oil the joints to keep the gate from rusting. He stepped over stones that Louise laid in the yard in the shape of the letter H.

When she first became a tenant of his, he felt guilty to charge her market rate but Black folk in Basin were already talking about their connection. He had to charge something. So, he collected pennies on the dollar every other year while he carried the property taxes. He'd vowed that no matter what happened to Louise or her Pretty Boy, he would never let his guilt blackmail him out of owning the property. He'd convinced himself that this is the best life for them, especially for a son he could never and would never acknowledge.

He walked to the door and knocked then waited. He waited for a couple of minutes and no one answered, so he knocked again, and then after a few more minutes he knocked a third time.

Knowing that Louise seldom left the house, Sheriff Golespy walked around to the back of the house. In the middle of the backyard, Louise had started a fall garden and was kneeling between the rows of vegetables.

"Louise!" He called out loud enough for her to hear but not to startle her.

She stood slowly, turned around, and dusted her hands on her overalls. Then, she picked up the bucket full of string beans.

"Hey, Roderick. What brings you here and it's not rent day?" She was always kind to him.

She reached the bucket to him and he carried it onto the back porch.

"I need to talk to you about James Horne. Where is he?" The sheriff asked and sat the bucket on the table.

Louise sighed. She knew if he was looking for Pretty Boy then he was in trouble.

"I don't know. He was here when I went outside but I don't know if he's still here. Let me go look in his room." She dragged her tired body towards the side of the house into another back entrance. The same entrance the sheriff had used for countless nights to wrap himself in her daughter's arms and have the most passionate sex he had ever known.

When Louise returned, Pretty Boy was walking behind her until he saw the sheriff. He quickly turned back towards his room, but he couldn't match Louise's reflexes. She quickly grabbed his shirt and pulled him toward the sheriff. Her strength shocked them both.

"Sit at the table, boy, the Sheriff has something he wants to talk to you about." The three of them sat at the wooden work table. Louise began breaking the tips off the string beans.

"Agnes Rosenthal was mugged the other night and some of her neighbors recalled seeing you roaming through the neighborhood several nights."

"Not me." He stared into his father's eyes, hating the feeling of looking at an older reflection.

"Where were you Wednesday night between seven and nine?"

"I was here, then my boy, Mickey, picked me up and we went out to find some white ass,!"

"Watch your mouth, James!"

"Louise, was he here at the time he just said?"

"Yeah. I saw him leave at about nine-thirty or closer to ten. I went to bed as soon as he left." She looked at her grandson, then the father that he so strongly resembles. Visibly frustrated, Louise cut off the tips and then snapped the string beans and threw them into a metal colander.

Sheriff Golespy watched her hands on the beans. To his surprise, his memory manifested the smell of her string beans blended with onion and garlic in her unique way. He desperately wanted to ask her to cook a pot for him to take back to the jail.

"Ok, James this friend of yours, Mickey Mouse, can he collaborate your story?" He asked hoping he had struck a nerve in return.

"I never said his name was Mickey Mouse." James hated looking at an older version of himself only paler, so he focused on the space between the sheriff's eyes when they talked. "His name is Mickey Gross, and yes you can ask him. He'll tell you we were together chasing ass." He crossed his arms.

Louise pointed her knife at James. "I'm going to tell you one more time, James. Mind your mouth and show some respect. The next time you curse in my presence, I'm going to slap you with this knife and I don't care if the Sheriff carries me to jail! Do you hear me?" She waved the knife left then right with each statement.

"Sorry, Mema. He's always coming here and talking to me like I'm not his son and he never brings a dime with him. Then he goes back on the other side of the tracks to his lily-white family and forgets my Black ass exists!"

Before he knew it, Louise slapped his lips with the flat side of the knife.

"Mema!" He jumped from the table "You almost cut me!"

"I told you to respect ME! I'm the one who has taken care of you all your life and I'm still doing it, so YOU will respect me!" While she yelled, he walked out of the kitchen and out the back door.

The sheriff watched quietly. This is some awful shit. "Louise, do you know where this Gross kid lives or who his people are?" He asked.

"Yeah. That's Gretchen Gross's boy. Do you remember Gretchen? Old man Luther Gross's daughter." She said.

"Yeah, I remember him. Didn't he die last year?" The sheriff asked.

"That's right. Gretchen lives on Lafayette Street. I don't know the house address but someone on that block will tell you where her house is."

Silence grew and stiffen between them.

"Louise, would you like to cook for the department—my men and the detainees? I'll pay you. I'm so sick of eating Patty's food. It's so bland. We can pay you a hundred dollars a week and whatever you charge for your vegetables. I'll have Williamson bring whatever other groceries you tell me."

Louise didn't look up from her work of chopping the beans

"What you say?" He asked

"Only those white chefs can cook and Patty is not a chef." She laughed.

"Well? What do you say?"

She looked at the way he lifted his eyebrow when he begged, just like James does when he tries to convince her to make pecan candy. "Okay. I'll accept your job offer, but you will purchase what I'll call and tell you and you will pay me my hundred dollars a week , pay for my produce, and you will pick up the food every day, and the days I can't cook the food I'll let you know. OK?" She said."

"Well, when do you want to start?"

"I'll start next week. We'll talk before then and I'll let you know what I need." Louise said.

The sheriff rose from the table and headed towards the back door. "Louise, keep an eye on James for me. The neighbors believe it was him who mugged Agnes."

He said as he walked out the back door. Not long after, Louise heard the gate open for him to leave. James had returned into the house through the front door and from his living room window, James watched his father leave again without saying goodbye or leaving a dime for him.

A Visit to Heaven

When Mrs. Agnes woke up, she felt dizzy. Her skin was clammy and gray. Her eyes darted around the bright room. She could hear strange voices talking around her. Then, she felt lightheaded and closed her eyes again, slowly. She felt the sensation of being lifted. Her body was levitating into a standing position. She floated near two bright lights that hung from the ceiling. From the ceiling, she could see the entire room. When she looked down, she saw her body lying on a table. A doctor and four nurses operated passionately on Mrs. Agnes as they tried desperately to remove the bullet from her head.

The doctor yelled, "I think we're losing her!" She heard a long loud beep, and as she looked in the direction that they were all looking, she saw a red line moving across a small television screen. Suddenly, she was floating higher, slowly moving into a black hole and toward a dim light.

As she drifted, the light before her grew larger and more beautiful. It was a full kaleidoscope sparkling and flickering a million colors at different times. She knew the light was special. It reminded her of the first diamond she had received from her husband. He had worked for three years and saved his "pocket money" to buy her the largest diamond ring he could find. When she wore the ring and deliberately held her hand at a certain angle, the stone reflected a full rainbow of colors. She loved looking at the ring in the sun and no matter where she was, she would hold her hand up to the sun so she could see the colors reflect.

As she moved farther into the black hole, she was into it and out of the other side. She saw people who were once a part of her life: her husband Morris, her mother, father, brother, uncle, and aunts. Everyone she had once loved was there. Suddenly, she felt an enormous weight lift from her body. She floated higher, lighter, and started to smile. She felt like she was flying in love.

"Agnes! Agnes!" She knew the voice but could not speak.

She grew fearful, then happy. Scenes of her life flashed in front of her. She recalled her wedding, she recalled baptism, she recalled the kids at school that she had hurt, she recalled having sex with her brother-in-law, and many other things, but mostly she recalled how she treated Mary Jean and T.P. She remembered them all. She wanted to cry; she could not believe that it was her that she was seeing.

"Agnes. Why can't you love?" The voice asked.

"I do love." She struggled to speak, ashamed and afraid.

"Agnes, you have hurt and destroyed a lot of lives." The voice spoke gently. "Why is it that you cannot love?"

"I miss my husband, Lord. He was all I had and after he died, I just did not care about anyone else. Besides, no one ever cared about me. From the day I was born until my husband came into my life, I didn't have a single soul who really loved me." Tears streamed down her cheeks. "My parents loved my sister more than me!"

"That is not true, Agnes. I have loved you before you were born. I have always been with you. Do you remember the day when you were born with an enlarged heart and the doctors said you would not survive? On that day, I said to you that you would have life abundantly, and that I would always be with you."

Mrs. Agnes remembered that day as if it had happened yesterday. The handsome man standing beside her bed holding her hand told her that exact thing. She nodded to acknowledge that she remembered.

"And don't you remember when you were five with a high fever? I sat beside your bed all the while you were sick. I held your hand and once again I told you not to be afraid that I would be with you always."

Mrs. Agnes remembered.

"Can you recall when you were fifteen years old? I helped you to escape the evil one who tried to devour you." Mrs. Agnes recalled the fear she had the day an old janitor tried to attack her. She knew he was going to kill her, but she broke free and ran.

She saw a man across the street looking at her as she ran, and she remembered that he did not say anything to her. She felt like she knew him. Without words, he told her where to hide and when it was clear for her to come out of hiding. As Mrs. Agnes recalled the moment, she nodded her head more in a bowing motion than affirmative.

"Agnes, when you miscarried, I was there with you in the hospital and I held your hand. I helped you to get through the loss of your child, who is here happy with Me even now. Did you see her?"

Mrs. Agnes looked and saw her child. She closed her eyes and cried.

"Lord, why didn't you let me have another child? All these years and I never had another baby. Why?"

"Your body wasn't strong enough to carry a child, Agnes. Your parents did not take care of their bodies and so when they produced you, they passed diseased genes to your body." The voice paused. "I sent children directly to you for you to care for and to love. I sent your nephew whom you abused. I can name many many more. Even today, you have the two best friends and sisters I've sent to you. Have you cared for them? Have you loved them?" Mrs. Agnes knew He was talking about Mary Jean and T.P. She felt awful knowing how she mistreats them. "My child, it has been I who have always been there for you and who have surrounded you with love despite yourself. You have not been alone during any moment of your life. I have always been here, and I will be with you even at the end."

Mrs. Agnes looked up. "What? Is this the end?"

"No, Agnes. There is work that you must correct on Earth. Your time is not now. I have much for you to do."

"But, I," She tried to hold in her cries. "Lord, I don't want to go back. Let me stay here with You."

"Sorry, My child. You must go back. You have tried to destroy lives. You've dishonored the name of My people and you have tried to condemn My sheep. You have time to correct yourself, then return to Me."

Immediately, a heaviness pulled down her body. Sadness flooded her. Mrs. Agnes wanted so badly to stay with God, with her family and friends. Without any control or thought, she slowly floated downward and returned to her physical body.

When the weight of her spirit form moved into her physical form, Mrs. Agnes wailed and cried. The nurse was shocked. She thought that Mrs. Agnes was so sedated that she did not have any pain yet.

"It's okay! It's okay!" One of the nurses rubbed her shoulder. She turned her head and searched the room for the hole. She looked for the kaleidoscope. She cried out for God. "Calm down, Mrs. Rosenthal. Please. Please calm down. We are here with you. You're going to be all right."

After a while of sobbing, Mrs. Agnes finally settled to the nurse's comforting voice.

The doctor quickly responded, "I will go speak to her friends in the waiting room. That was a close call."

Mrs. Agnes tried to sit up and pain struck through her head. She knew that she was back fully in her fragile body. She grabbed Donna's hand and squeezed it. Her eyes pleaded for relief. "I'm going to help you," Donna said and peeled Mrs. Agnes's fingers from around hers. She gathered a vial of medicine and a needle then gave Mrs. Agnes a shot in her shoulder. She drifted off into a deep restful sleep, feeling the euphoria of medicine and the time she floated into Heaven.

When Mrs. Agnes woke up, sunlight poured into the room. She heard people talking and slowly looked around the room. She had been moved into a smaller hospital room. Her head pounded and her body felt bruised and beaten. The more she tried to turn over, the more intense her head would pound. When she was able to turn to her left, she saw Mary Jean seated in a wooden chair, reading a book. She wondered how long she had been there. Then, Mrs. Agnes quickly closed her eyes. She did not want Mary Jean to see that she had seen her sitting there. Shame filled her chest. *My God, look at her sitting here with me even after how horribly I've treated this child of God for so long.*

Donna entered the room, said hello to Mary Jean, and checked each monitor.

"I see she's moved. Did she cry out?" She asked Mary Jean.

"No. She just turned over this way, looked at me, then closed her eyes again."

Surprised to hear that Mary Jean had seen her, Mrs. Agnes opened her eyes and moved her arm to get Donna's attention. She tried to let them know that her head hurt but no sound would come out of her mouth. Donna patted her on the back.

"Are you in pain, again, Mrs. Rosenthal?"

Mrs. Agnes slowly touched her head.

Donna rubbed Mrs. Agnes's hand and Mary Jean stood by the bed. "You can't talk just yet, but now that you are out of the Intensive Care Unit, Dr. Mortez will speak to you today, and he'll explain to you what your body has gone through in the last 48 hours." She nodded slowly trying to reassure Mrs. Agnes that things were better. "I'll get you something for the pain."

Tears began to flow down Mrs. Agnes's face. She needed her voice. She needed to speak. Mary Jean wiped the tears from Mrs. Agnes's eyes. She sympathized and hated to see Mrs. Agnes hurt despite the pain she'd caused her and her husband lately. Now would be a great time to find out why she's called the IRS on my husband and why she's been hell-bent on tearing down everything he has worked for. She stepped away from Mrs. Agnes and returned to her seat. She took two deep breaths, praying to stay in God's will even though she so desperately wanted to disassociate from everything connected to Mrs. Agnes. She sat quietly, staring at the same page of her book until Donna returned and administered the shot. Before Donna had even walked out of the room, the medication began taking effect and Mrs. Agnes dozed off.

She began dreaming immediately.

Just outside a large, white plantation house, Mrs. Agnes stood with Rev. Mical. Together, they'd proudly pilfered the home and robbed everyone in the house. Along with four men dressed oddly in suits, she and Rev. Mical loaded a van with silver and gold. Just as they were driving through the gates exiting the plantation, the weight of the gold and silver was so heavy that they sank into the earth.

Mrs. Agnes gasped awake.

Her body was turned on her left side. She saw Rev. Grant sitting in the chair where Mary Jean had once been sitting. He was asleep and she could tell that he was uncomfortable sleeping in that chair that was too small for his statue. He did not have any space to move around in. Once again, she felt bad, because she recalled how much she had done to try to destroy this man.

She wondered what day and time it was. She searched the room until she saw a small clock sitting on the stand next to her bed. She also saw a vase holding the most beautiful bouquet of mixed flowers. A stack of envelopes leaned against the vase. She had just enough strength to pull the cards onto the bed. She looked at the envelopes, sliding them aside one by one, and tried to envision the person who sent them. She searched to see if one had come from Rev. Mical.

Soon, Rev. Grant woke and saw Mrs. Agnes awake and trying to control her hands and fingers around the greeting cards. "Are you hungry, Mrs. Agnes?"

She nodded, still unable to speak.

He called out items from the cafeteria menu and she nodded at her choices. He touched her hand then left to get their meals. Mrs. Agnes watched him leave and began to cry. Like the rest of her body, Mrs. Agnes could not control her crying. She cried the twenty-five minutes that it took for Rev. Grant to return with her dinner. He noticed how her eyes had swollen since he left. It was a sorrow he'd seen many members carry when they were weighed by guilt. After they ate silently, Rev. Grant cleared away their trash and placed the trays on the rolling cart. She sniffed, trying desperately to not cry again.

"It's going to be okay, Mrs. Agnes."

She lowered her eyes and nodded. She wanted to apologize for everything and to promise that she would make everything right with the IRS and all the members who she'd run away from T.E.A.M. She wasn't certain if Rev. Grant understood her eyes, but he hugged her as if he did.

They sat quietly for a while until Rev. Grant offered to read the Sunday School lesson to her. She perked up and waved her hands. The thought of the Bible made her remember her visit to heaven. She wanted to tell him about her experience in the operation room. Since she could not speak, she swung her hands more, but he did not understand.

He offered her a pen and his notepad. "Can you write down what you want?"

Not sure if her hand could hold the pen steady enough to write, he suggested that she take her time and concentrate. "I'll be here to read it. Mary Jean needed to stay with the boys." He explained.

It took nearly two hours but Mrs. Agnes carefully wrote the entire experience and gave it page after page to Rev. Grant. He read each page, then glanced up at Mrs. Agnes. *My God, how awesome and forgiving You are. Thank you for loving us and speaking on our behalf, God. Thank You for saving her soul.*

Rev. Grant smiled and put the pages inside his notepad. *God moves in mysterious ways.*

Thanksgiving Dinner at T.P.'s

The day was cold—the kind of cold that penetrated the skin and chilled you to the bone. Sleet hung from the trees and ice layered the ground thanks to the nighttime rainfall. Louisiana weather was so unpredictable by lunchtime everyone will have to shed their coats and long sleeve shirts to cool off only to have to put them back on by nightfall. The wind howled making the cold colder, but the family was determined to make it to T.P.'s new home for Thanksgiving dinner. Each household showed up an hour before dinner and brought their delicious edible masterpiece for the feast.

Rev. Douglas and Demetric Douglas Junior iced the sodas, wine, and water. Demetric Junior had come home for the holidays. Then, they joined Rev. Grant, Lawrence Junior, and Robert Michael in the living room to watch football while T.P. and her mother dished the food into serving platters.

Although he hadn't shown up, George promised to be on time and bring dinner rolls. He knew her parents were going to be there, and he was expected to make a good impression. After a year of trying and failing to court her, George's deepest desire was to make T.P. his wife. Now that the drinking is becoming more and more frequent he felt like he was losing control again which meant he would soon lose all chance with T.P. since he was constantly telling her that she was going to be his wife.

Cynthia wanted desperately to ask about George but knowing her daughter, she knew that if George was of any significance he would soon appear. She decided to wait and see how the holiday unfolded. They finished dishing up portions of all of the food at 2:45 PM and called the men to the table. T.P. wanted everyone sitting and eating at three o'clock. Rev. Grant blessed the food and they all began to pass plates and bowls to pile their plates with the holiday favorites.

"This food is delicious! Ladies, we did an amazing job if I do say so myself. Better than any restaurant!" Cynthia said, waving a folk full of candied yams.

"Much better!" Rev. Grant said as he spooned more cornbread dressing onto his plate.

Mary Jean was enjoying the mustard greens that Shelia had prepared. She held in her tears as she savored the taste so much like Granny's mixed greens.

"Who cooked this green dressing stuff?" Robert Micheal asked and everyone laughed.

"That's mirliton, seafood casserole," Mary Jean said proudly. She had found the recipe in a stack of recipe cards in Stella's kitchen cabinet.

"I don't know anything about mirliton, but this is good," T.P. said dishing more into her plate.

The phone rang and T.P. excused herself from the table.

"Hello," she said.

"Hiiiiiiiiii, Pretty Lady," George said. "Ummm, I'll see you in about ten minutes." Then, he quickly hung up the phone to avoid answering any questions. T.P. had a premonition that George was drunk or full of marijuana and she didn't want to see him. She especially didn't want him near her parents. She could understand him needing to have a remedy for the nightmares—which he claimed was on occasion—but to be drunk on a night like tonight was unacceptable.

When T.P. returned to the table everyone was still talking about how good the food tasted, she thought to herself is there no other subject to talk about other than the food, and then she knew that she felt that way because she was not ready for what was coming.

"Was that your new man-friend?" Cynthia whispered.

"Yes. He's not himself, but he should be here in ten minutes," T.P. said nervously.

Mary Jean knew that something was wrong.

"T.P. come and help me to refill some of the Turkey and dressing platter. The food is so delicious we all need a second round," She said.

T.P. grabbed the turkey platter and Mary Jean picked up the empty dressing bowl and they headed to the kitchen. Mary Jean looked at Rev. Grant to cue him to be ready. Instinctively, he caught Mary Jean's look and shifted in his chair. His signal to her that he's alert and prepared.

"What's the matter?" Mary Jean asked as soon as they entered the kitchen.

T.P. shook her head, "George is on his way and I can tell by his slur that he is drunk or high and you know I am disgusted! This is the first time he will be meeting mom and dad and the first time he's stepped foot into my new place. At this rate, it'll be his last time!" T.P. said slicing more slices of turkey and dishing them onto the gold-trimmed, glass platter.

"Why didn't you tell him not to come?" Mary Jean scooped cornbread dressing out of the pan. She took a slice of turkey and quickly ate it. She had never realized that T.P. was a good cook just like her mother.

"I was, but he hung up the phone before I could tell him to stay away." T.P. was angry.

"Do you want me to ask Donald to go lookout for him and send him away when he arrives? But that is not a good idea because if he is drunk then if he's able to make it here he may not be able to make it home," Mary Jean said.

"Maybe he can get George to the guest bedroom and put him to bed before mom and dad get up from the table and they won't know that he's here," She said.

"They'll see another car when they get ready to leave, so they will know someone else is here," Mary Jean said.

"They don't know what car everyone came in."

"Yes, that's right. Go bring the turkey and dressing back into the dining room and tell Donald to help me in the kitchen." Mary Jean said.

When Rev. Grant entered the room, he knew he needed to run some sort of interference. "What's wrong, Baby?"

"George is on his way and T.P. doesn't want to see him while he's drunk or high."

"Dumb move, George!" Rev. Grant said. "He's drinking again, I wonder what happened?"

"He should be here any minute. Can you get him into the guest bedroom and put him to bed before dad and Cynthia see him?"

"Okay. I hear a car pulling up now. You go back to the table and I'll see what I can do, but I can't promise you anything. Lately, he's been inconsolable. You've seen how hard it's been to deal with him. Too many old demons—and too many secrets—are coming out of him all of a sudden," Rev. Grant said. He moved around Mary Jean and rubbed her back. She loved his random touches. He walked out of the side door and Mary Jean returned to the dining room.

"Robert Michael, why don't you tell everyone how your baseball season went this year." She picked a topic that she knew would keep the Douglases distracted.

Rev. Grant turned the corner of the house just in time to stop George from ringing the doorbell.

"Wel.........I hell.........o, brother." George's breath reeked, smelling like liquor and onions. He knew exactly where George had been. Only Jimmy Joe's had fried onions that smelled that strong.

"It is good to see you, man! Y'all finished eati.....n? I gotta meet my new family" He stumbled taking a step back to open the front door.

"Yeah, George, they are in there but you are not ready to meet them. Look at you, man. Do you want to lose T.P. on Thanksgiving?" He tried to talk casually to his younger brother so that he would not feel like he was being scorned.

"It's all good, Donnnald. Don't worry yooooself. I am in full control," George leaned on the house. For a moment Rev. Grant thought to get

George back in the car and leave. Instead, he said, "Okay, let's get you freshened up some before you meet everyone. You smell like ole Jimmy and his dead dog. You know you do not want T.P. to see you like this after all your hard work to clean up and she definitely doesn't want them to see you!" Rev. Grant looked his brother in the eyes. "Do you hear me, George? We are going into the bedroom quietly." He took George's arm and led him inside the house.

"I'm not in....tox....so...cated, Donald! I aaamm dr......unk and I'm high and I don't give a damn who knows it!" He said heading to the dining room.

"Good evening, everyone. I'm George. I'm so sorry that I am late for dinner. My brother here," He said looking back at Rev. Grant. "He thinks that I'm in....tox...so...cated but I am not I am dr......unk, and I apologize to T.P.'s parents because I love her and I'm sorry!" He said as he sat in Rev. Grant's seat and began grabbing food and placing it on Rev. Grant's plate. Mary Jean told the boys to go watch the game before they miss the best parts. They quickly left the dining room and ran to the back room. T.P. had designated one room as their playroom and library. They would gladly spend eternity there if they could.

Rev. Douglas looked at his son with a look that demanded get rid of this fool now!

"Let me see you in the kitchen, Demetria!" Demetric Douglas Jr. said. Damn, T.P.'s mind shouted. She knew her big brother was livid. As soon as the kitchen door closed, T.P. started explaining.

"Listen, D–."

"No, no, you listen," she was back sixteen again, whispering, pleading with her favorite sibling and hoping he'd trust her. "I'm going to tell him if he doesn't get help, we won't be able to go out anymore." She scanned her brother's angry face. "Listen to me. He has some deep problems, and he needs my help." T.P. said holding back tears.

"Listen to what you are saying, Demetria! You are saying you will stay in a destructive relationship! This just does not make any sense. Is the penis that good?"

She shot him an angry look. "We are not having sex, Demetric! You know me better than that!"

Rev. Grant tried to take George's arm and move him from the table, but George turned around and looked Rev. Grant in the eyes.

"Where were you Don....ald when he was raping me every day? Where were you!? Oh, I know, outside with your buddies. You never wondered why I was always inside when you were outside. You never wondered, mama never wondered, daddy never wondered, and Brother Maurice sometimes held me down in the church and they took turns raping me! Do you know how many times I called out to you, to momma, and to daddy?"

The room became noticeably quiet.

Just as T.P. and Cynthia entered the room, Mary Jean got up and Rev. Grant sat next to George and looked him in the eyes.

"I didn't know, George. None of us did! They were con artists! All of them!" Rev. Grant took a deep breath to calm himself. "I'm sorry. I'm so sorry that I didn't know because had I known I would be in jail today." Rev. Grant kept holding George's hand even though he was trying to jerk them away.

"He told me that if I told any one of you, he would kill you, and besides who would believe my little badass, and that's what mom and dad often said to me that I was a badass, so I believed him!" George said as tears ran down his face.

"Then that damn pastor down the street came in with his evil–."

Rev. Grant pulled George from his seat and hugged him close and tears flowed from their eyes. Everyone else in the room was quiet and seemed to be experiencing the brothers' pain.

"I am so sorry, and I apologize to you from the bottom of my heart. You have a beautiful lady who cares for you and you need to get well so that the two of you can have a productive relationship together." Rev. Grant said. "Come home with me, George. Time to get you the help you should have gotten years ago." He said.

"Demetric Junior, would you follow Mary Jean and the boys home?"

"No problem, Rev. Brother-in-law. You sure you don't want me to help you with him?" Demetric Junior said while gesturing toward George.

"Thank you. I can handle it," Rev. Grant said as he led his brother to the door helped him into his coat got his car keys out of his pocket, opened the door, and closed it behind them as they left.

After Rev. Grant and George left, the room was quiet Demetric Junior and Rev. Douglas went into the living room to watch the next game, and the ladies went into the kitchen to pack food for everyone to take home. The atmosphere was thick with anxiety as they cleaned the remaining dishes and packed away leftovers. T.P. was the least emotional of them all. Mary Jean held in her frustration. She didn't want to risk sounding judgmental and critical. Years ago, she decided that she would be the type of Christian who truly embodied the Fruit of the Spirit. For her, this was a tough year to be righteous.

Once Cynthia placed the last casserole dishes in the cabinet, the women gathered in the living room with the men and boys to say good-night. Mary Jean and the boys gave extra hugs to T.P. and Cynthia before collecting their bags. Rev. Douglas and Cynthia kissed T.P. and asked her if she needed them to spend the night. She assured them that she was safe and once they left, she would take a rose bubble bath and go to bed. They all left the house together with Demetric Junior trailing close behind Mary Jean's car just like he promised Rev. Grant.

After everyone left T.P. repositioned her chairs and sofa. She noticed George's coat had fallen from the dinner chair onto the floor. She gently picked it up—almost as if he was still wearing it. She decided to hang it up on the door hook. She could smell his cologne and a hint of whiskey and smoke. Sympathetically, she wiped the jacket with her palm. *You never know what demons some people are wrestling with. Secrets will eat you up, especially the secret lives of men.*

Driving home was too difficult for Mary Jean. The road was much more slippery than when they first arrived at T.P.'s dinner. For some time while they were inside, it lightly snowed and had started again.

"Look at the snow!" Robert Michael yelled.

"Wow! Mom it's snowing," Lawrence Junior echoed then moved across the seat to look out of the window with his brother.

"Sit back boys and be still!" Mary Jean instructed. "This is South Louisiana. Those flickers won't last."

"Ma! It's really snowing!" Robert Michael grew more excited.

"Just look out of your own windows" Mary Jean turned on her windshield wipers and checked her rearview mirror. She was relieved to see Demetric Junior following them. Once they made it home, Mary Jean pulled into the driveway and instructed the boys to grab their bags. She took the largest bag and headed up the steps. Demetric Junior beamed the headlights to help them see the path. Mary Jean waved her thanks, but he waited until she opened the door and walked inside before driving off.

As she entered the house, Rev. Grant walked down the stairs. He took the heavy bag from her and followed the boys into the kitchen where they sat the bags on the table.

"Did you enjoy Thanksgiving dinner at your Aunt T.P.'s house?"

"I liked the apple pie," Lawrence Junior said. "Did we bring some home, momma? Can I have another piece?"

"I liked the sweet potato pie!" shouted Robert Michael.

"No, sons, it's too late to eat. You will have nightmares, but I promise you tomorrow morning you can both have a slice of your favorite pie." Mary Jean stepped closer to Rev. Grant hoping he would embrace her.

Rev. Grant hugged Mary Jean then kissed her forehead. "Sons, go upstairs and get ready for bed." He said.

"Okay," they agreed.

As soon as the boys exited the kitchen, Mary Jean asked the question that Rev. Grant knew she would.

"How is George? Has he settled down?"

Rev. Grant led her into the living room. "He's calmer. We had another, um, exchange, but because he is still high and intoxicated, I'm not sure he really heard a word I said. Nevertheless, I helped him get comfortable in the guest room and the last time I looked in on him, he was asleep."

He hugged her again.

Mary Jean leaned into his chest. His love felt like heaven. For a moment, they stood quietly, breathing in each other's scent. "Let's just tell the boys that their uncle may be here for a while before they ask us a lot of questions."

He kissed her and agreed.

She walked to the wine cabinet and selected a bottle of 1965 Domaine Du Hout Bonneau. She poured a glass for each of them then sat on the sofa.

She sipped the wine and watched Rev. Grant walk to his favorite recliner."I knew something was wrong. I couldn't stop praying for George since the day he called looking to apologize to T.P. I never thought it was this bad." *And this makes me more careful with our sons because this can happen right under your nose.* Mary Jean wanted to add but she sipped more wine instead.

"Baby, right now. I just need our boys to understand that they can talk with us especially if someone even attempts to touch them in any place and in any way that makes them feel uncomfortable. I will make sure they know what those places are. But you better believe you, or, I will be with them as much as possible when others are around. They will know to tell us if an adult approaches them," Rev. Grant became irate. He gulped the wine and calmed himself.

"And we want to know if they are ever alone with an adult, without one of us," Mary Jean said thinking that this past situation with George had made her frightened for her sons—something she had never felt before. "So, what are your plans?" She asked.

"I'm going to make his appointments with Alcoholics Anonymous and make sure he gets there, I'll go with him. I'm going to get a good therapist for him to see on his off day from the store which, I think, is

Wednesdays. And I'll offer him to stay here for a while if that will make him feel better."

Mary Jean stood up.

"Is that okay with you?" He asked.

"You know that I'm with you in whatever you decide to do. George needs to be in our care. He is welcome to stay with us. You didn't even need to ask me that," she said.

"Yes, I did, I wanted to know how you feel. I know how I think you feel but I never want to take you for granted and think that I am going to always know." He walked to the front door and double-checked the locks and continued talking. "As we get older, our feelings change and people don't know if we don't tell them, right? We are not the people, we were years ago and we will not be the same people years from now that we are today."

She looked at him and wondered where his speech was headed. He chuckled, grateful that the wine and recliner had soothed his nerves. "Now, that I have preached that little sermon I'll go get my wife's bathwater ready so I can hold her tight. Then, I will tuck our sons in bed, then listen to their prayers, until you come and kiss them good night."

They laughed and walked up the stairs.

Kidnapping and Rape

Sheriff Golespy drove off towards the woods on Elm Street with Deputy Williamson on his heels as they headed towards the woods off Highway 91. The sheriff stopped at the Frost Top and got a hamburger; fries and a coke to go. Twenty minutes later they arrived at their destination and both stepped out of their cars and headed toward the cabin.

"Do you plan to tell Deputy Jones about this?" Deputy Williamson asked the Sheriff who was holding the hamburger and fries in his hand.

"Not, now, I have not been able to figure him out, yet he may be against the bootlegging and the women, I'm going to work beside him a little longer and then I'll know if I can trust him. What do you think about him?" The sheriff asked as they moved closer toward the cabin.

"I know he likes to follow the book and he's for what's right because when that preacher man called, I just laid the phone on the desk and I wasn't going to tell you anything until after you left, I was going to tell him that you had left for the day, but Mr. Do Goody got up and told you. So, I think he is too straight to understand our doings," Deputy Williamson said.

They both stepped onto the porch and opened the door to the stench inside the cabin smelling of urine and feces. They saw her lying on the sofa lovely as a flower even the bad smell did not take off from her beauty.

"Go get the liquor from the still and take your time, also bring this feces pot outside and dump it with you and take an hour before your return. I want to enjoy myself with this gal after she eats." He said.

The girl was Mavis Otter who worked in various bars from Basin to Baton Rouge to New Orleans and everywhere in between. She was someone that the two officers believed no one would miss. They waited long enough on the case for people to decide that she had run off with a band. The truth was locked inside the abandoned cabin. The sheriff had arrested her and given her the ultimatum to go to jail or be his slave for a week which had turned into three weeks and counting.

'Here, nigger gal," the Sheriff said throwing the hamburger and fries to her, which she grabbed and tore the wrapping off and began stuffing food into her mouth. As she ate the Sheriff sat in a chair across from her looking at her body. Her body is perfect, He thought. Niggers have the most beautiful bodies, rounded behinds, hairs full of crotch, firm tits, and full juicy lips. Just looking at her made his penis harder than his wife was ever able to do. When she finished eating the hamburger, fries, and drink, she threw the trash at him.

"Let me go! Unchain me!"

He liked it when she fought him because it made the sex even better. He stepped out of his underwear and headed towards her grabbing her by her long ponytail and snatching her naked body to his as he held her arms with one hand and took control of her body with his other hand. He pushed her and when she fell backward on the cot and he fell on top of her and placed his tongue inside her mouth then forced her legs open with his knees and as soon as his manhood touched her, he could not hold back the pleasure. She was the only woman who was able to do that to him. The mere touch of her body anywhere sent his body into uncontrollable spasms.

"Woweeeeeee!" He screamed and jerked off, but he was not finished he planned to do this again in an hour because she had that kind of effect on him.

An hour later when Deputy Williamson arrived back at the cabin, he could hear Sheriff Golespy still having a good time and he wondered when it would be his time. He decided to knock on the door anyway.

"Albert! Wait your turn!" The sheriff yelled.

"When is my turn? You're taking turns for both of us?" Albert was so angry he wished he was smart enough to blackmail the sheriff for kidnapping and raping teenage nigger whores.

Oscar Gets Out of Jail

When Judge Clark arrived, he was in a hurry because he had planned to play golf with his friend Don and a new guy that Don called "J.T". He smiled when he thought about it because Don was such a lousy golfer and he would beat him every time. *These games with Don are getting boring. I think I need to find another golf partner. Maybe the mysterious J.T. will do.*

'First case on the docket Your Honor is the State versus Oscar Smith for assault with a deadly weapon.

"Mr. Smith, what do you have to say for yourself?"

"Your Honor, he was trying to steal my money. I couldn't let him walk away with all my money in his pocket."

"What game were you two playing that caused you to lose the amount of money that would cause you to attack an innocent man?"

"We were shooting dice. He had won all my money and all I asked him was to loan me back a few of my dollars, so I could have a chance to win my money back."

The Judge took a few seconds and looked and Oscar. *This nigger must be crazy.* "You mean to tell me that you wanted someone who won your money fairly to give some of it back to you, so you can try to win your money back from them. Is that what you are saying, Mr. Smith?"

Oscar thought for a moment, and it still made perfect sense to him. "Yes! That's exactly what I'm saying, Your Honor. He owed me that much respect and when he refused, I just hit him on the side of his head to wake up his brain so he would do the right thing."

"You woke his brain up so much he had to be brought to the hospital emergency room." Judge Clark studied his notes. "That was quite an awaking, Mr. Smith."

"Attorney Condon. Where is the victim now?"

"We have not been able to locate him, You're Honor. He left a message with his aunt saying he wasn't pressing charges and he wasn't returning to Basin ever in life. We have her handwritten statement here, sir." The attorney handed the judge a sheet of yellow, ledger paper.

"I can't let him free just off of that but I will set bail at five hundred dollars and this will remain on his record." He slammed the gavel on his table. "Next case!"

Maude was glad that the bail was low because another week before Mrs. Golespy paid her. Maude paid the bail and waited in her car for Oscar to be released.

"Hi, Momma!" He kissed her cheek as if he had been picked up from a high school football game. "I'm so glad you came and got me out of that stinkhole! Golespy needs to clean that place up!" He lit a cigarette, blatantly ignoring his mother's asthma.

"Oscar, his name is Sheriff Golespy. That's exactly why he doesn't like you now. Speak to adults like I taught you!"

"Well, that's fine if he doesn't like me because the feeling is mutual. All he does is run after Black girls—him and that Deputy Williamson. They are doing something to those girls mark my word. It's going to come out one day and I'm going to make certain that he gets caught."

"Oscar, shut your mouth! You know nothing about that and don't be running around in this town telling everyone that lie because it will get you in a lot of trouble and my purse is running dry. I have breakfast for us ready at home. Are you hungry?"

"I could eat a horse right now, Momma. All those people fed us was sandwiches, chips, fruit, and a soda. I can't wait to eat some of your good cooking."

When they arrived at Maude's house, she had a breakfast buffet laid out in the kitchen. Nothing was too good for her Oscar. They both fixed a heaping plate then sat at the table.

"Where's Donna? Don't she stay here now?"

"She's upstairs, she should be down soon. She's been a little upset because Lawrence has been stalking her and he even had the nerves to come in the driveway when she wasn't looking and stab her in the arm." Maude quickly regretted the moment that fact came out of her mouth.

"He did what?! That nigger is dead!"

Maude instantly knew she had made a terrible mistake telling Oscar about Donna's problems. From childhood, he was always Donna's protector.

Oscar stopped eating and stood up. "Momma, where the keys to my car? I need to go make a run." He grabbed the keys from a hook by the kitchen door. He slammed the front door as he left. All Maude could do was pray.

Fifteen minutes later, Donna came downstairs dressed for work. Maude explained Oscar's demeanor and the conversation. "Oscar left in a huff, and I'm afraid that he's out there looking for Lawrence to kill him."

"Don't worry, Momma. I'll call around and find him. I should be able to cool him down." She picked up a muffin and headed towards the front door. She picked up the hall phone and dialed Oscar's constant partner in crime: Jonathan.

After the phone rang five times Jonathan picked up. She didn't give him time to say hello, " Hi Jonathan this is Donna is Oscar over there by you?"

"Yeah. Look like he brought Pretty Boy with him. Hold on. Oscar. Phone." Jonathan said. Donna could hear his hand rub the phone's speaker and the three male voices mumbled. One was shouting. Every time the three of them got together, someone argued or fought.

"Yeah. What do you want?" Oscar shouted into the phone.

Donna took a breath and tried to choose her words carefully because she knew the temper that Oscar possessed, "Oscar please, please, don't go do something stupid! You are already out on bail, do you want to go to jail for life?"

"I hear you, Sis, but that nigger put his hand on you. He should not have done that. You know I never let no one put their hands on you since you were born. I'm just going to rough him up a bit and shoot off one of his punk-ass hands that's all." He chuckled. Donna knew Oscar had very little experience with guns, so his chances of hitting Lawrence were slim to none unless he was in his face. So, she decided to call Jazz for him to warn Lawrence and convince him to stay away or he'll be shot. She hung up the phone, then dialed Jazz.

"Good morning, Jazz. How are you?" She asked sweetly. "Is Lawrence with you?"

"Nah, boo, what's going on?"

"Well, we have a problem. My brother Oscar is looking for Lawrence to kill him and I'm afraid Lawrence will end up killing Oscar or me because he is always high on something." Donna said peeping inside the living room to see if her mom was listening to her conversation.

"Don't worry. What type of gun does he have?" Jazz plotted.

"I remember him bragging that he had a Colt 357." Donna had only a few minutes to talk before she would be late for work.

He quickly envisioned getting a Colt to protect his friend.

"I am really afraid now, Jazz. This has gotten way out of hand. I can't even drive Im shaking so much right now."

"Okay. Let's hang up. Drive down to Broucher Avenue. I'll be there to get you to work safely."

Donna agreed.

Soon, Donna pulled up and he followed her to work and saw to it that she walked into the hospital safely. This had become a regular responsibility of his. Then, he went to Basin City Gun and Ammunition Shop to buy a worn-down Colt 357.

"How can I help you, young man?"

"I need to purchase a gun. I have some shady characters who have moved into the apartment next to me and I don't want to take any chances. They look like drug dealers." Jazz overtalked.

"Say no more. Those drug dealers are ruining the country and y'all colored act like yall don't have a Second Amendment right to protect yourselves, but you do. These lil trash heads will kill you just for looking at them." Mr. Poulain's peach skin was flaky and bruised red in spots thanks to old age and white rage. "You look familiar. Who is your momma?"

"You know my mom, Mr. Poulain, she worked for your mom before she passed, bless her soul," Jazz threw in the extra sympathy so that Mr. Poulain would be more relaxed and give him the gun he wanted without the long wait of a background check.

"Oh yeah. That was sweet lady Janice. She used to come clean, cook, and wash for my mama. She always smelled like sweet syrup." Mr. Poulain remembered when he had approached her for a date and she brushed him off, so he had to let her go and get another nigger woman who would be willing, and boy was Lillie Mae willing. After his mom died, he brought Lillie Mae over to live with him, and even though his wife was mad every day, he was happy every day. Soon his little good ride had to end and he had to fire Lillie Mae. She began to take over the house like she was his wife and not the help, but just the memory of her was sweet.

Mr. Poulain put a Smith and Weston on the counter and told him that should do the trick. Jazz asked him for another pistol and he refused every one of the pistols Mr. Poulain offered until he laid the Colt 357 on the counter.

"Now that's a cool-looking one, what is the name of this pistol?" Jazz feigned ignorance.

"That's a Colt 357. It's a very popular gun in this area. I don't know why but a lot of people buy this one." Mr. Poulain shook his head.

"Well, I don't want to be different from most of the people in town, so give me this one," Jazz said, happy that he was able to find a gun exactly like Oscar's gun.

"All right, it's cheaper than the rest because it sells so often. The price is one hundred and thirty-nine dollars Do you need me to wrap it for you?" Mr. Poulain said as he reached under the counter and pulled out some brown wrapping paper and began wrapping the gun before Jazz could respond.

As Mr. Poulain was wrapping the gun, a young girl around the age of fourteen walked into the store. When she saw Jazz, she started looking around like she wasn't supposed to be there. He turned around and gave the girl an angry look and she turned around and left the store. Jazz knew that many of the white men traveled to Basin to have sex with the young Black girls and many of the girls were missing.

Jazz paid Mr. Poulain, picked up the gun and three sheets of registration papers, and walked out of the store.

"Thank you."

Later that night he called Donna.

"Hey, Listen, Don't worry about Lawrence everything will be all right," He said proudly.

"Okay. Do you want to tell me what you have planned to do?" Donna asked with a softer tone.

"You just try to sleep and trust me." Jazz hung up the phone.

Leaving the Hospital

Sister Smith asked to ride with Mary Jean to pick up Mrs. Agnes from the hospital. Mary Jean was happy for the extra help since Rev. Grant had several important calls and another series of meeting with the accountant. She knew she would need help getting Mrs. Agnes in and out of the car and Sister Smith was strong enough to help her and not complain. Not only did Sister Smith want to help Mary Jean, she especially wanted to see the expression on Mrs. Agnes's face knowing that the only people who sat with her night and day were the people she was trying to destroy. She had also heard of Mrs. Agnes's close brush with death and wanted to see if this would have any impact on her.

When they entered the hospital room, Sister Smith was the first to greet Mrs. Agnes."How do you feel, Agnes?" She asked.

She just can't help asking a stupid question, thought Sis. Agnes and she almost told her that but decided that it would be nicer to just say, "Hello, Joyce. I'm still in pain, but it is not as bad as it had been."

Sister Smith was shocked to hear Mrs. Agnes's response. She just knew onery ass Agnes would have something smart to say. *Maybe she has changed.*

Mary Jean opened a small suitcase and unfolded a soft pink and lace housedress with silver snap buttons down the front. The store tag hung from under the sleeve with two buttons and a swath of lace. Mrs. Agnes smiled and thanked Mary Jean for her thoughtfulness.

Mary Jean helped Mrs. Agnes dress, while Sister Smith packed away toiletries, medicine, and Mrs. Agnes's quilt and pillows. Mary Jean thanked Sister Smith again for helping her and left to bring the car to the entrance. Just then, the nurse entered the room with a wheelchair and discharge papers. She and Sister Smith helped Mrs. Agnes into the chair and rolled her to the entrance.

They rode quietly to Mrs. Agnes's home.

When they pulled up to the house, Mrs. Agnes's neighbor Mr. Greenup waved and jogged over to offer a hand. He lifted Mrs. Agnes from the car seat and walked gently up the newly constructed ramp that lead to the side door. Gently he help her stand so the ladies could walk her into her bedroom.

Sister Smith smiled at his assistance. He looked too old to be strong enough to carry Mrs. Agnes, but he did so effortlessly.

Mary Jean and Sister Smith helped Mrs. Agnes get into her bed. Since this was her first time in Mrs. Agnes's bedroom, Sister Smith was surprised to see the beautiful white French provincial furniture that matched the furniture in the living room. The bed was queen size and the spread and pillow set were lavender. The bedspread was ruffled around the edge of the bed and at the foot of the bed was a spread holder to lay your spread over when not in use, and the curtains were a dark purple with lavender sheers in the middle. On the right side of the room was a large oval mirror dresser and on the left side of the room was the six-drawer vanity, she was surprised to see that Mrs. Agnes had a walk-in closet.

Sister Smith noticed how much Mary Jean cared for Mrs. Agnes she handled her as if she was her parent. She also saw that Mrs. Agnes was not her usual arrogant self. She seemed humbled and Sister Smith was happy for this because she did not think she would be able to deal with her if she would have been her same ornery self.

She and Mary Jean helped Mrs. Agnes give herself a sponge bath and fluffed her pillows so she could rest. Then, Mary Jean prepared a pot of vegetable soup while Sister Smith cleaned the house and bathroom.

While Mrs. Agnes ate, Mary Jean and Sister Smith cleaned the house and moved furniture for Mrs. Agnes to move safely through her home. The quilting club members decided that each night one of them would stay with Agnes until she was better. As soon as Sister Montgomery showed up for her shift, Mary Jean and Sister Smith left. Mrs. Agnes rested quietly and Sister Montgomery chopped onions and celery to start the next day's meal.

Around 8 p.m. Rev. Mical knocked on the door, looking like he had been drugged through hell and back. Sister Montgomery told him that Mrs. Agnes was resting, but he was adamant about seeing her, so Sister Montgomery stepped aside and let him in. He stormed through the house and headed straight to Mrs. Agnes's bedroom. Sister Montgomery thought it odd that he knew exactly where her bedroom was, considering there were three bedrooms in the house. Sister Montgomery decided to let them talk alone, so she turned on the television and sat on the sofa.

When Rev. Mical walked into Mrs. Agnes's room he strolled over to the bed and told her she needed to get strong fast, because they needed to get on with the business at hand. Mrs. Agnes looked at Rev. Mical. She looked deep into his eyes and what she saw frightened her, funny she had never seen it before; or perhaps she had, but at that time looking into his eyes was a reflection of what her eyes used to tell. She could not believe that he had not come to see her at the hospital, and he had not called, and yet, here he was standing in her bedroom still not asking her how she feels; his concern was in destroying Rev. Grant's church. She looked at him with clear eyes for the first time in a long time.

"And how are you Rev. Mical?" she asked him looking under-eyed thinking maybe he'll get the message.

"I'm okay Agnes." He said as he pulled a chair up closer to the bed. "How long do you think you'll be laid up?"

"Only God knows that Rev. Mical unless you know better!" She was amazed that this fool still had not asked her how she was feeling, he was just interested in helping himself.

"Agnes you know I need your help! I am going down to the IRS office at the end of the week and I need you to go with me. They called me and asked me to come in and bring the proof that I have about Grant's church. You need to get me some documents from the church. I know you can do it because they like you over there. So, you think you'll be able to get me some papers before Friday?"

"Rev. Mical looks like you'll be going without me and without any papers, because I'm not going to try to get any papers from Rev. Grant's office, nor am I going to get out of this bed until I am healed." Mrs. Agnes was becoming agitated at the arrogance of Rev. Mical.

Sister Montgomery headed to the bathroom and as she approached it, she heard Rev. Mical speaking about Rev. Grant, so she just stood in the hallway and listened to the conversation between Mrs. Agnes and Rev. Mical.

"Now don't tell me you've had a change of heart about that fool Agnes. You and I both know that it has been his unrighteous underhanded dealing that has kept his church this far. We are going to be the two with the anointing of God, which will bring his behind down. Now are you with me or has that bullet in your head caused your brain to malfunction."

Mrs. Agnes pulled her painful body onto the pillow; she wanted to make sure that Rev. Mical understood exactly what she was about to tell him; because she had no intention of ever having to have to repeat it. " Mical, when I was lying in that hospital, I was given another chance to make right all of the things in this life that I have done wrong and I thank God for this opportunity. You see sometimes bad things must happen to you, for you to see just what you really have become and what you can change about yourself to make you a better person. Thanks to you and my arrogance and sinful ways, I have been a total disgrace to my Lord and so have you."

" Now wait a minute Agnes!" Rev. Mical said getting upset.

"No. You wait a minute, Mical, you didn't put your foot down at the hospital to check on me. And as of this moment, you have not had the decency to ask me how I feel, all your talk has been about what you want to destroy. Do you know who was at the hospital for me the month I was there? No. You don't know, well let me tell you. It was Rev. Grant and his wife and other members of T.E.A.M., who sat by my bed and did for me, not you! Now, let you and I get something straight. I had a talk with God and that's some things I'm sure you have never had, and I hope you never have to, he spoke to me, and guess what, James Mical? He told me that he was giving me another chance to get myself right and I cannot do that with you in my life, so I'm asking you to get your hat off my furniture and your feet off my floor and your ass out of my house at this moment!"

"What? What did you say, woman? You cannot talk to me like that! You must don't know who you are talking to!" Rev. Mical rushed to the dresser, grabbed his hat, and headed toward the door.

"Sure, I do, Mical! I'm talking to the fool who is trying to destroy what God has built!"

Sister Montgomery had been shouting under her breath, "You tell him, Agnes!" Then, when she heard Mrs. Agnes tell Rev. Mical to get out she rushed to the front door and had it opened when he exited the room all huffed up. He looked at her knowing if she had the door opened ahead of time, then she had heard their conversation and he stumped out the door.

Meeting with the Deacons

Christmas would soon be here and I'm still struggling to heal. I've got to get better, Lord. Why do you have me here? Mrs. Agnes prayed and begged for answers but she could not shake the feeling that she had to do something about all the trouble she and Rev. Mical had caused Rev. Grant and his family.

After a month at home, she decided to call the IRS and try to explain to them how she and Rev. Mical had lied about fraudulent activities at T.E.A.M conducted by Rev. Grant. She talked to three representatives and each told her that the IRS had already begun investigating and would not be able to stop it based on her confession. One agent told her if the church records were in order it did not matter what she or anyone else had told them, they would drop the case. She knew that it was hopeless to try to convince them, but she was not going to stop there.

After contemplating a few days, she called the deacons from Rev. Mical's church and since the head deacon was a friend of her deceased husband, she knew he would come. She requested that he bring as many deacons as he could with him, and he did. After she had relayed the devious act that she and Rev. Mical had played on Rev. Grant, the deacons were appalled. Deacon Miller said he had never wanted Rev.

Mical as their pastor, but the others had been so intent on having him, so he just went along with them; however, he knew that the man was a snake, and he knew it would just be a matter of time before he showed his fangs.

A few of the other deacons, especially the younger ones who were loyal to Rev. Mical, did not believe the story; they thought that Mrs. Agnes was lying about Rev. Mical. Mrs. Agnes knew then that one of them would let Rev. Mical know what she had told them, but what they did not know was that before they were asked to come, she and Deacon Miller had devised a plan to catch Rev. Mical and would use his loyalist as bait. When they left, Deacon Miller told the deacons that he didn't believe what Agnes was telling them about Rev. Mical, he believed that she had made all of this up to cover up her sinful act, and they all agreed.

Deacon Tomas could not wait to call Rev. Mical and tell him about the meeting. He called him from the church's phone then he drove home and relayed to him that evening's event. Rev. Mical hit the ceiling he could not believe that Mrs. Agnes had betrayed him. He told Deacon Tomas not to worry Mrs. Agnes had a mental problem after her attack and that he would take care of it, all he needed him to do was to keep him posted about the other deacons.

After he completed, the call he slammed a paperweight that was on his desk on top of an ashtray and broke it into pieces. He then picked up the phone and dialed Mrs. Agnes's number. Just as Deacon Miller and Mrs. Agnes knew he would. Deacon Miller drove around the block, parked his car, and returned to Mrs. Agnes's house to wait for Rev. Mical's call. Deacon Miller showed Mrs. Agnes how to operate the black cassette recorder. He told her to insert the blank cassette tape into the recorder by pressing stop/eject and when the door opened to place the tape inside the machine and close the door by pressing down on it. Then he said once Rev. Mical started to talk she should press the record button and then start to talk with him on the phone but make sure her phone is close enough to the recorder that Rev. Mical could be heard as she could, too. He also told her that once they had hung up the phone then they would press rewind the tape back to the beginning and then press play. He also told her he would tell her what the other buttons were for later since the phone was ringing.

"Hello."

"Hello, Agnes. I hear you had some visitors at your home tonight and that you did a lot of lying on me. Why would you do that, Agnes? I thought we had a deal. I thought that you wanted to get rid of that fool just as bad as I did. I guess I was wrong."

"Rev. Mical, what you and I did to Rev. Grant was wrong! It was a sinful act and now we both have another chance given to us by God to straighten out this mess that we have caused, and we need to ask Rev. Grant for forgiveness. "Mrs. Agnes said as Deacon Miller listened on the extension phone and watched the recorder to make certain it was still recording.

"Agnes, you must be a fool! If you think that I am going to apologize to that fool, then you too are fools. Besides, you cannot prove anything! It will be your word against mine. And since your little near-death experience no one will believe you anyway. You know Black people don't believe in this nonsense as soon as the deacons hear about your little talk with God, I am certain they will think that you have lost your mind and they'll be right. And you know who will be the first one to give you this new title? It will be Deacon Miller." Rev. Mical was so sure of himself. He leaned back in his recliner and blew cigar smoke toward the ceiling.

"Well, Mical whether they believe me or not. I know what happened between God, and me just as I know that you wrote and sent the letter to the IRS on Rev. Grant's church and that it was mine and your idea to put the article in the churches bulletin with pictures of him and his family so that your members would see that his wife had children out of wedlock. That was wrong Mical. We were wrong! All I want to do is give my life to God and do right by people from now on and let me suggest that you do the same." Mrs. Agnes said.

"Look, Agnes! Do whatever the hell you want to do. You cannot touch me, woman. You are a fool, and just to think I was thinking about letting you head the deaconess board, but you blew it, fool!" It suddenly occurred to Rev. Mical that she might be taping this conversation and then he thought that she was not that smart.

"Rev. Mical if you can't do the right thing in this situation, then I would appreciate it if you would please not call my house again."

"That won't be a problem for me, Agnes. Just remember if I go down, then so will you. So, you best keep your mouth shut about this. Or, since you are so holy now, why don't you just say you set the whole thing up by yourself and then apologize? I am certain that will get you some points with God. What you say?" Rev. Mical laughed. "And I pray you get your ass shot again and it just might be by me, so watch your back!" He yelled.

Mrs. Agnes could not take anymore. She did not care if they had enough evidence about Rev. Mical or not, she was not going to listen anymore to this demon, so she slammed the phone down.

Deacon Miller took the tape out of the tape player and started making duplicate copies. He made five tapes, one for himself, one for Mrs. Agnes, one for the IRS, one for Rev. Grant, and one that he was going to play for the rest of the Deacons.

When Deacon Miller arrived home, he told his son, who is the director of the broadcast ministry, about his meeting with Mrs. Agnes, and about Rev. Mical's call. Deacon Miller told Max the details of the tape and instructed him to prepare to play it at the right time during the next meeting.

Max had been waiting for an opportunity to tell his father about the rumors spreading around the church. Max explained that Rev. Mical and Deacon Tomas were lovers and that they also liked women. Deacon Miller understood that to be bisexual. Even though he was shocked to hear that about Deacon Tomas because he was married, Deacon Miller was not surprised about Rev. Mical.

Max explained to his dad, that Rev. Mical and Deacon Tomas did not consider themselves gay, homosexual, or bi-sexual because they enjoyed sex with women and they enjoy sex with each other often. Deacon Miller sat in shock. He wondered how he could get evidence of this because this would be the best ammunition to destroy Rev. Mical and to let the unknowing ladies know that he was a true demon. He asked Max how he knew this was true and he told him that he had stayed over one evening in the tape room and Rev. Mical and Deacon Tomas were in his office and that Rev. Mical had forgotten to turn off the intercom and everything that they said was heard all over the church. When they realized what had happened, they were both upset, but when they came out to check and see if anyone had heard them, he had ducked down so they would not see that he was in the tape booth.

Deacon Miller wanted to know why he had not mentioned this to him before now. Max said he didn't have proof, and that there are so many guys that are doing it to pay for college that he didn't think about telling anyone, and besides. Max looked under-eyed at his dad to instantly show that it did not apply to him, he only liked girls. After the conversation, Deacon Miller decided to take his little tape adventure a little farther by getting a tape of them talking. He knew that they were always together and that on many nights when he and all the other deacons left the church the two of them would always still be there.

That Thursday night, Deacon Miller had Max connect the Panasonic video recorder inside Rev. Mical's office when he knew everyone would leave the church to watch part two of "The Young and The Restless."

Rev. Mical and Deacon Tomas could not wait for church to end on Thursday night. Deacon Tomas had purchased an expensive bottle of wine and they had planned to celebrate. Just before he walked out of the door Max pushed the record button on the cassette recorder that he had installed in Rev. Mical's office. Deacon Tomas checked the doors and rooms of the church and saw that they were all locked and that the lights were out, except in the main sanctuary and Rev. Mical's office.

Then he rushed and got the glasses he had placed in the back of the freezer to chill and returned to Rev. Mical's office. As soon as he opened the door, Rev. Mical was all over him pulling at his clothing. Rev. Mical told him that he was going to screw him like Mona the choir director had done to him a few days prior, they both laughed at this and got to the business at hand.

Early the next morning Deacon Miller and Max went to church, took down the video recorder, and retrieved the tape. After relocking the church, they returned home where Max placed the tape in their tape player. After excusing his son from the room, Deacon Miller sat down and pressed the play button on the video cassette recorder, and what he saw on that tape, he wished he'd never have to witness again in life. Two grown men tongue kissing and doing everything conceivable to each other sexually. Deacon Miller thought that the sound alone would be enough to get rid of both those demons. He called Agnes and told her that they had Rev. Mical and that he was going to expose him on Saturday afternoon and if she wished she could come and witness it for herself, but on second thought she told him that she did not want to see that happen, not even to Rev. Mical.

Deacon Miller Reveals Rev. Mical's Sexuality

This was the first meeting Deacon Miller had ever presided over that he did not feel good about his position. On his way to the meeting, he prayed and asked God to do his work righteously. He knew that this information would not sit well with most of the others and he knew that the embarrassment alone would be enough to cause the average man to want to kill. He did not want the church family to know about the sexual detail, but he knew they would have to tell them something and he wasn't looking forward to that either. The only thing he knew for certain was that it was going to be a long night.

Rev. Mical, took his time dressing that night. He and Deacon Tomas were going out to dinner after the meeting, which usually only lasted for about two hours at the most. After dinner, he had plans to meet one of his new converts for dessert. He smiled at himself in the mirror as he picked up his keys and headed towards the door. If he could he would have kissed himself.

Everyone was at the meeting on time; except for Rev. Mical as usual he was fashionably late. Deacon Tomas seemed a little edgy and kept looking towards the door, something he always did, but until tonight Deacon Miller had thought truly little about it, now that he knew Deacon

Tomas a little bit better, he knew why he kept looking at the door and it made him sick to his stomach. Just as he was about to leave the room and see if he could find an Alka seltzer, Sister Burch entered with snacks for the meeting, and right behind her was Rev. Mical who walked in the door uttering his usual words," Let us get this show on the road," he said and took a seat at the table.

After prayer, everyone got a cup of coffee and a slice of cake, and then returned to the table. Rev. Mical was joking with some of the other deacons when Deacon Miller sat at the table. Deacon Miller told the group that the meeting tonight was not about the Deacon ministry's usual business but was more on the order of the overall church business. When he said this Rev. Mical looked at Deacon Tomas to see if he could read his expression of knowing anything about this.

"I have in my possession two tapes that I would like to share with you, and after you have heard both tapes, we will vote." As he spoke, he walked over to the cabinet where the video player was located and opened the door, then Rev. Mical spoke up.

"Deacon Miller, everyone at this table knows about Sister Agnes's accusation. I called everyone and told them about it, so if you are going to play the recorder about her and me, then it will be a waste of our time." Many of the other Deacons agreed and said they did not believe anything that Mrs. Agnes had to say, after all, they knew her from when her husband was living, and they all knew that she cheated on him with one of his brothers.

As they were talking, Deacon Miller reached into his pocket and pulled out the tape player then turned the sound up, next he pressed the play button. When Rev. Mical saw this, he did not know what to think. He and Deacon Tomas just looked at each other.

The tape began sharp and graphic. The group heard Rev. Mical and Deacon Tomas having sex inside the church. The oldest in the group Deacon Anderson was so upset he jumped up and tried to take the tape out with his fingers, Deacon Miller had to push the eject button quickly before he would have broken the machine. Rev. Mical was yelling, "Where in the hell did you get this? It is all a lie. Someone's trying to frame me!" As he spoke, Deacon Tomas knew when he had been defeated, so he got up and walked out of the door.

"Where are you going, Tomas? Come back here and help me to make these fools understand this shit! You hear me, Tomas!" Rev. Mical was yelling into the air. When he looked around the table, the deacons looked at him with disgust. So, he too got up and walked towards the door and as he reached the door, he looked back and told Deacon Miller, "You win this time. I'll be here tomorrow to pick up my personal effects," then he exited the room.

The remaining deacons did not have to take a vote; the only thing that they had to do afterward was to decide what minister they could get to come to preach on Sunday until they could get a new pastor for the church.

Secrets Revealed

Deacon Tomas waited at Rev. Mical's home for him to arrive. He had been sitting in his car, trying to think of a way he would be able to live down the shame that this will cause his family. He knew his mom would be devastated, and his father-in-law would do his best to keep his family from him. He held in tears and tried to think of something he could say that would soften this mess as far as he and Mical were concerned.

As he sat waiting, he looked up at the large house that Rev. Mical owned thanks to the church members. He lived alone, but if you did not know who he was, and you just looked at his home you would think that a whole family lived in this house. He never particularly liked the house, it was not his style, but Mical thought it was better than any other minister in the area. It was more costly, but not better.

The house was light blue with a dark blue roof which had a fireplace.

The two stories looked like two rectangular sitting on top of each other. There were double windows on each side and another roof that was triangular sitting in the center. The bottom level was also rectangular and had double bay windows two on each side and a column on each end of the porch that helped hold up the top half of the house. The columns were half brick and half wood. The brick part was wider than the wood section.

The house sat off the ground and six wide steps were leading up to the door. The backyard was small for such a large house and Rev. Mical had fenced it in so his neighbor could not see when he decided to lie in the yard in his birthday suit, but he always wonder how he could think that, since his neighbors also had two-story houses, so if they were upstairs and looked out their window on his side of the house, they would see him.

Deacon Tomas remembered what Rev. Mical had told him about his neighbor Mr. Gibson who attempted to reprimand Rev. Mical for being nude in his backyard. He recalled what Rev. Mical told him.

———

As the story went, Rev. Mical heard the doorbell ring and wondered who would be at his house before breakfast. When he opened the door, it was his neighbor.

"Hello, Rev. Mical," Mr. Gibson said.

"Yes, Gibson. What brings you to my door this morning?"

"May I come in? I would like to speak with you about something," Mr. Gibson asked.

Rev. Mical was about to fix himself some breakfast and since he was hungry, he invited Mr. Gibson inside, but into his kitchen while he prepared his breakfast. When they arrived in the kitchen Mr. Gibson was surprised to see that Rev. Mical's kitchen was as nice as his living room. Rev. Mical saw Mr. Gibson looking around and he felt good that his home was just as nice as the neighbors and since they were not of the same race, he knew that Mr. Gibson did not like the fact that his house was as nice or nicer than his.

"Would you like some breakfast?" Rev. Mical asked.

"No, thank you," he said still looking around the kitchen in awe as he took a seat at the counter. "The reason I came over is to let you know that when you sunbathe in your back yard my kids have been looking at you, and I don't want them looking at nude men or women for that fact, so I'm asking you if you can cover up when you are in your yard, or let me know the time you will be sunbathing and I'll make certain that my kids are not around."

Rev. Mical was thinking while Mr. Gibson was speaking. *This fool must think I'm one of those Negroes who is afraid of him and don't know my rights.* He took a seat at the counter, with his plate of scrambled eggs, toast, jelly, and coffee. He looked at Mr. Gibson and places a fork full of eggs into his mouth, before speaking.

"Mr. Gibson, I'm sorry that your kids saw me nude, but it's my right to dress or undress however I please as long as I'm in my own yard. I suggest that you tell your kids to stop looking out the window and then they will not see me and as far as the time I choose to sunbathe, there is not any. The days I choose to go outside depend on my schedule and the weather. I am sorry that I am unable to help you with your problem. Good day," Rev. Mical said as he walked to the front door opened it wide, and waited for Mr. Gibson to leave.

―――-

When Rev. Mical pulled into his driveway, he saw Deacon Tomas's car. *Now, I have to deal with this pathetic fool! I do not know why he did not know about this. I told him time and time again, to touch bases with Deacon Jones, he had loose lips and would have told him this shit was going to happen and they could have been prepared for it.*

Deacon Tomas got out of his car and walked into the garage and the kitchen behind Rev. Mical. "What the shit happened, Mical?"

"How the hell you want me to know, Tomas! You dropped the ball; you were supposed to keep in touch with Deacon Jones." He said as he jerked the refrigerator open and dropped two cubes of ice into a glass.

"Hell, man, I didn't think I had to call him every day. I spoke to him the day before yesterday and he never mentioned anything about this," Deacon Tomas said as he took the glass out of Rev. Mical's hand and poured vodka into it. He turned the glass up and drank the vodka straight down. "Well, what do we do now?" He asked while walking behind Rev. Mical into the den, both of them now drinking straight vodka.

"I don't know what you plan to do, but I'm putting this house on the market and I'm leaving this hick town. I am a man of means and I know I'll find another church that will be willing to hire me as their pastor. Miller did not do anything to hurt me, even though he thinks he did. Did you know that fool never liked me, he was the only one who didn't want them to hire me in the first place and I can just see him now telling them they should have listened to him in the beginning?" He said as he plopped down on the sofa.

Deacon Tomas walked over, place his arm on Rev. Mical's shoulder, and asked him what about them. Rev. Mical looked up into Deacon Tomas's eyes and asked him,

"What about us!"

"Are you kidding? Look, man, there was never a US! We had sex and that was all it was. I told you in the beginning when we first started that I just like having sex with men, but I am no homosexual! I like having sex with women too and as soon as I'm settled, I'm going to find a nice little church lady and marry her, if I had done that here I wouldn't be in this mess."

"What are you saying, James? Do you think that just because you like having sex with women that makes you different? Man, you must be crazy! You are as much gay as I am. It was not me who always wanted it, it was you and you were not beating down any of those nice little church lady's doors to get with them. You might fool yourself, but you will never fool me. So, go ahead and leave this little hick town as you call it, but I guarantee you, you will be in the arm of another man regardless of whether you marry a nice little church girl or not." Deacon Tomas said as he walked out of the room and left.

Rev. Mical picked up a notepad lying on the coffee table and began jotting down the thing he needs to do to prepare to leave in a couple of days.

Lawrence is Murdered

Mary Jean thought it strange that for some unforeseen reason, she could not get Lawrence off her mind and she did not have another telephone number for him since Donna left. She thought it was odd that he had not called to persuade her to visit the boys for Thanksgiving or to make Christmas plans. She knew the boys had not heard from him but maybe her husband had and had forgotten to tell her. She made a mental note to ask him. An eerie feeling came over her just when the telephone rang, startling her.

"Hello."

"Hello, Mary Jean?" She could clearly hear trembling in the familiar voice.

"Yes, this is Mary Jean, who's calling?"

"This....... This..........is Donna, Mary Jean, I'm so sorry to call you like this, but...but Lawrence is dead!"

"What? What did you say?" Mary Jean just knew that she had heard the wrong name. "Did you say 'Lawrence'? Lawrence is dead?" She pulled a chair to the wall phone. "What happened, Donna? Are you okay?"

"It's a long story, Mary Jean, I can call you back later or you can call me when you're free. Do you have the time to hear it all?" Donna said trying to delay the inevitable.

"I am not busy, Donna, I need to know what happened to my sons' father! I'm going to have to explain this to them. I need to know the details." Mary Jean's hands trembled.

"Lawrence had been stalking me for a couple of months. No, wait, let me start from the beginning. I had Lawrence served with divorce papers about four months ago. When he got the papers, he called me, ranting, and raving, and cursing. He told me that he would see me dead before he would give me a divorce. I could tell by the tone in his voice that he had been drinking and I didn't tell you before, but I believe that he had started snorting cocaine, too."

Wonderful, just wonderful! This woman knew Lawrence was on drugs and she did not tell me. She let me send my boys to her house, knowing that they could have been killed riding in the car with him!

"A couple of weeks after I left, he showed up at my parents' home and pulled me out of the car. Then a month later he returned and tried to break the door down. He and my father had a few harsh words and later my mom mentioned it to my brother. Oscar is always on drugs and he had just got out of jail on bond and he told my mom to call him the next time that Lawrence showed up at the door uninvited. Well, about three weeks later when I backed out of my parent's driveway, I saw Lawrence parked across the street. The look he had in his eyes was pure hate. I did not tell my parents that I saw him that day, but for the next couple of weeks he would follow me, call me on the phone, and threaten me." Donna cried and tried to compose herself. Mary Jean waited, envisioning every memory Donna relayed.

"After days of this, I was frazzled. I told my parents about him stalking me and my mom told Oscar. It was strange because most of the time, he stared at me but didn't get out of the car until yesterday. As I reached my car, I thought I saw a shadow, but I dismissed it because I had been so nervous. Then, Lawrence grabbed me, and I felt something sharp and hot scratch my arm. Lawrence had cut me with his razor. Then, I heard a loud sound and he let go of me and sank to the ground. I turned around and saw Oscar holding a gun," Donna started sobbing again.

"Are you okay?" Mary Jean asked.

Donna continued crying. "My mom heard the gunshot and came running outside. She saw me and Lawrence both bleeding, she ran back inside and called for two ambulances. Oscar just stood there and grabbed Lawrence. I fainted before they arrived and was taken to the hospital. I had to have twenty-five stitches in my arm. He cut my ulnar artery severely. The injury caused loss of the ulnar and radial perfusion to the hand which will lead to loss of strength in my hand.

"And now Dr. Mortez says that I may have a time trying to use this arm or hand again." She cried more.

"I didn't deserve this! I'm a nurse! I need my arm. I need my hands!"

Mary Jean was speechless. She tried to think of what to say but no words would come.

"Everyone in my family is upset! My brother will probably go to prison for the rest of his life, and my parents are sick! Lord! I am so sorry that I caused everyone this grief. I feel so guilty I wanted to call you first! Them boys love their daddy and I'm so sorry that I'm responsible that they will never see him again." Donna said through long sobs.

"Donna, Donna, please slow down. Breathe."

Donna tried to catch her breath but by now her heart was racing right along with the tears.

"I am sorry, too, Donna. You are not responsible for what happened to Lawrence. It was not your fault. He is dead due to the bad decisions he made! The drugs and alcohol and your brother taking the law into his hands, that sin is theirs and theirs alone. Not yours." Mary Jean took a deep breath. Sharp pains expanded across her chest. "We will tell the boys. I know that they will be hurt, but God, in His mercy, heals our heartaches." Mary Jean said thinking about the events that had happened over the year and praying that this would be the last time she had to deal with death for a long time.

"I'm having his service at the end of next week. My parents don't want me to. They want me to give his body to his family. I told them that the only family that I know of is his uncle, so I am going to call him later tonight and tell him what happened. This is such a load. My body feels so weak. I had to relay all of this to the police, to you, and now I'll have to tell everyone who asks me. It's tearing me apart, Mary Jean, it's tearing me apart!" Donna cried and blew her nose.

"Breathe, Donna. Breathe." Mary Jean waited to hear if Donna would calm down. They both held the phone quietly, both thinking on their own time with Lawrence. Then, Mary Jean broke the silence. "Thanks, for calling and letting me know, if there is anything that we can do for you, call us, okay?"

"If it's okay, how would your husband feel about saying a few words at Lawrence's funeral? Do you think he'd do it?"

"I tell you what, Donna, I will speak to him and I'll let you know what he says, but I'm almost certain that he will do that. Let me check with him to see if he has any pressing engagements on the days ahead before I commit for him. I will call you tomorrow and let you know what he says. Once again, thanks for calling and I will be praying for you and your family. Goodbye." Mary Jean said still feeling uneasy.

"Bye," Donna said. She put the phone on its receiver, then picked the phone back up and called the one person who had been there for her through all of this.

When Rev. Grant arrived home, Mary Jean told him about her call from Donna. He was upset. For a while, he paced the room mumbling to God about how the boys needed the presence of their biological father and even though he felt honored to be their dad and try to fill the void for them, they really needed their father.

"Donna, wanted to know if you will say a few words over the body?" Mary Jean said. He gave it some thought then declined.

"I don't think that would be appropriate. I will attend the funeral with you and the boys, but I do not want to participate. It's more important for me to be with you and the boys." He sat in his favorite chair.

"For some reason, something just doesn't seem right. I know she told me that her brother shot Lawrence, but I just feel like there is more to her story than what meets the eyes. I think she is lying about some of it," Mary Jean said as she sat on the sofa next to his recliner.

Rev. Grant looked at her and scratched his head, "I was wondering the same thing. Reach me the phone." He said before asking, "What time is it?"

"It's six o'clock," Mary Jean adjusted the phone cord so it would extend beyond the couch to him.

"Let me try to call the sheriff, he's usually there until about six-thirty. He's become a little more tolerable now that Deputy Jones is part of his detective unit." Rev. Grant dialed the number to the sheriff's office.

"Basin Street Sheriff's department," The voice on the other end of the phone said.

"Good evening. This is Rev. Donald Grant. Is Sheriff Golespy in?"

"Yes. He's here, Donald," Deputy Albert Williamson said, refusing to acknowledge Rev. Grant's ministerial title. "Hold on."

Deputy Williamson laid the phone on the desk but didn't move. Deputy Jones overheard the conversation and knew that he was deliberately making Rev. Grant wait although on many other occasions Williamson would have gone outside if needed to catch the Sheriff on behalf of a white resident. Jones had a strong disdain for the racist responses in the small-town police force and as soon as he could catch these idiots on corruption or civil rights violations, he gladly would. Until then, he performed his job like the best of them.

He walked into Sheriff Golespy's office just as he was getting ready to leave for the day.

"Sheriff, you have a call from the minister whose wife we questioned about the Rosenthal case."

"Okay. That will be the Rev.......erend Donald Grant. He has that big church off Fourth Street, congregation seeping out the door. That nigger just evaded two audits from the I.R.S, got that young wife, and all them men flocking to his church. Somebody needs to shut him down. I know he's got secrets somewhere. He's got too much damn power." The sheriff talked casually and walked back to his desk to take the call. "Hello there, Donald, what can I do for you? I was just about to leave for the day."

"Well, this won't take long, Roderick." Rev Grant said deliberately stressing the sheriff's first name and sharing the same disrespect. "Can you tell me what's being done, if anything, about the murder of Lawrence Roberson Sr. and what's the status on Agnes Rosenthal's mugging and assault?" Rev. Grant asked.

"We are on the case, but it's not much of a case because we already know that Oscar Smith killed him and he's locked up in my jail again this time for Lawrence's murder the same day he got out on bond, but he'll be here awaiting Judge Clark next week," the sheriff said.

"I see," Rev. Grant said. "We feel that there's more to this than meets the eye. Would you investigate this further?"

"Now….Now…. Donald, why would I do that? I have the weapon and the murderer here in my jail. Do you have any other information that can help us with the case"?

"Not yet," Rev. Grant said looking at the hurt in Mary Jean's eyes. "Did you do ballistic on the gun to see if the bullet matched the one that killed Lawrence and if it matches the bullet fragments found near Mrs. Agnes? You know the doctors could not remove the bullet from her body."

"You listen to me, Donald! I do not need you telling me how to do my job. I do not tell you what to do in that big church of yours where you are collecting hundreds of dollars every Sunday, so do not tell me what to do on my job. If I find it necessary to run ballistics on the gun, I'll do that, but it won't be on a whim. You stick to preaching and focusing on your little wife. Me and my boys will handle the crime in this town!" The sheriff shouted. He looked at Deputy Jones in the doorway and continued, attempting to flex a false sense of control. "And don't go around acting like you're the sheriff! I know you have a lot of people in your church, but if something else happened I know we will find out and I will be glad to investigate it, but in the meantime let me do my job. Do you hear me, Reverend?"

"Sure, sheriff. And I hope that you heard me too. Enjoy your evening."

"You know that nigger thinks he can call here and tell me how to do my job, but that's not going to happen!" The sheriff said as he hung up the phone. "I'm going home now. Jones, aren't you on duty tonight? Louise Horne will have dinner ready tonight. You'll probably need to lock down and go out to get it. See that our guests are comfortable." He grinned believing he finally had something on Oscar that would tie him to the Roberson murder and assault with the same weapon that would keep him in jail. Now his wife nor Oscar's mom would be able to pull him out of this. Deputy Williamson left the precinct with Sheriff Golespy, leaving Deputy Jones behind. He listened as they exited the back of the building through two sets of metal doors. They were untrustworthy and Deputy Jones was pinning for an opportunity to catch them. They weren't smart by any means and he knew they would eventually slip up. He gave them enough time to travel several miles from the precinct before he decided to leave to pick up the night's meal.

Before entering Louise's neighborhood. Deputy Jones crossed the railroad tracks at Southern Avenue and stopped at the Scotlandville First Convenience store to make a private call from the outdoor pay phone. He parked the patrol car and walked to the front of the vehicle. He dropped a dime in the phone slot then aggressively pressed each button of the phone number. Before the first ring ended, the call was answered.

"The cats move in sync every evening. They don't go home. All cases remain open and investigations of new crimes lag. It's confirmed that Blacks have no rights as citizens. They stalk and prey on their control of Basin, Louisiana." He cleared his throat. "Standby for more." Then he hung up the phone and returned to the unit.

Louise Horne shouted her greeting from the kitchen then called Pretty Boy to answer the door. Instead, he grabbed the two large boxes of food and opened the door. Without a word, he gave the boxes to Deputy Jones then closed the front door. Yeah, that Golespy's boy all right. Deputy Jones smirked and loaded the car with the food that smelled like a Thanksgiving feast. Thank you, Mrs. Louise.

He walked into the jail in time to answer the ringing telephone. Oscar rose from the cot, hoping he would get the first bite of dinner.

"Jones here."

"Is the sheriff in?" Mrs. Golespy asked. Her words slurred like no sober woman's words should.

What the hell is in her mouth—tobacco? "No ma'am. He and Deputy Williamson left about an hour ago.

"Well, where the hell is he?"

"I don't know, ma'am, but when he returns here, I'll tell him to call you." He knew Golespy wouldn't return and it was only a matter of time before they all soon find out where the sheriff was strolling through the night.

Lawrence's Funeral

When Mary Jean and her family arrived at Lawrence's funeral, they were surprised to see so many cars. Mary Jean never met any of Lawrence's family except for his uncle, who came to see him in the hospital. It took them ten minutes to find a parking place and just as they were pulling into a vacant spot, they saw her dad and his family. Mary Jean was surprised to see her father; she did not know that they were coming; then it occurred to her that T.P. probably told them and gave them directions to the funeral home.

Tears filled her eyes when she saw how many of her family and church members had decided to attend. It confirmed in her the importance of having a loving and supportive family. They all waited for each other to park and entered the funeral home together. The boys were sticking close to her and Rev. Grant. They were grieving and it pained her to have had to bring them, but she knew that was impossible to leave them behind. *Not bringing them would cause more problems than bringing them,* she heard Stella's advice as clearly as if she were still alive. *Yes, ma'am.*

The funeral director ushered the family and close friends to the front seats. Mary Jean saw Donna crying, and as soon as she saw Mary Jean, she jumped up, rushed over to Mary Jean and the boys, hugged them all, and started sobbing.

"I'm so sorry," she tried to whisper between her sobs.

One of Donna's family members came and ushered her outside. Mary Jean stepped up to the casket with the boys and they began to cry, even Lawrence Junior, which was surprising to her because he was usually so reserved.

Seeing Lawrence lying there brought back the memories of her grandmother and the fact that Lawrence never had anyone close to him after his mother's death, except her and his uncle. She thought about all the things he had told her about his father, and she knew that the relationship between him and his father had such a profound effect on his life. At that moment, she knew the importance of having a caring mother and a caring father in a child's life.

All of her emotions were running rapidly, she felt sad for Lawrence. Sad that he never had a good life. She was livid that he was instrumental in destroying his life and in the process, he had deprived his sons of their interactions with their biological father. She breathed deeply and allowed herself to release the anger and feel relieved that his torment was finally over.

The service was short and a bit unconventional since the funeral home director was the only person in Basin willing to officiate. He didn't introduce himself and there were no programs printed in the memorial.

He cleared his throat with a dry cough and grabbed the mic like a club emcee ready to shout out an introduction to the next song. His voice was loud and startling.

"Today, we gather to lay to rest Mr. Lawrence Roberson. I never got the chance to meet Mr. Roberson, but I do know that he was the father of these two boys and for that, we are all grateful. This city can use some nice, respectful boys like these boys. I made some calls and Mr. Roberson's uncle told me that as a child he was very smart and often was the backbone for his mother. His uncle went on the say that his sister told him that Lawrence moved the sofa one night so that when his dad came home intoxicated, he would fall on the floor. She said they both regretted that move.

"They said Lawrence Roberson loved cars, but he hated working a long time on any job. He loved to party and when the family got together for holidays, he would drop by and get a plate of food and greet everyone then leave. Everyone knew it was because he didn't know them since he was not allowed to visit them when he was a kid.

"Every now and then, the uncle would talk to Lawrence and he knew the sadness Lawrence felt since his addiction problems were keeping him from being in his boys' lives like he wanted to be. He said Lawrence blamed himself because his sons' family always offered to help him. I bet he was a stubborn man and refused help. Well, I believe if everyone who knew Mr. Roberson could speak to him again, they would tell him to get his life in order and that pride comes before the fall. I'm certain his family wishes they just had one more day to talk him into rehab and to let him know how much they loved him because they said he never left their presence without saying I love you."

Mary Jean didn't know if she should feel disgusted by his poor choice of words or enraged. Either way, she'd hoped his so-called eulogy would end soon.

"So, family and friends gathered here today," he continued boisterously. "We know Mr. Roberson knew love. He loved his family and his sons, but that love was not enough to sustain him so he went to other places of turmoil seeking to meet his needs."

My God! Why won't he shut up! Mary Jean wanted to scream.

"I believe if Mr. Roberson were here, he would want us to tell of the goodness he felt for his co-workers who all expressed a deep liking of him. Even the bosses, whose jobs he just walked off from, said that he was a good worker, but something was always pulling him away from the things that were going right for him.

"Do you remember anything you particularly loved about the person? Everyone that I spoke to said Mr. Roberson was a sharp dresser and he loved fine clothing and was often seen in name-brand shoes and clothing. From talking to friends, loved ones, and relatives, I learned that Mr.

Roberson lived an incredible life and will be missed by many more people than those of you gathered today. And, I also learned about love by hearing the people who knew him speak about him.

"At last, my final statement is 'from dust we came and from dust we shall all return one day,' and today is Mr. Roberson's day, but tomorrow could be your day, so while we are upon this earth let us try to do that which is Godly and look out to help our fellow man who needs us. Sleep on, Mr. Larence Roberson, we will all see you one day." He raised his hands for the ushers to escort the body and mourners.

After the service, she met Donna's family, who were unfriendly to her as if she played a part in Donna's grief. One of Lawrence's old friends came over and spoke to them, but for the life of her, Mary Jean could not remember his name. He walked away after shaking her hand, then he and Donna walked off by themselves. Mary Jean noticed something odd about their interaction, they seemed close—almost intimate—because their demeanor shifted when they thought no one was looking.

They're a couple! Mary Jean made note of this and decided that she would call and ask Donna later about this because this would explain why Lawrence was so adamant about hurting her. She knew Lawrence had never had a problem getting women, so why was he still chasing after Donna? She knew that she would not be able to rest until she found out the truth and what Donna told her was not the truth, the whole truth and nothing but the truth so help her God.

Lawrence's uncle walked over and hugged Mary Jean and the boys. He gave her a notecard with his phone number and told her that he wanted to step in and help the boys. He tried to make small talk but Mary Jean was focused on Donna and her new beau's behavior to notice that Larence's uncle had taken her hand and was shaking goodbye. Once she realized it she smiled and said, "yes, sir. We will call you. Yes. Goodbye," He placed a piece of paper in her open hand and closed it gently.

"You take care," He said politely and released her balled hand. When she opened her hand, she saw the three hundred dollars he'd snuck to her.

—————-

On the drive home, Mary Jean wrecked her brain to recall the name of the man with Donna. It had been years since she'd seen him but she was convinced he was Lawrence's friend. She scanned her memory. *Jazz!* She hit her hand on the steering wheel. *That was Jazz! Lawrence's best friend!* She was sure of it.

When they arrived home, Mary Jean conveyed to Rev. Grant her misgiving about what she saw between Donna and Jazz. At first, she could not even remember his friend's birth name for some reason. Rev. Grant listened intently as she described the awkwardness of the service and the ramblings of the funeral director. He rubbed her shoulders as she explained the feeling of seeing Jazz and Donna together. He said he also thought their closeness was strange.

He offered to ask Deacon Johnny Anderson, who is an attorney for the church, to check the matter out if she wanted him to. She declined, knowing not much would come of it. Women move on with their lives the best way that they could.

"Right before you arrived." Mary Jean told him. "I called Sheriff Golespy's office and expressed to him that I have misgivings about Lawrence's death and that I thought there was more going on than meets the eye," She said as she took a seat at the kitchen table. Deep inside of her, she thought something was not right and even though she had no personal feelings for Lawrence, she felt that it was her place to check this out for the sake of her sons. She knew they said that Donna's brother had killed Lawrence. *But why was Donna so close to Jazz—Lawrence's best friend?*

Rev. Grant's voice interrupted her thoughts. "What did Sheriff Golespy say to you when you called him?" He asked.

"He said that Donna's brother, Oscar, was the person who killed Lawrence and that he was locked up in his jail waiting for the judge to decide on a bond and soon he would go on trial and then he would be shipped to Mississippi State Prison and that would be the end of that."

"That's almost exactly what he told me," Rev. Grant admitted.

"Well, did we expect any other response? Lawrence is Black and the guy who killed him is Black, so Sheriff Golespy feels that the case is solved. We know he has never done anything to protect or prosecute on Black peoples' behalf, so we'll just have to do what we do to get the whole truth in this case and the ones around the missing girls."

After winning the battle with the Internal Revenue Service and hearing about how quickly Rev. Mical had left town, Rev. Grant felt powerful enough to do just that: get to the bottom of all of this and clean up Basin, Louisiana—even if that included getting rid of a rogue sheriff. He especially understood cleaning up Basin also meant healing his own family trauma and that was not going to be an easy job.

Rev. Grant walked over to his wife and put his arms around her waist. So much had happened, so quickly that he hadn't had ample time to love on his wife and he was not about to miss any more time without her embrace.

They held each other silently for five minutes, taking in each other's breath and warmth.

Jazz and Donna Talk

The phone rang at eleven o'clock, one hour after the nightly news, just to ensure that Donna's parents were asleep and would not answer his call.

"Hi, Baby. How are you feeling?" Jazz asked.

Donna thought for a moment then when she was sure of her feeling she replied. "I'm better, now that I don't have to look over my shoulder all the time." She said as she fluffed her pillow.

"You should feel better about not being abused mentally or physically. Lawrence was my friend but I saw him slipping into insanity years ago. I tried to help him by talking to him but he was too far gone. Damn, it was like the inside of his head was clicked off and nothing I said mattered."

"Nothing we said mattered, Jazz. Nothing anyone said mattered."

"Yeah."

They held the phone for a moment.

"How's your brother doing?"

"They picked him up the day he was released. He was already out on bond for assault with a deadly weapon in that gambling fight on the Eastside. He hit that guy using the same pistol he came at Lawrence and me with. I don't know how momma and daddy got him out this time, but they did." Donna yawned.

"You did switch guns, right?"

"Of course I did. When Lawrence fell on Oscar, I grabbed his gun and slid it under the car seat. I was struggling to get up, but I got it done in time," Donna said, feeling smart. "I saw the other gun smoking on the ground before I passed out."

"Yeah, I dropped it trying to get them two fools off of each other. Hell, my back still hurts!"

"Well, I'm glad you did because apparently, the cops found it near Oscar while the paramedics tried to treat Lawrence. Thank you for being by my side, Jazz."

He stayed quiet, replaying the attack.

"Do you still have Oscar's pistol?"

"Nah. It's gone." Jazz said and Donna sighed with relief.

"Don't you feel bad about the fact that your brother could serve a lot of time for this murder?" Jazz listened closely to hear how she felt for her brother knowing that her feelings may one day apply to him.

"Oscar has been nothing but trouble for my mom and dad since he was a little boy. They were always going to school for problems he started, going to the juvenile detention home for other attacks, and constant street fights outside the house and inside. He puts us in more danger than Lawrence ever could. So as I see it, his doing time will be a blessing for all of us. Do you agree?"

"Yes, I 'spose so." Jazz began to wonder whether he had done the right thing and how long he would have to keep secrets.